where do i go?

BOOK 1

𝒜
yadayada
HOUSE *of* HOPE
Novel

NETA JACKSON

Thomas Nelson
Since 1798

NASHVILLE   DALLAS   MEXICO CITY   RIO DE JANEIRO   BEIJING

Published in Nashville, Tennessee. Thomas Nelson is a registered trademark of Thomas Nelson, Inc.

Thomas Nelson, Inc. books may be purchased in bulk for educational, business, fund-raising, or sales promotional use. For information, please e-mail SpecialMarkets@ThomasNelson.com.

Published in association with the literary agency of Alive Communications, Inc., 7680 Goddard Street, Suite 200, Colorado Springs, CO 80920. www.alivecommunications.com

Scripture quotations are taken from the following: THE HOLY BIBLE, NEW INTERNATIONAL VERSION®. Copyright © 1973, 1978, 1984 by International Bible Society. Used by permission of Zondervan Bible Publishers.

The Holy Bible, New Living Translation, copyright © 1996. Used by permission of Tyndale House Publishers, Inc., Wheaton, Illinois 60189. All rights reserved.

The New King James Version®. Copyright © 1982 by Thomas Nelson, Inc. Used by permission. All rights reserved.

The King James Version of the Bible. Public domain.

Ann Marie Rousseau, *Shopping Bag Ladies* (Pilgrim Press, New York, 1981).
"I Go to the Rock," words and music by Dottie Rambo. © 1977 New Spring, Inc. (ASCAP). Administered by Brentwood-Benson Music Publishing, Inc. Used by permission.

Publisher's Note: This novel is a work of fiction. Names, characters, places, and incidents are either products of the author's imagination or used fictitiously. All characters are fictional, and any similarity to people living or dead is purely coincidental.

Library of Congress Cataloging-in-Publication Data

Jackson, Neta.
  Where do I go? / Neta Jackson.
    p. cm. — (A Yada Yada house of hope novel ; bk. 1)
  ISBN 978-1-59554-523-7 (trade pbk.)
  1. Christian women—Fiction. 2. Shelters for the homeless—Fiction.
3. Chicago (Ill.)—Fiction. I. Title.
  PS3560.A2415W47 2008
  813'.54—dc22   2008035948

Printed in the United States of America

08 09 10 11 12 RRD 6 5 4 3 2 1

This series is dedicated to
the amazing staff of
Breakthrough Urban Ministries
and its "Joshua Center"
a shelter for homeless women in
Chicago, Illinois
who have literally created a "House of Hope"
for their many guests

In memory of
Dottie Rambo
whose song "I Go to the Rock"
provides both the theme for this series
and the titles of all three books
1934—2008

"To be without a home is to be invisible."
Ann Marie Rousseau, *Shopping Bag Ladies*

prologue

JUNE 1990, MONTPELLIER, FRANCE

The two American coeds stood at the apex of the tree-lined Esplanade, heads bent over their guidebook. Male passersby turned for a second glance, eyeing the youthful female bodies with lusty smiles. Tank tops, shorts, and Birkenstocks did little to cover the long, shapely legs and tan skin. Some slowed, hoping for a glance at the faces hidden by the straight, corn-silk hair of one and the rippling chestnut curls of the other, both worn long and whipping about in the wind coming off the large, open square sprawled before them.

"This is it—Place de la Comédie. See the fountain up there?" The young woman with the red highlights sparking in the sun pointed to the far end of the square. "Let's go up that way and find a café. It's after one already."

"But Gabby! The Polygone is right over there. It's like an American mall." The leggy blonde tugged her friend's arm, pulling her to the left of the Esplanade and away from the square.

Gabby jerked her arm free. "Linda! You and your malls. I didn't come all the way to France to *shop*. Come on. I'm hungry." She ran forward a few steps, then turned around but kept walking backward. "Come o-on! I'm going with or without you!" Then she ran on, laughing, backpack bumping on her back, threading through the other pedestrians filling the square.

Within moments she heard running footsteps and Linda's whine. "Wait up, Gabby!"

Laughing, Gabby locked arms with her companion as they walked to the far end of Place de la Comédie and approached the Fountain of Three Graces. They stopped, staring. The three graceful female figures stood atop a rocky mound of moss and green plants, with waterspouts pouring water into first one shallow basin surrounding the fountain, and then another. Several families with children sat on the smooth paving stones around the fountain, eating sandwiches and tossing crumbs to the pigeons that strutted about. A bald guy seated on a canvas stool nearby played a guitar, his guitar case open for the occasional francs. But the majority of warm bodies milling about the square or sitting on the ground around the fountain were young—late teens, early twenties—and multinational. University students.

"*Mmm*," Linda said.

"I know. It's beautiful."

"I meant those two guys over there. Sitting by the fountain. Do you think they're French?"

Gabby slapped her friend's arm. "*You* are impossible!" She laughed. "Come on. There's an empty table over there, see? At that café. We'll have a great view of the Opera House and we can watch the fountain—oh! Oh wait! Look!" Gabby clapped her hands. "It's a carousel!"

Linda rolled her eyes. "So?"

"I want to ride it! I've never ridden a carousel before!"

"Gabby! Don't be silly! Those things go up and down *and* around. You get dizzy riding a stupid escalator . . . Oh, brother."

A pair of eyes shaded by sunglasses followed the two young women as the curly-headed one ran up to the ticket booth, pointed at herself and her friend, paid their francs, and climbed onto the prancing carousel horses. The young man, sporting a loose shock of dark hair, poked his companion seated on the ground, his nose in a book, near the Fountain of Three Graces. "Hey, Cameron. Check out those girls."

"Where? The carousel?" His light-haired companion shaded his eyes and watched as the carousel started up, the horses lifted up and down, and the girls' laughter sailed over the square. "Silly Americans," he snorted. "Present company excepted, of course, Philip." Cameron went back to his book.

That got a laugh. "Stuffy Brit. Maybe we should go ride it too. Be good for you, my man. Too much studying can ruin your youth!" But Philip's eyes stayed on the young woman with the long, curly hair as she came around, up and down, on her prancing mechanical horse, her head back, laughing . . . disappeared . . . and came around once more. But this time the American girl clung to the pole, eyes tightly shut.

The carousel finally stopped and the girl climbed off unsteadily, almost falling. Her friend grabbed her and for a moment seemed to be holding her up. Philip started to his feet. Was she okay? But at that moment the young woman straightened and tossed her hair back, brushing off her friend's attention with a laugh. The eyes behind the sunglasses followed as the girls headed for the outdoor seating of the café between the carousel and the Fountain of Three Graces.

"Hey, Cameron. Let's get something to eat, okay?" Philip snatched the book out of the other's hands. "Come on."

His companion sighed, got to his feet, and grabbed for the book. By the time he repacked the book in his backpack and slung it over his shoulder, Philip had already picked out an outdoor table at the same café.

Gabby sucked on the straw in her lemonade and then sighed happily. "I could sit here forever watching people in this square. It's like . . . so international!"

Linda took a sip of her iced coffee and frowned at the menu. "Yeah, well, I wish you'd sat *here* fifteen minutes ago, rather than ride that silly carousel. I thought you were going to throw up back there . . . Hey! Where'd the sun go?" Linda squinted upward as a shadow moved across the open square. "Better not rain," she grumbled. "We haven't ordered yet."

"So what? If it rains this afternoon, we can go to a movie at the theater over there." Gabby pulled the straw out with her teeth and pointed the dripping end at the domed building that said *Cinema Gaumont*.

"Gosh!" Linda rolled her eyes. "Do you always have to be so cheerful?"

Gabby giggled. "Yes. And I'd be even happier if Damien, the jerk, could see me now—*in* France, having a ball, with only one year to go getting my BA. Without him actually *being* here, I mean." She tossed her hair back and snorted. "*That* would be a bummer."

Linda raised her frosty glass. "To Damien, king of the jerks—"

Gabby clinked her lemonade on Linda's glass. "—may he get seasick on that fishing boat with the captain's daughter, who no doubt smells a bit *fishy* by now."

The two young women collapsed into laughter, which stopped abruptly when a male voice said, *"Excusez-moi, ma'amselles?"*

"Ohmigosh," Linda said under her breath. "It's them."

Gabby looked up, startled. A tall young man with dark hair and sunglasses stood beside their table, accompanied by another young man with sandy hair. "Yes?" *Oh, dear. I should've said, "Oui?" or something. He sounds French.*

"May I introduce myself? *Je suis Philippe* Fairbanks, and this is Cameron Brewer, my housemate. Graduate students at La Faculté des Lettres." He pointed at himself. "Business." Then at his companion. "History." He flashed a smile revealing perfect white teeth. "And you are—?"

His French accent rolled off his tongue like melted chocolate. Gabby cleared her throat, hoping her mouth hadn't been hanging open. "Oh! Uh, I'm Gabrielle Shepherd—most people call me Gabby—and this is Linda Banks. University of North Dakota." She had never seen such a beautiful man. Tall, dark, and handsome. Literally! And French to boot!

"*Pardonne.* May we sit?"

"Uh . . . of course! Please. Sit down. Right, Linda?"

Linda nodded, eyelashes fluttering, licking her lips.

"Have you ladies ordered yet?" The dark-haired one pulled over another chair. "The lamb kebobs here are superb."

"*Mmm*," the other seconded, sounding decidedly British. "Absolutely scrummy."

Linda snorted. "*Humph.* Gabby needs a salad or something light. She nearly lost it on the carousel back there—ow!" She glared at Gabby. "What did you kick me for?"

The two young men laughed. Gabby flushed. "I am *fine.* Just a momentary dizzy spell. The lamb kebobs sound great."

"Excellent." The dark eyes gave an approving wink. "Lunch is on us—right, Cameron?"

And so they talked and laughed over succulent lamb kebobs and freshly baked bread. Gabby was aware that the dark eyes seemed to feast on her, and she flushed at the attention. His English was perfect—unlike her French—and his lovely French accent gave her goose bumps . . . until Cameron pulled the plug. "Aw, ladies, don't be fooled by this bloke. His name is Philip, not '*Philippe,*' and he hails from Virginia in the US of A. I, on the other hand, am London born and bred."

Gabby's mouth dropped. Then she laughed, grabbed a cloth napkin, and playfully whipped Philip's arm with it. "You imposter!"

He threw up his hands and grinned. "Ah, well. Fun while it lasted."

She was actually relieved at the joke. It would have been charming to be romanced by a Frenchman, but her small-town roots in Minot, North Dakota, were so . . . so *provincial.* She'd married her teenage sweetheart right out of high school, but a divorce two years later made her determined to get out of Minot and do something with her life. Until this junket through Europe with Youth Hostels International, the farthest she'd been was the University of North Dakota in Grand Forks. Big deal.

However, an *American* in Paris—or, Montpellier, in this case—put this charming looker on more equal footing. She tossed her curls back confidently. "So, why did you decide to study in Montpellier, *Philip?*"

Philip's grin was half grimace. "Oh, you know the story. Family business. Dad's got my life planned, wants me to follow in his footsteps." He shrugged. "It's a good business, but I want to broaden my horizons, explore some new ideas to bring the business into the twenty-first century."

Intrigued, Gabby leaned forward, chin resting on her hand as Philip talked. A slight shadow of a beard lined his strong jawline. His dark brown hair had a boyish way of falling over his forehead—though Damien had been drop-dead gorgeous, too, she reminded herself, and look where *that* got her. But . . . Philip was different. Damien was just a local pretty boy who'd swept her off her feet with empty promises. But this man . . . he had roots. A solid Southern family. (How romantic was *that*?) Heir to a family business. And he had new ideas. Vision. She liked that. He seemed so self-assured—the type of guy who would go places and do things—and that excited her.

"—been to Paris yet?" he was saying. "You must see the Eiffel Tower."

Gabby let slip a wry grin and an exaggerated sigh. "Probably not. Uh, heights don't agree with me . . . nor carousels, it seems."

"Oh, nuts." Linda jumped up, bumping the table and nearly spilling their drinks. "It's starting to rain." The leggy blonde joined the throng surging toward the inside tables of the café.

Gabby was feeling giddy and bold. "So, what's a little rain?" Instead of going inside, she ran into the square, laughing and twirling around slowly in the warm shower, arms outstretched, letting her damp hair twist up tighter, like a crown of curly ribbons.

Standing under the awning of the café, Philip Fairbanks watched the sprite from North Dakota swirl, laughing, in the rain. "I'm going to marry that girl," he murmured.

"Don't be barmy, Philip." Cameron hunched his shoulders against the damp breeze. "She's just a ditzy yank from North Dakota. What would your mum do if you brought home a girl named *Gabby*?"

Philip laughed. "Probably have a hissy fit. I'll tell her the girl's name is Gabrielle—that sounds French, don't you think? And I think she's charming. A free spirit. Different."

Cameron snorted. "Different, all right. Look at that hair. Little Orphan Annie grown up."

Philip *was* looking at Gabrielle's hair. The sun broke through the light rain, and raindrops sparkled on the mop of chestnut curls flying around and around. "Mm-hm," he murmured to himself. "I'm going to marry you, Mop Top. You wait and see."

chapter 1

Looking thirty-two floors down was almost enough to bring up my lunch. Philip *knew* I had trouble with heights. So what kind of sadistic joke made him buy a penthouse, for heaven's sake! Not to mention floor-to-ceiling windows that curved around the living room, like putting a glass nose on a Boeing 747.

I groaned. It'd take me a week to wash the inside of those windows. And who in the world washed the *outside*—?! My knees wobbled. Uh-uh. Couldn't go there or I'd lose my lunch for real.

But the view . . . oh my.

I stood in the middle of our new living room and tried to take it all in. Trees dotted the park along Chicago's Lake Shore Drive, wearing the fresh new wardrobe of spring. On the other side of the Drive, the western edge of Lake Michigan lapped at the miles of beaches separated by occasional rocky retaining walls and disappeared southward amid the misty skyscrapers of Chicago's Loop. Tall, billowy thunderheads caught the late afternoon sun. Earlier that day, cars had hurried along the Drive, like toys zipping along a giant track some kid got for Christmas. But now, at the height of rush hour, the far lane was packed solid as commuters headed for the northern suburbs.

O-kay. Looking *out* at the view wasn't so bad. I stepped closer to the window, keeping my chin up, refusing to look straight down. Near the beach, cyclists whizzed along a bicycle path, swerving around joggers. Dogs with their masters chased Frisbees or dashed into the water after a ball. No one was in the water—too early in the spring, I guessed. But the sand sparkled in the late afternoon sunshine. What I wouldn't give to—

"Is that all, Señora Fairbanks?"

I jumped. The sweet face of the maid, who'd been setting up the catered buffet in the dining room the past hour, looked at me expectantly. Dark hair. Dark eyes. Plain white blouse with a name tag that said "Camila." Black skirt hugging her chunky legs. A wedding band on her left hand. Obviously hoping to go home and take care of her own family.

"Oh. Yes, yes, I'm sure it's fine, Mrs. . . . Mrs. . . . ?"

She reddened. "Just Camila, señora. *Gracias.*"

"Well, then, call me Gabby." I glanced at the Fairbanks' heirloom grandfather clock patiently ticking away in the corner of the large room. Almost six o'clock. Philip had said to expect him between seven and eight. "What do I need to do when the guests arrive?"

The short, stocky woman smiled with relief. "No problem. Cold salads in the refrigerator. Beef tips and saffron rice in the warming oven set at one hundred fifty degrees. Will be safe. Just take them out." Picking up her bag, she disappeared quickly into the entryway—called a "gallery" in the Richmond Towers brochure—and out the front door of the penthouse.

Still standing in the middle of the living room, I suddenly felt bereft. I was alone. Again. Philip had been gone since seven that morning. The boys were still in Virginia at boarding school. Philip wouldn't hear of taking them out so close to the end of the school year. And so we'd moved, lock, stock, and oriental rugs, to Illinois so Philip and his new partner could hurry up and dream big dreams in their luxurious office in downtown Chicago. And here I was, not only alone, but stuck up here in the sky, like an eagle impaled on a flagpole.

I imagined Camila in the elevator, riding down, down, nodding at the doorman, going outside. Free.

Stepping close to the curved window, I steadied myself with my hand, daring myself to look down, hoping to see her emerge. The glass was thick and cool to the touch. Probably leaving a grubby handprint on the glass. Huh. I'd have to clean it before Philip's guests arrived. Had to have a clean prison wall, right?

Stop it, Gabby.

A jogger caught my eye as she ran through the park below, ran past the trees, did a sharp turn, and then suddenly disappeared. *Wait a minute. What just happened?* I squinted . . . then a movement on the other side of Lake Shore Drive caught my eye. The same jogger was now running on the path by the beach!

There must be a pedestrian tunnel under Lake Shore Drive. My eyes widened. Why hadn't I seen it before? We'd been here five days already, and all this time I thought the ubiquitous Drive cut us off from the sand and water unless we got in the car and drove somewhere.

I cast another furtive glance at the clock. Ten after. Philip wouldn't be here for another fifty minutes at the earliest—maybe longer. I was already dressed in a white pantsuit and gold-strap sandals. The temperature was almost eighty—warm for April. *What if*—

On impulse I grabbed my keys from the wooden bowl on the table in the gallery and headed out the penthouse door. I felt slightly giddy as I stepped into the elevator and pushed the button for the ground floor, like the time I'd ditched classes in middle school back in Minot, North Dakota. When the elevator doors opened, I pushed open the security door into the lobby and breezed past the African-American doorman, not wanting to chat, and found myself on the narrow frontage street that gave limited access to several high-rise condos besides Richmond Towers.

But beyond the street, beyond the park, beyond the pedestrian tunnel was sand and water. *Sand! Sand between my toes. Splashing in the miniwaves.* The desire drove me on like an urgent hunger. How long, how long had it been since I'd even been barefoot?

I burst out of the pedestrian tunnel under Lake Shore Drive like a runner carrying the Olympic torch. *Oh Gabby, you are so bad.* I laughed out loud. Kicking off my sandals, I ran barefoot across the grass and stepped down a low concrete wall to the sand, sending a flock of seagulls hopping into the air and landing a short distance away. Delighting in the feel of the warm sand on my bare feet, I ran at the birds, sending them scolding and hopping again.

I giggled, turning around and around, arms outstretched to catch the wind off the lake, wishing I was wearing a princess skirt to whirl. Hardly anyone was on this strip of beach, so who cared if I looked stupid? No one knew me anyway.

On a whim, I rolled up my pant legs and waded into the water—and screeched. *Ay ay ay.* That was *cold.* Hurting cold! I splashed back onto the warm sand, but now wet sand clung like chiggers between my toes and up my legs. I sat down on the concrete bench to brush off the sand when I felt the first drop. And the second. I looked up. The clouds now hung low and heavy and looked about ready to dump.

Grabbing my sandals, I climbed back up to the grass and started running toward the pedestrian tunnel, hoping the grass would clean off my feet. By the time I emerged on the other side, the rain had become a chilly shower. Forgetting the paved path, I made a beeline across the grass and between the bushes toward Richmond Towers—and the next moment pitched forward on my face.

"Hey!" A raspy voice shot out of the bushes two feet from my head. "Whatchu go kickin' my cart for?" This pronouncement was followed by several hacking coughs.

I was more startled than hurt—except for my toe, which was sending stabs of pain up my leg. I rolled over and grabbed my foot, even as the rain soaked into my clothes and hair. *Cart? What cart?* I squinted in the fading light toward where I'd taken my fall and vaguely made out something metal sticking out from under the bush. "Sorry," I mumbled. "Didn't see it . . . where are you, anyway?"

The bushes parted, and a head poked out, half covered with what looked like a black plastic garbage bag. "Keepin' dry is where I'm at, tha's what." More hacking. "Leastwise I was till Orphan Annie came along . . . uh-oh. That foot's bleedin', girlie. Here, lemme see it."

To my astonishment, an old woman crawled out of the bushes, holding the thin protection of the garbage bag around her shoulders like a Superman cape, and grabbed up my bare foot in a thin, sinewy hand, even as the rain steadied into a moderate shower. "Aiya. Gotta stop that bleedin' . . . hang on a minnit." The woman dropped my foot and pulled out a metal cart from under the bushes, set it upright, and began digging through whatever was stuffed inside, her cough grinding away like a waterlogged car motor.

I scrambled up, standing on one leg, holding up the offending foot. "Oh, don't bother," I protested. "I really have to get . . ." *Home?* I couldn't yet say the word.

She hauled out a long rag. "Oh, don't get your mop in a knot. Siddown." The woman practically pushed me down, grabbed my bleeding foot, and began wrapping the rag around it. I shuddered. How long had *that* been in her cart, collecting germs and vermin and who knew what—

"It's clean, if tha's wha's botherin' ya." *Hack, hack.* She dropped my foot. "Now git on with ya, an' leave me be."

"Wait!" The absurdity of the situation suddenly loosened my tongue. Me go home to my sky-high penthouse while she crawled back under that bush? "This is ridiculous. It's raining, and you've got a terrible cough. Come on with me. I can get you dry clothes and some cough syrup." What she probably needed was a doctor.

The old lady snorted, sounding more like a bullfrog than a laugh. "Nah, I'm okay . . ."

But she hesitated just long enough to bolster my nerve. I took her arm. "Please, I mean it. Come on. Just until the rain stops, at least."

Rheumy eyes gave me a long stare, then she turned, grabbed the handle of her cart, and started across the wet grass. I caught up, steering her toward Richmond Towers. "My name's Gabby Fairbanks. Yours is . . . ?"

She didn't answer, just plowed on, with me hobbling along on my rag-wrapped foot. We crossed the frontage street and somehow wrestled her cart through the revolving door of the high-rise. And stopped.

The doorman loomed in front of us. His normally pleasant expression had evaporated, replaced by an enormous scowl that would have done justice to a bouncer at a skin joint. "Hey! Get that rickety cart outta here. Lady, you can't come in here. Residents only."

I waved timidly from behind the old lady. "Uh, she's with me, Mr. Bentley . . . Mrs. Fairbanks."

"Fairbanks? Penthouse?" The man's eyes darted between us. "Whatchu doin' with this old bag lady?" He suddenly became solicitous, though I noticed he kept a wary eye on my companion. "Are you all right, ma'am? What happened to your foot?"

"It's all right, Mr. Bentley. I, uh, we just need to get up to the, uh, apartment and get into some dry clothes." I beamed a smile that I hoped conveyed more confidence than I felt, took the "bag lady's" arm, ran my ID card that opened the security door, and headed for the elevator.

I let out a sigh of relief as the doors slid closed behind us, and the elevator quietly hummed its way upward. Closing my eyes, I started to shiver. I really needed to get out of these damp clothes, get cleaned up and changed before—

My eyes flew open. *Philip!* Philip and his guests were due at any time. *Oh Lord, oh Lord,* I pleaded silently. *Keep Philip out of here until at least eight o'clock.* A new absurdity was standing right in front of me. For the first time I took a really good look at the woman from the bushes. Matted gray hair . . . wrinkled, mottled skin, hanging loosely like a beige mask over her facial bones.

Several layers of clothes topped by a shapeless shirt or blouse, hard to tell, hanging out over faded navy blue pant legs, rolled up at different lengths. And here in the elevator, she smelled . . . stale.

Oh God. What in the world am I going to do with this, this—

"Lucy." The old woman's eyes were closed, and it didn't seem as if she had spoken at all, except for the raspy voice.

"Lucy," I repeated stupidly. "Oh! Your name. Thanks."

The upward motion stopped. The heavy doors glided open to reveal the glistening ceramic tile of the top floor foyer. Our apartment door was the only one to be seen, flanked by two enormous pots of silk flowers. "Well, come on, Lucy. Let's get you into some dry clothes and do something about that cough." *And get you out of here—quick,* I thought desperately.

I pulled out my keys and shoved one into the lock. Good. Got the right one on the first try. The lock clicked, and I pressed the brass latch to open the door. It swung wide and I hobbled into the gallery, Lucy huffing right behind me . . . and stopped.

There, through the archway, in the middle of the enormous living room stood my husband, tall, dark hair, easy good looks even at forty-one, a glass of wine in one hand, talking in a big voice to a strange man and woman, gesturing as though showing off the penthouse view.

In the same instant, they must have heard us, because all three turned, staring straight at me. Silence hung in the air for a split second. Then Philip took several strides in our direction, his eyes wide. Horrified, actually. "Gabrielle!" he hissed between his teeth. "What's the meaning of this?!"

chapter 2

I opened my mouth—but a bump from behind nearly knocked me over.

"Hey, wha's the holdup?" growled Lucy. "Ya gotta bathroom 'round here? I gotta pee."

"Uh, uh . . ." I cast a pleading grimace at my husband, whose face had turned a decidedly unpleasant purplish red. "Be right back," I whispered frantically at him. I peeked around Philip and tossed a weak smile at his guests, who held their wine glasses like startled statues frozen by the wand of the White Witch in Narnia. "Sorry!" I sang out. "A little emergency here. Be with you in a minute."

I turned and hurried Lucy in the opposite direction. Shoving her inside the powder room in the hallway just outside the kitchen, I made a beeline for the master bedroom. Could I take a quick shower, hop into something presentable, and get back to our guests before Lucy—if that was really her name—made it out of the half bath?

Philip was right on my heels, shutting the bedroom door behind us firmly. "Gabby!" He grabbed my arm. "Are you trying to ruin *everything* before I even get things off the ground?" He gaped at my feet. "Wait . . . what's wrong with your foot? Is that blood?" His voice changed. "Are you okay?"

I pulled my arm away. "Yes, I'm *fine*. And no, I'm not trying to ruin your evening. I just got caught in the rain and cut my foot, and she . . . never *mind*. Let me clean up, and I'll be with you in a few minutes." I pushed him away. I'd forgotten about my bloody toe. "Go *on*. Go back to your guests. I'll be there."

He ran a hand through his hair, still frustrated, and sighed loudly. "All right. But that . . . that—" He flung his arm toward the hallway where I'd penned the old woman. "Get her out of here, Gabby. *Now.*"

With a final glare, he opened the bedroom door—only to catch a raspy voice floating our way. "Now, ain't this nice. Real nice. But say, now, this here cheese'ud be good wit some sandwich makin's . . . hey Gabby! Where are ya? Ya got some bread an' stuff?"

Both Philip and I flew down the hall toward the dining room—where Lucy was helping herself to the fruit and cheese platter on the buffet and stuffing handfuls of nuts into the pockets of her baggy pants.

"Out! Out *now*," Philip hissed—meaning the old woman, but directed at me—before heading back toward the living room where I heard him say with fake cheerfulness, "Please forgive our little interruption, ha-ha . . . must've followed my wife home when she got caught in the rain . . . have it straightened out in a few minutes . . . oh, here, let me freshen that for you."

I turned my attention to our other "guest," who popped a

green olive into her mouth, then immediately spit it out into her hand, followed by a disturbing cough or two. "Come on, Lucy. I'll get you some real food to eat."

The old woman followed reluctantly, as though she wasn't sure she should leave a sure thing for the mere promise of something more. But I quickly served a plate of the pasta salads in the refrigerator, topped with some of the beef tips and rice from the warming oven. She refused to climb onto the barstool at the granite counter, choosing to stand and shovel the food hungrily while I grabbed a phone book and looked up "Homeless Shelters." I couldn't just send her back out into the rain, Philip or no Philip, not with that cough.

No luck. Surely Chicago had at least one homeless shelter in this area! Grabbing the cordless off the wall, I dialed 01 for the lobby. "Mr. Bentley? . . . Yes, it's, uh, Mrs. Fairbanks. Top floor. Do you know the whereabouts of a homeless shelter for women in the area? . . . uh-huh . . . uh-huh . . . Is that nearby? . . . All right. Thanks—no wait. Could you call a cab for my, uh, friend? . . . Thanks."

I put down the phone. Lucy had stopped chewing and was looking at me under disapproving brows. "Did anyone ask *me* if I wanna go to some homeless shelter? Whatchu think I am, chopped liver?" Without waiting for a reply, Lucy turned her attention back to the rice and beef tips, mumbling under her breath.

Deciding that she was still occupied for another sixty seconds, I hustled into the master bath, pulled open the mirrored medicine cabinet, and grabbed a bottle of cough medicine. As I closed the cabinet, I raised my eyes—and saw for the first time the disaster pretending to be Gabrielle Shepherd Fairbanks.

I nearly screeched. My dark chestnut hair, already naturally curly, looked like it had been stirred up by an overzealous egg beater and left dripping. My "waterproof" mascara had smeared and left dark smudges under both eyes—complemented by a muddy streak that started in the middle of my forehead, ran straight down my nose, and skipped to my chin. Oh, right. Where my face had plowed into the muddy grass. My white pantsuit was rumpled and damp with grass stains in front and muddy splotches at knee level, and my feet were still bare—except for Lucy's rag, which was stained red around my big toe.

Tears sprang to my eyes. What had I been thinking?! I *knew* my husband was bringing guests, that he was eager to impress his new partner-to-be. So what do I do? I go on a fling out to the beach like an irresponsible ten-year-old! I come back looking like something the dog drug in, with a smelly old bag lady in tow, who hadn't even wanted to come anyway. And—

Lucy! I'd only meant to leave her for half a minute. What if she'd wandered into the living room, scandalizing Mr. and Mrs. Whatzit—what did Philip say their names were?—Fenton, or Fenchel, something like that. Clutching the cough syrup, I dashed out of my bedroom, through the hall and into the kitchen . . . only to slow down in relief.

Lucy the bag lady was leaning on her hand and elbow on the counter, eyes closed, snoring.

I felt a bit hysterical, unsure whether I was going to laugh or cry. *Oh God, this is too crazy!* . . . Was that a prayer? It'd been a long time since I'd really prayed, other than lonely prayers heavenward, asking God to protect my boys and bring them back to me soon, or to give me patience when Philip made me feel like a ball-and-chain around his life. Little did he know that I'd long ago become used to wearing the ball-and-chain that went along with the Fairbanks name. No, take that back. I never got used to it . . . which is why I was in the mess I was in today.

"Lucy?" I gently shook the old lady's shoulder. "Lucy, wake up. We've got to go. Here, take a spoonful of this . . ." I poured some purple syrup in the plastic cap that came with the cough medicine. She gulped it meekly, only half-awake, and let me lead her down the hall. I hesitated at the gallery but heard voices in the den. Smart man, my Philip. Sequester the guests so they don't have to see me looking like Cinderella *before* the ball, shooing out one of the Sisty Uglers. I stifled a giggle as Lucy, her cart, and I rode down the elevator to the ground floor. *Sisty Uglers.* That's what I used to call the "Ugly Stepsisters" when I was five.

Thankfully, the taxi was waiting when we got downstairs to the lobby. I handed Mr. Bentley a ten for the cabbie and let him take over, getting the muttering old woman and her cart into the Yellow Cab, giving the driver the address of the shelter, and waving good riddance.

A quick shower, a long simple dress in royal blue, a quick blow-dry to my damp curls, a touch of mascara and blush, and I finally felt able to present myself to our guests. Philip looked me up and down with a hint of approval. I relaxed. "I apologize for that little snafu."

Philip's new partner threw back his head and guffawed. "Haven't heard that one in a while."

Philip grinned, as if they shared a private joke.

Whatever. I extended my hand to his wife, who looked like the prototype for white female actors on all the cop shows:

blonde hair to the shoulder, "pretty" features, business suit with short skirt, willowy legs, high, pointy heels. "Guess I need to start at the beginning. I'm Gabrielle. Most people call me Gabby. And you are—?"

The woman laid long, limp fingers in my hand, her eyes drifting somewhere past my ear. "Mona. Mona Fenchel," she murmured. The manicured fingernails fluttered in the air. "Lovely penthouse. Really. Lovely."

Yeah, and your husband's going to get an earful on the way home. "Who do they think they are, these Fairbanks? Buying a penthouse along Lake Shore Drive! And they've been in Chicago all of one minute. Did you see her when she came in? And what kind of name is Gabby? She's nothing but a hillbilly from—"

"Well, I'm delighted," boomed a voice, cutting off my imaginary rant. Mona's husband, tie loosened, shirt collar unbuttoned, shook my hand firmly. He looked about Philip's age—forty-one—a little fleshy about the face. "Henry Fenchel. Don't you worry about your little, heh-heh, *snafu*." A wink in Philip's direction. "These things happen. Homeless people all over the city these days. But they don't do too bad now that the weather's warming up. Downright industrious, some of them, selling the *Streetwise* newspaper on every corner downtown. But others . . ." He shook his head. "You can take them off the street, but you can't take the street out of them."

I did my best to smile brightly and be the perfect hostess, whisking the cold salads Camila had prepared to the buffet and rescuing the hot food from the warming oven. I lit candles on the teakwood dining room table, Philip poured wine, and the men chatted. I tried to engage Mona Fenchel in conversation—*How long had they been in Chicago? Did they have family here? Would she like more of the beef tips and rice?*—but not once did she look me in the eye.

I was relieved when they left. The grandfather clock solemnly bonged out ten chimes as the door closed behind them. The apartment was suddenly silent. I turned and saw Philip standing in the middle of the marble-tiled gallery, hands in his trouser pockets, jacket open, looking at me. "Let's talk, Gabrielle."

Uh-oh. Now I was going to get it. I sat on a hassock in the living room and tried once more to explain that I'd thought I had plenty of time, I didn't know it was about to rain, the old woman seemed sick and had no shelter . . .

But Philip couldn't get past his bottom line. "You *knew* I was bringing my new partner and his wife home to dinner. You *knew* this was important to me!"

I nodded meekly. "You're right. I'm sorry, Philip."

But my apology only seemed to trigger a long list of my sins. Did I know how long he'd had to keep them in the den, refreshing their wine glasses while I did my little goody-two-shoes thing? . . . He was lucky Henry Fenchel had a sense of humor, thought the whole thing was amusing . . . But I had certainly offended the wife—something you just don't do in business partnerships . . .

Again I said I was sorry. And I was. The whole thing was inconsiderate of me, and my good intentions had certainly backfired. I assured Philip I wanted his new business venture to succeed, and I would make it up to him somehow.

But we still went to bed with our backs turned to each other.

As Philip's steady breathing turned into soft snores, I lay awake staring into the unfriendly darkness, trying not to think about the fact that we were lying prone, thirty-two floors above terra firma, like being levitated by an unseen magician. Instead, I tried to count the days until P.J. and Paul could join us here in Chicago. Mid-April now . . . middle school graduation at the academy near the end of May . . .

But in the darkness, a wrinkled face with alert, darting eyes kept appearing in my mind's eye.

Lucy.

Did she get to the shelter all right? Was she safe in a bed with actual sheets and blankets? What would happen to her tomorrow? She still needed to see a doctor for that awful cough. Would she go? Would someone take her? Or would she end up back out in the park under the bushes?

I felt a surge of anticipation. Once Philip went to work, I'd get on the phone and try to call the shelter. *No.* Even better. I'd take a taxi, go to the shelter, and find out for myself.

chapter 3

Daylight filled the muted Vienna shades like a bar of white chocolate. *Mmm. Chocolate.* My stomach rumbled. Must be time to get up. I flung out an arm . . . and realized Philip's side of the bed was empty.

What time was it, anyway? I squinted at the red digital numbers on our bedside clock. *Eight twenty?!* I tumbled out of the king-size bed and into the bathroom. I never slept this late! In fact, I was usually up before Philip, trying to make a decent breakfast and eat together before he left for work—though more often than not, he just took a couple of bites of scrambled eggs, grabbed his coffee and bagel, and dashed out the door after a peck on my cheek.

Gargling a shot of mouthwash and running a brush through my snarly hair, I grabbed my bathrobe from the back of the door and headed down the hall, hoping to find Philip before he was off for the day. But the house—*apartment? condo? flat? What in the world did one call this oversize tree house?*—was eerily silent. Padding into the living room, I pulled the cord on the floor-to-ceiling drapes. Drat. Cloudy and gray. But up here in the stratosphere, I couldn't even hear the traffic below. No treetops interrupted the sky. Only other tall, glitzy residential buildings and hotels to my right and left, standing at attention along Lake Shore Drive while life scurried along down below.

In the kitchen, a note was propped on the coffeemaker. "Gabrielle, remember we've got a theater date tonight, 7:00. And no bag ladies!" Then he'd added a PS: "Forgot to tell you the maid comes to clean on Fridays, 9 a.m."

What maid? Every Friday? Good grief, what else did I have to do except clean the house? The stove digital said 8:40. *Oh, great.* So much for a leisurely cup of coffee. I hopped into the shower and then pulled on a clean pair of white capris and a rose-colored cotton sweater. With an eye on the clock, I made the bed and plumped the shams. No way did I want some girl from Maids R Us thinking I couldn't even make my own bed.

The intercom chimed while I was drying my hair. I buzzed the security door downstairs, feeling smug that I'd accomplished so much in just twenty minutes. Two minutes later, the doorbell rang. I pulled open the door. "Oh! Camila!"

The round-faced Latina who had prepared our buffet dinner so expertly the night before stood beaming in the hallway, a snug gray cardigan her only wrap. "*Buenos días,* Señora Fairbanks." She held a bucket full of cleaning supplies in one hand and a mop in the other.

For some reason I felt like throwing my arms around her and giving her a hug. A familiar face! But I just grinned and let her in. "Please, just call me Gabby. We . . . I . . . uh, I'm not sure what to tell you to do. We only moved in last weekend. There are a lot of boxes still in the spare bedrooms." I laughed self-consciously. "We haven't been here long enough to get it dirty yet, but—"

"No problem, Señora Fairbanks. I cleaned for the people who owned the penthouse before you. And"—she hefted the bucket, chuckling—"I brought my own cleaning supplies today. In case yours are still packed. Where would you like me to start?"

"Uh . . ." My mind scrambled. "The kitchen, I guess . . . oh, no, uh, I still need to eat breakfast." For some reason, I felt my face flush. Camila had probably gotten up at six, eaten breakfast already, and traveled to Richmond Towers from who knows how far away, while the spoiled rich lady barely had her eyes open.

I felt like screaming at my husband. *Don't embarrass me like this!*

Camila started in the living room and the den, courteously giving me time to finish in the bathroom and make a fresh pot of coffee. As I perched on a kitchen stool, munching a toasted bagel at the marble counter, she bustled past me toward the bedroom. A moment later I heard her call out, "Oh, no, no, señora, you don't have to make the bed. I need to wash the sheets on Friday." I heard the muffled sounds of the bed being stripped.

So much for making the bed. So much for first names, too, I guessed.

I finished my coffee, put my dishes in the dishwasher, and wiped the counter, listening with frustration to Camila's happy humming coming from the other room. What in the world was I supposed to do with myself while she cleaned? I couldn't unpack boxes—that would get in her way.

At least back in Virginia, I'd been raising the boys, driving them to school and sports, helping them with homework, and volunteering at the League of Women Voters. And, oh yes, the

Petersburg Garden Club, thanks to a membership from my mother-in-law. A weekly cleaning lady seemed justified then . . . especially when I went back to school to complete my credits as a certified therapeutic recreational specialist—much to Philip's amusement, who thought a CTRS was a fancy name for fun and games.

But it stood me in good stead landing the job as a recreational therapist at the Briarwood Senior Center. Especially when Philip registered Philip Junior at boarding school two years ago. He'd only been eleven, going into sixth grade. And last fall, Paul had joined him, emptying the house of my heart.

At least I'd had my job, something that made me feel useful. Needed. Filled the long days and hours.

Hot tears rose up unbidden, thinking of P.J. and Paul. *Oh God, I miss them so much.* I grabbed a napkin, dabbed my eyes, and blew my nose. Good grief, they were still just *boys*, only thirteen and eleven. So what if the Fairbanks males "always" attended George Washington Preparatory Academy? They had Shepherd in them, too, and Shepherds went to school half a mile from home, like everyone else, wearing jeans with holes in the knee, and sporting a tie only at weddings and funerals, if then.

I slid off the stool. I had to get out of here. But go where? Do what? And then I remembered.

Lucy.

That's it! I was going to find that homeless women's shelter and see if they'd taken her in. Just inquire how the old lady's cough was doing. Tell the staff how we'd met in the rain. Laugh about it. Say hello and good-bye.

Grabbing my purse from the coat closet in the gallery, I ran down the hall and poked my head into the master bath, where Camila was scrubbing the shower. "Camila? I'm leaving now. Do you know how long you'll be? If I'm not back, can you just lock the front door behind you?"

She waved a hand ensconced in a yellow rubber glove. "No problem, Señora Fairbanks! Sí, you go. Everything will be fine."

Thankfully, Mr. Bentley was on duty again, though he pursed his lips and frowned when I asked if he would call a cab for me and find the address again for that same homeless shelter where he'd sent the bag lady last night.

"Now, what you want to go there for, Mrs. Fairbanks? Have you been to State Street yet? Or"—he glanced outside—"well, guess it's not the best day to go up the Sears Tower. Clouds too low. But how about North Michigan Avenue? Lots of shopping there."

I tried to keep impatience out of my voice. "Please, just call a cab, Mr. Bentley. And get that same address, if you would."

The cab pulled up in front of a brick church squeezed between other two- and three-story buildings. I peered out the window. "Is this it? Where—?"

"This is the address, lady." The cab driver pointed at the church. "Building burned down a couple of years ago. That one you see there is brand-new. Don't know why they put in that stained-glass window an' stuff. The old building hadn't been used as a church for years, much less this one. You want me to wait?"

I looked at the meter. $7.85. I handed him a ten. "No, thanks." I got out and stood on the sidewalk. Seemed like it had taken barely five minutes to get here. Must not be that far from Richmond Towers. Maybe I could walk back.

As the taxi pulled away, a stab of doubt weakened my resolve.

I didn't see a sign anywhere saying "Women's Shelter." Several broad steps led up to a set of double oak doors, flanked by stained-glass windows on either side. High above the doors, cradled by the peak of the building, the wooden beams of a cross stretched top to bottom and side to side inside a circular stained-glass window.

Not far away I heard the metallic rattle of the elevated train, catching my eye as it passed over the street a couple of blocks away. I craned my neck to see what else was on the block. Most of the buildings seemed to be two- and three-story apartment buildings, though to the right of the church building was a Korean grocery, a Pay-Day Loan, and a twenty-four-hour Laundromat, with apartments above.

A young couple with a baby in a stroller turned the corner by the Laundromat and walked briskly toward me. He was white; she was black. *Interesting.* That would raise a few eyebrows back in Petersburg. I stepped aside to let them pass, but they stopped.

"Hi." The young man spoke first. "Can we help you?"

"Oh. Well, yes, maybe you can. I'm looking for a"—*How dumb was this going to sound?*—"um, a women's shelter that's supposed to be around here."

The young black woman laughed as she bent down to pick up the baby from the stroller. "Well, you found it!" She tipped her chin toward the oak doors of the church, cradling the baby on her hip. "Come with us. We're going in."

She spoke with a Spanish accent, sounding like the cleaning woman, but Camila had creamy tan skin as I supposed most Hispanic-Americans had. This woman was dark skinned, with loose, black corkscrew ringlets caught back from her forehead by a broad, bright-orange cloth headband. And her whole face seemed to laugh—a wide, bright smile and dancing dark eyes.

"Josh, grab the stroller, will you?" The young mother skipped up the stairs. "Come, *niñita*, let's go find Auntie Mabel." She pulled open one of the oak doors and disappeared inside.

Was Josh the baby's father? He seemed so fair, sandy hair down around his collar, looking more like a college kid than anything else. The mother was definitely black, and the baby . . . hard to tell. Creamy tan skin, dark hair, but loose and curly. Well, daddy or not, Josh obediently folded the little umbrella stroller with a kick to the brace between the wheels, darted up the stairs, and caught the door before it closed, holding it open for me.

I followed, but only as I got to the top step did I see the simple brass plaque beside the doors that said Manna House.

chapter 4

Inside, the stained-glass windows on either side of the double oak doors filled the foyer with prisms of color and light. Large plants standing on the floor softened the large square entryway. In the open doorway of an office to my left, the young mother, still bouncing the baby on her hip, stood talking to an older black woman in a black skirt and soft, lime green sweater.

"Hi, Mabel. We have a guest," the young man announced.

"Oh, I am sorry. I did not introduce myself!" The younger woman shifted the baby and extended her hand. "My name is Edesa Reyes Baxter"—she dimpled at the young man—"and this is my husband, Josh Baxter. And this is Mabel Turner, the director of Manna House."

The baby in Edesa's arms let out a squeal and grabbed her mother's ear for attention.

"Oh, hush, hush, *mi niña.*" Edesa Baxter unhooked the baby's fingers, laughing. "I would not forget you! This is Gracie. God's miracle gift to Manna House."

What an odd thing to say, I thought. *Wait a minute. Does the baby belong to the couple? Or is she homeless and staying at the shelter? No, that couldn't be. But why—*

My thoughts were interrupted by the director, who shook my hand firmly. "Can we help you in some way, Mrs. . . . ?"

She must have seen the wedding ring on my left hand. "Gabby Fairbanks. Actually, um, I was looking for an older woman I ran into yesterday. She had a cough and was sitting under a bush in the rain. She said her name was . . . um, her name was—" For some reason, I totally blanked.

"Ah! You must mean Lucy." Mabel smiled. "So you're the mysterious person who sent her here by taxi. I think she's still here. Josh, would you check to see whether she signed out?"

Josh Baxter sauntered over to the receptionist's cubicle on the other side of the foyer—a glass-enclosed cubby with an open window into the foyer, and a wide ledge on which lay a big notebook. Suddenly I felt foolish. What in the world was I doing here? I half hoped the old woman had signed herself out. If she was here, what would I say? *How are you?* . . . *Fine.* . . . *How's your cough?* . . . *Fine. Or worse. Whatever.* And then our "conversation" would be over.

Oh, suck it up, I told myself. I was here now. Might as well just do it. I smiled, trying to look self-confident. "That would be nice. I was just concerned about her. Uh, do you have many women staying here?"

Mabel Turner shrugged. "It varies. We have beds for forty-eight residents—but that includes a few with kids, who we try to put in a room together as a family, if possible. Some stay for two weeks or two months. Longer than that, we try to find transitional housing. Sometimes they just disappear back onto the street. Especially when the weather gets warmer."

Residents. She called them residents. I needed to remember that.

"Lucy didn't sign out," Josh called over. "Guess she's still here."

"I'll find her." Edesa shifted little Gracie to her other hip. "I've got fifteen minutes until I lead Bible study. Would you like a tour of Manna House, uh—I'm sorry, I forgot your name already." She seemed genuinely flustered.

"Gabby. Short for Gabrielle." I smiled reassuringly. "That's all right. You've got your hands full." I followed her through the double swinging doors into a large room. "Gracie . . . that's a pretty name. How old is she?" I was fishing, I knew.

"Eight months. Or thereabouts." Edesa kissed the top of the baby's soft black hair. "Her mother was a drug addict, and she never actually told us a birth date. Josh and I are adopting her. Takes a long time, though." She made a face at me. "Too long."

Well, okay. That was a successful fishing expedition.

"This is our multipurpose room." Edesa swept a hand around the large, bright room. Several women of various ages and colors were looking at magazines or talking in "seating groups" created by overstuffed chairs and small couches draped with colorful covers. A large woman—Mexican maybe?—hovered over a cabinet by the wall, pumping hot coffee from a large carafe into an over-size Styrofoam cup. Two young women barely out of their teens played cards at a table along the opposite wall.

"Yeah," fussed a voice, lounging somewhere within the cushions of the closest love seat. "An' Edesa been sayin' for months we gonna rename this room. Sheeze Louise! What kinda name is 'multipurpose,' I axe you?"

Edesa laughed. "Okay, Precious. Show yourself. Have you seen Lucy?"

A dark face appeared over the back of the love seat, a woman I guessed was somewhere in her thirties. Rows upon rows of tiny braids clung tightly to her head and hung down to her shoulders. "Take a guess where Miz Lucy's at! Down in the kitchen, eatin' breakfast leftovers. . . . Oh, 'scuse me." The woman hopped up, came around the couch, and held out her hand to me. "Name's Precious McGill. Didn't mean to be rude."

I shook her hand. "I'm Gabby Fairbanks."

"What are you doing here?" Edesa asked her. "You don't usually come till three." She turned to me. "Precious is one of our volunteers. She and her daughter Sabrina help supervise our after-school program—such as it is—three days a week. We need more tutors."

I blushed slightly. I'd assumed she was one of the "residents."

"Girl, ain't no school today, an' ain't no after-school program, neither. It's Good Friday. An' Jewish somethin' too—oh, yeah, Passover. Wait till Gracie starts school. Then ya gonna be scramblin' for child care two, three extra times a month 'cause it's this or that holiday again. Equal opportunity religious holidays, ya know. Can't ya hear them kids downstairs?"

Now that she'd mentioned it, I did hear muted squeals, thumps, and the general hubbub that goes along with kids at play coming from below.

Edesa made a face. "Speaking of Good Friday, I'm supposed to lead a Bible study on those scriptures in a few minutes, and I was giving Mrs. Fairbanks here a tour. Could you . . . ?" She looked hopefully at Precious.

I almost said, "Please. Just call me Gabby." But I gave up. Did I have "Mrs. Fairbanks" tattooed across my forehead or something?

"Oh, sure. Got plenty of time till I need to throw lunch

together. Fillin' in for Estelle today." Precious reached for Gracie. "Gimme that baby too. She need changin' or anything?"

And so Gracie and I were both handed over to Precious McGill, who cheerfully chatted nonstop as she showed me the toddler playroom populated by two toddlers and one mother on a cell phone, a schoolroom with two computers (deserted), a small TV room with a news station blabbing away to no one, and a small prayer chapel, all on the first floor. On the second floor, six medium-sized bedrooms held four bunks in each, plus showers, bathrooms, and a small central lounge. I felt embarrassed peeking into the sleeping rooms when someone was there, even though the doors were open, and Precious didn't bother to introduce me to anyone. She just said, "Hey there," or "Say hi to Tanya, Gracie," waving the baby's hand.

My tour guide did a quick change of the baby's diaper, using a stash of disposables in the second-floor lounge. Then we headed for the basement, where we peeked into a large recreation room. A handful of kids ranging in age from maybe six to eleven were sprawled in the beanbag chairs, watching cartoons, though a teenage girl and a little boy were playing foosball. Precious poked me. "That's my Sabrina over there, getting whupped by little Sammy."

The lower level also boasted a well-equipped kitchen and dining room, and that's where we found the old woman I'd met yesterday, hunched over a paper plate, wiping up the last drips of syrup with a rolled-up pancake.

"Someone to see you, Miz Lucy . . . Nice to meetchu, Miz Gabby. I'm gonna go catch Edesa's Bible study while I have a chance. Don't get to sit in too often, 'cause I'm usually waitressin' at this café, but this week they give me Friday off. Come on up later, if you want." And Precious disappeared up the stairs with the Baxter baby.

Lucy looked up at me with her watery eyes. *"Humph."* The old woman finished mopping up syrup, coughed a couple of times into a napkin, stuffed the last bite of pancake into her mouth, then looked up at me again. "You gonna jus' stand there? Go on. Siddown." It was the same raspy voice. "You hungry?"

"No, I'm fine." I pulled out a molded plastic chair and sat. "I . . . I just came to see if you made it okay to the shelter last night. I was worried about your cough. And . . ." I felt my face flush. "I wanted to apologize for my husband's rudeness yesterday. I didn't know he'd be home."

Lucy just stared at me again. She was wearing different clothes than yesterday, a pair of yellow pants, gym shoes with no socks, a large white T-shirt, and a brown, nubby-knit cardigan. Her frowzy hair looked as if it had been washed. Good. At least she'd gotten a bath and clean clothes. And food. I smiled inwardly.

Finally she spoke. "Yeah, well. He can't help it. I shoulda known better'n ta go up ta that fancy penthouse wit' you." She coughed and cackled a laugh. "Man, that was some highfalutin place you got there. Ain't never seen one o' them. An' that bathroom smelled mighty good. Didn't have no bathtub in it, though. You must be payin' through the nose for that place, an' they don't even put a bathtub in there?"

I laughed, feeling more at ease. "Don't worry. It has two more bathrooms with bathtubs *and* showers." I didn't mention the Jacuzzi tub. "But I'm sorry the situation was awkward. We just moved here to Chicago, and my husband was entertaining his new business partner. And then we come in, all drippy wet, and me barefoot, bleeding on the rug . . ."

Lucy grinned, showing a few missing teeth. "Heh-heh, gotta admit. The look on they faces was priceless." And then she laughed, a series of snorts and guffaws, punctuated by a few more raspy coughs. I couldn't help it. I started to laugh too. It *was* funny. I just hadn't had anyone to laugh about it with yet. Until Lucy.

After a few moments, she wiped her eyes with a well-used napkin and struggled upward out of her chair. "Well, I'm goin' upstairs to sit in somethin' more comfortable than this plastic chair. You comin'?"

I followed her up the stairs to the main level and into the multipurpose room. Edesa had pulled several of the couches and chairs into a bigger circle, where she sat with a Bible open on her lap, talking earnestly to a group of five or six women. The baby was nowhere to be seen; Josh neither. Maybe he had Gracie in the toddler playroom while Mommy taught the Bible study. *That's sweet.*

Lucy sank with a wheeze into an overstuffed chair outside the circle, feigning disinterest, but I noticed she sat close enough to hear what Edesa was saying. I did too.

". . . no accident that *Jesús*"—she pronounced it *Hesús*—"was celebrating the Passover feast with His disciples that night, the day we now call Good Friday. For centuries, this Jewish feast had commemorated their deliverance from bondage in Egypt, that old, old story when Moses told the Hebrew slaves to put the blood of a lamb on their doorposts, and the angel of death would *pass over* them when he saw the blood . . ."

Something stirred in me. *Good Friday.* I hadn't thought much about it for years—not since that knucklehead, Damien Spencer, superstar youth leader at Minot Evangelical Church, had married me right out of high school and then dumped me two years later.

I refused to go to church after that, even though it upset my parents. In fact, I'd been pretty mad at God all through college—until I met Philip. And then it seemed my storybook dreams were all coming true, and God just didn't seem important anymore.

Oh, sure, our names were on the membership roll of Briarwood Lutheran Church, and Philip and I took the kids to church on Christmas and Easter—even sometimes in between, especially when my parents came to visit—because that's what the good, solid, God-fearing Fairbanks family had done for generations.

But it'd been a long time since I'd thought much about Good Friday. Philip said he didn't understand people who acted all gloomy and sad, as if Jesus had just died that day, and I kind of agreed with him. Christians believe He'd risen from the dead two thousand years ago, right? Why not skip right to Easter, with its joyful resurrection music and traditional brunch and egg-rolling races on the church lawn? So that's what we did.

But all that was yesterday. Today we were in a new town, a big city where we didn't know anyone, didn't have anyone to impress, didn't even know where the churches were. Where would we go to church Easter Sunday? Did it even matter?

I almost wanted to laugh. Or cry. Here I was, sitting in the multipurpose room of a homeless women's shelter in Chicago, with the only "friend" I'd met so far, listening to a twenty-something black woman with a Spanish accent talk about Jesus and the angel of death and why the Jewish Passover was important to Good Friday—and for some reason I didn't understand, I was hanging on every word.

". . . and now Jesus, the Lamb of God, was about to sacrifice Himself and spill His blood to deliver *all* of us from death. He broke the bread that night and said, 'This is My broken body.' He filled the cups with wine and said, 'This is My blood,' fulfilling the true meaning of this Passover feast, once and for all.'"

"Sounds gory ta me," Lucy muttered loudly.

Edesa grinned. "*Sí*. You're right, Lucy. Jesus' death on the cross wasn't pretty. But He took the punishment for our sins so we don't have to be separated from a holy God, either in this life or when we die—oh, praise You, *Senŏr!*"

To my surprise, the pretty young woman got choked up and had to grab a tissue and dab her eyes. After a moment she recovered and ended with a short prayer. The few shelter residents who'd attended the Bible study just got up and wandered away, although one pole-slim woman went up to Edesa and said, "That was good. Real good. Thanks." And then, "Is it time for lunch yet?"

"Lunch is in half an hour!" Mabel Turner's voice chimed in from the back. "Tina, Tanya, Carolyn, and Lucy . . . you're on setup and serving." She glanced around the room. "Where's Carolyn? Would someone remind her she's on setup? . . . Thanks, Tina."

I made a few mental notes: Tina was the big Hispanic, Tanya was the tall, skinny black woman who seemed to be Sammy's mother, Lucy was Lucy, didn't know who Carolyn was.

"Hey, I got this cough," Lucy growled. She hacked a few times to prove her point. "You don't want me coughing all over the food, do ya?"

"Hmm. All right. Cleanup instead."

"*Humph*." Lucy made her way toward the stairs to the lower level without a backward glance at me.

I looked around for Precious, but she must have slipped out to start lunch. I made my way over to the director and smiled. "Like summer camp. Everyone has chores?"

Mabel arched an eyebrow. Her skin shimmered like polished oak, with just the right amount of blush and burgundy lipstick for a businesswoman. "No to summer camp. Yes to daily chores. One of the rules. Everyone needs to contribute in some way to their room and board while they're here."

I nodded in the direction of Edesa Baxter, who was gathering up her Bible and notes. "You have a Bible study and an after-school program . . . I didn't realize a homeless shelter had activities." I gave a self-deprecating laugh. "Guess I assumed it was just a bare-bones bed-and-breakfast for the homeless."

The director shook her head. "To tell you the truth, Mrs. Fairbanks—Gabby—we'd like to do more. Manna House has only been back in operation since last Thanksgiving. And it's a long way up from the streets to a productive member of society. Even when the women are getting off drugs, learning how to work the system, getting some job training . . . there's a lot of downtime. Hurry up and wait. What I'd really like to find is a program director to give our residents life skills and enrichment experiences. But . . ." She shrugged. "We can't pay much, so it's hard to find someone qualified."

I nodded my head and smiled like a robot. But all over my body, nerve endings jumped to life like a racecar with all pistons firing.

Program director? *That's me!*

chapter 5

I opened my mouth and then closed it again like a stupid gold-fish. *Don't be a nut, Gabby!* I told myself. *You don't know anything about homeless women or what they need. Not to mention Philip would never hear of it.* Ignoring the voices in my head, I opened my mouth and blurted, "Program director? I'd like to hear more—"

"Mabel? Mabel Turner! Phone!"

The young woman manning the reception desk overrode my tentative inquiry. Mabel headed swiftly for her office off the foyer, calling to me over her shoulder, "Please feel free to stay for lunch, Gabby. We enjoy visitors!" And she disappeared through the swinging doors.

I stayed, hoping I'd get a chance to speak to the director again. But I felt awkward, standing in the lunch line in my Calvin Klein capris and Esprit hooded sweater, along with women who had probably never seen the inside of Nordstrom's or Marshall Fields. I said hi and smiled at some of the kids, but they were more intent on filling their paper plates with taco salad and tortilla chips, and balancing large plastic glasses of Hawaiian punch. I noticed that most of the other women left one or two seats between them, eating without much conversation.

When I got to the counter, a middle-aged white woman, who was serving the taco salad—hairnet covering her hair, plastic gloves on her hands—looked me over, frowning. "You just come in today? Did you sign in with Ms. Turner?"

Precious, bustling back and forth behind the counter, came to my rescue. "This is Miz Gabby Fairbanks, Carolyn. She's a visitor. Friend of Miz Lucy's."

"Oh really."

I could tell she believed *that*. Lucy had been first in line and was already in a corner of the dining room, shoveling in mouthfuls of salad and washing it down with punch.

I bypassed the red punch for a glass of water instead, wondering where I should sit. Well, darn it, I came to see Lucy, so I was going to sit with Lucy. I sat. We ate. The silence was punctuated only by the sound of crunching chips, slurps of punch, and the occasional raspy cough.

Might as well try to get better acquainted. "The people here seem to know you, Lucy. Have you been here before?"

I got The Look. *Okay, dumb question.*

"Have you lived in Chicago most of your life?"

This time I didn't even get a look. Lucy got up abruptly and headed for the counter, returning a minute later with another glass of punch and a handful of oatmeal cookies, which she held out to me with just one word: "Nope."

"*Nope?*" Oh, right. Her reply to my question about living in Chicago.

"Thanks." I took a cookie and nibbled the edges.

Guess I wasn't going to get much with yes and no questions. I wanted so much to ask about her story. Lucy couldn't have been homeless her whole life! How did she end up on the street?—or to be more exact, under a bush in the park along Lake Shore Drive? I looked at her rough, wrinkled skin and wondered what she'd looked like as a girl. Had she been married? Did she have any children? If so, how could they let their mother end up like this?!

Lucy stood up, piling my paper plate on top of her own. "Huh. If ever'body cleaned up after themselves, wouldn't be no need for a cleanup crew. Well, thanks for comin' ta visit me. If I don't see ya again, been real nice." She turned away.

"Wait. Lucy. I'd, um, I'd like to see you again. If I came back—"

"Nah, don't bother. If it don't rain this weekend, I'll prob'ly be outta here."

Boldness took over common sense. "But what about that cough? You really ought to get medical help."

Lucy rolled her eyes. "Lady . . . Gabby . . . whatever you wanna be called. I been takin' care of myself 'fore you came along, and I intend to do just that after you leave. But if it makes you feel any better, the nurse comes here ever' Wednesday, an' I'll probably let her fill me up with that red stuff an' a bunch o' pills, if it ain't gone already by then. Satisfied?" And she stalked off with our paper plates and plastic glasses.

My face burned. I felt like shouting after her, *"Well, good for you!"* But it was obviously time for me to leave. Mabel Turner hadn't shown up during lunch, and asking about the program director job was a dumb idea anyway.

I waved good-bye to Precious behind the counter and scur-

ried upstairs as quickly as I could, now eager to be gone. I'd
overstayed my welcome as it was. Should I call a cab? Or just
walk? It hadn't seemed that far. Maybe the receptionist had a map
and I could figure it out . . .

Luckily for me, she did. But while the receptionist—who
looked slightly Asian to me, but mixed, yes, definitely mixed—
was pointing out the location of Manna House on the map, in the
neighborhood just north of Wrigley Field, a male voice said, "You
leaving now, Mrs. Fairbanks?"

I turned. Josh Baxter stood behind me, holding the baby. "Yes.
I'm trying to figure out if I can walk back to Richmond Towers
without getting myself lost. It's not that far, is it?" I pointed out
the area on the map.

"Mm-hm, about two miles straight up Sheridan Road. But I
was just outside; I came back to get an umbrella. Could rain any
minute. Hey, Gracie and I are going to catch the northbound El
up to Rogers Park. If you don't mind riding the El, I could tell you
where to get off. It's just a couple of stops north." He grinned and
waved the umbrella. "Besides, we've got cover."

Which is how I found myself walking two blocks to the
Sheridan El Station, pushing a baby stroller, while Josh Baxter
held the umbrella against the light drizzle. "You're going home
without Edesa?" *Obviously.* I might as well have asked *why*, as if it
was any of my business.

He laughed. "Okay, you're not going to believe this, but she's
staying to study. She'll come home later, in time for Good Friday
service tonight. But it's easier for her to find a quiet corner to do
her homework at the shelter—the chapel usually works—than it
is in our tiny studio apartment with Gracie. She's trying to get
her MA in public health, but Gracie kind of interrupted that last

fall . . . didn't you, kiddo?" Josh bent down to tickle Gracie's neck, making her giggle, but in the process, the open umbrella nearly knocked me into the gutter. "Sorry!" he said, and grabbed me back onto the sidewalk.

At the El station, Josh showed me how to buy a CTA pass in the machine, insert the card into the turnstile, and grab it when it came popping out while pushing on the bar. He handed the stroller to me over the top of the turnstile, then came through carrying Gracie. I followed them up the stairs to the El platform, which stood eye to eye with the second-floor windows of nearby buildings.

My stomach got queasy as I glanced over the edge of the platform and realized how easily one could stumble (or be pushed) off the platform, down onto the tracks in the middle with no way to get back up. I backed as far away from the edge as possible, though that didn't help much. Behind me, only a short wall stood between me and the two-story drop to the street below.

An elevated train rattled and squealed its way into the station, stopped, and the car doors slid open. People got off. People got on. "This is ours. Red Line," Josh said, beckoning to me. Feeling foolish for my wobbly knees, I stepped gingerly into the car across what seemed like a big, wide crack and grabbed the nearest pole. Josh and Gracie swung into one of the molded plastic seats. "Come on. Sit down. It's safer."

I sank into the seat beside them as the elevated train jerked and picked up speed. I blushed. "Sorry. Heights are sometimes a problem for me."

"That's all right. Is this your first time on the El?"

I repeated my story about just moving to Chicago a week ago, we didn't really know anyone, we had an "apartment" in one of the high-rises, my husband was going into business here with a partner . . . while Gracie pulled herself up on her foster daddy's lap and stared at the people in the seats behind us.

"What about you, Josh?" I cocked my head so I could see his face. Nice-looking kid. College age, if you asked me. Sandy hair, a bit shaggy, but that seemed to be the style these days. "How long have you and Edesa been married?"

He laughed. "Since Christmas! Let's see . . . almost four months."

"Four months! But . . . how long have you had Gracie?" Didn't these kids know it made sense to wait awhile before starting a family? Even a honeymoon pregnancy would've given them nine months to get used to each other.

He grinned again. "Five months. She's the reason we got married. *When* we did, I mean. We were engaged but planning to wait till we both finished school."

"And Edesa? She speaks such fluent Spanish! What is her background?—Oh, I'm sorry, Josh. I know I'm asking too many personal questions."

Josh laughed. "It's all right. She's from Honduras. Came to Chicago on a student visa. Just like there are African-Americans, there are African-*Central*-Americans—oh. This is your stop, Mrs. Fairbanks. Berwyn, see? When you get down to the street, just walk two blocks over to Sheridan, then turn left—that'll be north. Should only be a block or so to your high-rise. You'll be all right? The rain doesn't look too bad."

I nodded, shoring up my confidence. "Thanks, Josh. I appreciate it. Best wishes with Gracie's adoption." I stood and was swept out the door with other disembarking passengers. A moment later, the train was gone.

Down on the street level, I walked the two blocks to Sheridan Road, crossed the street and turned left. Sure enough, I saw Richmond Towers up ahead, jutting into the air like a giant glass tube that had been fast frozen. But Josh was wrong about the rain. I managed to get downright soaked by the time I pushed through the revolving doors of the Sheridan Road entrance into the lobby.

Mr. Bentley looked up from behind the half-moon counter that gave him full view of both entrances. I'd already figured out that the true urbanites—the ones with no cars, who walked everywhere or used public transportation—used the Sheridan Road entrance. Those with cars used the frontage road entrance, near the parking garage. I felt proud of myself, going out and making it back again *sans* car.

The bald doorman with the wiry gray beard rimming his jawline peered at me over the top of the reading glasses he'd been using to read the newspaper. "Mrs. Fairbanks." *Not hello or good afternoon. Just saying my name, the way a teacher might if I walked into class late.* "You are wet again. You seem to have a knack for getting caught in the rain without an umbrella."

I didn't have the guts to say, *"So? None of your business."* Besides, maybe the man was just joking with me. I chose joking. "Yep. Except this time I have my shoes on, and I'm not bleeding." I tossed him my best grin.

The eyebrows went up. "Uh-huh. *And* you did not bring home any strays today. Mm, three out of four isn't bad for a new-comer." He grinned at me. "You'd better get into some dry clothes, Mrs. Fairbanks, before you catch a whopping Chicago spring cold."

I left him chuckling and headed for the elevator. But he had it wrong. I'd managed to avoid *four* out of *five* of yesterday's "sins." Today I was getting home *before* my husband, and I had plenty of time to get out of my wet capris and sweater, take a long, hot bath, and get gussied up for our theater date tonight.

chapter 6

Philip was pleased that I was dressed and ready to go when he got home. I freshened my makeup while he showered and changed clothes, watching as he dressed in dark gray wool slacks, a black silk shirt, and a light gray two-button sport coat. At forty-one, he was still incredibly good looking, no paunch, with a hint of that boyish glint in his eye that had first attracted me.

"Did the cleaning woman work out today?" he said, pulling on a pair of Gucci loafers.

"Yes, fine." I decided not to mention that I'd left her alone a good portion of the time she was here on her first day. Would he mind? Good grief, cleaning services had to be bonded or something, didn't they? "Her name is Camila."

"Oh. Got the tickets?"

I could tell he wouldn't remember her name. He might never meet her. Even her check would go to the cleaning service, not to her personally.

As Philip drove our Lexus through the wet streets, I was captivated by the way each drop on the windshield briefly captured glints of streetlights before it was swiped away. My thoughts drifted with each swipe . . . how had Camila ended up in Chicago in the first place? Had she always cleaned other people's houses? Did she have a husband? Kids? Uncles and cousins living in the same house? That was the stereotype, anyway—

"What's that address again?"

"What?—oh." I squinted at the ticket packet. *Blue Man Group. Briar Street Theater.* "North Halsted . . . there, isn't that it? Wow, I didn't know it'd be so close." We'd only been driving ten or fifteen minutes. Could this be near the Manna House shelter? For a moment I felt as if I'd come through a time warp. I'd spent a good part of the day at a shelter for homeless women, eating taco salad off a paper plate with a crusty old woman named Lucy . . . and now here I was, attending a popular show on Chicago's hip north side, if the number of restaurants, good-looking folks in late-model cars trolling for parking spots, and people in evening dress, dashing about under umbrellas on a rainy Friday night, meant anything.

Parking was terrible. Philip finally let me out in front of the theater and told me to look for the Fenchels while he parked . . . which was crazy, given the crowd inside the foyer, waiting for the doors to open. The chatter sounded like a false-teeth convention—not exactly the opera crowd, which was okay by me. Finally I spotted Henry Fenchel at the bar, flirting with the barista while she twisted the cap on a bottle of Sam Adams and handed it to him along with a glass of white wine.

As he turned, Henry's eye caught mine. "There you are! Philip parking the car? Say, would you like a drink? You can have this one. I don't know where Mona disappeared to."

"Right here, darling." Mona Fenchel seemed to appear out of

nowhere and took the glass of wine. "But we can get another one." She smiled sweetly. "Chardonnay?"

I shook my head. A glass of wine with no food in my stomach, and I'd be loopy enough to dance on the piano if they had one. "Thanks anyway. Philip will be here shortly." I hoped. I wasn't sure I could handle two Fenchels by myself.

Mona raised her glass happily. "Good thing it's Holy Week or whatever they call it. Otherwise I don't think we could have gotten weekend tickets at the last minute. Thank God for keeping the Christians and Jews occupied elsewhere." She giggled.

It was all I could do to keep my mouth from dropping open. If God wanted to strike her dead right then, it would be all right with me. Although if I remembered my Bible stories correctly, the earth opening up or fire falling from heaven usually consumed a good many bystanders too. *Forget it, God,* I muttered silently. *Do it when I'm not around.*

To my relief, Philip finally showed up, a bit damp. Mona looked him over and then glanced at my outfit—silk mauve blouse, contrasting fawn-colored slacks and jacket, and sling-back heels. "You're both so dressed up," she purred. "We should have told you to come casual."

For the first time I noticed that both she and Henry were wearing jeans—designer jeans, but denim nonetheless. She giggled and sipped her wine. "Sometimes the audience gets a bit splattered during the performance. But . . ." She fingered the material of my jacket. "If you get it dry-cleaned right away, any stains should come out."

I could feel my back arch. *Get your hands off my jacket! Did it occur to you to tell us how to dress for this show?* But I said nothing, slipped my hand through Philip's arm as the doors opened, and followed an usher to our seats.

I had no idea what to expect from the Blue Man Group, but the stone-faced trio, covered head to foot in blue paint, put on a freewheeling performance that left us feeling giddy and breathless—a circus of wacky percussion, banging on drums, and "making music" with PVC plumbing tubes. We couldn't help but laugh until our sides ached.

It felt good to have a good time. I was aware of Philip's arm resting across my shoulders and the occasional squeeze he gave me as we shared laughter. We'd laughed a lot before the boys were born . . . before the business started to take up more and more of Philip's time. Or more of his heart.

I was starving by the time we were seated at Jack's on Halstead after the show, and I ate more than my share of the crab cakes we ordered for an appetizer. I knew better. Should have eaten something before we left home. Even after fifteen years of marriage to money and nightlife, I wasn't used to eating dinner at ten o'clock at night.

I'd genuinely enjoyed the show—bizarre as it was—but after the four of us rehearsed all our favorite acts through asparagus-tips-and-spring-greens salad, my gas ran out and I barely ate the grilled lemongrass-encrusted salmon I'd ordered. Talk turned to business, and I tuned out, suddenly feeling bushed. Philip didn't seem to notice, as long as I added a seemingly alert "Mm" or "Uh-huh" from time to time.

Mona's comment about Holy Week still bothered me. The

young couple I'd met today—Josh and Edesa Baxter—said they were attending Good Friday services tonight. And Edesa's little Bible study at the shelter had actually been interesting. I'd never thought about how the Jewish Passover fit hand in glove with Jesus and what happened on Good Friday so many years ago. *What was their Good Friday service like?* I wondered. A far cry from the Blue Man Group performance, I was sure of that! Which had been a lot of fun . . . but I squirmed inside, thinking maybe it wasn't the most appropriate thing on the night Christians were remembering the terrible crucifixion of the Son of God.

You hypocrite, I scolded myself. I'd parked my Christianity on a backseat years ago. Why should it bother me what we did on a weekend night, Good Friday or not? Still, just being at the Manna House shelter today had touched a nerve—touched something—that felt a little tender.

"You're awfully quiet," Philip said on our way home. The rain had stopped, and we actually had the windows down, breathing in the cool, damp air.

I tried to read his tone. Just commenting? Asking why? Annoyed? *Whatever.* "Mm. Just tired." Then I added, "I enjoyed the evening." *In spite of Mona Fenchel.*

He looked at me sideways. "Good. I'm glad. I know the move happened pretty fast, Gabby, but I think you'll like it here. Chicago's an exciting city. Henry was telling me . . ."

Hm. Philip was certainly being pleasant tonight. Should I tell him about finding my way about the city on my own today? Of course, then I'd have to mention that I ended up at the homeless shelter to see Lucy. But maybe that was okay. At least she was at the shelter and not in our penthouse! I smiled to myself, remembering how Lucy had laughed at the little scenario when we two drowned rats had come barging in on Philip and the Fenchels . . .

"I think 'Fairbanks and Fenchel Development Corporation' will make a good name for the business, don't you?" Philip was saying. "Has a nice alliteration. 'Fairbanks and Fenchel' . . . We're going to sign the partnership papers on Monday. Just . . ." He paused and looked at me sideways. "Just don't do anything stupid, Gabrielle. Like, you know, the business with the bag lady. Things like that can sour a business relationship in a hurry."

I pressed my lips together. I wanted to shout, *Her name is Lucy!* But decided, no, this wasn't exactly the time to tell my husband I'd eaten lunch with the bag lady.

I called the boys Saturday morning—the second weekend my boys were spending their weekly break from the academy with their grandparents in Petersburg, Virginia, instead of with their father and me. I tried to be upbeat and positive on the phone. "Hey, how'd your Latin test go, P.J.? . . . You're going to try out for lacrosse next year? That's neat, kiddo! . . . Yeah, yeah, I know you gotta go. What are you and Granddad doing today? . . . Oh, wow. Virginia Beach! Sounds like fun. What are you going to—the aquarium? Yeah, I heard it was great . . . Wait a minute, P.J. Put Paul on for a sec, will you?"

As I waited for my youngest to get on the phone, I started to bristle. What was wrong with this picture? Sure, *one* weekend with the grandparents now and then, doing special things, was great. But was this the way it was going to be for the next six weeks? The senior Fairbanks pulling out all the stops to entertain my sons, while I got a two-minute report on the phone, like a parent who'd lost custody?

"Hi, Mom." My eleven-year-old's plaintive voice rattled my cool. "I miss you."

"I miss you, too, kiddo." It was all I could do to keep my voice from quivering. "Only six more weeks, right? We'll come to P.J.'s eighth-grade graduation and bring you back with us to Chicago."

A short silence. "But what about my friends here?"

"I know, hon. It's . . . it's hard to move away. But you'll make good friends in Chicago too."

Another silence. "Guess I gotta go. Granddad's calling us to get in the car."

I wanted to hug him so badly. But I put on a bright voice. "Sure, honey. Have a good time at the aquarium. Happy Easter tomorrow! You going to church with Nana and Granddad?"

"I guess. They haven't said anything about it. I . . . I gotta go, Mom. Say hi to Dad for me, okay?"

The phone clicked in my ear.

Hitting the Off button on the handset, I sank back into the deep cushions of our wraparound couch. Philip was in the den, working on his laptop. I probably should have gotten him on the phone too. But right now I didn't want Philip's company. I just wanted to remember P.J.'s and Paul's voices in my mind . . . in my heart . . .

All too soon, their voices faded. I tried to get the sound back—P.J.'s confident prattle, Paul's pensiveness—but I couldn't. Hot tears squeezed out of my eyes, and I grabbed a tissue from the end table. *Oh God! I am so lonely . . .*

After a few minutes, I blew my nose and went into the bathroom to repair my face. Seemed like I'd been talking to God a lot more since we moved here to Chicago. Huh. Not sure if He was listening, though. It'd been a long time since I'd done any praying, and the connection was probably pretty rusty.

I took a long, hard look at myself in the bathroom mirror. Dark reddish-brown hair—"chestnut" sounded better—a naturally curly mop, best worn short or it got out of hand. Oval face. Minimal makeup. Philip used to say my hazel eyes were my best feature—long lashes, dark eyebrows, nicely shaped. Even at thirty-nine, I knew I could turn a few heads. But for some reason I felt as if I were looking at a stranger. Who *was* this person? Did I know her? Who in the world was the real Gabrielle Shepherd Fairbanks?

I felt frozen in time, staring at the stranger in the mirror. Then, like a dog coming out of the water and shaking off every last drop, I mentally shook myself and got out of the bathroom. *Watch it, Gabby,* I told myself. *You could easily end up a basket case, and what good would that do? Get busy. Do something.*

Cookies. I'd make chocolate-chip cookies and send them to P.J. and Paul. Not exactly the same as coloring eggs and putting all sorts of goodies into their Easter baskets like I did when they were younger. I wished I'd thought of this sooner, so they'd have them for Easter, but . . .

I started pulling measuring cups and measuring spoons out of the drawer. Tomorrow was Easter. And I wanted to go to church. Might just go crazy perched up here on the thirty-second floor all weekend. But where in the world would I go?

Could always ask Mr. Bentley. Who else did we know? Camila, the maid? Well, I would, but I didn't have a phone number for her, only the cleaning service, and I was sure they wouldn't give out Camila's personal number.

Who, then? The Fenchels? I rolled my eyes. If Mona Fenchel were the last person on earth, I wouldn't ask her where to find a church.

So that left . . . the people at Manna House. Well, why not? They were familiar with the city. Someone would remember me from yesterday.

I peeked into the den. Philip was deep in thought, a spreadsheet on his computer screen. I picked up the bedroom extension, dialing the number Mr. Bentley had given me. A bright voice on the other end answered, "Manna House."

"Hi. This is Gabby Fairbanks. I visited Manna House yesterday—"

"Oh, yes, I remember. This is Angela. The receptionist."

"Yes, of course." The Asian-something girl. At least now I knew her name. "Uh, this might sound like a strange request, but we're new to Chicago, and I'm wondering if you could recommend a church for us. Tomorrow's Easter, you know."

"Well, uh . . ." There was a long pause. "I don't know where to begin, Mrs. Fairbanks. There are a lot of churches. Depends on what you want, you know, Methodist or Baptist or—"

"Where do you go, Angela?"

She giggled. "I go to a Korean-speaking church. I'm sure you'd be welcome, but I don't know how much you'd get out of it."

Oh, for heaven's sake. This isn't going anywhere. I tried not to sound exasperated. "What about Mabel Turner? Or that young couple, the Baxters. Do you know the name of their church?"

"Mm. Not sure about Ms. Turner. But Josh and Edesa . . . all I know is that some folks from their church are coming here tomorrow night to lead our Sunday Evening Praise. SouledOut something or other."

"Coming there?" Well, that was a thought. "In the evening, you said. Well, thanks, Angela . . . oh, what time?"

"Six o'clock," she said. I clicked the Off button. Not exactly Easter Sunday morning. But something inside me said, *Go.*

Maybe it was time to get the rust off that God connection.

chapter 7

To my surprise, Philip got up early the next morning—well, early for a Sunday—and said he was going for a run. "Henry goes to the gym," he grunted, tying his running shoes. "Might as well take advantage of the jogging path before those thunderheads get serious." He winked at me. "Send out the hounds if I'm not back in an hour." The door closed behind him.

I gave him two minutes to ride the elevator and cross the frontage road to the parkway; then I went to the wall of windows to watch his shiny blue warm-up jacket and matching shorts heading for the underpass. He reappeared moments later, a tiny blue dot, heading south along Foster Avenue Beach.

Maybe I should go for a walk too. But I had second thoughts when I saw the large thunderclouds piling up over the lake. Breathtaking . . . but I'd had my fill of coming home soggy and chilled to the bone. Besides, it was Easter Sunday and I really should call my mom. She'd been alone two years now since Dad died. That was another thing that made me mad at God. Why a heart attack at seventy-two, for heaven's sake?! Noble Shepherd had kept working at the carpet store he'd owned for over forty years until "Mama Martha," as the locals called her, put her foot down and said it was time for them to enjoy some retirement, buy a motor home, take the Alaska Highway, do something before they had to hang it up.

They never did buy that motor home.

I sighed and hunted for the cordless. At least my mom was young enough to manage on her own. I was the youngest of three, a "happy accident," Daddy used to tease—though they hadn't been very happy with me when I dropped out of college, got engaged to a man I met in France (whom they met for the first time at a lavish Virginia wedding), and settled in that foreign country called The South.

I finally found the phone in the cushions of the wraparound couch where I'd talked to the boys the day before. At least we were Central time now, same as most of North Dakota. I dialed.

The phone picked up on the other end. "Hello?"

"Happy Easter, Mom."

"Oh! Happy Easter to you too. I'm so glad you called, honey. I thought about calling you, but didn't know about the time difference in Alaska."

"Mom! It's Gabby. I'm in Chicago, remember?"

My mother seemed flustered. "Oh, well, that's right. You'll be leaving for church soon, I suppose."

Even though that's exactly what I'd been wanting to do, I felt a tug of irritation. "We just moved here, Mom. Haven't found a church yet."

"Well, sure. But I bet there're some good Easter services on the TV. How are the boys?"

That did it. I started to blubber and ended up having a good cry. Nothing like talking to your mama when you're feeling homesick and missing your kids.

When I hung up twenty minutes later, I picked up the remote to the plasma TV embedded in the wall and clicked it on. Sure enough, a large choir in white and gold robes was joyously singing, *"Christ the Lord is risen today-ay, Ha-ah-ah-ah-ah-le-eh-lu-u-jah!"* I got a fresh cup of coffee, tried two or three other channels, and finally settled on the Chicago Community Choir, taped earlier that week, singing Handel's *Messiah*. The choir looked like a ten-bean soup packet, all sorts of colors and shapes. The choir wore white blouses and shirts topping black skirts or pants—except for the occasional blue shirt or orange blouse of someone who forgot the dress code. I closed my eyes and just listened as the majestic music took over our living room.

Surely He hath borne our griefs, and carried our sorrows . . .
He was wounded for our transgressions, He was bruised for our iniquities. The chastisement of our peace was upon Him . . .
and with His stripes we are healed . . .

"Whooee. What a run!" Philip's voice broke into the choral music. "I'm starving. Is breakfast ready?" Flushed and sweaty, my husband stuck his head into the living room. "What's this?"

I held up my hand for quiet. I wasn't ready for Philip to return.

. . . All we like sheep have gone astray; we have turned every one to his own way; and the Lord hath laid on Him the iniquity of us all . . .

In the background, I could hear stuff being banged around in the kitchen, and minutes later the shower running in the master bath. Well, he could just wait for breakfast or get his own. Why did he expect me to jump up and take care of him? It was Easter Sunday, after all. And right now I was mesmerized by the familiar and yet strangely new words and music . . .

How beautiful are the feet of them that preach the gospel of peace, and bring glad tidings of good things! . . .

Humph. My own feet were tucked up under me, pretty much not caring if my husband got any breakfast or not.

"Bring glad tidings of good things?" Oh well, why not. I reached for the remote, turned down the volume, and pushed myself off the couch. By the time Philip got out of the shower, shaved, and appeared dressed in khakis and a sport shirt, I had batter sizzling in the waffle iron, frozen strawberries thawing in the microwave, and a fresh pot of coffee dripping.

He grinned and pecked me on the back of the neck. "Smells great. Say, what do you want to do today? I know I've been busy all week. What say we take in the Art Museum? Or the Museum of Natural History? Something indoors anyway. Day's going to get nasty."

That kiss on the back of my neck melted all my defenses. I perked up, practically purring. "Do you mind doing Natural History?" After all, I was a North Dakota girl, more at home with animals and geologic formations than great masterpieces. But this was perfect. Spend a quality day with Philip—and then tell him I wanted to attend the Sunday Evening Praise service at the Manna House Shelter for Homeless Women.

Getting out of the backseat of a taxi in heels and trying to get an umbrella up at the same time took more coordination than I was born with, but somehow I managed to get up the steps and into the door of Manna House just before a huge flash of lightning and a twin crack of thunder threatened to kill me on the spot.

Maybe Philip had been right, telling me I was stupid to go out in this storm. After that comment, my courage had faltered and I'd been rather vague about exactly where I was going. *"To this church nearby that has an evening service."* Well, the building *did* look churchy, didn't it?

"Mrs. Fairbanks!" Mabel Turner turned away from the group she'd been talking with in the foyer and extended a welcoming hand. "How delightful to see you. I didn't know you were coming tonight."

"Gabby, please." I returned her warm handshake. "Yes. I called Manna House wanting some suggestions of where to attend Easter services, and the receptionist—Angela?—kindly told me about the, uh, service here tonight."

"Yes, yes, of course. We have a Sunday Evening Praise service here every week, hosted by different churches. Our residents really enjoy it, and of course guests are more than welcome. Avis! . . . Avis and Peter, I'd like you to meet someone. And bring C.J. with you."

Mabel motioned to the attractive African-American couple she'd been talking to earlier, and they approached smiling, along with a sullen-faced black kid, maybe thirteen or fourteen. To tell the truth, I wasn't sure if the youth was a boy or girl. Hair braided tight to the head all over in a unisex style, jeans, sport warm-up jacket, and a heartbreaker face.

"Gabby, I'd like you to meet Avis and Peter Douglass and"—

Mabel pulled the youth into a hug—"this is C.J., my nephew. Say hello, C.J."

C.J. mumbled "hello" and shook my hand limply. Okay, *nephew*. That answered that.

"And this is Gabrielle Fairbanks, a newcomer to Chicago who stumbled on us by accident . . ." Mabel suddenly looked at me and then burst out laughing. "Oh! That was unintentional. But funny, oh yes, very funny."

By this time, Avis and Peter were looking a bit bemused. So I had to explain about tripping over Lucy in the park and coming to the shelter later to see her. We all laughed, and Mabel finally finished her introductions. "Avis comes with the worship team from SouledOut Community Church once a month to lead our Sunday Evening Praise, and Peter is one of our board members. Oh—I think we'd better let Avis go. The praise team looks like they're about ready to begin. C.J., go sit down."

We pushed through the double doors into the multipurpose room, following in Avis's wake, who excused herself with a whispered, "Nice to meet you, Gabrielle." The couches and overstuffed chairs had been pushed aside and folding chairs set up, though many of the residents were still milling around, getting coffee from the coffee urn, or chatting loudly in their seats. Several men and women with instruments—an electronic keyboard, saxophone, and two guitars—were looking around as if wondering how to get everyone's attention.

Another window-rattling crack of thunder did the trick. "Praise the Lord, sisters—and brothers too!" Avis called out in greeting. "It's Resurrection Sunday!"

Several people responded loudly: "That's right! Hallelujah!"

"We can't let the rocks cry out in our place—or in this case, thunder." Several residents snickered. "If Jesus Christ can sacrifice His own life so that we can live, we can bring Him a sacrifice of praise."

Turned out that was the title of the song, but I didn't know the words, so I just hummed along as best I could. It was hard to make out the words over the saxophone, anyway. I wasn't alone. Only about half the shelter residents sang along, and many of those were mumbling. *Sacrifices of thanksgiving? Sacrifices of joy? Hmm.* If the only bed I had was a bunk in a shelter, I might be able to drum up a sacrificial "thanks." But joy?

When was the last time I felt joy? A smile tickled the corners of my mouth. Running barefoot in the sand a couple of days ago, sending the gulls fluttering like dancing girls with gauzy white scarves. *Yes, that was joy.* My prelude to that strange encounter in the park with a metal cart belonging to a bag lady under a bush—

Lucy. I glanced quickly around the room but didn't see her. *Oh Lord, she's not out in this storm, is she?* No, no, surely not. She'd find shelter somewhere . . . wouldn't she? But I did see lanky Josh Baxter and his cute wife, Edesa—a poster couple for racially mixed marriage. A white man and woman stood next to them, the woman holding baby Gracie and nuzzling her affectionately as the singing group launched into a new song. Josh's parents, if I had to take a guess.

Interesting. Did the Baxter clan go to this SouledOut Community Church too? If so, this church certainly had a mixed group of people. The praise team had both blacks and whites too.

The next hymn was more familiar. "Up from the grave He arose!" I wasn't used to singing without a hymnbook, but I'd sung this one many times growing up, and it was also a staple when we made our Easter appearances in Petersburg. The guitars

and sax gave it a rather funky flavor, though. Even the tinny piano
at my home church in Minot, North Dakota—not to mention the
majestic organ at Briarwood Lutheran—seemed more appropriate somehow.

We finally sat, and the woman who'd seen right through my
claim to buddy-ness with Lucy in the lunch line two days ago—
Carolyn, I think Precious had called her—stood up and read from
a paperback Bible. "For we died and were buried with Christ by
baptism. And just as Christ was raised from the dead by the glori-
ous power of the Father, now we also may live new lives." She
read several more verses, which basically said the same thing in
more words, then lifted her head. "That's from Romans, chapter
six. Amen." And sat down.

What was her *story?* I wondered. Pallid skin, middle-aged,
thirty pounds too heavy, slicked-back brownish-gray hair worn in
a ponytail, but quick on her feet, and she read smartly. Obviously
not a high school dropout. But why homeless?

After the Bible reading, Avis Douglass gave what she called a
short devotional on the meaning of "new life." She was certainly
an attractive black woman—hair swept up into a sculpted French
roll, black pantsuit, silk blouse, very professional looking. Her
husband wasn't bad either. Salt-and-pepper hair cropped short,
dark gray flannels, black open-necked shirt. I caught him eyeing
his wife with a little smile.

"Jesus didn't rise from the dead just to prove He was God,"
Avis was saying. "There was one reason, and one reason only, that
Jesus came to earth, went to the cross, and rose from the dead—
and that was to take the death penalty for our sins, so that we
might have new life. New life for me, new life for you."

Oh sure, I thought. *Easy for you to say. You have a good-looking husband, probably have a good job. You seem happy. But what about all these women here? No man, no family to take them in, no home . . . not much hope of a new life here.*

I was startled by my thoughts. Good grief. Who was I to pit this Avis Douglass person against these women? Look at me . . . Philip and I lived on a six-figure income, we just bought a penthouse, I arrived here tonight in a taxi. I didn't grow up rich, but we weren't poor either. Never missed a meal in my life. So what in the world was going on?

Only later, after the service was over, after I met Josh Baxter's parents—a friendly couple who seemed to kid around with each other and laugh easily, even though they had to be married longer than Philip and me—and after I was back in the taxi alone with my thoughts, did I realize why I had reacted so cynically to Avis's devotional.

Even though we had just moved to Chicago, it didn't feel like a new start or a new adventure or a new opportunity or a "new life" to me.

In fact, I wasn't sure I had any kind of life at all.

chapter 8

Philip was in the den with the phone to his ear when I came in. I could tell he was talking to his mother. I waved a hand to get his attention. *"Boys okay?"* I mouthed.

"Just a sec, Mom." He looked up with exaggerated patience. "The boys are *fine*, Gabrielle. Dad took them back to the academy this afternoon"—and then he turned back to the phone, his desk chair swiveling so that his back was to me.

What's wrong with this picture? I muttered to myself, stalking off to the bedroom. *We* should be telling the grandparents that our boys are fine—not getting the news from them. And why hasn't Mrs. Fairbanks talked to *me* about the boys? . . . though I knew perfectly well the answer to that. Philip's mother had been less than enthusiastic about his son's rash decision to marry "that girl from North Dakota." *"It was France,"* I overheard her tell a guest on our wedding day. *"Men don't think straight in France. The place is so quixotic, the first girl they meet, they think it's love."* And her friend had said, *"You'd think he would have fallen for a French girl. I love a French accent, don't you?"*

Well, howdy. I'd barely made it through France with my *Travelers' Guide to English/French Phrases*. So what? I was the mother of the Fairbanks grandchildren, and that ought to count for *something*!

I slammed the bathroom door on "something" and decided I needed a long soak in the tub. Running the water as hot as I could stand it, I found a bottle of bubble bath and shot a stream of golden liquid under the gushing faucet. Sliding under the bubbles until only my head and my knees poked out of the water, I wondered if this was how a crocodile felt, poking its eyes up out of the water and scoping out the territory. My eyes traveled around the room, the marble wall tiles, the glass-enclosed shower, the marble counter with two sinks—and no windows, thank God. I didn't need any reminders that *this* crocodile pond was thirty-two floors deep.

I flicked a bubble that floated past my knees, then another, bursting all that came within fingernail reach. *Story of my life . . . bursting bubbles.* First there was Damien . . . even now I got goose bumps remembering his dark lashes, lopsided grin, hair falling over his forehead like an Elvis clone. He was top banana of the pep squad at school, and had the same *rah-rah* attitude at the Minot Evangelical Church youth group. Even the mothers at church loved him, blushing when he paid attention to them. *"That color brings out the blue in your eyes, Mrs. Rowling"* or *"That's your grandson? You don't look old enough to be a grandmother, Mrs. Talbot!"* Oh, how puffed up I felt when he chose *me*—a mere junior—to go to his senior banquet. He used to love my curly hair, which I wore long in high school, twining it around his fingers, pulling my head back gently so he could kiss me . . .

I flicked another bubble. We got married the same summer I graduated high school. My dad even gave him a job at the carpet store as a salesman. I thought all my dreams had come true—married to the most popular guy at Minot High School's Central Campus, and his family went to our church, so my folks were happy. We had a little fixer-upper on the edge of town, with room for his hunting dog and my two cats. Damien said he'd take care of me so I didn't have to work, so I sewed curtains and mowed the lawn, joined the Junior League and impressed everyone with how I organized the Junior League Thrift Shop, and threw baby showers for my friends who were already starting families.

But Damien just kept flirting—old or young, it didn't matter. Women were like ice cream to him, his flattery dripping over their egos like thick chocolate sauce. And then one day he found a flavor he liked better than me, I guess. He decided we'd gotten married too young, quit the carpet store, and took a job on a fishing boat out of Puget Sound in Washington State.

I learned later that the boat was owned by Priscilla Tandy's daddy. Priscilla was the homecoming queen in the class before me. Damien's class.

I ran a little more hot water, then settled back into my pond. I'd been devastated. Cried for weeks. Married and *jilted*? Since when had they rewritten the fairy tales? My parents comforted me as best they could. "At least you didn't have a baby you're left to care for." *Humph*. Small comfort. Right then, I would have welcomed a baby to be mine, to love me back, to love me forever.

"Hey." Philip poked his head into the door, giving me such a start that I splashed water over the side of the tub. "How long have you been in there? You'll be a prune." He snickered suggestively. "Don't want a prune in bed. But clean is nice . . . very nice. Maybe I'll take a quick shower." He disappeared into the walk-in closet between bath and bedroom to strip.

I drained the tub, toweled off, and crawled into bed *sans* night-gown. I'd just have to take it off anyway. This had become Philip's intro to lovemaking. An announcement. "Hurry up and come to bed." Sometimes I got the feeling we made love because he felt the urge and I was the available female. But was he making love to *me*?

Philip was off early again the next morning, tossing down his orange juice, pouring coffee into a travel cup, and grabbing the plain whole-wheat bagel I toasted for him. "Oh, can you come by the office this afternoon, Gabby? Like two o'clock? Henry thought you and Mona could give some decorating ideas—window treat-ments, wall color, plants, that kind of thing. Needs to look profes-sional, but we want our clients to feel welcomed. Just take a taxi to the Aon Center downtown. Here's the address if you need it. Okay?" He handed me a brochure with a picture of a ramrod-straight building on the front. Peck on the cheek. "See you at two." He disappeared into the gallery, and I heard the front door open. And close.

So Henry wanted my decorating ideas, did he? I groaned. I couldn't imagine anything I'd rather *not* do than decorate the offices of Fairbanks and Fenchel with Mona Fenchel. Maybe I'd call in sick . . . plead female troubles . . . a migraine . . . a death in the family. *Something!* Let Mona do it.

Sighing, I embraced the inevitable. *Stiff upper lip, Gabby,* I told myself, tossing dishes into the dishwasher helter-skelter and heading for the bedroom to get dressed. *Think of it as a way to support Philip's new business venture.* Besides, I had all morning to go online and familiarize myself with commercial decorating terms, ideas, and color schemes . . .

Which I did, feeling pretty smug as I gripped my briefcase and wheeled through the revolving doors of the Aon Center—second-tallest building in Chicago after the Sears Tower, the brochure had informed me. In the elevator I faced the bank of floor buttons. *Wait a minute. No button for the sixty-second floor.*

Noticing my bewildered expression, a woman in an oxymoronic "business" suit—tailored jacket, masculine tie, tight short skirt—said, "This elevator is only for odd-numbered floors. What floor do you want?"

Well, duh. I got off, feeling stupid, and found the even-numbered elevators. This one did have a button marked "62" . . . *and* "72" *and* "82." I felt dizzy even thinking about eighty-two floors. *Oh, Lord, help me, please.* "Sixty-two." I nodded to the person closest to the panel, and hummed like Pooh Bear trying to fool the bees until the bell dinged, the door slid open, and there I was.

Sixty-second floor. I followed the numbered signs pointing this way and that until I found the suite number Philip had given me. Company name wasn't on the door yet, but when I turned the knob, I could hear Mona Fenchel whining. "Well, of course, you have a *view*. But couldn't you get a suite facing east toward the lake? Or even south would give you more of a grand sweep of the city. North is so . . . well, not the best parts of the city." She turned as I closed the door, and the whine turned to sugar. "Don't you agree, Gabrielle?"

Philip, as usual, had a phone to one ear, finger in the other to shut out distractions. Henry stood in the middle of a mishmash of polished cherry office furniture, a plastic smile attached to his face. I ignored the question. "So this is it!" I said brightly. "Wow, right downtown. Very exciting. How many rooms do you have in the suite?"

Henry's smile widened. "Aha. I knew you'd be impressed. This is the reception area, natch. Two offices—that one's mine." He pointed. "Conference room is bigger than we need, but we're going to divide it, make half into a drafting room. Of course, heh-heh, it's a mess right now. But once we get painters in, finish ordering the furniture, and hire a secretary, we'll be in business."

Philip turned, flipping his cell phone shut. "We've got business right now, Henry. Robinson's people want to meet us at the Sopraffina Market Caffe in the lobby in half an hour." He gave me a nod. "Glad to see you made it, Gabrielle. You two okay for an hour or so? Give you time to come up with some ideas about the décor." He was halfway out the door. "Come on, Henry. Robinson could be a really big client. Oh, grab those sample spec sheets." And they were gone.

I stood face-to-face with Mona Fenchel, who seemed to be sizing me up, trying to make up her mind if I was a worthy opponent. I didn't blink. She wasn't a natural blonde, I decided, though the color was good. But I had her beat. My kid-red hair had darkened over the years to a nice auburn-brunette, all mine.

"Well!" she said, tossing her head. "They expect us to do something with this mess? What do they *want*, for crying out loud?"

I cleared my throat. "I think what they want is ideas. I came with a few color photo samples"—I snapped open my briefcase and withdrew the pages I'd printed out from the Internet—"but obviously I hadn't seen the space yet."

Clearing a place on the desk in the middle of the room, I spread out some of the color pictures of various office décors I'd found. Mona gave them a glance. "Obviously." She sounded bored.

I counted to ten. Then made it twenty. "All right. Where would you like to start?"

She didn't answer, just walked into the office Henry had indicated was his. She went room to room, then back to Henry's office. "A theme. An eye-catching theme, carried from room to room . . . something bold. Daring."

Oh brother. "Well, um, that's a thought. I was thinking of using neutrals, which can actually be very alluring if done right." *Ha. What did I know?* But I blabbered on, determined not to go down without a fight. "I'm not talking beige. Rather, sandstone, with browns and ochre reds—here, take a look at this photo." I pushed a sheet of paper at Henry's wife. "What I read suggested adding contrasting or seasonal colors with plants and fresh flower bouquets. I think that would go well with the cherry furniture Philip and Henry already ordered."

She took the sheet of paper reluctantly. "Mm. Nice . . . if this was New Mexico. No, I'm talking seascapes, greens and blues. Not pastels, either. Emerald and azure, flowing in curves to represent waves and movement . . ." She waved a hand to indicate a tsunami-sized wave rising from one side of a wall to another, ending at the windows—the very, very high windows—looking out over the north end of Chicago with the ever-present Lake Michigan far, far below.

My stomach lurched.

"Excuse me . . ." I bolted. I needed the bathroom . . . fast.

chapter 9

Philip glared at me over dinner that night—baked catfish, wild rice, steamed broccoli—which we ate in the formal dining room. The room was large enough to seat all Twelve Days of Christmas. Made me feel like the lonely partridge in the pear tree. At least we were eating at the same end of the table.

"Why didn't you override that crazy 'wave' idea, Gabby? For crying out loud, we'll look like an aquarium."

So this fiasco was my fault? "I tried, Philip. Really I did! I suggested neutrals—sandstone, with red ochre and brown accents. Mona just turned up her nose."

"Whatever." He attacked his fish. "Henry loves it, but it's not going to happen. Not if my name is Philip Fairbanks. My mother would throw a conniption . . ."

Let your mother do it, then. I swallowed my smart remark and adjusted my attitude. He needed encouragement. "Look, Philip. You need a professional decorator, an impartial third party. Don't pit Mona Fenchel and me against each other. We don't know each other well enough to buddy-buddy over decorating your offices. I backed off because I know it's important to you that we get along." *And besides, I had a sudden date with the toilet.* But I wasn't about to tell Philip I got seasick in his new restroom.

He brooded over his glass of chardonnay. Philip was not a drinking man, but he did love good wine with his dinner. However, I couldn't help but snicker at the glowing description of the Italian brand he'd brought home. *"The nose reveals bright pear, apricot, and fig aromas with hints of cinnamon, allspice, and vanilla."* Give me a break.

Finally he set down his glass. "Well, we'll just have to get a professional decorator. Henry was sure you two women would get a kick out of decorating the suite together. Would have saved us some big bucks too. I should have known you weren't up to it."

I strangled the hot words that flared up on my tongue. So the professional decorator was his idea now? Wasn't that what I just said? And did anyone ask *me* if I wanted to decorate the offices of Fairbanks and Fenchel?

Standing up abruptly, I stacked my dishes and marched into the kitchen, dumping my plate and silverware into the dishwasher without rinsing or scraping. The fancy-smancy dishwasher could clog up for all I cared. Clog up and spill soapy water all over the penthouse . . . out the door . . . down the elevator . . . flood the whole building . . .

The TV news came on in the living room. *"—attacked a Tel Aviv restaurant today, killing nine people and wounding many more. The group calling itself Islamic Jihad claimed responsibility for the suicide bomber, who . . ."*

I gripped the edge of the kitchen counter, suddenly feeling small and selfish. What was a spat with my husband over what color to paint his new offices compared to families who'd just gotten word that their son or daughter or husband or aunt had been blown to bits while eating out in a favorite restaurant? And what about the suicide bomber? Dead too. What would make someone do something so drastic, so utterly bloody and violent?

Glancing into the dining room, I noticed Philip's empty dishes still sitting there . . . and for a nanosecond, I felt an urge to do a little *jihad* myself. *Good grief!* Was it really too hard for the man to bring his own dishes to the kitchen?

How Philip talked Henry into hiring a professional decorator, he never said—and I didn't ask. But at least I wasn't the one who had to stand up to Mona Fenchel. Underneath all the tension of the past few weeks, I knew Philip was worried about the launch of his new business. He'd chafed at Fairbanks Brothers, Inc. back in Petersburg, frustrated when his fresh design ideas had been turned down by the conservative philosophy of his father and uncle, the "Fairbanks brothers" who'd started the commercial development company back in the late sixties. Mike Fairbanks had been twenty-nine then, was sixty-six now. His motto was, "If it ain't broke, don't fix it." The commercial buildings he and Matt Fairbanks had designed and built over the last thirty-odd years had a reputation for quality, durability, and function—and they weren't about to tinker with that formula just to stand out in the crowd with some funky design.

I knew leaving the security of a position in a stable family company was a risky leap for my husband. To his credit, he didn't want to start a competing company in Virginia, so he chose Chicago. But that left the question of who would inherit his father's share in the company when Mike Fairbanks retired. Philip's two sisters were married and settled elsewhere and had no interest in running the business. His father had threatened to sell out when the time came, ". . . since you don't want to help me build it up," he'd told his only son.

"Aw, he'll come around," Philip had boasted to me. "Then we can merge the two companies, and do twice the business." But after fifteen years of being married to the man, I suspected all that bluster hid a smidgen of insecurity, though he covered it up with all the fervor of a Rottweiler burying a bone.

On Tuesday, Philip went to work with no instructions for me to carry out, so I spent the day exploring the environs around Richmond Towers. Ohh, it felt good to walk. The sun was out, and the temperature hiked to a comfortable sixty-five . . . though at Mr. Bentley's suggestion, I went back for a small umbrella "just in case." Well, not a suggestion exactly. He just said, "Goin' out, Mrs. Fairbanks?" while turning the pages of his newspaper as if I wasn't standing there. "Chicago weather has a way of sneakin' up on you." I took the hint.

I spent the morning checking out the shops along Sheridan Road, asking if Tedino's Pizzeria delivered, chatting up the staff of Curves—though I felt a bit dizzy by all that spandex going great guns on those exercise machines—and familiarizing myself with the local Dominick's grocery store two blocks away, bringing home two top sirloin steaks and a movie I rented at their kiosk. Philip would like that.

After putting the steaks to marinate in some olive oil, balsamic vinegar, and minced garlic—lots of garlic—I topped off my day with a brisk walk through the pedestrian underpass to Foster Beach, took off my sneakers, and wiggled my toes in the damp sand. The soothing sound of waves lapping on the shoreline drained the last of yesterday's tension out of my spirit. I just needed to work harder to adjust to our new life here in Chicago, I told myself. Find ways to be supportive, take care of things so Philip could give his full attention to developing the new business. And after all, P.J. and Paul would be here in six weeks. There should be lots of fun things to do in the city during the summer. We'd explore, take in the ethnic festivals, go to the beach. I was just lonely for them, that was all.

That's what I told myself. I only wished I believed it.

I might go crazy before the boys even got here.

On the way home—my feet safely ensconced in my gym shoes this time—I passed the bush where I'd met Lucy . . . did she frequent this part of the park? I wandered up and down the jogging path both ways, but didn't see anyone except a few mothers pushing strollers and talking on their cell phones, and an older Asian man sitting perfectly still on a bench. The yuppie joggers must all be at work this time of day.

But this was Tuesday . . . didn't Lucy say the nurse came to Manna House on Wednesday? And that she might come to get her cough "checked out"?

I walked this time. Two miles straight down Sheridan to the north edge of Wrigleyville. Weatherman had said thunderstorms later in the day, but I could return by El if I needed to. I knew I was getting close to the shelter when I passed the Sheridan El Station, where the El crossed over the street, then passed Rick's Café, a few other eateries, and the Wrigleyville North Bar, which was obviously a sports bar for die-hard Cubs fans.

Took me forty minutes to walk the two miles, though. Turning the corner by the Laundromat, I gratefully dragged myself up the steps of the church-turned-shelter and pulled open one of the large oak doors. Man oh man, I couldn't wait to sit down.

"Hello again, Mrs. Fairbanks. Welcome!" Angela's sweet voice, carrying only a slight trace of a Korean accent, met me in the cool foyer. "Everyone is downstairs. Mrs. Enriquez the nurse is here." She laughed behind the open window of the reception cubicle and went back to her computer.

"Thanks." I smiled. For some reason, a sense of—*of what? well-being?*—settled over me as I headed into the multipurpose room. Maybe it was just familiarity. After all, this was the third time I'd been here in less than a week.

Well, *everyone* wasn't downstairs. A thin person, covered by a gray trench coat, was sacked out on one of the couches, a brown hand hanging limply over the side. The ponytailed woman named Carolyn and another resident with a big, loose Afro were hunched over a game of chess near the coffee carafes. I gave Carolyn a wave as I headed for the stairs, but her attention was obviously on how to slaughter her opponent with her knights and pawns.

Downstairs, the dining room resembled a Greyhound Bus Station waiting room. Fifteen or more women sat scattered around the tables, chatting or talking in a loud voice to someone across the room. Several were filling out forms, while two or three jiggled a young child on their knees. A bored-looking young black woman sat in a corner, leg crossed and swinging, filing her nails. Another, lighter-skinned, maybe Latino, tight-lipped and nervous, paced back and forth. She probably needed a cigarette.

I pulled out the closest chair, hoping to see someone I knew by name, but came up zero. A "privacy booth" had been created in one corner of the dining room with a simple room divider. Nearby, an array of medical supplies had been stacked on the closest table. A fifty-something African-American woman wearing a food worker's hairnet sat at the end of the table, knitting something blue and bulky from a bag of yarn at her feet, her elbow resting on a clipboard.

The pacing woman was making *me* nervous. They needed some activities going on while people waited. Something to entertain the kids . . . a "learn to knit" group . . . a nail salon . . . a book club . . .

A woman wearing typical blue hospital scrubs came out from behind the screen, pulling on a fresh pair of latex gloves. "Who is next, Estelle?" The nurse had dark, wavy hair and a round, pleasant face. A motherly look about her.

The knitting lady peered at the clipboard. "Aida Menéndez . . . Aida? You here?"

A young girl—she looked eighteen at the most—got up and let herself be trundled behind the screen by the nurse. The two began talking a rapid stream of Spanish.

"Hey! Miz Delores! You said I was next!" The loner in the corner waved her nail file.

"Pipe down, Hannah. She said no such thing." The woman named Estelle thumped the clipboard with a knitting needle. "I got your form right here . . . three more ahead of you."

The bored young woman shrugged and went back to doing her nails.

"Ya gotta fill out a form if you wanna see the nurse," a growly voice said in my ear. I jumped and turned. Rheumy blue eyes met mine.

"Lucy!" I couldn't help grinning. "Where'd you come from?"

"Question is"—the old woman squinted at me suspiciously— "where'd *you* come from? Seems like you poppin' up all over the place." She turned her head, hacking a few jagged coughs into a faded red bandanna.

I decided to make light of it. "Came to ask if you wanted to go out for coffee. Couldn't find you under the bush in the park, so I decided to try the next best place."

She darted a look sideways at me, bandanna still over her mouth, and a sudden pang clamped my mouth shut. What if she thought I was making fun of her? But before I could say anything, Estelle called out, "Lucy Tucker? Lucy! Get over here, darlin'."

Lucy shuffled off, muttering into her bandanna.

"Be sure to use the cream on that rash," the nurse was saying to the young girl as she left the makeshift examining room. Then her attention turned to Lucy. "About time you got yourself in here, Lucy. Still got that cough, don't you?" She shook her head and rolled her eyes behind Lucy's back. *"Obstinada."*

They disappeared behind the screen—but Lucy was anything but quiet. "All right, all right, don't rush me! . . . Get that thing outta my mouth, I'm gonna choke . . . whatchu mean, hold my breath? A person's gotta breathe, don't ya know . . ."

Estelle hollered over her shoulder, "Don't make me come in there, Lucy! You want lunch or don'tcha?" Several of the women waiting for a turn snickered.

After a while, Delores Enriquez came out alone, bent down, and talked in a low undertone to Estelle. Estelle frowned and scanned the room. "Anyone know where Miz Mabel is?"

"She's out," someone said. "Saw her leave a while ago."

I made my way over to the table. "Is something wrong? Can I help?" *And just how do you think you can help, Gabby Fairbanks?*

The nurse straightened up. "And you are . . . ?"

I held out my hand. "Gabrielle Fairbanks. I'm, uh, a friend of Lucy's."

"No she ain't!" a raspy voice hollered from behind the screen.

Estelle looked at me with a smile of recognition. "Oh, that's right! Precious told me about you." She turned to Delores. "This is the lady who found Lucy out in the rain, sent her here last week."

"She cut her foot an' I was helpin' *her*!" Lucy hollered.

"Actually, that's right," I admitted.

Delores raised her eyebrows hopefully. "Do you have a car?"

I shook my head. "Sorry. I walked."

The eyebrows fell. "Lucy needs to go to the clinic at Stroger Hospital. She's running a fever, could be pneumonia or bronchitis. And she needs someone to go with her." She lowered her voice. "To make sure she *goes*."

"That's all right. I'll take her. We'll get a cab or something."

I had no idea what I was doing. But it couldn't be that hard, could it? Just give the cabbie the name of the hospital, no sweat.

chapter 10

The clock on the clinic wall of the county hospital inched its way toward four thirty and Lucy's name still hadn't been called. I couldn't believe this! The waiting room still looked as full as when we came, though maybe half of those were family members of people waiting to see a doctor. A huge percentage of the people in the waiting room were Latino, if the swirl of Spanish going on around me was any indication.

"G'wan, Gabby," Lucy growled. "Get outta here. I don't need no babysitter."

It was tempting. If I left now and took a cab, I could get home before Philip . . . but I'd promised. And the fever must be sapping Lucy's strength. She'd been quiet for a long time—though this was the fourth time she'd told me to leave.

"Nope. I'm fine. They've got to call you soon—"

"Lucy Tucker!" a nurse barked from the doorway.

"See? What did I tell you?"

"Yeah. Whatever." Lucy hauled herself out of the molded

plastic chair and took her sweet time following the nurse. The door closed behind them.

I waited. The clock passed four thirty. Sighing, I realized I couldn't avoid the inevitable. Fishing for my cell phone, I walked out into the hall for some quiet and called Philip.

His voice mail gave me a beep. "Hi, Philip. It's me. Just wanted to let you know I might not be home when you get there and don't want you to worry. I'm at Stroger Hospital, just brought someone to the clinic down here. I can explain later. Sorry about supper. But maybe you could get some takeout or something, okay?"

I flipped the phone closed. *Whew.* Philip was not going to be a happy camper.

Well, so what. He left me alone all day to my own devices. He could manage a few hours by himself in the evening.

A few more people were called in, then a nurse came out and said, "I'm sorry. The clinic is closed. The rest of you, go on home and come back tomorrow." Her announcement met with groans and protests. "If you can't wait until tomorrow, go to the ER. That's it, folks. Go on home, now." I felt badly for the families who had been waiting several hours already. Some all afternoon. At least Lucy got in to see the doctor.

It was nearly five thirty when Lucy finally came out, clutching a sheaf of papers. "Bronchitis," the nurse said. "Make sure she follows those instructions."

"Any prescriptions?" *Anything to make her well instantly?*

The nurse shook her head. "No antihistamines, decongestants, or cough suppressants, either. She just needs an expectorant to get that mucus up. A vaporizer and hot showers will help. And drink plenty of water, Ms. Tucker. You can take Tylenol for the fever."

But as we walked the long halls toward the main entrance, the nurse's words to the other patients rang in my ears: *"Go on home, now."* Trouble was, Lucy didn't have a home. Hot showers? A vaporizer? Drink lots of water? That meant you had to pee a lot. Where was a sick homeless woman supposed to do that?

I thought of the two extra bedrooms in our penthouse, waiting for the boys, the unused bathroom . . . and quickly dismissed the idea. Philip would never stand for it. And he'd probably be right. You didn't just take homeless people off the street into your home. The police, the mayor—and surely Mr. Bentley!—would all say it wasn't wise. What did I know about this woman, anyway?

It had started raining while we'd been in the clinic. "You'd think we moved to Seattle," I muttered, holding my umbrella for Lucy as the taxi finally pulled up. I gave the driver the address of Manna House. I didn't know if they could put up someone who was sick. Lucy really needed a private room. But where else were we going to go?

The *swish-squeak, swish-squeak* of the windshield wipers and Lucy's sporadic coughs were the only sounds inside the cab for the next ten minutes, lulling me into a kind of stupor, so I was startled when Lucy poked me with her elbow. "How come you ain't praying for me 'bout this bronchitis? Ain't that what the Bible says to do when someone's sick?"

"Uh, sure, Lucy. I've been praying for you." That was a lie, but maybe I could send up a prayer now and make it retroactive.

Lucy turned her head toward the other window. "Huh. Ain't what I meant."

Good grief, what did she want me to do, pray out loud right here in the cab? The driver would think we were nuts!

Silence reigned until the taxi pulled up in front of Manna

House. I asked the cabbie to wait and tried to hustle Lucy into the doors of the shelter, though Lucy wasn't hustling. To my relief, Mabel Turner's office door was open, and she was talking to Estelle, the knitting woman. Estelle's hairnet was gone, revealing loose, kinky hair with streaks of silver, caught into a knot on the top of her head.

"Oh, thank goodness you're back." Mabel came quickly into the foyer. "Delores Enriquez said you'd taken Lucy to the clinic, but she didn't get your cell number, so we couldn't call." She turned to Lucy. "What's going on?"

"I'm hungry, that's what," Lucy snapped, but the coughs took over.

"Come on." Estelle took her arm. "They're serving supper downstairs. Meat loaf and baked potatoes tonight. How's that sound, Your Highness? You hungry too, Mrs.—? Sorry, I forgot the name."

"Just Gabby is fine. Thanks anyway, but I need to get home and the cab is waiting."

Estelle shrugged and followed Lucy, who was heading for the lower floor. "Hey, Aida. How ya doin'?" Estelle called out to the young Latino girl curled up in one of the overstuffed chairs. I'd seen her earlier in the shelter's makeshift clinic. The girl glanced at Estelle with dull eyes, but said nothing.

I wanted to ask about her—she seemed way too young to be out on the street, or even here in the shelter—but Mabel was looking at me expectantly. "So . . . ?"

"Nurse said bronchitis. No medication, but she's supposed to drink plenty of water. They said hot showers and a vaporizer would help."

Mabel frowned. "She needs a separate room. *Hm*. Can't do

that here right now. But maybe . . ." She turned back into her office, got on the phone, talked a little while, then came back out into the foyer, smiling. "The Baxters will take her for a few days. He's driving down to get her and Estelle."

I was confused. "Josh and Edesa Baxter? He said they lived in a tiny studio. How do they have room for—"

"No, no, not Josh." Mabel laughed. "His *parents*, Denny and Jodi Baxter. They were here Sunday night. You met them, I think. Josh told me on the sly to call them if I ever needed temporary space. With Josh married and his sister at college, they have a couple of empty bedrooms right now."

"Wow. That's generous."

Mabel laughed. "Well, Josh said his mom might not officially *volunteer* to take in somebody but would probably say yes if asked. And Estelle lives upstairs in the same two-flat. So she can look in on Lucy during the day."

I was glad . . . but at the same time felt a strange sense of loss, like something had died. The Gabby I used to know would've volunteered to take Lucy. At age seven, that Gabby had brought home a cardboard box with a litter of abandoned kittens. The mama cat had been run over in the road. My mom let me keep them out on the back porch if I *promised* to feed them six times a day. I was all over those kittens, feeding them with an eye-dropper, watching them get fat and spill out of the box until they were old enough to take to the pet shop. And then there was the dog with only three legs, and the box turtle with the cracked shell . . .

What had happened to that Gabrielle? Weren't people more important than kittens and box turtles?

I tried to refocus. "So Estelle is not a resident here?"

"She was, once upon a time. Ask her about it sometime." I noticed how Mabel's ready smile highlighted how attractive she was—smooth brown skin, straightened hair cut short but full and brushed off her forehead in a wave, simple gold loops in her ear-lobes, full lips colored with a creamy tangerine that matched her sweater. "Now she's licensed to do elder care, but between jobs she hangs out here and helps however she can." Mabel extended her hand. "Thank you so much, Gabby. I'm afraid I don't have the budget to reimburse you for the cab fare you spent today, but I want you to know how much we appreciate it."

I took her hand, afraid that if I spoke I might cry. Something was churning up inside me, and I didn't even know what it was. I just nodded and turned to go, then suddenly turned back. "Mabel." The words pushed out in a rush. "The other day you mentioned you were looking for a program director. I . . . well, I'm a CTRS—Certified Therapeutic Recreational Specialist—and I directed programs for seniors back in Virginia. I'm wondering . . . I think I'd like to apply for the job."

Mabel stared at me. "Well, well. If the Lord doesn't work in mysterious ways." She went into her office, consulted an appointment book, and then looked up. "Could you come back tomorrow, Gabby? We can talk about it then, and I'll have an application for you to fill out. Eleven?"

I nodded without speaking and dashed out to the waiting cab.

Oh Lord, Oh Lord . . . I didn't exactly know how to pray in the moment, but I knew I was going to need some supernatural help. *I'd really like this job. In fact, I need it. And if You help me get it, and pacify Philip, I promise I'll go to church more often. And read my Bible. If I could find it. Packed somewhere. And P.S., please be with Lucy and help her to get well.* There. That ought to cover my butt with Lucy.

But first I had to explain to Philip where I'd been all day.

"I just don't get it, Gabrielle." Philip was pacing. A bad sign. "What in the world were you doing at that homeless shelter in the first place? Then you volunteer—volunteer!—to take a perfect stranger who has pneumonia, or bronchitis, or whatever, something contagious anyway, to the county hospital, of all places, which is probably full of who-knows-what diseases flying around in the air. Sitting in a roomful of sick people all afternoon!" He stopped pacing right in front of me and shook a finger in my face. "You don't *think*, that's what wrong with you, Gabrielle. You . . . you just up and *do* things, willy-nilly, whatever comes to your mind. Did you think about how this would affect me? Affect *us*, affect getting this new business off the ground if you got sick? Not to mention that it's seven thirty, and we haven't had supper . . ." He spiked the air with an expletive, rolled his eyes, and flopped down on the plush sofa.

"I'm *sorry*, Philip. I didn't realize it would take so long. I thought we'd be in and out in an hour or two. I tried to let you know, left a message on your cell phone."

"Yeah, yeah, I got it. What was I to think? Maybe you'd been in an accident or something. All you said was you were at Stroger Hospital. Henry said it's the county hospital, over on the west side, not a good neighborhood."

"That's not true. I told you I brought someone to the clinic. Didn't you listen to the whole message?"

"Whatever." He pushed himself off the couch. "That's not the point. You still haven't explained what you were doing at this . . . this homeless shelter in the first place. Yeah, yeah, you ran into an old bag lady last week, you did the right thing and sent her to a shelter. *Period.* You don't need to go running over there to check up on her. Let them take care of the homeless. That's what shelters are for!"

I pressed my lips together. This was pointless. Telling him right now that I intended to apply for a job at this shelter would be like volunteering to be the human sacrifice in an ancient Aztec ritual.

chapter 11

The weather forecast still said rain, but today I didn't care. It was April, after all! The air was warm and moist, the kind of weather that sprung all the buds on the trees and sprinkled green kisses on the grass in the parks along Lake Shore Drive.

I allowed myself an hour to get to Manna House, but it was hard to wait until ten o'clock to leave. In spite of Philip's upset at me the night before, I woke up excited, my mind already spinning with ideas for activities and programs at Manna House. Job skills . . . word processing . . . parenting classes . . . cooking . . . maybe even field trips to the museums. Had Lucy ever been to a Chicago museum?

Well, probably. Surely she hasn't been homeless all her life.

I stood in the middle of our walk-in closet. It was a job interview . . . should I wear a suit and heels? But this was a homeless shelter; maybe that would be too spiffy. I finally decided to go with "business casual"—tan slacks, jade-colored blouse, black blazer, flats for walking, a bag roomy enough for a small umbrella.

And I'd take the El. If I was going to be working at Manna House, I'd need an inexpensive way to get back and forth. Might as well learn how to do it on my own now as later.

I was actually whistling as I bounced through the lobby of Richmond Towers and headed for the west-side doors spilling out onto Sheridan Road.

"Where are *you* off to, Mrs. Fairbanks, all twinkletoes today?" Mr. Bentley's bald dome and grizzled chin beard made him look as if his head was on upside down.

I laughed. "I'm interviewing for a job, Mr. Bentley. Wish me luck!"

He eyed me suspiciously. "What are you up to now, might I ask?"

I paused at the semicircular desk, eager to let the excitement within me bubble out. "That shelter you told me about needs a program director—and I'm it!" I giggled at my self-confidence. "Seriously, Mr. Bentley, I'm a qualified CTRS, and this job seems just right for me."

He peered at me over his reading glasses. "Oh, it does, does it?" He pursed his lips. "What do you know about homeless people, Mrs. Fairbanks?—no disrespect intended."

My confidence wobbled. "Well, good point. Not much. But I'd like to learn. And one thing I do know, Mr. Bentley—*everyone*, rich or poor, male or female, young or old, needs to feel useful, needs purposeful activities or work to occupy their time." I chewed on my lip. "Including me."

His expression softened. "Good luck then, Mrs. Fairbanks. I'll be lifting up a prayer for you today. Want me to call you a cab?"

For some reason, his blessing buoyed my confidence again. "No thanks. I'm taking the El. I did it once, think I can do it again." I waved and pushed through the revolving door for the three-block walk to the elevated station.

The Red Line. That's what Josh Baxter had told me. *Take it south to . . .* I squinted at the transit map on the platform at the Berwyn El Station, trying to keep my eyes from straying to the street below. *Sheridan. That's it. One . . . two . . . three . . . only four stations. Shouldn't take long.*

But I was still anxious once I was on the train, counting the stops, craning my neck at each one to be sure we hadn't passed it yet. The train bent around a big curve just before pulling into the Sheridan station. *Okay, that's my clue,* I thought, relieved to get out the door before it slid shut again.

Once back down on street level, I stood uncertainly, looking both ways. Did I turn right or left? Then I saw Rick's Café and the Wrigleyville Bar down the street to the right. *Aha. Back on course.* I glanced at my watch . . . only ten thirty. Good grief, I had a half hour to kill. Was there any place around here to get a cup of coffee?

I glanced around—and had to laugh. The Emerald City Coffee shop stood right under the El tracks next to the station, so close it could have bit me on the rear. Pushing open the door, I smiled at the decidedly casual décor. On one side, couches and comfy chairs circled around a beat-up coffee table. On the other, small tables were occupied by individuals busy at their laptops. At the counter I ordered a medium-size coffee with cream. The proprietor—a slender older woman with spiffy gray hair—looked at me oddly, as though trying to place me among her clientele as she poured the steaming coffee. "Just made a fresh pot. You want a muffin or anything with that?"

The lemon poppyseed muffins looked good. I took my coffee

and muffin to a comfortable chair near the front window, sank into the cushions, and sipped the hot coffee slowly. Now that I was safely back on the ground, uneasiness niggled at the edge of my excitement. *I shouldn't be doing this without telling Philip.* Especially after he'd made his feelings about me just visiting the shelter abundantly clear.

But, darn it, what else am I supposed to do? He took me away from a job I enjoyed back in Petersburg, left our boys in the academy there, hung me in a penthouse like a pair of panties on a clothesline . . .

I snickered at my mental image of the penthouse panties and pushed the problem of Philip into the recesses of my mind. I'd deal with that *after* the fact. No point getting him all stirred up if I didn't even get the job.

After enjoying a refill, I paid my bill and walked the few blocks to Manna House. It had started sprinkling, but not enough to need my umbrella. *10:55*, I noted smugly, grabbing the handle of the heavy oak door. Early but not too early.

The door didn't budge. I tried the other one. Locked too. *What in the world?* I hunted for a doorbell and found a white button beside the brass plate that said Manna House. I pushed and was rewarded by a shrill ring inside. But no one came to the door.

I pushed the button again . . . and finally the door cracked opened. "Oh, Mrs. Fairbanks!" Angela peeked around the door, her straight black hair swinging over her face. "Sorry the door was locked. I was on the phone and couldn't—oh, come on in. Did you want something?" She locked the doors behind me.

"Well, yes. I have an eleven o'clock appointment with Mabel Turner. Is she here?"

Angela grimaced. "Actually, no. I mean, she's not back yet. She had some kind of emergency with her nephew, C.J., at his school. But that was her on the phone. She's on her way. Do you want to wait in her office?"

Hiding my annoyance, I agreed to a seat in Mabel's office. I'd tried so hard to be on time, and Mabel Turner just blew me off. Did she go running to school every time her nephew had a problem? What about his parents? Couldn't they take care of whatever? Besides, I had a son about C.J.'s age and one even younger, and *we* didn't go running to school every time—

I stopped myself. I didn't even know if my boys *had* problems at school. Parents weren't supposed to call during the day, only in the evenings, before study hall, and weekends. But I no longer saw P.J. and Paul on weekends, either, because we'd moved a thousand miles away. *Admit it, Gabby, you're jealous of Mabel, that she can go to school and check up on her nephew.*

Reaching for a tissue box on Mabel's desk, I blew my nose, took a deep breath, and tried to think of something else. It wouldn't do for Mabel to walk in and find her new program director blubbering away.

Mabel Turner bustled in at eleven thirty. "I'm so glad you waited, Gabby." She dumped her bag and umbrella on the floor and hung up her trench coat on the back of the door. "I didn't forget you. Did Angela explain?"

"Just said it was something about your nephew, C.J."

Mabel nodded. "I'm his legal guardian, so when anything comes up at school . . ." She sat down at her desk, moved a few papers out of the way, and leaned forward, hands folded. "Now, tell me about yourself."

I blinked. That wasn't exactly the question I was expecting to start the interview. "You mean, my qualifications and work experience?"

"No, just tell me about yourself. Let's get acquainted."

Well, this was different. But I kind of liked it. Relaxing, I rehearsed the story of our recent move to Chicago from Virginia . . . the new business . . . two sons still in private boarding school back in Virginia until the end of the school year . . . I'd left college to marry my husband, but finished my BA degree and CTRS a few years ago, and had been working as activities director in a senior center in Petersburg . . .

"Did you always live in Virginia, Gabby? What about your parents?"

I squirmed a little. "No, actually, I grew up in Minot, North Dakota, a small town of about thirty-five thousand. My father owned a carpet store, but he, um, died a couple of years ago. My mom still lives alone in the home I grew up in." *Alone.* Kind of knew how she felt.

"Siblings?"

"Two older sisters. Celeste lives in Alaska, her husband works for the Park Service in Denali National Forest, one daughter in college. Honor has two kids, is divorced, and moved to San Diego so she wouldn't have heating bills." I skipped over my disastrous two-year marriage to Damien. What was the point? Water under the bridge.

Mabel put a hand to her mouth in an unsuccessful attempt to hide a smile. "Celeste? Honor? And Gabrielle? Your parents must have been very heavenly minded." The smile turned into a chuckle.

I grinned wryly. "It gets worse. My dad's name was Noble . . . Martha and Noble Shepherd. I think the names were my mom's idea. The three of us endured a lot of teasing at school and church when we were kids, but"—I shrugged—"we've all gone separate ways. It's mostly Christmas letters and birthday cards now." *Another sore point, but why go into it?*

Mabel studied me. I squirmed. What was she thinking? What did she want from me? What did all this have to do with applying for a job at Manna House?

The director leaned forward once again. "Gabby, as you're probably aware, Manna House is a privately funded, faith-based shelter for homeless women—which is a politically correct way of saying we are unabashedly Christian in our outreach and ministry. You say you went to church growing up . . . can you tell me about your own faith journey? Then and now?"

I stared at her, my hopes crumbling. Sure, I could tell her I grew up in the Minot Evangelical Church, attended Pioneer Girls clubs—a Christian version of Girl Scouts—from third through seventh grades, gave my heart to Jesus at age eight in my first summer camp, had memorized all the books of the Bible and my weekly Sunday school verse too. But she'd see right through my lame attempt to explain my insipid adult "spirituality" . . . *"Well, before we left Virginia, Philip and I were members of the Briarwood Lutheran Church all our married life, and we always took the boys to church on Christmas and Easter . . ."*

I studied my hands in my lap, twisting the tissues I'd been holding into tiny shreds. Finally I looked up. The compassion in Mabel's face brought tears to my eyes. There was nothing to do but tell her the truth.

"To be honest, Mabel, I gave up on God after . . ." I told her about Damien, about getting married right out of high school and dumped two years later by my supposedly "Christian" husband. When I'd married Philip, God had taken a backseat. After all, where had that gotten me with Damien? "But . . ." I twisted the tissues some more. "Ever since I walked in here last week, something has been stirring up in me. I . . . I've been praying again, though I have to admit I'm pretty rusty. Sitting in on Edesa's Bible study, and coming to the worship service Sunday night . . . well, I just wanted more. Almost like God tapping me on the shoulder and asking, 'Hey there, Gabby! Where've you been?'"

Mabel just looked at me, chin resting on her hands, elbows propped on the desk, as if trying to read my heart.

"I guess that sounds pretty dumb," I admitted. "Like I'm trying to say the right thing just to get this job."

"No. I believe you're being honest with me." Mabel sat back in her desk chair. "Now, I'm going to tell you something which may sound just as dumb. From the first time you walked in here, Gabby, I had the sense it was God who sent you. And He kept bringing you back. Maybe you don't see it this way, moving here because of your husband's business and all, but I believe *God brought you to Chicago* because He has a purpose for you"—she tapped the desk firmly with her finger—"right here at Manna House."

My lips parted. I blinked. What was she saying?

"But," she acknowledged with a small smile, "we do have to get approval by the board, and they are going to want to see this application." She pushed a couple of pages stapled together across the desk at me. "You fill that out, and I'll go get us some coffee. We still need to talk about what your job responsibilities would be as program director."

chapter 12

Mabel Turner made it clear that I didn't officially have the job yet. "But I'm going to bat for you, Gabby," she'd said, as we left her office and headed downstairs to see if there was anything left from lunch. "If this is God's doing—and I believe it is—we don't have to worry about it."

I thought about what she'd said all the way home on the El. I mean, I wanted the job, knew I had the right credentials, and was pretty sure I could put together a good program for the residents of Manna House . . . but what did she mean, *God* brought me to Chicago? And He had a purpose for me at Manna House?

"Bryn Mawwwr! Next stop is Bryn Mawr!" the loudspeaker squawked.

Wait a minute. I peered out the window. Was Bryn Mawr one of the stops before Berwyn, or had I gone past it? I stood up on the moving train, holding tight to the nearest pole, and scanned the row of advertisements and No Smoking signs running above the windows, looking for a transit map. *Not there . . . not there . . . rats!*

As the train slowed, I turned to the nearest person moving toward the door, a young black teenager with iPod plugs in his ears, nodding his head in time to some music in his head. "Berwyn!" I said loudly, trying to get his attention. "Up ahead?"

Without skipping a beat, the teenager jerked a thumb over his shoulder, back the way we'd come. The train jerked, stopped, and the doors slid open.

Oh, brother. I got off with the flow, finally found a map on the platform, and realized I'd only gone one stop too far. I decided to go down to street level and walk back—it only added a few more blocks.

But not even my stupid mistake could dampen my spirit today. Mr. Bentley peered at me over his reading glasses as I came through the revolving door. "Ah. There she is. Are you now gainfully employed, Mrs. Fairbanks?"

I simpered a little. "I'll find out Monday. But in the meantime, I'm going to work on my business wardrobe—shred a few of my jeans, forget to wash my clothes . . . what?"

Mr. Bentley's scowl stopped my spiel. "Homelessness is not a joke, Mrs. Fairbanks. If you don't know that by now, forget the job. They don't need do-gooders down at that shelter."

My face reddened. What was up with *him*? Wasn't he the one who didn't want me bringing Lucy into the building that first night? "I was just kidding around, Mr. Bentley." Miffed, I headed for the elevator, which, for some reason, took its own sweet time getting down to the ground floor. But as I waited, my irritation subsided. Next to Lucy and Mabel, Mr. Bentley was one of the few "almost friends" I had here in Chicago. I couldn't afford to let some minor comment become a wall.

I walked back to the lobby. Mr. Bentley was talking to another resident in the building who was upset because someone else had dared to park in the parking space he'd been guaranteed. I waited until Mr. Bentley had calmly assured him that he would contact the manager and get it taken care of immediately. The man went off in a huff, muttering about the hassle of having to park on the street.

I sidled up to the half-moon desk before the doorman could pick up the phone. "Mr. Bentley? You were right. My comment was inappropriate. I apologize."

The dark eyes studied me. "That's big of you, Mrs. Fairbanks. Maybe you'll do all right in that job after all." A grin escaped above his short, grizzled beard. "You've got guts, gotta say that."

Guts. I grinned as the elevator whisked me up to the thirty-second floor. When was the last time anybody had said that to me? Probably the time snotty Marvin Peters dared me to go up to the front door of "the old witch's house" on the outskirts of town when I was in fifth grade and still wearing my hair in braids. All the kids whispered about the old lady who lived there, saying she kept twenty cats and rode out on her broom at Halloween, and anybody who knocked on her door got a spell cast on them. I'd pooh-poohed the whole thing, marched up to the porch, and knocked on the door. The old lady invited me in, offered me cookies and hot chocolate, and we had a nice chat. Ruby was her name, and she invited me to come back anytime. But when I went out to the cluster of wide-eyed kids, I put my nose in the air and said. "You were wrong. It's twenty-*one* cats."

Marvin Peters never pulled my braids after that.

The answering machine light was blinking when I let myself into the apartment. I dumped my bag on a chair and touched the button. *"Philip, darling. Call home when you get a chance—oh. I'll try your cell."* I rolled my eyes. "Call home" indeed. Why couldn't Philip's mother get it into her head that he wasn't her baby anymore? I felt like pushing the Redial button and telling Marlene Fairbanks that Philip's "home" was with his wife and children now and had been for fifteen years.

Except—my children were spending their weekends at *her* house, not ours. A mad that lay dormant most of the time popped out and burned behind my eyes. Well, that was going to stop! P.J. and Paul were *not* going back to George Washington Prep in the fall. If Chicago was our home now, that meant the kids too.

I was so busy fuming about the first message, I almost missed the second. *". . . need your next of kin and emergency info. Please call ASAP so I can get copies of your application to the board before we meet on Saturday."*

Had to be Mabel Turner. I fished in my purse for her card.

"Manna House."

Didn't sound like Angela. "Mabel? Is that you? This is Gabby returning your call. What are you doing at the reception desk?"

A laugh echoed in my ear. "Oh, we all cover for each other. Especially the front desk. Thanks for calling back. You forgot to fill in next of kin and that kind of thing. Your husband's name, I presume . . ."

I hesitated. Did I want Manna House to call my husband for some emergency? *Of course, you dodo-head,* I scolded myself. "Uh, his name is Philip Fairbanks, and you have our home number. But his cell is . . ." I rattled it off.

Mabel repeated his name and number absently as she filled in the information. "Gabby, what does your husband think of your application for this job?"

Good grief. The woman was as perceptive as Merlin the Wizard. I hesitated again, then realized there was no way around being straight up with her. I already had the sense that Mabel Turner didn't stand for any baloney. "He . . . doesn't know about it yet." I took a deep breath. "To tell you the truth, Mabel, his nose has been out of joint ever since I brought Lucy home. He's trying to establish a new business in Chicago and is very sensitive about our, um, 'connections.'"

"Gabby." Mabel's voice was firm. "You need to talk to your husband—now. Do it, girl. But, here, let's get God on the job." And Mabel began to pray right in my ear. I was startled. We didn't pray out loud in the Fairbanks household. In fact, even back in the evangelical church when I was growing up, people might say, *"I'll pray for you,"* and they probably did . . . later.

"—and Lord God, give Gabby the courage to share her heart with her husband. And prepare his heart to receive this direction You are leading her in. I pray for a blessing on both Philip and Gabby. Pour a blessing on Philip's new business, that it will flourish and prosper. And a special blessing on Gabby, as she seeks out Your purpose in her life. I believe You have sent her here, Lord . . ."

I barely heard the end of Mabel's prayer, because I started to cry, silently at first, and then shoulders shaking, my nose running, and tears messing up my makeup.

"I'm scared, Mabel," I finally hiccoughed. "Scared Philip will say no way. But if the board will have me, I really want—no, I need—this job."

"Girl, didn't we just give the whole thing to God? Now, you go pull yourself together, call up your husband, and take him out to dinner tonight. Ask him how things are going with his business . . . what did you say it was again?"

When I hung up with Mabel, the tears had dried with a flicker of hope. *Take Philip out to dinner.* What a good idea. For one thing, he couldn't yell at me in a restaurant. For another, she was right. I needed to take an interest in *his* business if I wanted him to support me in mine.

I picked up the phone again. "Okay, God," I murmured. "I hope You heard Mabel's prayer and that You're on the job."

The cab let me out in front of Bistro 110 on East Pearson Street just across from Chicago's historic Water Tower. The sidewalk outdoor eating area was empty—chairs stacked, tables glistening with the recent rain, flower boxes empty. *Would have been fun to sit outside,* I thought, pushing through the door into the restaurant. Another time, when the weather wasn't so iffy.

The restaurant was surprisingly full for a Thursday evening. Good thing I'd made a reservation. "Fairbanks for two, seven o'clock," I told the maître d' who looked at me questioningly. He consulted his list, smiled, and led me to a table covered with a white cloth. The fresh daisies tucked into a tiny vase were a nice touch.

A waiter appeared and handed me a menu. "Are you waiting for someone, or would you like to order?"

"I'll wait. He should be here soon. But hot tea would be nice. Thank you."

The tea soothed my jumpy nerves. Philip had been surprised when I'd called and suggested going out to dinner tonight. "Tonight? Why not the weekend?"

"Why not tonight?" I'd said sweetly. "You've worked hard all week, I'm sure you could use a break. I found a nice French restaurant downtown. We could meet there."

"I don't know, Gabrielle . . . I've got a five o'clock meeting with a new client, don't know how long it'll last."

My heart had sunk. Five o'clock meetings usually meant drinks and "unwinding." But I'd pushed forward. "I'll make the reservation for seven. Just the two of us," I'd added. No way did I want Henry and Mona to "just happen" to come along.

As my watch ticked closer to seven thirty, I was just about to change my mind and order some soup when Philip appeared, tie loosened, and sank into the cherrywood chair opposite me. "Sorry I'm late. Meeting went almost to seven. Whew! I need some coffee." He signaled a waiter and then leaned forward, a grin cracking his face. "But if we get *this* account? Oh baby! We're in. On our way."

"That's great, Philip!" My spirit rose. This was a good start. "See? This is a little celebration."

Philip shook his head. "Uh-uh. When we *sign* this account, *then* we'll celebrate—the four of us. We should know next week."

Next week? Hopefully I'd be working by then. But it shouldn't matter, although the staff and volunteers at Manna House seemed to be in and out all hours of the day and night. And I caught "the four of us." Well, I had a week to psych myself up for an evening with the Fenchels.

The waiter brought Philip's coffee, along with a pad to take our order. I selected the French onion soup, a romaine salad with apple *batonnet*—whatever that was—and roasted pecans, and the angel hair pasta with chicken.

"I'll have the *escargots en croute* . . . mm, skip the salad . . . and the roasted duck confit." Philip handed back the menu.

I laughed.

"What's so funny?"

"Your French! You're amazing. You do the accent so well."

Philip rolled his eyes. "Restaurant menus. That's about it for my French now. I was fairly fluent after two years at the university in Montpellier, though."

"I *know*, silly." My voice was flirty. "That's where we met, remember? You pretended you were French just to knock me off my feet."

He nodded, but I could tell his thoughts were still distracted by his meeting.

I gave up on the romantic angle. "So tell me about this new client. Is it a big project?"

"Huge." Philip seemed glad to talk. I nodded, trying to understand the jargon of commercial real estate development as we polished off our appetizers, and asked questions now and then until our entrées arrived along with a lull in the conversation.

"I'm excited for you, Philip." I was trying to eat the slippery angel hair pasta in a ladylike manner, but somehow more fell off my fork than got into my mouth. I should've ordered a steak. "Hopefully, I'll have some good news next week too."

The words were out of my mouth before I had time to think about how to bring up Manna House. For a moment, what I said didn't seem to register. Then Philip looked up from his roasted duck and potato ragout. "Good news? What do you mean?" His face paled. "Gabrielle. You're not—!"

I laughed. "No, no. Nothing so earthshaking." *Good move, Gabby. Scare him with a pregnancy, maybe he'll be relieved when I tell him about Manna House.* "I mean, I applied for a job, and I should know in a few days." I reached across the table and laid a hand on his arm. "I would be able to use my skills as a recreation therapist."

Philip dabbed his mouth with his napkin and then put it down, frowning. "I didn't know you were applying for a job. Shouldn't we have talked about this? We don't need the money, Gabrielle. You know that. Especially if this new client comes through."

"It's not the money, Philip. I had to quit my job at the senior center pretty abruptly to move to Chicago. Which is okay," I hastened to add, "but the boys are at the academy, you're busy with your work . . . I want to get on with my career too."

He threw up his hands. "Good grief. We've been here less than two weeks. I thought you'd appreciate time to get settled, finish unpacking, get familiar with the city. Mona knows downtown Chicago better than the cabbies. I'm sure she'd be glad to show you around, introduce you to some of the clubs she belongs to, that kind of thing."

I took a slow breath. In and out. Should I tell him I would absolutely *hate* to hang out with Mona Fenchel, and I'd be bored silly at her stupid clubs? . . . *Nope.* I sent up a desperate, *Help, Lord!* and hoped Mabel was still praying.

Philip wasn't through. "At least you could've waited until I've got this new business on a firm footing before jumping into your own game. There will be social events we're expected to attend . . . I don't know." He pushed his plate aside as if I'd ruined his appetite.

I tried to ignore his pouting. "I'm sorry, Philip. I hadn't planned to go job hunting yet—it just happened. Kind of fell in my lap. And it seemed so perfect, I jumped on it. But I should have talked it over with you before applying today. That's why I'm telling you now." I shrugged, trying to pass it off lightly. "For all I know, I might not get the job."

"So what is this job? Is it full-time? I sure hope not."

No way around it. "Um, I don't know about the hours yet. It might be part-time. The job would be program director at Manna House—you know, the homeless shelter in the Wrigleyville neighborhood just south of us. Where we sent Lucy last week."

Philip stared at me. "Lucy!" He spit the name out like a bone stuck in his teeth. "I should have *known* you'd do something stupid like this."

chapter 13

Now it was my turn to stare at Philip. I didn't care if we were in a restaurant. I wasn't going to just let him kick me into a corner. "Stupid? *Stupid?*" I kept my voice low, but I spat out the words with the intensity of a couple of knife jabs. "Philip Fairbanks, that's unfair. There's nothing stupid about a homeless woman—an *elderly* homeless woman, for heaven's sake!—and there's nothing stupid about admiring the people who run shelters and thinking I can make a contribution!"

Matter of fact, it was a good thing we *were* in a restaurant, because I felt like throwing something. My leftover pasta would have made a good weapon—*splat!*—right in the middle of his Fairbanks-perfect face.

Philip threw up both hands—almost as if he knew I was tempted to take aim. "All right, all right. I shouldn't have said 'stupid.' But admit it, Gabby. You've been *obsessed* ever since you tripped over that woman. I mean, you could have ruined our relationship with the Fenchels right then and there when you brought her in that night! The smell alone was enough to make me puke." He rolled his eyes. "Then you go checking up on her at the shelter and end up playing nursemaid, taking her to a clinic in the ghetto—"

He reached across the table and grabbed my wrist. "Look. We came to Chicago to start a business. I expect—I need—your support. To put Fairbanks and Fenchel first, to make decisions that will help ensure our success! For us, Gabby." Philip released my wrist and leaned back. "Sure, maybe a job in a few months would be all right. But a job that enhances our standing in the community, maybe gives us connections that could prove profitable. We've got to think about these things, Gabby."

I looked away, envying the other restaurant patrons, laughing, talking, enjoying their meal and the easy camaraderie of Bistro 110. Where did I go from here? Philip made it sound like I, personally, was about to bring down his hopes of making it here in Chicago by taking on this job.

Are you praying, Mabel? I hoped so, because I knew we couldn't leave the conversation here. I needed time to think, to approach with a different perspective . . .

The waiter appeared, like a God-inspired interruption. "Dessert, *monsieur? ma'moiselle?* We have crème brûlée, lemon and apple tarts, and if you like chocolate—"

Philip waved his hand as if brushing him away. But I spoke up. "The apple tart sounds good. And coffee, please." Didn't Mary Poppins say a spoonful of sugar helped the medicine go down? "Go on, Philip. You love chocolate cake."

He shrugged.

"Make that an apple tart and a slice of chocolate cake. And two coffees." For some reason, ordering dessert for both of us helped get my feet back under me. I had to steer down the middle lane here, or we were going to be barreling down the highway in opposite directions.

I made my voice bright. "Philip, honey, I do want to support you in this new venture. Tell you what, if Manna House offers me the job, I'll tell the director I'm only available part-time—and hopefully that can be flexible, so if you want me to be available, I can be." *Whew.* I was going out on a limb here. Would Manna House be open to a part-time program director? "But"—I didn't flinch—"I do want this job. *This* job."

The desserts and coffee arrived, once again giving us breathing space. The small talk about extra cream and dessert forks poked holes in the balloon of tension around our table. The waiter disappeared.

The Ping-Pong ball was on Philip's side of the table.

"Fine." He tackled the thick slice of dark chocolate cake. "You're going to do what you're going to do anyway. Just"—he waved his fork at me, loaded with chocolate—"just don't get any notions about bringing your homeless 'friends' home with you. And certainly not to the office. Never."

Could be worse, I told myself as the weekend loomed. At least Philip and I were still speaking. Agreeing to disagree, or something like that. And maybe it was all for nothing. I could get a call from Mabel saying, *"Sorry, Gabby. The board doesn't feel you're the right person."* Or, *"Wish we could, but we just don't have the money."* Huh, if it was just the money, I'd do it for free.

Camila had come again Friday morning, so the penthouse was sparkling. While she was cleaning, I'd tackled the boxes still stacked in the two extra bedrooms, doing load after load of sheets and towels. I made up the boys' beds—a bunk bed for Paul, and a single bed for P.J.—and stocked the second bathroom, even though they wouldn't be here until the end of May. "I can do that, Señora Fairbanks," Camila had protested, when she saw me making the beds. "It is my job, no?"

"No, my job." I'd laughed to make sure she knew I was teasing. "I want to do this for my sons, my—how do you say it?" I'd grabbed a photo of P.J. and Paul that had surfaced from one of the unpacked boxes.

"Ah. *Sus muchachos.*" She'd pointed to me, then to the photo. Then she held up two fingers. *"Dos muchachos."*

This is good, I'd thought. I might learn a little Spanish. And by the end of the day, I'd unpacked most of the boys' bedrooms, had dinner ready when Philip got home, and decided it was worth wasting an evening watching TV just to sit together on the wrap-around couch.

I was going to suggest we visit a church or two come Sunday, but when Philip said he had to go back to the office on Saturday, I scratched that. Doubted he'd want to spend his only free day of the weekend going to church. Besides, I'd gotten out of the habit of going to church every week. Was I ready to jump back into that discipline? Give up a lazy Sunday morning having coffee in bed, reading the paper, making crepes or omelets for brunch? At the same time, I felt a tug—a tug that was getting stronger. At Manna House, even homeless women had a chance to study the Bible and go to church on Sunday nights.

With no cleaning chores to do Saturday morning, I decided to make brownies for the boys and get them in the mail if I could find the closest post office . . . and tried not to feel too anxious about the Manna House Board of Directors meeting that morning to discuss my job application.

Mr. Bentley wasn't on duty in the lobby when I came out of the elevator and pushed through the security door just before noon with my packages. This doorman was practically a kid, a white guy somewhere in his twenties, shirt collar unbuttoned, cracking gum, and twirling in the swivel chair behind the desk as if bored out of his mind.

"Excuse me. Sir?" *Humph.* "Dude" *or* "whippersnapper" *would be more like it.* "Can you tell me where to find the closest post office?"

"Nope. Don't live around here." Another swivel.

Good grief. What good was a doorman who couldn't help the residents? I managed to finagle a Chicago phone directory out of him, but that was a dead end because I didn't recognize the street names and had no idea which one was close to Richmond Towers. Finally, I walked to the small branch bank down the street and asked for directions. Didn't sound like such a long walk to me . . . but I hadn't counted on the wind whipping off the lake. By the time I mailed the two boxes of carefully packed brownies and got back to Richmond Towers, I felt as though I'd run a marathon.

No messages on the answering machine. Should I call the boys? But what if Mabel called? Besides, it was already afternoon. The boys would probably be out and about . . .

That set off a good cry, realizing I had no idea what my sons were doing that afternoon. And Paul was only eleven! Still just a kid who should be watching Saturday morning cartoons or playing his PlayStation 3 or imitating the older boys on his skateboard. For that matter, Philip Junior was still a kid, too, though what thirteen-year-old didn't think he or she should have all the privileges (but none of the responsibilities) of adulthood?

I snatched up the phone. We had call waiting. If Mabel called, I'd just tell the boys I'd call back.

No luck. I just got Marlene Fairbanks' charming voice mail telling me to leave a brief message. *Beep.* "Paul and P.J.? This is Mom. Please give me a call as soon as you get in this afternoon. By the way, I sent you something special in the mail today. Should get to school by Monday or Tuesday. Love you!"

Mabel hadn't called by the time Philip got home from the office at eight. I didn't say anything—I was pretty sure I wouldn't get any sympathy if I wailed, *"Why hasn't she called?!"*—but I did wonder out loud why the boys hadn't called back.

"The boys? Oh, sorry, Gabby, I forgot to tell you. Mom called me at the office yesterday, no, maybe it was Thursday . . . anyway, she said she and Dad were taking the boys on a quick trip to Colonial Williamsburg and spending the night in a hotel. It sounded like fun."

My urge to send a book sailing at his head was stifled by a stronger urge not to sink the boat, not when I had his tacit permission to accept this job if it came through. *("Use words to say you're angry, Gabby,"* my mother used to say when I was throwing a tantrum. *"You don't have to yell and slam doors.")*

"You *forgot*?! Good grief, Philip! I've been dying to talk to them all day, wondering if they're okay! You could have told me—better still, why doesn't your mother ever call *me* and talk to me about the boys?" By the end of my little rant, I'd worked up a decent mad.

"Calm down, Gabby. Good grief. I said I was sorry. Besides,

you worry too much. They're fine. They're probably having a blast with their grandparents."

That wasn't the point. I needed to hear my sons' voices, to tell them I loved them, to hear them say they loved me. But I dropped the conversation, went into the bathroom, and bawled silently into a towel.

I finally heard from the boys on Granddad Fairbanks' cell phone as he was taking them back to the academy on Sunday afternoon. They passed it back and forth, telling me all about Colonial Williamsburg, how they got to whittle a whistle, and the cool indoor swimming pool at the hotel. "So what did you send us, Mom? Our own cell phones?"

I shouldn't have told them I'd mailed something. Let it be a sweet, simple surprise.

It was all I could do not to call the shelter to see if Mabel was there after the call from the boys. I didn't want to seem too eager . . . though why not? It'd been twenty-four hours since the directors met. Surely she could tell me something.

Philip was watching baseball on the big plasma TV, kicking back with a bag of chips and a jar of mango salsa. I settled at the kitchen counter with a cup of chamomile tea to soothe my nerves and dialed.

"*Hola!* Manna House. Can I help you?"

Definitely not Angela. "Uh, hi. This is Gabby Fairbanks. Is—"

"Oh, hello, Señora Fairbanks! This is Edesa Baxter. How nice to hear your voice."

Edesa's lilting sunshine seemed to spark from the phone and

brighten the room. "Hi, Edesa. So they've got you on the desk this afternoon, I see."

She laughed into my ear. "Actually, I came to translate for the worship service this evening. Iglesia Cristiana Evangélica is doing our Sunday Evening Praise—the pastor is on the Manna House board."

I glanced at the clock. Ten past five. "It starts at six?"

"Give or take." She laughed. "Depends on when the band arrives. Are you coming? We'd love to see you."

Band? Maybe she just meant the musicians, like last week. "Thanks, Edesa. Maybe I will! But I called to see if Mabel is there. She around?"

"Mm, haven't seen her, but she usually shows up for Sunday Evening Praise. That woman doesn't know how to take a whole day off!—oh, must go, Mrs. Fairbanks." I could hear Gracie screaming in the background. "Precious is waving wildly. Where Josh is, I have no idea. Adiós!"

The phone went dead. But I was already making up my mind. I quickly changed into a black jersey dress, multicolored cinch belt, and dress boots, touched up my makeup, and grabbed my trench coat. "Philip?" I poked my head into the living room. "Mind if I take the car? I'd like to go to church tonight."

He half turned his head as a batter swung. When the ball sailed out of bounds, he looked my way. "Church? Now?"

No sense beating around the bush. "Actually, it's a worship service at Manna House. Different churches come in each Sunday evening. A Spanish church tonight. Could be interesting. Would you like to come with me?" *Did I really say that?* For a nanosecond, I panicked. *What if he said yes?*

"Honestly, Gabby. Isn't this a bit much? Good grief, if you

want to go to church that bad, I'm sure there are decent churches around Chicago—oh! Oh! Oh! That's a homer! Go, man! Go!" The action on TV grabbed his eyeballs and let me off the hook.

I crossed to the couch, kissed him on the cheek, and grinned. "I assume that's a no. Don't worry, I won't be late. I have my cell."

This would be my first time driving in Chicago, but I wasn't worried. Straight down Sheridan Road . . .

It was just the parking that was bad. I had to park the Lexus two blocks away from the shelter. The dense residential neighborhood, mixed with small businesses and eateries, had few garages, just street parking. Not a problem now, but it might be dark when I started home.

The band must have arrived in good time, because the music was already loud and joyous when I entered the foyer at six fifteen. From the doorway I saw a lively group of young Latinos playing guitars, tambourines, a trombone, and a conga drum. The multipurpose room was packed tonight, and everyone was on their feet, moving and clapping. I didn't recognize the song— they were singing it in Spanish—but my feet certainly felt like tapping.

To my left, the door to Mabel's office suddenly opened and she came out, followed by a stocky man in a dark suit and tie, clutching a Bible.

"Oh! Gabby!" Mabel said. "I didn't know you were coming tonight. But I'd like you to meet Reverend Carlos Álvarez, pastor of Iglesia Cristiana Evangélica, who is leading our worship tonight. Reverend Álvarez is a member of our board . . . we were just praying together before he speaks tonight. Reverend Álvarez, this is Mrs. Gabrielle Fairbanks."

A wide smile showed off two gold teeth hiding among his

molars. The pastor tucked his Bible under his arm and took my hand in both of his. "Ah! Señora Fairbanks. I'm delighted to meet you." Still holding my hand, he turned to Mabel. "So this lovely woman is our prospective program director?"

chapter 14

Prospective program director? My eyes darted to Mabel as the pastor took his leave for the multipurpose room. Did he mean—?

Mabel held me back a moment. "I was going to call you tomorrow morning and ask you to come in for a second meeting." Her tone was low, confidential. "But since you're here, can you stay a few minutes after the service? We can talk then, save you a trip." She smiled, gave me a little squeeze, and left me to find my own seat.

Now I was thoroughly confused. Rev. Álvarez acted like I had the job—or practically. *Prospective* was the word he'd used. But Mabel said we needed a second meeting. Was that why she hadn't called?

Precious, standing in the back row with her teenage daughter on one side, was waving at me, pointing to the empty chair next to hers. Josh Baxter was walking back and forth behind the last row, bouncing a wide-awake Gracie in his arms. He nodded hello and smiled as I slipped past him—stepping over the feet of

Hannah the Bored, who had confiscated one of the overstuffed chairs pushed against the back wall and was sitting on her tailbone, feet stuck out, arms crossed, eyes closed—and dumped my shoulder bag and coat on the chair next to Precious.

"Hey ya, Miz Gabby. Ain't this great?" Precious grinned at me, clapping along to the beat of the band and joining in on the occasional *aleluya*s that peppered the Spanish gospel song. "One of these days I'm gonna get Miz Edesa to teach me Spanish."

I nodded and smiled. But my mind was such a jumble, I didn't really pay much attention to the worship going on around me for the next fifteen minutes. Hardly any of the music was familiar, even the songs sung in English. But when Rev. Álvarez stood to speak and people settled into the odd array of folding chairs, I tried to focus. No sense getting myself stirred up. What was so unusual about two interviews for a job, anyway? Actually, it was usually a good sign when you got called back.

Rev. Álvarez called out something in Spanish as the band put down their instruments. Edesa Baxter, looking very American in her skinny jeans and nubby green sweater over a black tank top, translated. "How many of you have ever been hungry?" Murmurs and nods went around the room. Nearly all the residents held up their hands.

The pastor spoke again, and Edesa translated. "There are many kinds of hunger—hunger for food, hunger for love, hunger for God . . ."

Back and forth they went, first in Spanish, then in English. "Ever notice how what you feed on affects you? . . . If you eat junk food, your body suffers . . . If you're starved for love, your spirit dies . . . If you don't feed on God's Word, your soul shrivels up." Heads nodded, and a few *améns* popped around me.

Rev. Álvarez opened his big Bible, then nodded at the band members, who dug into a box and started passing out paperback Bibles. "These Bibles are a gift to you from Iglesia Cristiana Evangélica," Edesa translated, "so that we can all feed on the Word of God together. Some are in Spanish, some in English. Just say which one you want."

The teenager I'd seen on the nurse's visiting day—last name was Menéndez, I remembered that much—eagerly waved her hand until she got one of the Spanish copies. Precious leaned over at me. "You got a Bible, Miz Gabby?" she stage-whispered.

"Uh, at home, sure. Still packed, I'm afraid." Good excuse, anyway. To tell the truth, I wasn't sure where my Bible was—the one my parents had given me for high school graduation with *Gabrielle Shepherd* embossed in gold on the leather cover. Still in mint condition, if I could find it. It hadn't occurred to me I'd need a Bible tonight. Hardly anyone carried their Bible to church back at Briarwood Lutheran. The text was always printed right in the bulletin.

Precious caught the attention of the trombonist, who was still handing out English Bibles, and held up two fingers. She handed one to Sabrina, slouched in the seat beside her, and the other to me. I took the paperback, but my face heated up like a hot flash. Precious was just a bit too zealous looking out for me, as far as I was concerned.

The text was Psalm 103, verses 1 through 5. It took people helping each other or looking it up in the table of contents at least five minutes to find it. But Rev. Álvarez was patient, pointing out something in his Bible and talking quietly in Spanish to Edesa, who nodded eagerly. I sighed. *Why don't they just get on with it?*

But Rev. Álvarez never did preach a sermon. What happened next was more like a poetry reading plus prayer meeting plus therapy session. The pastor invited different volunteers to read each verse, after which he said we would turn the verse into a prayer—all of which Edesa translated for us.

"I'm with that." Precious stood up and read the first verse. "Praise the Lord, O my soul! All my inmost being, praise His holy name!"

The pastor prayed in Spanish, after which Edesa translated: "*El Señor*, sometimes I have to tell my heavy soul to praise You. Wake up, soul! Pay attention!"

Precious nodded vigorously. "Uh-huh. Got that right. Don't wait for Sunday to get your praise on!"

Volunteers among the residents were slow in coming, so Mabel Turner read the second verse. "Praise the Lord, O my soul! And forget not all His benefits."

The pastor lifted his face, eyes tightly shut, visibly moved as he prayed in Spanish. Again Edesa translated: "Oh God, how easy it is to look at all our problems and forget all the good things You have given each and every one of us."

I squirmed, unsure this would go over with women who had no home, no money, no health care, no—

"Who forgives all your sins—" someone read.

"Oh, *Jesucristo!* This is the greatest benefit of all! No matter how far we stray from You, You welcome us back and cover our darkest sins with Your blood of forgiveness!"

"—and heals all your diseases," the same person finished.

Ouch, I thought. *Most of these women aren't the healthiest specimens around. Thanking God for healing might come across a bit hollow.*

"*Señor Dios*, our bodies are broken, and we have abused

them," Edesa translated as the pastor prayed. "Give us the strength and wisdom to stop our bad habits, to take care of this holy temple where Your Spirit lives. We also ask healing for the diseases in our spirit—resentment, anger, bitterness, pride—which are the cancers of the soul."

I heard someone weeping . . . and then another.

The reading went on, back and forth, phrase by phrase. The weeping was getting louder. But the pastor pointed to another reader to read the last verse: "Who satisfies your desires with good things, so that your youth is renewed like the eagle's!"

His prayer in Spanish. Then Edesa's translation: "Oh God, we long to recapture the years stolen from us that we have so easily given to the enemy. Thank You, *Dios,* for all these benefits, wrapped like gifts at Christmas, just waiting for us to receive them. Amen and amen."

"Whew. That was quite a service." I sank into a chair in Mabel Turner's office. Some of the women were still in the multi-purpose room, crying and praying with Pastor Álvarez.

Mabel closed the door and sat down at her desk across from me. "Yes. Pastor Álvarez has led Sunday night service here before, but nothing like this." She seemed distracted, head averted toward the other room as if listening. But finally she looked back at me. "I'm sure you want to get home. Let's get to business . . ."

I sat up straight and crossed my ankles. Yes, this was business. She put on a pair of reading glasses and picked up my application. "The board was impressed with your credentials and experience, even though it hasn't been that many years—"

I flushed. "Yes, I finished my degree just a few years ago." I bit my lip. Should've finished it back in 1990 instead of marrying Philip so quickly—but I'd already plucked that chicken. No point shaving it again.

"Before finalizing the decision, the board would like to follow up on the references you provided, and get a chance to meet you—don't worry, nothing formal. Actually, you already met Peter Douglass—Avis Douglass's husband, who was here with her when she preached last Sunday night. And it was serendipity that Pastor Álvarez got to meet you tonight. But there are three other board members—another pastor here in the city, one of our social workers, and the former director, Reverend Liz Handley, who just retired." She smiled mischievously. "That's how I got *my* job."

My insides sank a little. So I still had to wait for an answer. How long would it take for these "informal meetings"? I'd been hoping—

"The main thing they recommended is that you spend a week just hanging out here at Manna House, getting to know the residents, talking to the staff and volunteers, and developing a sense of what the needs are. Then, if your references don't turn up a warrant for your arrest or that you've got a second job as a call girl"—she said this with a totally straight face—"we'll include this get-acquainted week in your first week's pay. So . . ." Mabel looked at me over the top of her reading glasses. "How would you like to start tomorrow?"

"Tomorrow!" I couldn't help the happy screech. So what if the first week was a trial balloon! "Absolutely—oh." I suddenly remembered my promise to Philip. "Uh, is it possible to start out part-time?" . . . and ended up explaining the whole tension with Philip starting up his business and wanting me to be "available." *Whatever that means.*

Mabel chewed on her pen. "Tell you what. We'll start at thirty hours and make the hours flexible." She smiled wryly. "We all work flexible hours anyway, Gabby. Manna House is a twenty-four-hour operation, remember?"

A knock interrupted our laughter. Josh Baxter stuck his head inside the door. "Edesa and I are about ready to leave, Mrs. Turner. Wondered if Mrs. Fairbanks wanted us to walk her to the train."

"That'd be great." I gathered my coat and shoulder bag. "Except I drove. Would you mind walking me to my car?"

The prayer meeting had dispersed. The band had packed up and gone home. The couches and chairs had been arranged back into their "conversational groups." A few of the shelter residents were playing cards, others stood around talking, while some slouched on the couches with unreadable expressions.

Excitement tickled my chest. Tomorrow they would have names. I'd have permission to talk to Carolyn, Tina, the Menéndez girl, and Hannah the Bored.

Gracie had fallen asleep in the stroller, her loose, dark curls peeking out from the blanket as we walked toward my parked car. Edesa was bubbling about the "church service" that evening. "Josh, did you see? I had a chance to pray with Aida, that *pobrecita* who came in last week. She wouldn't talk, just cried. But she let me pray for her."

I was curious. "She seems so young. How did she end up here at the shelter?"

"Don't know the whole story," Josh said. "But unfortunately it's not uncommon. Foster kid, in and out of foster homes, most lasting only a couple of months. But when a foster kid turns eighteen? The state washes its hands. Okay, kid, you're on your own. Aida literally had no resources, so she ended up at the shelter."

"Good grief," I murmured. "So young . . . and then there's Lucy, who's got to be in her seventies, at least. Still don't know her story. By the way, how is she doing at your parents' house, Josh? Lucy, I mean."

"Ha." He snorted. "She stayed two nights and then disappeared . . . what?"

I'd stopped short. The SUV was right where I'd parked it. The silver Lexus gleamed in the arching glow of a streetlight just above. But a beat-up two-door had squeezed into the parking space just behind and pulled up bumper to bumper. In front, an ancient Cadillac had backed up to Philip's pride and joy, packing it in like the baloney in a sandwich.

"Uh-oh." Josh walked from front to back of my parked car, as if measuring the inches. I looked around frantically, prepared to run house to house, knocking on doors, until I found the owners and got them to move their cars. But only the flat brick walls, locked doors, and dim windows of apartment buildings on both sides of the street stared back at me.

Josh shook his head. "This car isn't going anywhere tonight, Mrs. Fairbanks."

chapter 15

I could *not* believe this was happening to me! Pounding my fists on the car, I wailed, "I *have* to drive this car home, or Philip will shoot me!" Tears threatened to spill over, but I kicked the tires instead and muttered a few choice words under my breath, while Edesa and Josh stood there helplessly, letting me make a fool of myself.

Reality finally sank in, and I let the Baxters talk me into riding home with them on the El. "I'm sure the car will be fine till morning," Josh said as we settled into our seats on the northbound Red Line. "You can come back and get it then. A bit of a hassle, but at least it wasn't stolen or a window bashed in."

Oh great. Thanks a lot. He has no idea.

I leaned my head against the cool window, eyes closed, dreading the confrontation I knew was ahead of me.

"Gabby?" Edesa's soft accent tickled my ear. "Your stop is coming up. Would you like us to walk you home and pray together about the car?"

I didn't answer, letting the squeal-and-clatter of the train wheels fill up the space. I'd give anything for them to walk me home. It was already nine o'clock and dark, and even though Sheridan was a busy street, I'd feel so much better not walking the three blocks to Richmond Towers by myself. But pray? I hadn't thought about that.

I opened my eyes as the train slowed. "That's all right. You've got the baby and everything. You two need to get on home and get her to bed." I got up, grabbing a pole in the swaying train with one hand and clutching my shoulder bag with the other.

Josh and Edesa exchanged a glance. The train stopped and the doors slid open. "We'll come with you," Josh said, grabbing Gracie's stroller and helping Edesa, who was holding the sleeping baby, out of her seat. There was no time to protest. *Doors open. You get out. People get on. Doors close.* No time to diddle around.

Had to admit I was grateful for the company. The night was chilly, but Gracie was wrapped in several layers of blankets in the stroller. As we approached Richmond Towers, I started to thank them, but Josh was already wrestling the stroller through the revolving door. What were they doing? Again I expected to say good-bye in the lobby, but they waited with me as I opened the security door, then we all got on the elevator.

"Really, you guys. I'll be fine." I put on a smile.

"Mm," was all I got out of Edesa.

When the doors slid open on the top floor, they got out with me. Edesa looked around. "Only one door? Yours?" I thought she was making a comment about me living in a pampered penthouse, but her face lit up. "Good! Here we can pray." She grabbed my hand and one of Josh's and squeezed her eyes shut. "*Jesucristo,* we come to You with thanksgiving that no harm was done to

Gabby's car tonight. You are so good! We praise You, Lord and Savior! But we know it will be an inconvenience for her poor husband, who depends on it for work . . ."

I blinked my eyes open in astonishment at her prayer. Thanking God when our car was held captive miles from home? Praying for my "poor husband" who would be "inconvenienced"? I squirmed. What if Philip heard us out here?

Edesa's prayer, though intense, was quiet and short. I said thanks and unlocked the door, but realized they were still standing there. "Uh, do you want to come in?"

"No, no." Josh shook his head. "But maybe we can help explain."

"Gabby?" Philip's voice sailed from somewhere within. "That you?" He must have heard our voices, because he actually came to the door. "Oh. You have visitors." He stood there in his robe and slippers over sweats and a T-shirt, newspaper in his hand.

"Uh, yes. Um, Philip, this is Josh Baxter and his wife, Edesa, um, from Manna House. Volunteer staff," I hastened to add, remembering Philip's decree to never bring people home from the shelter.

Josh stuck out his hand. "Pleased to meet you, Mr. Fairbanks. We just wanted to make sure your wife got home safely. When we left Manna House tonight, cars had parked so tightly in front and back of your wife's SUV, she couldn't get it out. A real bummer! But that block empties out during the day, so she should be able to get it easily tomorrow morning."

Before Philip had a chance to react to this information, Edesa also shook his hand. "I am pleased to meet you, Señor Fairbanks. We have so enjoyed getting to know Gabby."

I wondered what my husband was thinking, seeing this tall,

white college kid and his dark-skinned wife—who looked African-American but spoke with a Spanish accent—at his door. Virginia born and bred, mixed couples were not "the usual" in Philip's world. Mine either, for that matter.

"And this," Edesa continued happily, pulling back the blanket from the baby's face, "is Gracie, who needs to get home and get to bed. So we will go now." She gave me a hug. "I'm so sorry for this *problema*, Gabby. But it will all work out. *Dios te bendiga.*"

The young couple said their good-byes, got back into the elevator with a wave, and the doors slid closed behind them. Philip had not said a word.

We were still standing outside our front door in the large foyer of the top floor. Finally he spoke. "You mean . . . you didn't bring the car home."

I shook my head.

"It's parked somewhere down around that homeless shelter, jammed in like a sardine, and it's gotta stay there all night."

I nodded.

"Oh, for—" He whacked the doorjamb with the newspaper. "So what am I supposed to do in the morning, Gabby? Huh? Tell me that."

For some reason, my anxiety was gone. Sucked down the elevator shaft with Josh and Edesa. "Take a cab, I guess. Believe me, Philip, I'm really upset about this! But . . . I'm supposed to go back to the shelter tomorrow to begin my training, so I'll get the car first thing, park it where it won't get hemmed in, and bring it home tomorrow afternoon."

That got his attention. "Training?"

I nodded, and couldn't help the smile. "Yes. They offered me the job. Just waiting on references. And good news! They agreed to part-time. The hours are flexible too."

"Oh." He seemed confused by the turn in the conversation. "Guess you got what you wanted." He turned abruptly and disappeared inside the door. But a moment later a parting salvo flew back at me. "That car better be in one piece when you get back tomorrow!"

I lay in bed that night, thanking God for Josh and Edesa Baxter, who had somehow defused the whole situation . . . and I was still thanking God the next morning when I got off the El at the Sheridan station in bright sunshine, walked to where I'd parked the car the night before, and there it was. Still parked, but now lovely in its loneliness. And as far as I could tell, no scratches, bumps, or dings. Edesa would be squealing *"Gloria a Dios!"* or something like that.

I moved the Lexus and parked it in front of the Laundromat next to the shelter, making sure I was in the last parking space on the corner so I could back out. The sun warmed my back a few moments later as I rang the doorbell and was let in by a disgruntled Angela. "New policy. Doors always locked. Sure keeps me running."

"You need a buzzer or something you can push from your desk."

She looked at me, almond eyes widening, her mouth making an O. "That's it! I'll ask if we can do it at the next staff meeting." She gave me a playful poke with her elbow. "You're the bomb, Mrs. Fairbanks!"

There we go again. "If you're going to be so formal, I'll have to call you *Miss . . . Miss . . . ?*"

She laughed. "Kwon. Angela Kwon. But don't you dare. Angela is just fine."

"Then call me Gabby. Staff is on first-name basis, right?"

Angela nodded, then tilted her head. Soft, straight hair swung forward like a lady's silk scarf. "You working here now?"

I grinned. "Hope to be. This is my get-acquainted week, or something like that. In fact, do you mind if I hang out with you a little bit? Find out what you do?"

She laughed again. "Feel free! Here's the key to the staff closet—you can store your coat and purse in there if you want." She pointed. "Multipurpose room, far side."

I wanted to roll my eyes. *Precious is right. We've got to find a new name for the gag-awful "multipurpose room."* Mabel Turner's office door across the foyer was closed, but I knocked anyway, thinking I should check in. She might have other plans for me.

"She's not in," Angela sang out from behind the glass of the receptionist's cubby. "Out strong-arming local businesses to cough up funding for the shelter." The phone rang. "Manna House . . ."

O-kay. Guess when Mabel told me to come "just hang out," that's what she meant. I pushed through the double doors into the large sitting area, threaded my way around the couches and chairs and their occupants to the closet on the far side, stowed my stuff, and turned . . . suddenly realizing several pairs of eyes had followed me.

The woman closest to me peered up at me from the depths of an overstuffed chair, with small eyes in a rough, brown, leathered face. "Seen you here before, woman." Her accent was heavily Jamaican. "De city send you or someting?"

"No." I smiled and sat down nearby. I couldn't guess her age—somewhere between thirty and fifty. Wiry hair pulled back into a stubby ponytail with a rubber band. Fifty extra pounds encased in a sweatshirt and faded jeans. "I'm volunteering this week. My name's Gabby." I held out my hand. "Yours?"

She left my hand hanging in midair for a few seconds longer than was comfortable, but she finally shook it. "Go by Wanda . . . Gabby? What kind o' name is dat? You talk *jabba-jabba* or someting?"

I grinned bigger. "Something like that. Short for Gabrielle."

"Ah!" Recognition flickered in the tiny eyes. "Like de angel."

"Have you been at the shelter long, Wanda?"

She scowled. "Long enough. Waitin' to get me state ID so me can get a job. Dey get you coming an' going, ya know. Can't get a job witout an ID. Can't get an ID witout an address. Can't pay for a place to live witout a job. Dat's de drill."

I blinked, not knowing what to say. Getting an ID had never been an issue for me. Once you learned to drive and got your license at sixteen, that was it. "I'm sorry, Wanda. That's tough." I stood up. "See you around, I guess. I'll be here all week."

"Yeah, yeah. Me too. *Cha!*" She waved me off.

I wondered if I should introduce myself to the handful of women scattered around the room, but I'd already asked if I could hang around Angela's den and figure out how to work the front desk. So I just smiled, nodded, and said, "Hi," until I was back in the foyer with a folding chair I'd grabbed on my way.

The phone seemed to ring every few minutes. But during short lulls, Angela tried to acquaint me with the phone system. Extension one for Mabel Turner . . . two for the kitchen/dining room on the lower level, which supposedly also covered the rec room . . . another in the childcare room on the first floor . . . a fourth upstairs on the sleeping rooms level.

"Everybody who comes in or out needs to sign that day's log." She hefted the big notebook sitting on the shelf of the cubby's "talk-through" window.

"Oops." I grimaced. "I forgot." I signed my name and time in. A lot of names were signed out already that morning. Reason given: *job . . . job hunting . . . job interview . . .*

"Mrs. Fairbanks? I mean, Gabby. Would you mind taking over the phone for twenty minutes or so?" Angela stood up and squeezed past me. "I need to pick up some things at the drugstore on my break. Want me to bring you some coffee or something?"

"Uh, sure. Coffee would be great, a little cream. But answering the phone . . . I don't know people's names or where they are in the building."

Angela bent over the log, her long, dark hair flowing. As a kid I'd envied straight, silky hair like that. Mine was always a curly mop top. "Estelle should be coming in to make lunch today . . . lucky us. That woman is one good cook! As for the rest, maybe just take messages. I'll run them around when I get back."

The young woman grabbed her sweater and purse, and disappeared through the front doors with a wave.

And there I was, at the front desk of Manna House, without a clue what I should be doing. The phone rang. For Mabel. That was easy: took a message. Two more calls—one, a volunteer who couldn't come in to help with lunch that day, and the other for someone named Diane. I glanced at the log. *Diane . . . out.* I took a message on both.

The door buzzer rang at the same time as the phone. I

grabbed the receiver. "Manna House . . . Ms. Turner? I'm sorry, she's not in right now. Can I take a message?"

Blaaaaat. Someone was leaning on the buzzer. "All right, all right," I muttered under my breath as I scribbled the number for Mabel and hurried for the door. If that was Estelle—

It wasn't. A young woman stood on the stoop, a mass of tangled hair tucked up under a baseball cap, hands shoved in the pockets of her skinny jeans, and jiggling nervously. A ring pierced the side of her nose, and strings of hair streaked brown and blonde escaped the cap and fell around her ears and neck. Her gray eyes darted at me uncertainly.

"This the women's shelter?" Her voice had an edge. "They told me to come over here, I could get some help." She hunched her shoulders and shivered as if she were cold, although the day was mild and temperatures were supposed to head into the low seventies today.

What in the world was I supposed to do? Mabel wasn't here, and Angela was off who-knew-where. And who was "they"?

I swallowed and swung the door open wider. "Yes, this is Manna House Women's Shelter. Come on in. I'll try to find someone to help you." Where was Angela? *Oh God, send her back soon!*

The young woman followed me inside, slinking like a feral cat. *Get her name, something . . .* Glancing around Angela's desk for a pad of paper and a pen, my eyes fell on a clipboard with a folder that said "Intake Forms." I grabbed it, pulled out a sheet, and stuck it back in the clipboard. "Here, fill this out. You can sit over there." I handed her a pen and pointed to the folding chair now sitting just outside the reception desk.

The phone rang. Another message for Mabel.

"What if I ain't got no current address?" The woman was frowning at the page in her lap.

The door buzzer made us both jump. "Whatever . . . fill out what you can." *That better be Angela—or Mabel Turner. "Just hang out" indeed!*

Estelle Williams loomed in the doorway, plastic shopping bags hanging from both hands. "Here, take these quick," she huffed, slinging a couple of bags at me. "I need to get one of those little shopping carts on wheels—oh. Who do we have here?"

The fifty-something black woman glanced at the newcomer tapping her foot so hard she was making the chair shake, took in the clipboard, then looked back at me. "Lord have mercy, you're learning quick," she muttered under her breath. "That girl is high on somethin'. Amphetamines, likely. Keep her busy here till we can get someone to stay with her."

She trundled through the swinging doors, lugging her plastic shopping bags, then called back. "Oh, yeah. Sign me in, will ya?"

chapter 16

High? On what? Was she going to do something crazy? I wanted to call out, *"Wait! Don't leave me."* But Estelle was gone.

Oh great. I knew diddly-squat about the aftereffects of addictive drugs. Fortunately for me, Angela came back five minutes later while the newcomer was still tapping and frowning over the clipboard. "Good, you found the intake forms."

"What happens next?"

Angela shrugged. "Right now, just stay with her till Mabel comes in. Stephanie Cooper's our case manager, but she's usually only here Tuesdays and Thursdays."

I got another folding chair from the big room and set it up next to the tapping foot. The young woman handed me the clipboard. Most of it was still blank, but she'd filled in her name. "Naomi?" I tried a smile on her. "That's a pretty name."

"It's okay." She tucked her hands under her jean-covered thighs, as if sitting on them to keep them still.

"My name's Gabby. Sorry you have to wait. The director should be here soon."

As if on cue, the buzzer went off. I practically vaulted out of my chair to get the door. Mabel Turner, a bit more dressed up than usual in a pale green suit and heels, stepped in. I handed her the clipboard. "Thank goodness it's you. You have a new guest."

Mabel glanced at the intake form. "Naomi Jackson?"

"Yeah. That's me." *Jiggle, jiggle. Tap, tap, tap.*

"Come into my office. Let's talk, okay?"

The young woman followed Mabel into the office and the door shut behind them.

I looked at Angela back in her cubby. "Is Mabel going to be okay in there?"

"Oh, sure. Someone will stay with her while she comes off her high. Then she'll be assigned a case manager—Stephanie's good—she's a social worker, also one of our board members. Mabel does case management, too, but I think we could use a few more."

"So what's Mabel doing in there right now?"

"Probably getting more information out of her, then going over the rules for staying at Manna House. No drugs, for sure. It all depends on whether she actually wants to get help." The phone rang. Angela picked up. "Manna House . . . Yes, she's here, but she's in a meeting. Can I take a message?"

Messages! *I better tell Estelle her lunch volunteer isn't coming.*

I found her in the kitchen downstairs, putting away the groceries. "Guess that makes you my helper then," she grunted, dumping a ten-pound bag of flour into a large container. "You okay with that?"

"Sure." Making lunch would seem like a vacation in the Bahamas after manning the front desk.

"Here." She handed me a pair of latex gloves and an ugly

hairnet cap. "Better tuck that mop of yours under this. Don't want no hair spicin' up the soup. They gonna know the red ones are yours, for sure."

For the next hour Estelle kept me busy peeling and chopping vegetables for a vegetable-beef soup, while she mixed up several batches of biscuits and a large flat pan of brownies. But she caught me off guard when she said, "Mabel tell you I used to be homeless?"

"Just that you were once a resident here." I didn't admit I'd assumed she was homeless *now* when I first met her.

"Oh, yeah . . . before the fire took this place down." She laughed. "But, Lord, Lord, He is so good, because that fire turned out to be a blessing for *me*."

My knife paused in midair. "What do you mean?"

She chuckled. "This white girl, Leslie Stuart, kinda like you, 'cept she's got long blonde"—*wink, wink*—"California hair . . . anyway, she took me in after the fire. Turned out she was lookin' for a housemate and, knock me over with a cotton ball, we hit it off like the Odd Couple, so . . ." She laughed again, a big *hee hee hee*, while she slid the pan of brownies into the commercial-size oven.

"Did you know her or something?" I couldn't quite imagine the scenario. "Or did she just show up on the sidewalk the night of the fire and invite you to sleep over?"

Estelle scooped up my chopped carrots and potatoes, threw them in her soup pot, and handed me a bag of onions and a bunch of celery. "Nope. Didn't know her. But this church north of here, SouledOut Community, took all of us in the first night, then farmed us out to various church members till the city could find other shelters that had room."

"SouledOut?" The name was familiar. "Isn't that the church that did worship here on Easter? Avis Somebody preached. I think her husband is a board member here."

Estelle's shoulders shook with amusement. "That's the one. That's where I worship now. Not only that, I'm part of this prayer group called Yada Yada. Stu and me and about ten others, more or less. If you hang around here long enough, you'll meet most of them at one time or another. Edesa Reyes—I mean Baxter . . . she's a Yada too."

My eyes were swimming from cutting the onions. I grabbed a paper towel and dabbed. "Sounds weird," I sniffed. "Like a Greek sorority or something."

"Nah, it's Hebrew. From the Old Testament—uh-oh. Time creepin' up on us. Can you run upstairs and see if these two are around?" She pointed at names on a chore sheet. "They need to get down here to set up. And—*hee hee hee*—you better fix your face. You look like one of them raccoons we had back in Mississippi."

So much for waterproof mascara. As I repaired my makeup in the common bathroom, a thought popped into my head. *Funny. She didn't say anything about* why *she'd been homeless . . .*

I left at three o'clock, anxious to get the Lexus home and safely in the parking garage before I got tied up in traffic. Besides, I was exhausted. I'd helped serve lunch, which was fun, giving me a chance to chat with each resident and staffperson who came through the line, trying to memorize names and faces. Many were out for the day—Mabel said some of the residents at the shelter had jobs of one sort or another, or had appointments at public aid—so it didn't take long. Then I took my soup to a table and sat with Wanda, who turned out to be a lot more talkative the second time around while she polished off seconds on brownies. Took me a while to understand her patois accent, but it was fun trying to catch the gist.

I'd stayed for cleanup, along with Aida Menéndez and Tina, a large, good-looking Latina, but the two of them talked rapid Spanish to each other as they washed pots and pans, so I just concentrated on scooping leftover vegetable-beef soup into two large plastic containers and wiping down tables with a spray bottle of disinfectant.

As I drove north on Sheridan Road, Estelle's comment, *"You're learning quick,"* rubbed up against my spirit like a purring kitty welcoming me home. Even Mabel seemed pleased that I'd handled things at the front desk, though she'd apologized later for not letting me know what the intake procedure was. *"I didn't think you'd need it in the first hour!"* she'd laughed. *"Go ahead, call it a day. We'll see you tomorrow."*

I could see Richmond Towers and the other lakefront high-rises coming up in the distance. But my thoughts were still back at Manna House. I'd noticed Mabel made a point to stick with Naomi at lunch, talking and laughing with others across the table even though the newcomer hunched silently over her food, still tapping her foot under the table. By the time I left, Naomi was zonked out on a couch in the multipurpose room while Tina sat nearby, flipping through a magazine, keeping an eye on her.

Had to admit, I was surprised they let someone who was high come into the shelter and sign up for a bed. I probably would have told her to come back when she's sober . . .

I parked the car in the Richmond Towers parking garage but bypassed the door directly into the secured elevator area in order to walk outside to the frontage street along the park. Such a beautiful afternoon! The time-and-temperature sign I'd seen on a bank coming home had said seventy-two degrees. Blue sky arched overhead with only a few wispy cirrus clouds to catch the eye. I couldn't see the lake from here—my view blocked by the trees in the park and Lake Shore Drive—but suddenly I had an urge to stick my toes in the sand and splash in the water again. Should I change? I was still in my slacks and cotton sweater I'd worn to work . . .

Nope. Once thirty-two floors up, I'd probably see stuff I needed to do and that'd be it.

On impulse, I pushed through the revolving door. "Mr. Bentley!" The bald-and-bearded doorman standing in the lobby, hands behind his back, was just the person I wanted to see. "Could I leave my purse with you for a little while? Half an hour, max, I promise."

"Now, Mrs. Fairbanks." He arched an eyebrow at me. "What would I be doing with a purse? What would people think?"

I giggled. "Didn't take you for a man who cared what people think. But, I mean, don't you have a drawer or something behind that desk I can put this in? Doesn't have to be locked. You'll be here, right?"

With a shrug, he took the bag, stuck it in a drawer behind the half-moon desk, and said, "Go on, get out of here. That purse ain't going anywhere."

Feeling free and lighthearted, I walked briskly through the park across from Richmond Towers, half-ran through the underpass under the Drive, and in no time stepped onto the stone retaining wall. Slipping out of my flats and knee-high nylons, I walked through the warm, dry sand, then rolled up my trouser legs and waded into the lapping water. *Brrr.* Still numbing cold. Didn't Lake Michigan ever get warm?

Sitting on the two-level stone wall that made a convenient seat facing the lake, I let the sun warm my back and dry my feet. Something Mabel had said last week during my interview warmed me inside too. *"From the first time you walked in here, Gabby, I had the sense it was God who sent you . . . I believe God brought you to Chicago because He has a purpose for you, right here at Manna House."*

I wasn't sure what she meant. But it made me feel . . . wanted. As though God hadn't forgotten me, even though I'd ditched Him years ago. Even though the afternoon was slipping away, I felt reluctant to take the elevator to our sterile penthouse. Right now my heart felt full and I didn't know what to do with it. The staff and volunteers I'd met at Manna House—Estelle, Precious, Edesa, and even Mabel—seemed to so easily say, "Praise God!" or "Thank You, Lord!" That didn't come easily to me, but something deep inside wanted to tell God "thank You."

So I just closed my eyes and said it. "Thank You!"

"For what?" A gravelly voice behind me caught me off guard. I twisted around and found myself face-to-face with a beat-up shopping cart overflowing with bundles, bags, bits of carpet, plastic tarp, and assorted junk. Then a wrinkled face framed by flyaway, graying hair peered over the top and looked down at me. "You lost again or somethin'?"

I grinned up at her. "Hi, Lucy."

chapter 17

I scrambled to my feet. Lucy was dressed in yet more mismatched layers of clothing, but her eyes seemed brighter. "You're looking better! Hope that means you're feeling better. How's the cough?"

She ignored my comment. "Put on your shoes."

"What?"

"Shoes. Put 'em on. Didn't your mama tell ya not to go barefoot in the park? That's how ya cut your foot—an' I ain't got any more clean rags to spare mopping up blood after you."

"Yes, ma'am." I grinned, sat back down, and pulled on my nylons and flats. I patted the stone wall. "Sit down a minute. I'm glad to see you."

"Nah. Don't have time. I'm on my way somewhere."

I got to my feet again. "Where? Can I walk with you?"

"No, you can't. But turn around . . . now, see? Ya got a grass stain on the seat o' your good britches. Huh. Some people don't have the sense they was born with." She started off, pushing her cart ahead of her, shaking her head.

"Lucy! Wait." I ran after her. "When will I see you again?"

She shrugged and kept walking. "Maybe tomorrow. Maybe never. All depends."

"But I wanted to tell you something."

That got her. She stopped and cocked her head. "So tell me."

"I—I applied for a job at Manna House. I'm going to be there all week learning the ropes, then hopefully start next week. That's why I was saying 'thank You' to, uh, God."

Heavy-lidded eyes studied me. "What kinda job?"

"Program director. Planning activities for the residents." Why was I telling Lucy this? Why would she care? But I blathered on. "I used to do it for a senior center, but the shelter is a new situation for me. I could use some ideas."

She snorted. "Sorry. Ain't interested in bingo. Or shuffleboard. Big waste of time, if you ask me." She started off again.

"I *am* asking you, Lucy!" I called after her. "Think about it!"

She marched on as if she hadn't heard. Then she suddenly turned, marched back, and growled at me. "Now you git on home and take care o' that grass stain 'fore it sets. An' next time ya come to the beach, wear somethin' ain't goin' to get ruin't."

I chuckled at Lucy's bossiness all the way up the elevator to the top floor of Richmond Towers—but I took her advice, changed into my jeans, treated the stain on my slacks, and tossed them into the wash. I wanted to share the joke with Philip when he came home that night, but hesitated. Lucy's name might still be a sore point between us. Besides, he seemed distracted that evening, spending an hour on the phone, talking business.

"Is everything okay?" I asked when he finally got off the phone.

He flopped into an armchair that matched the curving couch. "I don't know. Maybe." He ran a hand through his hair. "Hope so."

I perched on the arm of the couch and waited . . . which paid off.

"It's this new account we bid on last week." He sighed in frustration. "Found out on the sly that another company is bidding for the contract. Big rep for underbidding on projects. Fenchel and I are trying to decide whether to lower our bid right now. We really need this deal. A big one."

"I'm sorry, Philip." I had a brief urge to say, *"Maybe we should pray about it."* But I was sure it would sound odd coming out of my mouth, as if I was trying to be superspiritual or something. "Anything I can do?"

He shook his head, sinking deeper into his thoughts. I left him alone, but fifteen minutes later brought him a cup of fresh coffee. I was pretty sure he'd be up half the night crunching numbers.

I never did hear him come to bed, and he was gone when I woke up. I still felt the urge to pray, but wasn't sure exactly for what. So I just prayed silently over my morning coffee. *"God, help Philip today. He'd really like to land this job to kick-start the new business."* I found myself adding, *"And I'd really like him to get this contract, so he won't be so tense and touchy."*

I set out for my second day at Manna House, but to my shock, the temperature had dropped thirty degrees overnight and it was misting again. I was definitely not dressed for cold and damp. When I got to the shelter at nine o'clock, I was shivering. And the hot water pot and coffee urn in the multipurpose room were cold and empty. *Well, I'm here to learn, so I might as well make the coffee.*

Wrapping my cold hands around a Styrofoam cup fifteen minutes later wasn't exactly down-home comfort, but at least the coffee was hot. The pungent smell seemed to draw people out of the woodwork, including Mabel and a woman I hadn't seen before, carrying a clipboard. White, medium height, a few extra pounds. Straight, light-brown hair hung just below her shoulders, bangs brushed to the side. Jeans, clogs, and a blue sweater. Not scary at all.

"Oh, good, you're here, Gabby." Mabel took the Styrofoam cup I handed to her. "I want you to meet Stephanie Cooper, our case manager. Stephanie, this is Gabby Fairbanks, who is applying for our new position of program director."

I shook Stephanie's hand. A nice grip. "You're also on the Manna House board, I've been told."

Stephanie laughed. "Yes, Estelle's housemate shanghaied me. Stu and I both work at DCFS. I'm glad to meet you, Gabby. We need some new blood around here. You're from Virginia, I hear?"

"Not if you asked my mother-in-law. I grew up in North Dakota, which cancels out the last fifteen years, I think."

Stephanie laughed again. "Now, that's an interesting vita. Wild West meets Old South."

I grinned. "Oil and water." I liked this woman.

"Sorry I can't talk more. I've got an appointment in a few minutes with a new guest who came in yesterday." She consulted her clipboard. "Naomi Jackson."

I nodded. "We've met."

"Really?" Stephanie looked at Mabel and then at me. "Say, would you like to sit in? It'd be good orientation. I'll have to ask her, of course."

Which is how I found myself in the TV room a few minutes later with Stephanie and the young woman who was still wearing her baseball cap, but not tapping. "Sure, fine. Whatever," she said, when Stephanie asked if she minded me sitting in. I parked myself in a corner and tried to be invisible as Stephanie got down to business. Fast.

"Naomi, we're here to help you any way we can. But to do that we need some help from you. Do you have a picture ID?"

A shake of the head. Stephanie wrote something down.

"When was your last TB test?"

"Can't remember . . . last year maybe?"

"Hm. All right. The nurse comes in tomorrow. You need to see her and get the test. No ifs, ands, or buts. Understood?"

Naomi nodded sullenly.

Stephanie handed her a couple of sheets stapled together. "These are the house rules. Read over them, and if there's anything you don't understand or have a question about, just ask. But let's go over some of the highlights, okay?"

Whew. As I listened, I realized I needed to know the rules too. *If you are assigned a bed, you must be here by 8 p.m. . . . . all guests must have a physical and a mental health assessment within one week of being assigned a bed . . . must meet weekly with your case manager . . . must be actively working on goals as determined by your case manager . . . must take a shower daily . . . laundry is available on a sign-up basis . . . no profanity, no violence, no drugs, no smoking inside the building . . . personal belongings may be searched at any time . . . staff may conduct random drug tests . . .*

Stephanie set aside her copy of the rules. "What are your goals, Naomi? I don't mean way off in the future. I'm talking about this week. This month."

Naomi scrunched up her face. "Get a job so I can have my own money. And stay here till I can get my own place."

Stephanie leaned forward. "Naomi, we don't have time to play games here. Staff says you showed up here yesterday high on something. Amphetamines? The first question is: are you at a place where you want to stop?"

"Guess so."

I thought that answer would shoot the whole interview. Who was this Naomi person fooling? Even I could tell she wasn't ready to give up whatever her addiction was. But to my surprise, Stephanie's voice softened. "Naomi, I'm not here to judge you. But I'm not here to enable you either. If you can set some realistic goals for the next few weeks, and you make progress toward those goals, I'm willing to be here for you 24/7. You can call me any time you want—here's my cell number." She handed the young woman a card. "But first you need a plan. What are you going to do later today when you get a craving for those pills?"

The bill of the cap hid her eyes. "Try not to use."

"Wrong answer."

I half expected Naomi to walk out. But she seemed to reach deep somewhere, as if facing her own reality. A few seconds passed. She sighed. "Get into detox. Right away."

"That's right. I can help you with that. We'll try outpatient first, and you can stay here. If you can't handle that, then it'll have to be inpatient. You good with that?"

Naomi nodded.

"If you stay clean for two weeks, then we can work on getting you a job. But you'll need a picture ID. So . . . what's the plan?"

Naomi's mouth tipped into an almost-smile. "Get into detox. Get an ID."

"Good plan." Stephanie smiled. "I'm starting to hold you accountable as of right now. You and me, okay?"

The interview was over in thirty minutes. After Naomi left the room, Stephanie sat back and turned to me. "We'll see what happens in the next twenty-four hours. If she's still here by curfew tonight, we'll have a good chance of taking a few steps forward. But"—she shrugged—"it's up to her."

The days passed so fast, I almost felt dizzy by the end of the week. I dressed for the chilly weather on Wednesday, but by late afternoon the temp was back in the sixties and stayed there the next several days. Mr. Bentley teased me almost every morning on my way out. "Got your bathing suit? Umbrella? Snow boots? Might need 'em all before evening." At the shelter, I had the sneaking suspicion that Mabel was making sure I got a good feel for the place, because I ended up doing a bit of everything, from cleaning toilets to supervising the rec room after school— and somewhere in there, getting a chance to talk to some of the women in residence.

Like Carolyn. Gray cells popping beneath that brownish-gray ponytail. "Know what this place needs?" She had just whipped me at chess in thirty minutes, and I used to think I was pretty good. "Books. I like to read, but all they got here are a bunch of old magazines. And the Bible, of course. Heck, I cut my teeth on Dostoevsky."

Dostoevsky! She must have seen the shock on my face, because she grinned. "My ma fell for a door-to-door salesman selling Great Books. One gullible woman. Kicked him out but kept the books, which was fine by me."

I laughed and made a note. *Start a library. Maybe a book club?*

And Tina. The woman was big boned and carried her weight well, and she had a classic Latina face with golden skin. She'd taken the teenage Aida under her wing, and I saw her going over the house rules with the teenager, helping her with the English words.

"Tina, would you be interested in teaching an ESL class? English as a second language?"

"Who, me? A teacher?" But her eyes lit up.

I added another note. *Get basic ESL materials.*

Even Precious, who was a volunteer, not a resident, had hidden talents. She showed up three afternoons a week to supervise homework in the minimal after-school program, but I heard rhythmic music coming from the rec room and went to investigate. Precious had all five of the Manna House kids, ages six to eleven, on their feet, dancing in perfect rows and steps—stepping forward, back, to the side, half turn, do it again . . .

I clapped in the doorway.

"All right, back to the books!" Precious yelled, turning off the CD player. "We're busted!" The kids giggled and scurried back to their chairs around the single table. "Gets the blood goin' to their pea-brains—ain't that right?" She laughed and high-fived the eleven-year-old.

"That looked like a lot of fun. Why don't you teach it to everybody? You and the kids? For a Fun Night or something."

"For real?"

Another note. *Plan a Fun Night, with dancing and games.*

Thursday was another case management day for Stephanie Cooper, who showed up again in jeans—and I realized I hadn't seen Naomi Jackson since her meeting on Tuesday. I sidled up to

Stephanie in the lunch line. "What's happening with Naomi? Did she go to detox?"

Stephanie shook her head. "Walked out of here Tuesday, haven't seen her since."

"Oh no!" I'd felt a connection to Naomi, since I'd been the first one to meet her at the door, and I'd been hoping for the best.

"Just pray for her," Stephanie said. "She knows we're here. One of these days she'll be back. And she'll be ready to do business. But . . . it might get ugly between now and then. A lot of these young women are turning tricks for their drugs. She's going to need our prayers."

Pray for her. Funny. As soon as Stephanie said she'd skipped out, I assumed there was nothing Manna House could do until she came back. But these people actually prayed for the women who came to the door—whether they stayed at the shelter or not.

Another note. *Start a prayer list.* This one just for me.

On my way out the front door later that afternoon, Mabel called me back. "Oh, Gabby. Two of our board members you haven't met yet are going to drop in about lunchtime tomorrow. They'd like to meet you. Clyde Stevens is pastor of New Hope Missionary Baptist, and Liz Handley was—"

"Former director of Manna House. I know." I smiled. "I promise I'll be on my best behavior. What's for lunch?"

Mabel laughed. "Who knows? But Pastor Clyde has a weakness for macaroni and cheese and fried catfish, and Estelle knows it."

I walked toward the El smiling to myself. My first week at Manna House had almost come to an end. After tomorrow, hopefully I'd hear that I had the job. I was excited to get started, to sort through the ideas I'd been collecting and see which ones were viable.

Friday. Wasn't that the day Edesa Baxter led a Bible study in the morning? I smiled even broader. Tomorrow was going to be a good day . . .

The "William Tell Overture" erupted in my bag. I fished for the cell phone, flipped it open, and glanced at the caller ID. *Fairbanks, Philip.* I had a sudden ominous feeling. He'd been tight-lipped and silent most of the week, working late at the office or at home in the den, not wanting to be bothered. I'd given him a wide berth, not wanting the cloud over his head to rain on my parade. I almost let the call go to voice mail, but caught it on the fourth ring.

"Hello? Philip?"

"Gabby? Where are you?"

His voice was upbeat. My spirit inched upward a notch. "On my way home from work. Where are you?"

"Still at the office. But I've got great news. We sign the Robinson deal tomorrow morning, eleven o'clock!"

I squealed. "You got the contract! Oh, Philip, I'm so happy for you."

"You better believe it, Mop Top. That's why I'm calling. The Fenchels and Fairbanks are going to celebrate! How about that neat little bistro you took me to last week? Can you make a reservation for the four of us for lunch tomorrow?"

chapter 18

❋ ❋ ❋

I stopped dead on the sidewalk. *Lunch?! Tomorrow? This can't be happening!* No way did I want to call Mabel and tell her I couldn't show up to meet the last two board members on Friday. My mind did a quick spin. "Ah . . . sounds great, Philip. But, uh, why not make it tomorrow night for dinner, make a real night of it?"

"What are you talking about?" Philip sounded irritated. "The signing is at eleven, Mona is bringing a bottle of champagne to the office to celebrate, and then what . . . we diddle our thumbs till six? Besides, the Fenchels have tickets to something or other tomorrow night. Just do it, Gabby. Make it one o'clock. Gotta go."

I flipped the phone closed and felt like throwing it. *Unbelievable!* I stalked into the Emerald City Coffee Shop near the El station and ordered coffee to calm my nerves. Thoughts collided like pinballs behind my eyes. Should I go back and talk to Mabel? What would it look like if she had to call the board members and tell them, sorry, our prospective program director can't make it? On the other hand, if I told Philip about my dilemma, he'd just use it as ammunition as to why this job at the shelter wasn't going to work out. All he needed was an excuse to be down on it.

"You want another, miss?" the owner called from behind the counter. I shook my head absently.

Weren't things supposed to fall into place when God was on board? Mabel seemed to think God had sent me to Manna House—and I was glad to accept her view of it, since the job seemed perfect for me, though I had to admit her take sounded a bit *hocus-pocus*. But if I missed showing up at the shelter tomorrow, my dependability rating might skydive before it'd even gotten off the ground.

Wait a minute. I corralled my thoughts into a neat little row. If Philip wanted a reservation at Bistro 110 for one o'clock, why couldn't I do both? Lunch at the shelter was usually noon, straight up. I'd go to the shelter in the morning, let Mabel know my little conflict, meet the reverends at twelve for half an hour, make my apologies, catch a cab at twelve thirty, and be at the restaurant before Philip and the Fenchels even arrived.

Perfect.

I settled back into the chair, downing the last of my coffee in its "tall" cardboard cup with the plastic sippy lid. Maybe God had a way of untangling these little *snafus* anyway.

Only when I was on the El, watching the wall of buildings and windows fly by, did a nagging thought step out of line. Philip had said Mona Fenchel was coming to the *office* with a bottle of champagne . . . did he expect me to be there for the signing too?

By the time I let myself into the penthouse, I was pretty sure I knew the answer. This was a big deal for Fairbanks and Fenchel, and I should be glad Philip wanted to include "the wives," shouldn't I? He and Henry could just go out to celebrate and come home with a hangover.

But, I argued with myself, kicking off my shoes and flopping onto our king-size bed, getting this job at the shelter was a big deal for me too. Maybe I should just tell my husband I had an appointment at noon, but I'd be at the bistro with bells on at one. Get it all out on the table. After all, there was no reason both things couldn't happen, right? Except . . . it was hard to reason with Philip once he decided things should happen in a certain way. He'd see it as making my petty agenda more important than his big moment. By wading straight into the water, I risked getting sucked in by the undertow that swept so many of our communications out to sea. If not setting off an actual tsunami.

Okay, maybe I wouldn't say anything, just do it and deal with the fallout later. After all, Philip didn't actually *say* he wanted me to come to the signing. Just asked me to make a reservation at that cute little bistro I'd taken him to before. Why not leave it at that?

I got off the bed. I'd feign innocence. Tonight, I'd raid the freezer—there should still be a package of king crab legs in there—make a lovely dinner, light the candles, rub all the tension from last week out of his neck. Tomorrow, I'd go to the shelter, meet the board members, show up for the celebration at the restaurant. And cross my fingers.

But first, I better make that reservation, or my name really would be mud.

Unlike most weekdays, Philip didn't dash out of the house at seven thirty the next morning. In fact, he was still there when

Camila arrived to clean at nine, trying to choose between his gray Armani suit, white shirt, and conservative maroon tie, or a tan suit with blue shirt and tan and brown striped tie.

I was glad for the interruption—anything to distract Philip from going over his plans for the day with me. We'd made it through dinner and the evening the night before, mostly because I kept asking questions at the table about the new job—a combination residential-office multiplex with more than one hundred one- to three-bedroom condos, twenty-five work studios, ten high-end shops on the first level, and underground parking. "Everything from the design to managing the construction, Gabby! Robinson Inc. is primarily an investment firm, putting up the money." Philip had happily picked his teeth with a toothpick after sucking out the meat from the last crab leg. Then he'd excused himself from the table and spent the next two hours on the phone.

I poked my head into the bedroom. "Camila's here, Philip. I'll get her started at the other end of the house. Mm, the tan and blue looks nice." I closed the bedroom door and steered Camila toward the living room. "Can you start up front? My husband is still dressing for an important day at work." I gave her an apologetic smile. "Sorry. We'll both be out of your way in a few minutes."

"*Sí,* no problem, Señora Fairbanks." Camila gave me a nervous smile. "But I have a favor to ask, *por favor.* Next Friday is Cinco de Mayo, fifth of May, a big celebration in my country. I would like to take the day off to be with my family . . . if that is okay with you and Señor Fairbanks?"

I tipped my head curiously. "Cinco de Mayo? What holiday is that, Camila?"

Camila must have taken my question as hesitation, because her words came out in a rush. "If it is a problem, I could make it up to you by coming to clean Thursday or Saturday after my regular—"

"No, no, it's fine." As little time as we spent in the penthouse, we could easily skip a week. I hoped it was okay with the cleaning service, but who cared. We were the employers, weren't we? "Tell me about this holiday—"

"What are you going to wear, Gabby?" Philip appeared in the archway between gallery and living room in the gray Armani. "How about that purple outfit I bought you?" He glanced at his watch. "Oh—gotta run. Don't be late, Gabby."

"Go on, go on, I'll be there." I pushed him out the door, at the same time pushing down the niggling suspicion we were talking about two different times. I leaned against the door and closed my eyes. The purple outfit. *Plum* would be the fashion word. A clingy, long-sleeved top with soft folds falling around the scoop neckline, and flowing pants that could pass for a long skirt. It was lovely . . . and completely wrong for my chestnut hair. Not to mention it would be totally out of place at the women's shelter.

But the purple outfit it would be. I'd have to shave off another five minutes to change in Mabel's office. And forget the El. I picked up the phone and dialed 01. "Mr. Bentley? Would you call a cab for me? . . . Twenty minutes would be fine."

I got to the shelter at ten wearing casual slacks (I decided against jeans today, even though most of the staff—except Mabel—dressed down) and carrying a bulging bag with the purple outfit and dressy shoes. Colorful prisms reflecting from the stained-glass windows on either side of the oak doors splashed over the tile floor of the entryway and decorated the walls. I drank in the colorful welcome. The sun was out. All should be well.

Mabel wasn't in her office, so I went hunting—and found her comforting a sniffling Edesa in the toddler playroom behind the multipurpose room. Gracie was on the floor, rocking on all fours, as if trying to get hands and knees coordinated for The Big Crawl.

"Oh. Excuse me." I started to back out of the room.

"No, no, you're just in time." Mabel waved me in. "I have an appointment soon, but I don't want to leave Edesa alone. She needs some help pulling herself together before leading the Bible study at ten thirty. Can you . . . ?"

"Of course." Except it was Mabel I needed to see, and she was disappearing down the hall. I turned my attention to the young mother. "What's wrong, honey?"

Edesa sank into a molded plastic chair, leaned over to place a squeaky toy in front of the baby, and then blew her nose into a well-used tissue. I fished in my bag and handed her an unused travel pack.

"I . . . I . . . I just got a call from our . . . our . . . social worker," she hiccoughed. "She says someone claiming to be *el papá del bebé* has come forward and . . . and . . . and wants to stop the adoption and take . . . take . . . take Gracie." A flood of fresh tears shook her body, and she buried her face in her hands.

"Oh, Edesa." I pulled over another chair and put my arm around her. I could only imagine how she must feel. "Oh, honey." I had a dozen questions—Who was he? Why was he only coming forward now? Where was he when the baby was born?—but I just hugged her to me and let her cry.

After a few minutes, Edesa blew her nose again and looked at me with a wry twist to her full lips. "And I'm supposed to—*hic*—lead a Bible study on trusting God this morning! Me! I'm a mess . . . and I don't have time to call Yada Yada."

She must have caught my funny look. "S-sorry. That's my prayer group." She hiccoughed again. "We meet every other week. I'll e-mail them later, and I know they'll shake heaven with their prayers. But I—*hic*—need prayer right now—and . . . and Josh doesn't even know. He has a test today, trying to test out of a class for next semester." Her dark eyes lifted and met mine. I'd hardly ever seen Edesa Baxter without a sparkle in her eyes, but even wet with tears, her eyes struck me as alive, honest, open—as though they were truly windows to her soul. "Will you pray with me, Gabby?"

"What?"

"Will you pray with me? And then, I hate to ask, but could you take care of Gracie for the next hour? Josh couldn't come today . . ."

"Of course." I meant, take care of Gracie. The Bible study only went to eleven thirty. But Edesa took my hand in both of hers, our light and dark fingers entwined, and she bowed her head. I realized she was waiting for me to pray.

I suddenly felt like an adolescent at my first Spring Fling, standing against the wall, terrified somebody would ask me to dance. And then someone did. And now was the moment of truth. "God . . ." I swallowed. I couldn't remember the last time I had prayed aloud. I used to pray, "Now I lay me down to sleep . . ." with the boys when they were small. But people around here didn't pray memorized prayers. They just talked to God.

I tried again. "God, Edesa's pretty broken up over this news about a relative showing up. But if anyone I know trusts You, God, it's Josh and Edesa. And they love this baby so much . . ." I stumbled on for a few more sentences and then said, "Amen."

Edesa gave me a hug. "Thank you so much, Gabby. I . . ." She grinned shyly. "I'm so glad you're going to work here. Nobody's married on staff except me. It will be *muy bueno* to have someone around who's been married a while to talk to about . . . well, you know." She grabbed her Bible. "Gotta go. Bye, Gracie, honey." She blew the baby a kiss and was gone.

My skin prickled. Me? Have marriage advice for those two lovebirds? Fat chance. Though . . . once upon a time, Philip and I were in love too. Smiles and glances across the room, hilarious pillow fights, finding a single rose on my pillow. One time I'd talked him into driving to Virginia Beach on the spur of the moment—at ten at night!—just to wade in the ocean by moonlight. He had laughed and told me I was good for him, good for their "proper" Southern family. I still remembered his strong arms around me as the tide swirled around our feet, his fingers in my "mop top" and his kisses soft on my lips, my eyes, my hair.

But that was then. This was now . . .

Now. *Yikes.* I still needed to find Mabel and tell her about my crunch. I scooped up the eight-month-old and cuddled her on my hip, smelling the softness of her dark hair as I glanced at the clock on the wall.

Ten forty. The signing at Fairbanks and Fenchel was in twenty minutes.

Just to be safe, I fished for my cell phone and turned it off.

chapter 19

Except Mabel was not to be found. "Oh, she went out," Angela informed me from her cubicle. "Had a hair appointment or something. Taking an early lunch."

I felt like rolling my eyes. Flexible schedules was right! Was she even going to be here when the two board members came? What if she came sauntering in at twelve forty, thinking there was no big rush for this meeting with the "reverends"? After all, she didn't know I had to leave at twelve thirty. But scooting out when she expected me to be here would be worse than telling her I couldn't make it at all.

Gracie started to squirm and squeal, annoyed at my inattention. I jiggled her in my arms and made absentminded cooing noises as I paced around the foyer, wondering what to do. Too late to make the eleven o'clock signing at Philip's office. No one here knew about the split-second timing needed to enable me to get to my second rendezvous . . . *Drat!* My coy conniving had lit a fuse burning at both ends, and I'd be apologizing for the mess in two directions.

Dear God, if I haven't totally blown it, I could use some help—"Ouch!"

Gracie had grabbed a handful of my hair. She kept her grip at my outburst, but the rest of her body pulled back in my arms, and the giggle on her face slid down to a quavering pout of her bottom lip.

"Aw, sweetheart, it's all right." Suddenly the baby in my arms came into focus. This little girl was oblivious of the storm swirling around her—her birth mother dead, a fight brewing between her loving foster parents and the supposed father over her adoption. And here I was, acting as if juggling my tight schedule was the linchpin of a Middle East peace proposal. And nothing had even gone wrong yet! I was getting carried away, praying about such trivial stuff.

"Come on, Gracie," I whispered in the baby's ear. "Let's go play. But we gotta be quiet, 'cause Mommy's leading the Bible study." I squeezed through the double doors and was heading quietly toward the toddler playroom when the lilt of Edesa's accent from the circle of chairs on the other side of the multipurpose room became actual words . . .

"The psalmist said, 'When I am afraid, I will trust in God.' And then, in the same psalm, he turned it around and said, 'I trust in God, why do I need to be afraid?' And do you know what, *mis amigas*? Those are God's words to *me* today!" Edesa caught sight of Gracie and me slinking out of sight and blew a little kiss. "Because today I learned there is a big problem in the way of Gracie's adoption . . ." Her voice caught, but she blinked, smiled, and went on. "So I have to admit, *sí*, I am *asustada*, but I will trust in God."

The women slouching in the sloppy circle of chairs and old

couches seemed to straighten, lean forward. A few murmurs reached my ears, and then a voice spoke up belonging to Diane, with the big Afro. "An' if you trust in God, you don' *need* to be afraid, girl. We gon' keep you covered in prayers, so we got your back, 'Desa. Know what I'm sayin'?"

Nods and murmurs of "Got that right."

I slipped out of the room with Gracie, my eyes blurry with sudden tears. Destitute women without homes and family, some separated from *their* children, praying for one of the volunteers and her child . . .

Whew. Manna House was certainly an upside-down place. In fact, maybe God heard my piddly prayer after all, because Rev. Liz Handley popped in at eleven thirty as the Bible study was breaking up—all five-feet-two of her, a stocky white woman in her sixties, wire-rimmed glasses, salt-and-pepper hair cropped so short it might have passed military muster. As I returned Gracie to her foster mom, several of the residents gave "Reverend Liz" big hugs, and they laughed when she blustered, "Where's Estelle? I hope she's cooking."

Mabel still hadn't shown up, so I stuck out my hand. "I've been looking forward to meeting you, Reverend Handley. I'm Gabby Fairbanks, hopefully the new program director."

"Liz is fine, Gabby." The former director of Manna House cocked her head. "So you want to get mixed up with this crew?" She laughed and we sat.

We chatted about the typical stuff—where I was from, past experience, how I stumbled upon Manna House. She seemed genuinely interested in some of my ideas for life enrichment—setting up a library, getting ESL materials, field trips to museums, even the occasional Fun Night for starters. "But I'm so new to

Chicago, I'm not sure how to find resource people, or even resource materials." I hoped my confession wouldn't disqualify me.

"You'll learn. Start with putting the word out to the board, the staff, and the volunteers. We all go to different churches. Who knows what we can come up with!" She peered over her wire frames. "And don't forget to look under your nose, Gabby. Some of these residents have talents and connections you wouldn't believe. Talk to them. Find out what they like to do."

"I can do nails!" Hannah the Bored popped her head up over the arm of a nearby chair and waggled her long, purple nails.

I gave her a smile—but lowered my voice. Why were we having this conversation in the multipurpose room, anyway? "But . . . aren't the residents here temporarily? I mean, people like Lucy Tucker come and go like will-o'-the-wisps. Others stay here, what—a few weeks at most?"

Liz shrugged. "Some. But many stay the full ninety days allowed. And some, when they get on their feet, come back to volunteer. Look at Precious and Estelle. Both were residents at Manna House before the fire, and now look at them. Giving back. I'd start with them. Pick their brains for ideas too—oh, hey, Angela. What's up?"

The receptionist appeared waving a couple of sticky notes. "Sorry to interrupt, but Mabel just came in, said to tell you she'd be here in a minute. And Pastor Stevens's secretary called. He can't make lunch today because a teenager in their neighborhood got shot this morning—he's with the family. Oh, and there's a taxi waiting outside for you, Mrs. Fairbanks."

I leaped up. "Oh no! What time is it?" I glanced at my watch . . . 12:32! How had the time gotten away from me? "Tell him to wait! I need five minutes." I turned to Rev. Liz and blurted out that I needed to run, I was so glad to meet her, and please let Mabel Turner know I'd explain later . . . and suddenly realized I had no idea where I'd left my bag with the purple outfit.

By the time I found my bag in the toddler playroom, wiggled into my outfit in a toilet stall and freshened my makeup, I'd kept the taxi waiting ten minutes—with the ticker ticking. And by the time the taxi pulled up in front of Bistro 110, it was five after.

Late.

But I put on a brave face and breezed into the restaurant. No familiar faces waiting to be seated. I started to relax. Maybe they weren't here yet.

"Name please?" The maître d' looked at me inquiringly.

"Fairbanks, party of four, one o'clock?"

"Oh yes. Come this way, please."

My chest tightened. They were already seated! They even had drinks and a bread basket. Henry Fenchel leaped up as I approached the table for four tucked in a front corner with windows. "Gabrielle! Now this party can get started." Philip's partner gave me a flirty grin and pulled out the empty chair for me.

No such grin from Philip. My husband took a long drag from a stein of beer and leveled a long gaze at me over the top.

I'd rehearsed a little speech in the taxi. *"So sorry I'm late . . . had a meeting with the board at my new job . . . you know how that goes!"* But a glance at Mona Fenchel's simpering face changed my mind. I was not going to grovel in front of this woman for only being five minutes late.

Instead I laughed. "You won't believe what I had to do to get here! Had a meeting with the board this morning at my new

job—had to practically walk out. But I told them this was important." I turned a bright look on my husband. "How did the
signing go? I want to hear all about it!—oh. Waiter? Can I have a
lemonade please?"

Philip still held me with his gaze. "You'd know how it went if
you'd been there, Gabrielle."

"If I'd—?" I managed to look astonished. "Honey, you didn't
say anything about coming to the signing. Just asked me to make
a lunch reservation for one o'clock to celebrate." I made a puppy-
dog face. "Oh, dear. I'm sorry . . . one of those communication
snafus." I turned to Henry and Mona. "You two never have those,
right?"

Henry guffawed. "Never. Ha-ha." He slapped Philip on the
shoulder. "See? I told you it was just a mix-up. A little *snafu,* the
lady said. Heh-heh. I like that. Besides . . ." He winked at me.
"Mona made sure your glass of champagne didn't go to waste.
Ha-ha-ha."

Mona Fenchel rolled her eyes. "Oh, pipe down, Henry." She
took a sip of her double martini. "You didn't miss much, Gabrielle.
Boring, actually. The bigwigs from Robinson wanted some last-
minute changes to the contract, so I had to sit around for forty
minutes while they argued, with nothing to do in that—how do I
say it kindly?—*provincial* waiting room. So . . . suburban. And not
even one magazine to read." She shook her head at the offense to
her sensibilities.

I couldn't believe it. Mona Fenchel had unwittingly let me off
the hook. But I turned to my husband. "Changes to the contract?"
My concern was genuine. "Is everything all right?"

Philip shrugged. "Just last-minute nonsense was all."

"Don't you believe it, Gabby." Henry shook a finger at me.

"Philip, here—he's the man. Philip refused to budge on the main points, and they backed down." He raised his stein of beer. "Here's to Philip. He saved our hides."

My lemonade had arrived. We each hefted our glasses in acknowledgment. I could tell Philip was starting to thaw. I got brave and laid my hand on his arm. "So everything's okay? You signed the deal?"

He nodded and broke into a smile. My heart squeezed as the tension evaporated. Gosh, he really was handsome.

"I'm so glad, honey." And I was. Very, very glad. I lifted my glass again. "Here's to Fenchel and Fairbanks!"

My husband stiffened. Three pairs of eyes stared at me. Philip paled. Then Henry threw back his head and guffawed. "'Fenchel and Fairbanks' . . . I like that. Yes, indeed. I like that!"

chapter 20

My face heated like a hot flash. Never had I so desperately wished a hole would open up and swallow me. *"Fenchel and Fairbanks"* . . . How could I have turned the names around like that?! In front of my husband! Worse, in front of my husband *and* the Fenchels!

Henry would never let Philip forget it. Worse, Mona would probably never let Henry forget it. *"You jerk! I told you not to let Philip bully you into putting the Fairbanks name first! Well, if Gabby Fairbanks can call it Fenchel and Fairbanks, so can I!"*

My tongue felt like cotton candy. I couldn't look at Philip. I knew my husband saw me as a traitor . . . and I felt like one too. *Oh God,* I moaned inwardly. *If only You'd rewind the last few minutes and let me do them over.*

Huh. While I was begging, might as well rewind the past twenty-four hours and take another shot.

The waiter—that God-sent apparition in black pants, white shirt, and black tie—penetrated my misery with his notepad. "How are you folks doing? Ready to order?"

I grabbed the menu, but the words swam before my eyes. I heard Henry order the bistro steak and *frites*. Mona went for the baked artichoke and arugula chicken salad. Philip was forced to speak. "Shrimp cocktail. Spinach salad. The salmon." He flipped the menu closed like a snap judgment.

I'd lost my appetite. "Just the quiche, thank you."

Somehow we made it through the "celebration lunch." Henry tackled his steak and fries with concentrated attention. Philip drank too much and avoided talking to me. Mona Fenchel dripped sweetness into the chasm. "I didn't know you started a job, Gabby. Can you tell us what you're doing, or is it a deep, dark secret?" She simpered at me over a second double martini.

I did not want to talk about Manna House after my faux pas. It might feel like sticking Philip's nose in it. So I mumbled something about doing a program for a nonprofit and let it go at that.

But Mona had the subject in her teeth. "And what nonprofit is that, dear?"

I counted to ten while hiding behind a long glug of lemonade. "Manna House. A shelter for homeless women."

"Well." I could feel Mona's pitying eyes on me. "That's sweet."

Philip and I walked to the car in total silence. As the doors closed and the locks clicked, I knew I needed to say something.

"Honey, I am so sorry."

He started the car and revved the engine like a sixteen-year-old.

"I know I put my foot in my mouth, Philip, but it was totally unintentional. I'm so embarrassed."

"Whatever." Philip pulled into traffic, stone-faced.

I plunged on. "When I realized what I'd done, I didn't know how to make it right! It was so awkward. I was afraid saying something would just make it worse. Give it more attention than it deserved. I . . . I was hoping it'd just blow over."

Philip snorted. "Oh, right. Just blow over." He swiveled his head toward me, eyes dagger slits, pinning me to the passenger side door. "Awkward for you? What about me, Gabby? You know Fenchel will goad me about this, my own wife putting his name first—as if you were disagreeing about the decision to name the company Fairbanks and Fenchel."

A horn honked. Philip jerked his eyes back to traffic, hit the steering wheel with his hand, and cussed out the other car. Or maybe me.

"I'm . . . I'm really sorry, Philip."

Silence stuffed the car like an inflated air bag the rest of the way to Richmond Towers. And the rest of the weekend passed pretty much the same way . . . two bodies taking up physical space in the same condo, but not *sharing* it in any real sense. We went through the motions of Saturday—calling the boys at separate times, Philip talking to his mother in the den, me running clothes through the laundry, shopping for groceries at Dominick's a few blocks away, Philip taking the Lexus for an oil change.

Sunday was much the same. Gray clouds had dampened the climate outside, as well as in. Philip went for a run between sprinkles, came home, showered, went out again for hours, and then came home and holed up in the den.

I thought I might scream if I had to stay inside this tomb another hour. But where could I go? The on-again, off-again drizzle made a walk along the lake a soggy prospect. I didn't have anyone to talk to, to vent, to let off steam. Even Mr. Bentley was off duty until Monday.

As the hands on the grandfather clock inched toward four o'clock, my spirit lifted. The Sunday evening worship at Manna House . . . I'd go there, just to have *somewhere* to go. But when I called the shelter, a voice I didn't recognize picked up, then yelled to someone else, "Lady wants to know if there's a church service here tonight! . . . Oh, yeah. Okay." The voice came back on the phone. "Sorry, it's the fifth Sunday this month. They ain't having nothin' tonight."

I slammed the phone into the charger, pulled my hoodie and a windbreaker out of the closet, and headed for the elevator. Rain or no rain, I had to get out of here!

Lake Michigan was calm in spite of the gloomy day. I walked along the jogging path, hands jammed in the pockets of my windbreaker, letting built-up tears mix with the light rain on my face. "Oh, God . . ."

My moan escaped out loud. Well, so what? I pretty much had the path to myself, save for the occasional die-hard biker zipping around puddles at breakneck speed. "God, what am I going to do? I really let Philip down! I tried to tell him I'm sorry, but . . . I don't know how to fix it! I can't live with his mad forever. Help me, please."

I'd reached a stretch of large boulders creating a retaining wall between lake and park. Carefully climbing up the slick rocks, I stood huddled inside my hoodie and windbreaker, listening as the sprawling lake licked gently at the craggy rocks.

"When I am afraid, I will trust in God . . . I trust in God, why do I need to be afraid?"

Where did *that* thought come from? Oh, yeah. Edesa's Bible

study at the shelter Friday morning. And she had bigger troubles than I did. If she could trust God under the threat of losing little Gracie, could *I* trust God to take care of this mess with Philip?

I snorted. Looked like it was my only option.

". . . why do I need to be afraid?"

Exactly! If Philip wanted to sulk, well, let him. I blew it. I said I was sorry—really sorry. What more could I do?

Let God handle it. If He could.

Philip took himself off to work early Monday morning, much to my relief. The weekend from hell was over—I hoped. The TV weather guy said it was still drizzly, but temperatures were supposed to climb back into the seventies this week.

Perfect for the month of May. For some reason, turning the kitchen calendar to a new month made me feel positively giddy. Today I would know if I had the job or not . . . the sun was bound to come out . . . and in three and a half weeks we'd drive to Virginia to pick up P.J. and Paul. "And if I have anything to say about it," I growled at the mirror in the gallery as I headed for the front door, "they aren't going back either!"

The African-American doorman was back at his post as I came through the main lobby. "You can relax, Mr. Bentley," I sang out, patting the large tote bag over my shoulder. "I've got an umbrella."

"Humph." The bald-headed gentleman kept turning pages of the *Sun-Times*. "One of those itty-bitty collapsible things? How's that supposed to keep you dry if a thunderstorm rolls through?"

I laughed. "That's what I like about you, Mr. Bentley. You care what happens to me even if nobody else does."

He looked up sharply. My face reddened, and I quickened my step. "Have a good day," I called back, disappearing through the revolving doors that spit me out on the Sheridan Road side. *I'll be answering questions about* that *if I'm not careful.*

The commute by El was beginning to feel familiar. I even recognized faces on the El platform. Businessmen and smart-suited women of assorted hues carried briefcases, newspapers, and cell phones. A tall young woman with Caribbean good looks could, I decided, be a model. A short, round—okay, fat—woman with a babushka always lugged three or four plastic bags, puffing up the stairs to the platform one step at a time. I nodded and said hello to anyone standing nearby and usually got a nod or hello in return—except for the under-thirty-year-olds, who all had iPod buds in their ears.

Today I sat next to the babushka—well, she sat down next to *me* with a *whoomph*. I gave her a smile. She pulled a transit schedule out of her bag and fanned her face. "In ze old country," she said with a heavy accent, maybe Russian, "ze trains stay on ze ground. I tell you, *dyevushka*, those stairs will be killing me one day."

I didn't have time to find out where she was going at this time each day, because by the time she arranged her bags, accompanied by several *oomphs* and wheezes, the train was rolling into the Sheridan El Station.

"Hi, Mrs. Fairbanks—I mean, Gabby!" In the receptionist's cubby, Angela tossed her black, silky mane off her face and pointed at Mabel Turner's door. "Mabel said to come on in when you got here."

Uh-oh. I'd meant to call Mabel on Friday and tell her where I'd disappeared to! And here it was Monday, and she had no idea where I had gone in such a hurry.

Might as well face the music. I knocked, opened the door, and peeked in. Mabel had the phone to her ear, but she motioned me in and held up a finger. I sat in the chair across the desk from her, feeling as if I'd been called to the principal's office. A moment later, the finger came down, and the phone returned to its cradle. She looked at me, puzzled. "What happened on Friday, Gabby? Liz Handley said you went running out to a taxi after a quick change to a fancy purple outfit. And you'd call to explain."

Once again my face heated, and the tops of my ears burned. "Oh, Mabel, I am so sorry I didn't call. Philip and I had a major meltdown—well, I guess more like a deep freeze. And I was so busy navigating the icebergs, I totally forgot to call." I suddenly teared up. "Seems like all I've done the past few days is apologize."

Mabel handed me a tissue . . . so I blew my nose and started at the beginning with Philip's phone call Thursday, just after I'd left Manna House. "Guess I handled the whole thing badly. I should have called you right away to explain my dilemma, not try to juggle things on my own." I wagged my head. "I let everybody down, didn't I? My husband, you, Reverend Handley . . ."

"Gabby Fairbanks, next time you get yourself in a pickle and need somebody to talk to, *call me.* Here's my card with my cell phone." She pushed a business card across the desk. "Day or night. I'm serious."

I looked at the card stupidly. "Does that mean . . . you haven't given up on me yet?"

A tiny grin tipped the corners of her mouth. "Honey, if we gave up on people that easily, we'd be in the wrong business. Besides, Liz Handley took a liking to you. And she may be the *former* director, but around here, what Liz says carries a lot of weight. And she told me, 'Hire that woman, Mabel. Don't let her get away.'"

Mabel held out her hand to shake mine. "So congratulations, Mrs. Fairbanks. Welcome to the Manna House staff." Then she waved me out. "Now, go find the office Josh Baxter set up for you off the dining room downstairs."

chapter 21

❀ ❀ ❀

In a daze, I walked downstairs to the lower level. A couple of the shelter residents were still in the kitchen, cleaning up after breakfast. I recognized Diane—her big Afro was hard to miss—and waved hello. Carolyn, hairnet askew, ponytail sticking out the back, was wiping down tables. I stood uncertainly in the dining area. *Office? What office?*

"Hear you're movin' in." Carolyn grinned at me. "They put you in the broom closet." She snickered and pointed toward a door standing slightly ajar near the stairway, then squirted disinfectant on yet another table.

A sheet of orange construction paper was taped to the door. In childish bubble letters, it said Ms. Gabby's Office. I pushed the door open wider. The room was dark, no window. I pawed around for a light switch and clicked it on . . . and caught my breath. On my left, a lush bouquet of spring flowers—irises, tulips, and daffodils—sat on an ancient wooden desk in the tiny room. (Had it really been a broom closet? Big broom closet.

Small office!) Next to the bouquet, a computer monitor blinked at me, hiding a simple laser jet printer. Keyboard and mouse pad were in place, as was a padded office chair pushed into the chair well. A phone (my own phone!), a legal pad, and several pens had been arranged neatly to one side. There was just enough room beside the desk for another chair and . . . that was it.

"Look behind the door!" Carolyn yelled behind me. "I didn't help lug that thing in here for nuthin'!"

I peeked around the door. A beat-up file cabinet with four file drawers stood against the other wall, along with a wastebasket. On top of the file cabinet sat two boxes, one marked "Hanging Files" and the other "File Folders."

A lump caught in my throat. Josh Baxter had set up this office for me over the weekend? Not just Josh, either, if he rounded up Carolyn—and probably others—to help him move the stuff in. And the computer . . . I sat down at the desk and manipulated the mouse. Instantly a background of the Chicago skyline at night filled the screen, along with program icons—Microsoft Word, Internet, e-mail, dictionary, streets and maps, even a Bible search icon.

"Go on, try it out." Carolyn had leaned into the doorway. "Mr. Josh was here all day Saturday programmin' that thing. Signed you up for e-mail an' everything."

It was true. When I clicked on e-mail, my name came up, and several e-mails popped into the in-box. My eyes blurred as I read Mabel Turner's welcome *("We praise God for sending you!")*, Josh Baxter's helpful advice *("Don't forget to store our e-mail addys in your address list so you can contact us")*, and Edesa's encouragement *("Check out Proverbs 3:5–6")*.

Oh, great. She's making sure I dig out my Bible.

I had to laugh at Liz Handley's e-mail. *"Welcome to the broom closet, Gabby Fairbanks! My office was in a broom closet, too, before the place burned down. Hopefully nothing that drastic has to happen before you get a window. 'Beauty for ashes,' you know. On behalf of the Manna House board, welcome!"*

I sat at the desk a long time, staring at the delicate bouquet of flowers and sorting through my jumbled feelings. The Manna House staff, and even some of the residents, had been fixing up this office and getting me "operational" this weekend, while I'd been sitting up in my luxury penthouse surrounded by silence, being punished for all my sins. Even though I hadn't called Mabel to work out my dilemma . . . even though I'd run out on Rev. Handley with no explanation . . . even though I hadn't called Mabel afterward to explain, like I'd said I would . . . what did they do?

They gave me flowers.

It took me close to an hour to get past being blubbery and able to start thinking critically about my new job. I pulled the legal pad close and began to scribble notes. Recreational needs for homeless women were certainly different than for the residents of the retirement center where I'd worked back in Virginia. The elderly needed fun and stimulation to keep their minds and bodies active. But homeless women needed life skills, an expanded vision of what life could be beyond the streets, as well as stimulating activities to fill listless hours.

I feverishly jotted down every idea that came to me—*budgeting, etiquette, cooking, dressing for success, word games, ESL (Tina?), Fun Nights/dancing (Precious?), book club (Carolyn?), making jewelry (other crafts?)* . . . I paused, then wrote: *literacy? GED classes?*

Finally I put down my pen. Maybe I was getting out of my

depth. I was a recreational therapist, not an educator. Still, my title was "Program Director," not "Recreation." And a variety of educational classes certainly seemed needed. But . . . I should back up. What did *Mabel and the board* expect of me? So far, they'd left me on my own to just "get acquainted." But I needed to set goals, construct a balanced program, find resources . . . Good grief, did I even have a budget?

I flipped to a new page on the legal pad and wrote: *(1) Meet with Mabel! Job description? Responsibilities? Accountability? Budget? . . .*

A knock on the door made me jump. A brown face, damp with perspiration beneath a puffy hairnet, peeked in. "Door ain't locked, you know. You can come out and eat lunch now. We don't do room service." Estelle smirked at me and disappeared.

Sure enough, I heard the clatter of aluminum pans and plastic glasses, and the chatter of women moving through the serving line. I'd been oblivious to time passing. As I came out, Mabel was already sitting at a table with a few of the "day residents" who didn't have jobs or job prospects. But she stood up and started clapping, urging everyone around her to do the same. "Cheers to our new program director, Gabby Fairbanks!"

Several of the women clapped or waved. Back in the kitchen, Estelle banged on the bottom of a pot with a metal spoon. My face surely turned beet red, because I could feel my ears burning. "So if you've got ideas for activities we need here at Manna House," Mabel added, "see Gabby."

From a corner of the room, a familiar voice growled, "Already told her we didn't need no shuffleboard or bingo 'round here—hey, Estelle! You got any more of that 'noodle surprise' over there?"

Lucy. Swathed in the usual layers of sweaters, knit tops, and cotton blouses, and a new knit hat in purple yarn jammed on her head. I wanted to laugh. If Lucy was here, it must be raining. Well, good. I wouldn't have to chase all over the park to find her.

"Thanks, everybody. I'm excited to join the staff here at Manna House." I grabbed Mabel in a hug before she could sit down again. "Thanks so much for the flowers," I whispered in her ear. "You have no idea what they mean to me." Then I hustled to the counter for my own plate of "noodle surprise" and sat down next to Lucy.

"Nice hat, Lucy. Looks new." I meant it. The hat was stylish, with a slightly wavy knitted brim and a clever rose made of yarn on one side. Even on Lucy's grizzled head, it lent a certain charm.

"*Humph.* Estelle made it. Glad ya like it."

I glanced across the room at Estelle, still behind the counter. That's right. The first time I'd met her, Estelle had been knitting. I'd thought it was probably your basic long scarf—every beginner's first project. But this hat was the cat's meow. *Hmm . . .*

Mabel and I got our meeting, and to my relief, she had already worked on a job description and list of responsibilities. I was happy to see that the list was specific without being limiting: *"Assess resident activity needs through questionnaires and personal interviews"* . . . *"Establish attainable goals for weekly and monthly activities"* . . . *"Establish budget needs within overall operating budget"* . . . *"Oversee interpersonal interactions during group activities"* . . . *"Educate residents in resources in the larger community"* . . .

I was so excited about my new job, I was tempted to stay into the evening and meet the women who were usually out during the day, maybe even try a brainstorming session to get their ideas.

Decided against it. Staying late today probably wasn't the

wisest thing. I still had fences to mend at home and didn't want to build them higher. Besides, I should probably work on a questionnaire and talk personally to staff and residents before throwing the discussion wide open.

As I walked into Richmond Towers at four thirty, I tried to keep Edesa's psalm that had encouraged me yesterday in focus. *"When I am afraid, I will trust in God . . . I trust in God, why do I need to be afraid?"* "That's right, Gabby," I murmured to myself. "You don't have to be afraid. You made a mistake, you apologized, what Philip does with it is his problem—"

"Evening, Mrs. Fairbanks." Mr. Bentley tipped his cap at me with a wink. "You always talk to yourself like that? I'm thinking you've been hanging around our friend the bag lady too often."

"Sorry about that, Mr. Bentley. I was thinking out loud . . . but I've got good news. I've been hired by the Manna House Women's Shelter as their new program director. I even have an office!" I had to grin. "Used to be a broom closet."

He laughed. "Well, congratulations. Have to admit, not too many of the residents of Richmond Towers have such a, uh, colorful job." He winked again.

"That's exactly what I like about it, Mr. Bentley!" I could feel the excitement returning to my voice. "Homeless people on the streets seem so colorless, so . . . gray. Even our friend Lucy—you remember, the bag lady. But at the Manna House shelter, there's so much"—I searched for words—"so much *life*, so much *color*."

Even as I said it, I realized how true it was. Not just the multicolored population of staff and residents, but something indefinable I'd felt the first time I'd walked through the double oak doors. And suddenly I knew what it was . . .

"The color of hope, I guess."

chapter 22

Philip usually got home around six thirty, which gave me a couple of hours to fix supper. I pounced on the two sirloin steaks in the freezer and popped them into the microwave to defrost. *Perfect.* "The way to a man's heart is through his stomach," so they say—whoever "they" are. I snickered at the dorky cliché as I mixed a simple olive-oil-and-red-wine-vinegar marinade. "But a good steak dinner can't hurt—"

I stopped, holding in midair the fork I was using to tenderize the steaks. *Good grief, Mr. Bentley is right. I am talking to myself.* I blew a stray curl off my forehead. I needed a dog. Or a cat. Something to talk to.

My whole chest tightened. No, I needed my children home. With me. And a husband who didn't shut me out.

At six forty I heard the key in the front door and tensed. Philip called out from the gallery, "Smells good! What's for dinner?"

I slowly let out my breath. *Score one for the dorky cliché.* I turned and smiled as my husband came into the kitchen, loosening his tie. "Marinated steak," I said. "Roasted potatoes with garlic and rosemary. And some fresh veggies. Have a good day?"

"Mm-hm. Got another promising prospect, a smaller job, but this way we won't be putting all our eggs in one basket." He leaned his backside against the counter and popped a cherry tomato into his mouth. "You?"

I blinked. Philip was asking about my day? Like a normal conversation? Had God heard my prayer?—though it hadn't even been a prayer, just an ache. I took Philip's cue and relaxed against the counter, too, snagging a strip of raw red pepper from the veggie plate. "Yes, a very good day. In fact, Manna House offered me the job. They even gave me an office." I didn't mention it had a former life as a broom closet. "I have a new e-mail to give you, and a work phone number—though my cell is still the best way to reach me."

He pursed his lips, as if considering my news, then shrugged. "Okay. Glad it worked out, I guess. Just . . ."

I touched his arm. "I know. Philip, I'm really sorry about Friday. I'll try not to let this job interfere with things that are important to you."

"Important to *us*, Gabby. Us! See? That's what upset me on Friday. You didn't show for the signing, you showed up late at the restaurant . . . and then you—you flippantly rearranged the name of our company. That hurt." His voice held an edge. "Are you on my side, or aren't you?"

No, no . . . I couldn't let this conversation slip back into the chasm between us. But I heard something new. He was hurt. Hurt was different than mad. I grasped at it. "I am on your side, Philip. I was incredibly thoughtless. And that's what I'm sorry for. That I hurt you. Will you forgive me?"

My words hung in the air between us. Then he nodded. "Yeah, well . . ." He pushed off from the counter. "Do I have time to change before dinner?"

"Steak will take ten minutes max!" I called after him, turning the oven to Broil. While I waited on the steak, I squeezed my eyes shut. "God," I whispered, aware I was talking out loud again, but wanting to do more than just a vague "thought prayer." "God, thank You. For my job. And for Philip forgiving me." Well, he had, hadn't he? Not in so many words, but . . . "And, God, please help this to be a new day for us."

I woke early the next morning before Philip and wandered into the front room, my mind already spinning with program ideas for Manna House . . . and caught my breath. A stunning sunrise over Lake Michigan filled the wraparound windows. Feathery cirrus clouds flung streamers of brilliant pink fluff across the sky, as though a flamingo were shedding its winter down. Lake Michigan, smooth and glassy, captured a mirror image of the brilliant sky.

Oh my. Between rainy days and my fear of heights, I'd been keeping the drapes pulled in the front room. But the TV weatherman on the nightly news had said the next several days would be in the low seventies and mostly sunny. I might have to give the view from up here another chance.

Philip actually ate the eggs I scrambled for him and pecked me on the cheek before heading out the front door. I smiled as I loaded the dishwasher and got ready for my own exit. Maybe things *would* be different now that the business was getting a toehold here in Chicago.

At the front door I paused. My Bible . . . where *was* it? I'd been meaning to look up the verses Edesa had put in her e-mail. Most of the boxes had been unpacked. Maybe it was with the books, most of which were in Philip's den. It took me five minutes to find it, but there it was, with *Gabrielle Shepherd* stamped in gold letters on the brown leather cover.

I sniffed—the cover still had a leathery smell—and opened it to the presentation page. *"To Gabrielle, our angel . . . on your graduation from high school. Love, Mom and Dad."* On the facing page, my mother had written in her beautiful script: *"Only one life, it will soon be past. Only what's done for Christ will last."*

I shut the Bible and stuck it in my bag. Didn't really want to think about Mom's sweet little proverb right now. Life—at least for me—had turned out to be a little more complicated. After all, it hadn't been *my* plan to be divorced after only two years by my sweet-talking-youth-group-leader-supposedly-Christian husband, had it?! And my second marriage to Philip had seemed more honest at the time. Just enough religion to keep my foot in the church door, but without all the hypocrisy.

I hadn't counted on the big hole in my life, though.

Forty minutes later, I rang the bell at Manna House—9:00 a.m. on the button—signed my name on the in-and-out log, and smiled a greeting at the handful of residents lounging around the multipurpose room before heading downstairs. I unlocked the broom closet and flipped on the light. Flowers, computer, legal pad—everything was just as I had left it. Too bad about not having a window. The prisms of sunshine coming through the stained glass in the foyer upstairs had been a delightful greeting. But I was soon so absorbed in creating a questionnaire for the board, staff, and volunteers, I wouldn't have noticed anyway . . .

Name three activities you think would benefit Manna House residents. (List the resources needed to create those activities.)

What skills, hobbies, or interests do you have that might be shared with MH residents?

Would you be willing to conduct an activity (a) once a week; (b) every other week; (c) once a month; (d) a one-time event . . .

"*Hola.*" Edesa Baxter peeked into my office, her warm brown skin a contrast to the chubby latte cheeks of the Latina baby she held in one arm. Gracie rode her foster mother's hip like she'd been glued on, eyeing me shyly.

"Hey! Where's that handsome husband of yours? I want to thank him for setting up this computer for me—" I'd started blabbing before I noticed that Edesa's usual megawatt smile was missing, and the baby hiccoughed as if she'd been crying. "Um . . . are you okay?"

Edesa shook the little twists crowning her head. "I think the *bebé* has an ear infection. She kept tugging on her ear and screamed half the night." Her own dark eyes puddled. "Josh had to go out in the middle of the night for some infant Tylenol. None of us got much sleep—and he has classes at Circle Campus this morning."

"You're taking Gracie to the doctor today, right?"

The young mother nodded. "But we cannot go until later this afternoon. We have an appointment with the social worker at one o'clock. Josh is supposed to meet us there." She hugged the little girl a bit closer. "We need a lot of prayer, Gabby."

"Oh, Edesa." I pulled her into the office, crowded as it was, and shut the door. "Will the father be there?"

"No, *gracias a Dios.* But the social worker is going to go over the petition to stop our adoption"—her lip quivered—"and tell us what must happen next. We have to go to court, I think. But . . . I have hope, Gabby. God brought Gracie to us, I believe that." A glimmer of smile returned. "I have a friend—one of my Yada Yada Prayer Group sisters—who told me, 'God didn't bring you this far to leave you, 'Desa.'"

"Of course not." No way was I going to dump my doubts on her. The courts always ruled in favor of a relative, didn't they? "I'll be sure to pray for you this afternoon."

At least Edesa didn't ask me to pray right then. I still wasn't comfortable praying out loud, especially on the spur of the moment. In fact, I wasn't sure my connection to the Almighty was all that reliable just yet.

During the next few days, I felt as if I accomplished a lot. I printed my questionnaire and passed out copies to as many staff and volunteers as came in that week, and I sent the rest by e-mail attachment to the board. I even got a few back, though Precious handed hers back blank. "I don't like forms ya gotta fill out. Too much like public aid." She rolled her eyes. "Just let me talk atcha, and *you* write it down."

I laughed and grabbed a pen. "Fire away."

"Okay, first, you gonna get a bunch of well-meanin' stuff from some people, doing cut-an'-paste crafts, which, let me tell ya, it's just busywork any three-year-old can do. Just 'cause these women ain't got homes, don't mean they ain't got brains too." She tapped her head, which was braided all over so tight it looked like it must hurt. "An' those pastors on the board, bless 'em, they probably gonna say we should be havin' group devotions at six a.m.—or maybe a Bible class from Genesis to Revelation."

I repressed a smile. The Bible class idea had already come back from Pastor Stevens, whom I hadn't met yet.

"Nothing wrong with that, I'm just sayin'. But take it from somebody who's been there—correction, somebody who's been *here*—that ya really need to ask the women themselves what kinda things they like ta do. An' don't dis ideas like doin' nails and fixin' hair—yeah, I heard Hannah harpin' at you ta let her do nails. But when you been living on the streets, a bit of pamperin' is pretty nice. Homeless women need ta *feel* like women, too, ya know."

I wrote down "Pampering—nails and hair," feeling duly chastened. I had indeed totally ignored Hannah's harping about doing nails. In fact, I'd basically been ignoring Hannah in general, because for some reason her bored mannerisms bugged me.

"What about you, Precious? Supervising homework for the kids a few times a week is great, but I know you've got more talents hiding under the rug that could perk up the lives of the residents."

"Hidin' under what rug? You talkin' 'bout my hair?" She patted her braided head.

I'm sure the color of my face clashed with my hair. "No, no, it's only a saying. I meant—"

Precious hooted. "Heh-heh! I'm just messin' with ya, Miz Gabby. I'll think about it. Meantime, didn't you say somethin' 'bout having a Fun Night where we could do dancin' an' stuff? How 'bout next Friday?"

"Next week? Uh . . . sure. Let me look at the calendar." I clicked the organizer icon on my computer, and a calendar popped up. "Week from Friday would be . . . oh, that's Mother's Day weekend. Maybe that wouldn't be such a good—"

"And why not?" Precious leaned both hands on my desk. "You think these women have someplace else to go Mother's Day weekend? Maybe fly to California, visit the grandkids? Huh." She snorted. "Them that still got their kids—ain't too many of them here anyway—are the lucky ones. Them that don't, a Fun Night might be a good way to dull some of the pain doggin' the holidays."

I bit my lip. *Mother's Day* . . . Last year, even though P.J. had been away at the academy, the school had scheduled a three-day leave for Mother's Day weekend. But this year, both boys were at the academy, and we were a thousand miles from Virginia. I wouldn't get to see either of them. Unless . . .

But I didn't say anything to Precious, just nodded my head and typed in "Fun Night."

chapter 23

I took Precious McGill's advice and asked for a gab session with the shelter residents on Thursday evening. This was the first time I'd met some of the women who were out during the day, some of whom had jobs or sold the weekly *Streetwise* newspaper. Others, I'd been told, spent their days standing in lines at public aid or the Social Security office, or trying to get their names on the long waiting lists for subsidized housing. "'Course a little panhandling on the side comes in handy now an' then," Precious said with a smirk.

I was disappointed when only a dozen or so showed up in the multipurpose room at seven o'clock, even though Mabel had announced it at both lunch and supper. She must have seen the look on my face. "I'm sorry, Gabby," she murmured. "We can't make them come. You'll just have to make do with the ones who show up."

"Why? Don't they want a say in what activities are offered here?" *Huh.* I'd left my husband to fend for himself that evening, probably using up some of my capital in the "good graces" department. The least these women could do was show up to make it worth my while.

The director shrugged. "Some are just tired, Gabby. They've been pounding the pavement all day. And I'll admit, some don't care. Food, shelter, clothing—that's the bottom line. The rest is 'whatever.'"

Okay, then. Whatever. I pulled some of the furniture into a semicircle, hoping for a cozy chat, but a few of the women—including Hannah the Bored—sat off to the side, arms folded. I was determined to make this work. I introduced myself as the new program director, thanked them for coming, and said I'd like to hear their ideas for activities. "And please say your name when you speak, since I haven't met several of you. This is a brainstorming session, so all ideas are welcome—"

"What she sayin'?" An old woman with a mouth so puckered it looked as if she'd swallowed her teeth turned to the person beside her and spoke loudly, drowning me out. "Can't hear a word!"

"Pipe down, Schwartz!" someone muttered, accompanied by several snickers. Mabel hustled over and sat down beside the old lady, patting her on the hand.

"—and I'll, uh, list them here." I uncapped a black marker, indicating the pad of newsprint propped on a chair.

Silence yawned. Not even the old woman spoke.

I could feel my underarms getting wet. I should have told Precious to be here. She was so sure this was what I needed to do. *Huh.*

In desperation I said, "Here are a few ideas to get us started. Carolyn suggested a book club . . ." I wrote it down and underneath added *Fun Night/Dancing, Budgeting Your $, ESL (English as Second Language), Trip to Museum,* reading off each one. "We want a variety of activities—some just for fun, others to help with practical skills, even some outings. Obviously, we won't be able to do everything, but let's brainstorm."

It worked. A woman named Kim—slender, light brown skin, soft voice, neatly dressed—suggested "Typing Class." Hannah the Bored wanted a "Spa Day" (no surprise there). Soon other ideas flew about—"Movie Night" . . . "Can we go see Oprah?" . . . "I like to make jewelry"—and I wrote them all down, in spite of a few arguments among the group. ("Why just ESL? Why not Spanish for gringos?" "Because this is America, stupid, not Mexico." But I wrote down *Spanish for Gringos* and got a laugh.)

Kim timidly waved her hand. "Some of us work during the day but need more job skills. Can you do those on the weekend?" A few heads nodded.

Weekends. I'd been hoping to keep my part-time hours to weekdays, when Philip was at work. But her suggestion made sense . . .

By the time we wrapped up at 7:45, I had a pretty good list. "That was, um, interesting," Mabel deadpanned, offering to drop me off at the Sheridan El Station, even though it was still light outside. "But just so you know, tickets to see the *Oprah* show may be free, but you can spend a whole day on the phone trying to get a couple . . . let alone enough for a group."

I laughed. "Really? Drat. That was my favorite suggestion."

I showered quickly the next morning, eager to get back to work and sort through the ideas I'd been collecting, choosing a good balance of activities to start with and drawing up a possible calendar. Then I'd have a proposal to present to Mabel and could start to work on a budget.

Not bad for my first real week on the job.

As I was toweling my wet hair, Philip poked his head into the bathroom. "Gabby, tell the cleaning woman to be sure to wash the inside of the windows in the front room today. I deliberately specified inside windows on the contract with the cleaning service, but I don't think she's . . . what?"

I'd stopped toweling when he said "cleaning woman" and grimaced. "Uh, Camila isn't coming today. It's Cinco de Mayo—some kind of holiday for the Mexican community. She asked me about it last week. I'm sorry. I should have told you."

He gaped at me. "What kind of holiday? You agreed? Gabrielle, she only comes once a week! Did you arrange for her to come tomorrow? What if we want to entertain this weekend? The place is a mess!"

"Philip." I tried to keep impatience out of my voice. "The house looks fine. I thought missing one week wouldn't matter. Neither of us is here much during the week. If we entertain"—*Where did that come from? He hasn't said anything about entertaining this weekend*—"I'll do whatever needs to be done to be presentable."

"*You* thought . . . ! Did you remember I've already paid a month ahead?" He withdrew his head, but I heard him cursing in the bedroom. "Stupid Mexicans. They come here wanting jobs and then don't show up when you need 'em."

I pressed my lips together and turned on the hair dryer, staying in the bathroom longer than I'd intended to avoid getting into it any further with Philip. *What a jerk.* Good grief, Camila probably worked longer hours than both of us put together and undoubtedly deserved a day off, holiday or no holiday. Still fussing with my hair, I finally heard the front door slam. Good, he was gone.

But it was obvious *some* kind of holiday was afoot. As I walked to the El, cars flying green, white, and red flags zipped past, their sound systems blasting Spanish music as young people hung out of the windows, waving and shouting. Now I was curious. I still didn't know what the holiday was all about. As soon as I got to my office at the shelter, I turned on my computer, called up Google, and typed "Cinco de Mayo" into the search box. Lots of Web sites. I clicked on one, then another.

"Not to be confused with Mexican Independence from Spain on 16 September, 1810" . . . *"Cinco de Mayo, the 'Fifth of May,' celebrates the victory of the 4,000 Mexican troops over 8,000 French forces in the Battle of Puebla in 1862"* . . . *"A minor holiday in Mexico, but celebrated in the U.S. by Mexican-Americans with parades and festivals with the same cultural pride as St. Patrick's Day by the Irish."*

Parades? Shoot! Wish I'd thought of this sooner! It would've been neat to take some of the women from the shelter to the parade today. Still browsing, I clicked on a site that said, "Cinco de Mayo Festivities, Chicago 2006." *Wait a minute* . . . The parade was on *Sunday?* Strange. I'd assumed Camila wanted the day off because the festivities were today.

My mind started spinning. If the parade wasn't until Sunday noon, I might have time to get it together after all! I'd need a car—no, a van. Didn't Josh Baxter say he used their church van sometimes? Maybe—

Excited, I went hunting for Edesa. I hadn't seen her since Tuesday, hadn't even heard how the meeting with the social worker went, but today was Friday, and she usually led the weekly Bible study. Sure enough, the young black woman was pulling chairs into a small circle with the help of Tina, who looked strong enough to pick up one of the overstuffed chairs and heft it over her head single-handedly. The two of them were talking rapidly to each other in Spanish as a few of the shelter residents started to straggle in.

"Edesa, I don't mean to bother you, but I need to get hold of Josh—" I suddenly realized she had no "papoose." "Where's Gracie?"

Edesa made a face. "Sick. Home with Josh. Double ear infection. But at least you'll be able to find him. *¿Qué pasa?*"

Quickly I shared my idea of taking some of the shelter residents to the Cinco de Mayo parade on Sunday, but needing a van. "How about you, Tina? Would you like to go? Maybe you could tell the rest of us what it's all about."

The big-boned Latina drew herself up, looked down her nose at me, and muttered something in Spanish. Edesa giggled.

"What?" I looked from one to the other.

Tina thumped her chest. "I am *Puerto Rican*, not Mexican. It is not *my* holiday."

I could feel my ears getting hot, and Edesa laughed right out loud. "Cut Gabby some slack, Tina. She's new to Chicago. Besides, I know you'd love to go, right?" She gave the larger woman a playful poke in the ribs, then scribbled a number on a scrap of paper. "Here's our phone number, Gabby. See what Josh says about the van. What a great idea! I'd love to go, too, but . . . well, depends on Gracie."

I skipped the Bible study to make my call. Thirty minutes later, Josh called me back and said the church van was available, but had I ever driven a fifteen-passenger van? "I could if I have to,"

I said. "I learned to drive on my dad's utility van in North Dakota—he owned a carpet store. But I don't know Chicago streets. I was hoping you'd drive." Talk about understatement.

"Can't promise," he said. "Gracie's pretty sick. We plan to lie low this weekend. I could probably get the van down to the shelter, but don't count on me to be the chauffeur. But for what it's worth, I think this is a great idea, Gabby. Be sure to take in the festival at Douglas Park after the parade. Lots of great food and bands. In fact, Delores Enriquez's husband will probably be there with his mariachi band. Don't miss it!"

Well, so be it. I'd drive if I had to. Maybe I'd take our car on Saturday and practice the route.

By the time Estelle banged on a pot, signaling lunch, the plan was falling into place. Josh Baxter would deliver the van and the keys to the shelter by Sunday morning. The first twelve residents who signed up would get a seat on the van. (I was still hoping for another staff person or volunteer to go along.) We'd leave at eleven, park as close to Douglas Park as we could, take in the parade along Cermak Road, then hang out for the festivities. I even printed out a map that gave me the best route from the shelter.

So far everyone I'd talked to had loved the idea. Even Mabel had given her somewhat dubious blessing to my seat-of-the-pants idea—"As long as you're back in time for Sunday evening service," she'd said. "It's Pastor Stevens's church"—and let me announce the outing at lunch. Aida Menéndez was especially excited, jumping up from her chair and throwing her arms around my neck. "Oh, *gracias,* Señora Fairbanks!"

Tina told me later that Aida's first foster mother had taken her to the parade when she was five, but the girl hadn't been to a festival since. "This is *muy bueno*. She needs to connect with her culture."

I spent the rest of the afternoon working on my proposal for the first set of activities and a list of resources needed. I was just getting ready to hit the Print button when my "William Tell" ringtone went off. Grabbing the cell out of my purse, I flipped it open. "Hello? Hello?" Only crackling on the other end. *Rats!* No signal down here. I looked at the caller ID . . . It was Philip.

I called him back on my desk phone. "Philip? Hi, honey. Sorry about that. Couldn't get a signal on my cell. What's up?"

"Don't plan anything for Sunday, Mop Top. We've been invited by a new client to go sailing on his new sailboat—a thirty footer! The weather is supposed to be great." His excitement oozed from the phone—an insidious gunk clogging up everything I'd been doing that day. Not Sunday . . . not Sunday!

I felt as if I might need electric paddles to jump-start my heart. "We who?" I squeaked.

"The Fenchels and us, of course. They said we'd need some good windbreakers and boat shoes—"

"But . . . but . . ."

"—and I offered to bring some good wine and cheese, that kind of thing . . . Gabby? You still there?"

"Uh, sorry, Philip. I've gotta go. Talk about it later, okay?" I hung up the phone. My head sank into my hands. Why didn't I just say, *"I'm sorry, Philip. I can't go. I have to work Sunday. Part of my job. I've already made a commitment to take—"* Oh, sure. After Philip's rant this morning about Camila taking the day off, he'd just love to hear that I couldn't go sailing—with his client, no less, which made it "business"—because I'd be taking a vanload of homeless women to the Cinco de Mayo parade. Not to mention the icy silence I'd had to swim through all last weekend when I didn't move heaven and earth to be at the contract signing. Did I want to go through that again?

"Argh!" I grabbed fistfuls of my hair with a sudden urge to pull curls out of my head, roots and all.

"Gabby? ¿Qué pasa, amiga?" Edesa slipped into the room behind me and shut the door.

I rolled my eyes. I didn't even want to repeat the phone call, cementing my dilemma into reality. But I finally told her, hot tears sliding down my face. I grabbed a tissue and blew my nose. "What am I going to do, Edesa?! Go back out there and chirp, 'Sorry ladies, the outing's off, I'm going sailing?' Or tell my husband, 'Sorry, I'm going to a parade, see you later'?" I didn't bother to explain the edgy dance Philip and I had been doing around work issues.

Edesa was quiet for a long moment. "Gabby, did you look up the scripture I gave you in the welcome e-mail on Monday?"

I shook my head. "Sorry."

"Do you have a Bible here?"

I started to shake my head again—then remembered the Bible I'd stuck in my bag a few days ago. "Uh, yes, right here." I pulled it out.

She paged through it and stopped someplace in the middle. "Here it is. Third chapter of Proverbs, verses five and six. Here. You read it." She shoved the Bible at me.

"You read it." I shoved it back. I knew I sounded petulant, but I didn't feel like reading "Obey your husband" or "Thou shalt not lie" right now.

"Okay." She picked up my Bible and read with her Spanish accent. "'Trust in the Lord with all your heart and don't lean on your own understanding'—"

The words were familiar. Probably one of the verses I'd memorized in Sunday school as a kid.

"—'In all your ways acknowledge Him, and He will direct your paths.'" Edesa closed the Bible.

I sat silently, picking apart my soggy tissue, digesting what I'd just heard. *Trust in the Lord . . . don't lean on my own understanding . . . He will direct my paths . . .*

Finally I glanced sideways at Edesa and gave a snort. "You think?"

She smiled, the beautiful grin that seemed to stretch ear to ear. "*Sí*, I think. God is going to show you what to do, *mi amiga*. I will pray." She gave me a hug and slipped out of my broom closet.

Huh. Easy for her to say.

chapter 24

To my relief, no one was in the dining room or kitchen when I left at four o'clock, and I scooted through the multipurpose room without waving to the two women who sat sprawled in a corner, playing cards. I took a deep breath and stopped by Mabel's office . . . *Drat! Not in!* I wasn't sure if I was relieved or vexed. Just delayed the inevitable confession and flagellation.

I signed out and scowled my way home, going over my options. Not that I had any. I'd practically promised Philip—okay, I *had* promised—that I wouldn't let my job interfere with things connected to his work. But I hadn't anticipated having to break a promise to *my* "clients," after getting them all excited about our first outing.

Should I tell him my dilemma? If I told him I canceled an outing at the shelter to go sailing on his client's boat, maybe he'd quit harping at me about whether I was "on his side" or not. Or would he get ticked off that I'd even planned something on the weekend? Maybe "don't ask, don't tell" was a better policy. Just go, try to have fun . . .

I groaned inwardly as the buildings and shops along Sheridan Avenue slipped past the train windows. What was this going to look like to Mabel and the board? The new program director makes plans for an outing, gets everyone all excited, then turns around and *cancels* because she and her husband got an invitation to go sailing . . .

Argh! I felt like banging my head against the window of the El. Not the greatest way to kick off my program plans. Maybe I should write a book: *The Idiot's Guide to Starting a New Job—How to Get Fired the First Week* by Gabrielle Shepherd Fairbanks.

But instead of head banging, I leaned my cheek against the cool window. When was God going to show me *the* path I should go? Felt like I was in the soup either way—

"Thorndale! Next stop Thorndale!"

What? I scrambled for the door of the train car. I'd overshot my stop by two stations this time.

Sunday. Eleven o'clock. Sunny. Breezy and mild. Perfect day for a parade.

But instead of loading up the borrowed van with Manna House residents, I was walking behind Philip along a dock in Waukegan Harbor north of Chicago, carrying a picnic basket with two bottles of Shiraz, three kinds of cheese, and a couple of boxes of good crackers. We were wearing his-and-hers white deck pants, new navy windbreakers, "boat shoes" with good rubber soles, sunglasses, and white baseball caps—except my bushy chestnut curls stuck out from under the cap, making me look like Bozo the Clown.

I'd finally sucked up the courage to call Mabel on Saturday

morning and told her I had an unavoidable family conflict—
something my husband had arranged—that put the kibosh on the
Cinco de Mayo outing on Sunday, and would she please tell those
who had signed up that I was so, so sorry. She'd been quiet on the
other end for several beats, a yawning gap that made me want to
crawl in a hole and pull dirt down over my head. But all she said
was, *"Of course, Gabby. These things happen. I'll pass the word."*

I'd been hoping she'd say, "Oh, no problem, someone else
can drive the van, we'll still go, don't worry about it." But she
hadn't.

"What's wrong with you?" Philip had asked when he got
home Friday night. "You practically hung up on me! Don't you
want to go sailing? You can be such a wet blanket, Gabby." Keeping
my voice even, I told him the sailboat invitation was very nice,
but I'd been planning an outing for the homeless women at
Manna House for Sunday, and now had to cancel, which put me
in a very awkward position, thank you very much.

He'd just shrugged. "Just reschedule for another day. It's not
like those women have corporate jobs they have to go to next
week."

I'd decided to drop it. It wasn't going to help anything to
point out that the Cinco de Mayo parade *only* happened on
Sunday. He'd just ask, then why did Camila take Friday off?

I had a few dark words with God about the whole mess. Was
this the right thing to do? Edesa had been so sure God would
show me the "right path."

However, once I'd made the decision, a certain smugness settled into a corner of my spirit. The sacrifice I was making might
come in handy when I brought up my idea for Mother's Day
weekend . . .

As Philip hunted for the slip number he'd been given, I tried to take in the harbor in panoramic snatches: clubhouse with a nautical-themed restaurant, gift shop, and large restrooms with showers and dressing rooms. Rows and rows of docks with all kinds of power boats and sailboats lined up side by side, from glitzy yachts to weather-worn, chunky fishing boats, tied up in their individual slips. And beyond the harbor, Lake Michigan stretched blue-green and vast, broken only by small whitecaps like so much dotted-Swiss material.

A voice hailed us from the deck of a sleek sailboat bearing the name *Rolling Stone*. The man was a very tan fifty-something, dressed casually in shorts, windbreaker, captain's cap, rubber-soled shoes, no socks. No Fenchels to be seen, but a thirtyish brunette peeked out from the cabin and smiled a welcome. Introductions were made: Lester Stone, Sandy Archer. *Hmm. The boat and the owner have the same name, but not Sandy.* I didn't see any wedding rings.

Lester helped me cross from the dock to the fiberglass deck, and Sandy took me below to the cabin. Everything fit like a miniature puzzle—two-burner gas stove, fridge, sink, drop-leaf table wedged between two padded benches that supposedly made into a single bed on one side and a double on the other. Toward the bow, Sandy pointed out the "head"—a flush toilet and a vertical, coffinlike shower—and more bunks. Everything was trimmed in wood, the curtains royal blue. Taking my picnic basket, she lashed it to the counter with a bungee cord and handed me a sleeveless jacket-style life vest.

For the first time, it occurred to me sailing might be a bit different from putzing along on my uncle's outboard fishing boat on Devil's Lake in North Dakota.

"Ha-ha-ha. How are ya, Lester?" I heard Henry Fenchel's voice booming above deck. "Mona, this is Lester Stone, our new client . . . ha-ha-ha, *Rolling Stone,* I like that. Hey, Philip, where's Little Orphan Annie?"

Thanks a lot, Henry. Did he think I hadn't heard that old joke before?

"*I* think all those curls are pretty," Sandy whispered to me before going back up the three-step ladder. I followed, deciding Sandy was a friend for life. For the next fifteen minutes, I scrunched in a corner of the blue padded seat of the open cockpit, trying to stay out of the way while Lester gave instructions to Philip and Henry about casting off from the dock and how to unfurl the sails once we reached open water. Sandy seemed at home scooting around the boat, unsnapping the blue cover from the main sail and stowing it below, checking ropes and wires. Mona lounged opposite me, looking perfectly cool in a light blue jumpsuit and gold-strap sandals. I noticed she did not put on the life vest Sandy handed to her.

Well, so what if I looked like Winnie the Pooh with a bulletproof vest. Sandy was pulling the straps tight on hers, and I was going to take my clues from a sailor.

Sail untied but not raised, Lester stood at the wheel and effortlessly piloted us out of the harbor using an inboard motor. I relaxed, smiled at Philip, who was casually sitting on the slightly rounded deck above the cabin, feeling the warm sunshine kiss my face. Might as well just enjoy the day.

Once out on the lake, Lester shouted instructions, Philip pulled quickly on the line to raise the sail, the boom swung out, and as Sandy secured the line—*snap!*—wind filled the large sheet and the boat picked up speed. My stomach did a couple of flip-flops, but I tried to keep my eyes focused on the flat horizon. *Okay, okay, I can do this.* After a while, Lester yelled, "Coming about!" Laughing, the guys ducked, the boom swung to the other side, the sail snapped—and immediately Mona's side of the boat tipped up. *Wa-a-ay up!* My stomach leaped into my throat, and I tasted bile. I grabbed at the rail behind me, though the waves seemed dangerously close.

Lester grinned at me from behind the wheel. "When we heel up like that, Gabby, just move to the other side. Brace your feet on the opposite seat."

I was afraid to let go, but Sandy reached over and gave me a hand. Once on the high side, I sat sideways between Mona and Sandy, clutching at the rail, one leg straight out, foot planted against the fiberglass bench where I'd been sitting. Mona just lifted her chin and let the wind tousle her golden hair, but to my satisfaction, I noticed she did put on her life vest.

Every ten minutes or so, Lester changed direction, tacking back and forth, farther and farther from shore. The higher we "heeled up," the more Philip and Henry seemed to be enjoying themselves. "What a great day for a sail!" Philip shouted to Lester, and the "captain" grinned back at him.

But when we heeled up so far the opposite railing brushed the water, I had to fight a rising panic. My knuckles were white clutching the railing behind me. My ankles and thighs ached from pressing against the opposite bench. And finally my stomach rebelled, and I turned, retching over the side.

Mona recoiled. "Ohhh, *gross*. If I'd known you were going to be so much fun on the water, Gabrielle, I would've stayed home."

Sandy simply handed me a roll of paper towels.

I didn't dare look at Philip.

That sail was the longest, most miserable two hours of my entire life.

When we got back to the harbor, I excused myself, climbed onto the dock, and walked on wobbly legs back to the clubhouse, where I locked myself into a toilet stall, stuffed a few paper towels into my mouth, and had a good silent cry. What a wimp I was! I should have known. If I got queasy from heights, it was a straight jump across a checkerboard to being seasick-prone.

I finally pulled myself together, repaired my face, and went back to the *Rolling Stone*, where the others were passing around plastic tumblers of wine, the cheese and crackers, and sliced apples. Sandy made coffee and brought out a tin of rich, dark brownies. The men talked business, Mona and Sandy chatted about people and parties in Chicago, and I smiled and nodded, wishing I'd spent the afternoon with my feet on the ground, watching the Cinco de Mayo parade.

Once back in the car, Phillip and I rode in silence back down to the city, passing the occasional car with Mexican flags attached to the windows on either side. Finally I said, "That was really nice of Lester to invite us out on his boat."

Philip flipped on his turn blinker and moved into a faster lane.

"Sorry I got seasick. That was my first time sailing. I didn't know what to expect!"

Philip grunted and just kept driving.

I watched his profile—sculptured, handsome, smooth—but couldn't read his eyes behind the sunglasses. I decided this wasn't the time to bring up Mother's Day weekend.

But once we got back to Richmond Towers, showered and changed, and settled at the kitchen counter with hot roast beef sandwiches, I said casually, "You know what I was thinking, Philip. Next Sunday is Mother's Day, and the boys have a three-day weekend. Why don't we fly them here to Chicago, introduce them to their new home, and do something special all together as a family next Sunday? We haven't been to any of the museums yet. Best Mother's Day gift I can think of!"

Philip looked at me as if I'd just suggested climbing the Swiss Alps. "Gabby, that's silly! Philip Jr. graduates from eighth grade in a couple of weeks, and they'll be coming here for the summer. It doesn't make sense to spend the money to bring them now."

Unbidden, my eyes watered and I had to grab a napkin. "But I really miss them, Philip."

"Aw, Gabby, don't go crying. I miss the boys too. But it's only a couple more weeks! We'll fly down for his graduation, stay a few days with my parents, and bring them home with us then."

I stared at him. I'd just rearranged my whole weekend for him and humiliated myself getting seasick in the process. That should earn me *some* brownie points. "Is that a no?"

Philip rolled his eyes and got up from the kitchen stool. "Be reasonable, Gabby. You can wait another couple of weeks." He headed for the front room, and I heard the TV come on.

I sat at the kitchen counter for a long time, my thoughts and feelings so convoluted I hardly knew how to untangle them. I had to get out of this house! Go somewhere, do something . . . before I said—or did—something I'd regret later.

chapter 25

My ears pricked up as the grandfather clock in the front room bonged five thirty. Sunday Evening Praise at Manna House was at six . . . Mabel had said Pastor Stevens's church would be there, and he was the one board member I hadn't met yet. As for the shelter residents, I might as well face the music tonight and get it over with. Aida Menéndez and the rest deserved a personal apology from me, if nothing else. Never could tell who'd be around tomorrow.

Suddenly determined, I pulled on a sweater, grabbed my purse and the carry-all bag with my Bible, and headed for the front door. "I'm going to church!" I yelled into the living room, loud enough to be heard over the TV but not waiting for an answer. *Like I'm really dressed for church,* I thought wryly on my way down in the elevator, looking at my jeans and loafers. But I didn't care. And I knew the "church" at Manna House wouldn't care either.

Lively gospel music could already be heard clear out on the

street by the time I'd waited thirty minutes for an elevated train on its weekend schedule and walked to the shelter. Using my staff key to let myself in, I snuck into the multipurpose room and found a chair in the back. The room was surprisingly full, with quite a few unfamiliar faces, many clapping and shouting, "Glory!" or "Praise You, Jesus!" as the song came to an end. Many of the unfamiliar folks were wearing dresses and heels, even a few hats. Must be members of New Hope Missionary Baptist. I wished I'd taken time to at least put on a pair of slacks and a nice sweater.

A young African-American man with a few too many pounds for his age—this couldn't be Pastor Stevens, could it? He seemed too young!—bounced back and forth at the front of the room as an electronic keyboard and set of bongo drums filled in the lull. "C'mon now, church, c'mon," the young worship leader said, "let the redeemed of the Lord *say* so!"

More shouts, clapping, hallelujahs, and lifted hands. Couldn't say I was used to all this raucous enthusiasm during a worship service—so unlike the formal liturgy of Briarwood Lutheran back in Virginia, or even the more informal but still sedate services at Minot Evangelical Church growing up. But it was impossible to just sit there. I clapped with the others. Clapping for God—well, why not?

"Okay, now, you all heard our girl Whitney sing Dottie Rambo's song 'I Go to the Rock' on *The Preacher's Wife* soundtrack—c'mon now, don't pretend you didn't see that movie." Laughter. "But even if you didn't, you'll pick it up mighty fast. On your feet, everybody! One-two, one-two—"

Right on the beat the keyboard player and drummer, both young black men barely out of their teens, struck up the lively gospel tune and the Missionary Baptist folks helped carry the words . . .

Where do I go . . . when there's no one else to turn to?
Who do I talk to . . . when nobody wants to listen?
Who do I lean on . . . when there's no foundation stable? . . .

I'd seen the movie, though couldn't say I remembered the song, but now it echoed in my head as if putting words to all the aches, confusion, loneliness, and anger sitting like crud in my spirit. *No one to turn to . . . nobody wants to listen . . . who do I lean on . . .*

Suddenly the tension in my spirit uncoiled like a live wire, unleashing a torrent of tears. I couldn't stop. Shoulders shaking, eyes and nose running, fishing for a pack of tissues, I sank back into my chair as the shelter "congregation" all around me kept singing . . .

I go to the Rock I know that's able,
I go to the Rock! . . .

A light hand touched my shoulder, then two thin arms went around me, and Aida Menéndez was whispering in my ear. "It is okay, Miss Gabby. We're not mad at you. Miss Mabel said you couldn't help it. Next time, maybe. *Sí?*"

I nodded, still mopping my face, and hugged her back. "Thanks, Aida. I am so sorry I had to cancel our plans to go to the parade."

As the song finally wound to a close and a middle-aged black man in a suit and tie got up to speak—this must be Pastor Stevens—Aida, the young girl who'd been kicked out of the foster-care system at eighteen, who'd probably been disappointed by people like me all her life, slipped back to her seat. Aida had presumed my tears were guilty ones—and maybe some of them were—but she had no idea how deep and dry the well was from which they'd sprung.

I liked Pastor Stevens. He made a point to introduce himself after the service. "You must be Mrs. Fairbanks," he said, shaking my hand and smiling, a slight tease in his deep brown eyes. "They said you had curly hair. Mm-mm. They weren't kidding." He laughed.

I only hoped my nose wasn't bright red after the crying spell during the service. We chatted, he apologized for missing our lunch date a week ago, and I assured him I understood. He said he appreciated the questionnaire I'd sent to the board and was sure several members of his congregation would be glad to sign up as volunteers. He didn't seem to know about the Cinco de Mayo fiasco, didn't mention it anyway, so I left it to Mabel to inform the board if she felt it necessary. But I was grateful it didn't come up in my first meeting with Pastor Stevens.

The pastor also introduced me to his wife, a sweet-faced woman who looked at least six months pregnant, and several members of his congregation who, Mabel explained later, enthusiastically showed up whenever their pastor had to speak somewhere else.

That kind of loyalty must be nice, I thought.

As soon as I was able to slip away, I went downstairs to my office, closed the door behind me, and booted up my computer. Then I called up the Internet, typed in the travel site we often used, and filled out the necessary information:

Departing from:	Chicago O'Hare Airport
Destination:	Richmond, VA
Date of departure:	Saturday May 13
Date of return:	Monday May 15
Number of passengers:	1

I didn't say anything to Philip when I got home later that evening, but the next morning as he was leaving for work, I handed him his travel mug of fresh coffee and a folded piece of paper.

"What's this?"

"My flight info. I'm going to Petersburg this weekend to see the boys. Wanted to let you know a week ahead of time so it doesn't interfere with any last-minute plans." I kept my voice light, matter-of-fact.

"What? Gabby, we should have talked about this!"

"I tried. Don't worry. I'm working now, so I can pay for the ticket. Have a good day." I smiled and walked out of the gallery back to the kitchen.

Behind me I heard, "Of all the—" and then the front door slammed.

My smile grew even wider.

There was something else I had to do before I could leave for work. I picked up the phone and called Philip's parents in Virginia.

"Hello, Marlene? This is Gabby . . . No, nothing's wrong. Philip's fine. I'm calling to let you know that I'm coming to Petersburg this weekend to see the boys—Mother's Day, you know . . . Yes, I *know* Philip didn't call to let you know. I thought I should call you myself . . . No, just me. We'll both be coming in a couple of weeks for P.J.'s graduation, but I thought—"

I repressed a sigh and listened while Philip's mother fussed for a full minute about having to change plans now and I should have let them know sooner. "Yes, I'm sorry about that, it was kind of a last-minute decision. I'd like to spend some time with just the boys since I haven't seen them for a whole month, but of course I'd love to see you and Dad Fairbanks too . . . No, don't worry about picking me up, I can rent a car . . . Of course, I understand. I'll get a room at the Holiday Inn Express . . . Yes, two nights, Saturday and Sunday. I'll fly to Chicago Monday after the boys go back to school . . ."

I was so exhausted after navigating the phone call with Philip's mother that I felt like crawling back into bed. But I drank a second cup of coffee, gathered up my stuff, and headed for the elevator. Hopefully Mabel would have had time to look at my program proposal and we could get started lining up volunteers and resources. *ESL materials—they shouldn't be too hard to find . . . and typing—Kim's idea is probably the most practical of all . . . the shelter already has two computers in the schoolroom . . . there are probably self-help programs available, but a teacher would be nice . . . probably more available on the weekends anyway—*

"Mrs. Fairbanks! Wait a moment . . ."

Mr. Bentley had been busy giving directions to a trio of Japanese men, who seemed to be having trouble understanding their Chicago map. But the men nodded and bowed and waved as they pushed through the revolving door to the sidewalk, where they stood in a huddle, looking at the map and pointing in different directions.

"They thought this was a hotel," the doorman explained, shaking his head. "I'm glad they have all day to find what they're looking for. They're going to need it." He looked me over, noting my khaki jeans, tooled leather belt, and ankle boots. "How's the job going? Is this Casual Monday?"

I laughed. "Pretty much. Manna House is casual seven days a week. Besides, my office is a former broom closet."

The house phone on the half-moon desk rang; he answered, but held up a finger for me to wait. I tried to stem my impatience. I really did need to get to work. But a moment later he came back. "I just wanted to tell you I saw your, uh, friend Saturday—you know, the old bag lady."

"Lucy?"

"Yeah, that one."

"Where was she? I haven't seen her for a while. I've been kind of worried."

He scratched his graying beard, which outlined his jaw and chin. "Behind the Dominick's grocery store, just south of here. My nephew works in the back unloading trucks, and I was supposed to pick him up. So I drove around back, and the old lady was picking through the Dumpster. The stuff they throw away could feed an army, I tell you! And she was stuffing her bags left and right."

"Was she all right? How did she look?"

He shrugged. "I guess she was all right. I didn't talk to her, didn't want to scare her. She kept lookin' around, like somebody was goin' to tell her to get out of there. Just thought you might want to know I saw her." His voice softened. "Ever since you brought her in here soakin' wet that day . . . well, wouldn't want that to be my mother, livin' like that."

"Is your mother still living?"

"Eighty-eight, goin' on ninety, and feisty as ever." Now he laughed.

"That's great." Would my own mother live to be ninety? She was only in her seventies, but my dad had died at seventy-two. And I had no idea how old Lucy was . . .

"I don't know why Lucy doesn't stay at the shelter! She could sleep in a bed, get three decent meals a day." I shook my head. "Anyway, thanks, Mr. Bentley. I better go. I've got a new program to implement and a Fun Night to plan for Friday night."

"A Fun Night! What's that?"

I laughed. "Just what it sounds like! Having fun, playing games, doing group dances . . . you know."

He grinned. "You mean, like the Mashed Potato, stuff like that?"

I grinned back at him. "I don't know about that. Wasn't that a sixties craze? You're showing your age, Mr. Bentley. But maybe you ought to come, show some of our residents a good time. Not all of them are old ladies, you know." I gave him an exaggerated wink.

The bearded doorman shook his head. "Nah. I'd be the only guy—"

"Oh come on. There'll be some other men there." I was sure Josh would come, and Mabel had said she was going to ask Peter Douglass to bring a few other "brothers" to give security. I laughed. "Just think about it."

But Mr. Bentley didn't look convinced.

chapter 26

The week seemed to fly by quickly. My spirits had lightened considerably—partly because I was going to see my boys in a few days, partly because I'd stood up to Philip and bought a plane ticket, whether he liked it or not. Was it that easy? I mean, it wasn't like I wanted to be at odds with my husband, but in this case, *he'd* been the one who hadn't been acting reasonable. Good grief! I hadn't seen my boys for a whole month! Mother's Day was coming up! I'd be gone all of two days.

It made perfect sense to me.

But for some reason I forgot to tell him I would be staying at work Friday evening too. Forgot? Or was some part of me still scared to upset him? He'd grumbled about me "going off and doing things on your own," but he'd seemed to accept that I was going to see the boys. I was reluctant to push my luck.

I'd busied myself all week putting the first few programs in place. Josh Baxter said his mother was an elementary teacher in the public school system and could probably get me some ESL materials. When I talked to her—her name was Jodi, and she sounded friendly enough on the phone—I found out that Avis Douglass, the beautiful black woman who spoke at the Sunday Evening Praise the first time I'd shown up, was the principal at her school, and between the two of them, they could surely come up with materials, both basic English and basic Spanish. Since she's a teacher, I got brave and asked Jodi if she might consider coming in on Saturday to teach typing to some of the women like Kim who wanted to increase their job skills. She said she'd pray about it.

That took me aback. I expected her to say she'd think about it. It made me feel funny. Had *I* prayed about anything this past week? Edesa had said she'd pray that I'd trust God and He'd show me "the right path." But had I prayed about the sailing-or-parade dilemma?

Maybe not. I did what I thought was right . . . or had I just gambled on who would be madder at me if I let them down—Philip or the shelter residents? To put it bluntly, would Philip have forgiven me like Aida did if I'd disappointed him?

There was no way I was going to disappoint the residents *this* weekend. I screwed up the courage to tell Philip on Friday morning that I'd be late getting home that evening because I'd organized a Fun Night.

"Tonight? Good grief. You're going to be gone clear till Monday, Gabrielle. The least you could've done was save tonight so we could go out to dinner or a movie or something."

"I'm sorry, Philip. That's just the way it worked out. I should have told you sooner." I felt like gritting my teeth. I was so sick of apologizing.

The intercom interrupted, and I hustled to open the front

door for Camila, leaving him muttering, "So what am I supposed to do all weekend while you're off gallivanting?"

A few minutes later, the short, squarish cleaning woman came into the gallery bundled up in a jacket, her head scarf and round face glistening and damp. "Good morning, Camila! Oh dear, you're wet. Is it raining this morning?"

"*Sí*, Señora Fairbanks. And getting colder again. Be sure to dress warm—"

"And where were *you* last week?" My husband's voice cut her off as he came into the gallery with his suit coat and briefcase. "I heard you asked for the day off because it was a Mexican holiday last week. But the parade and festivities weren't until Sunday!" He glared at her.

Her eyes rounded in fright. "No, no, *señor*, it wasn't for the parade. *Mi esposo* is a cook for a restaurant, good Mexican food, and I help him cook food in the restaurant booth during the whole festival—Thursday to Sunday! I did not even get to see the parade."

I smiled smugly. I knew she'd have a good reason.

"Well . . . don't expect me to pay you for work you didn't do." Philip grabbed a felt dress hat from the hat rack and huffed out the door.

Camila looked at me, her eyes frightened. "Oh, *señora*, I did not expect you to pay!"

"I know you didn't, Camila. Don't mind him; he's just in a bad mood this morning." I helped her out of her jacket and hung it up in the coat closet. "I wish I'd known you had a vendor's booth at the festival. I would have loved to come."

"Oh, you should have come! We would have cooked *carnitas* or *chamorros* for you special." As we chatted, I felt a little guilty and grateful at the same time. Her arrival had deflected Philip's rant at me and given him something else to be mad about.

Camila was right. The warm temperatures of the past several days had taken a dive, and it was barely in the forties again—and raining, to boot. Forewarned, I took along an extra pair of slacks, socks, and shoes to work, as well as my umbrella, and by the time I got to Manna House, I'd determined to forget about Philip and his infantile behavior. Which I did, because a pleasant surprise came walking through the door right after the morning Bible study . . .

Lucy showed up again.

"Lucy!" I gave the old woman a hug, though she was badly in need of a bath. "I see you decided to show up for our party!"

"What party? Who has time for a party?" But her eyes glittered.

The old woman's cough was back; otherwise, she was as feisty as ever. After lunch, Estelle Williams rounded up several of the other residents who were "in" that day to help make snacks for the evening, while Lucy poked her nose into their business and snitched a sample of everything. Precious McGill and her daughter Sabrina showed up after school and organized the after-school kids to twist crepe paper decorations and tape them to the walls of the multipurpose room. By the time supper had been cleared away—a simple affair of macaroni and cheese, sausage links, and applesauce on paper plates—excitement for the evening ahead had pumped up, and the multipurpose room was filled with chatter long before seven o'clock.

Josh and Edesa Baxter showed up with Gracie, who was always a hit with the shelter residents. I was surprised how easily they let the baby be passed from person to person. Wasn't Gracie just getting over ear infections? Estelle, who'd changed into a royal blue caftan she'd made herself and put on dangly gold earrings, finally stole Gracie and kept her. "You just want an excuse not to dance and get all sweaty," I teased.

She arched an eyebrow. "Exactly. This has to be dry-cleaned."

Peter Douglass showed up with another "brother" named Carl, and Josh said he thought his parents might come too. I felt good. This party was getting a lot of support.

To kick off our Fun Night, we started with a game of Steal the Bacon for anyone who wanted to play, and ended up with two teams of eight big-and-little people each. I numbered off each team, put them behind masking-tape lines at opposite ends of the room, tossed a dish towel tied into a knot into the center, then called a number—"Six!"—and the two "Sixes" ran toward the middle, danced around and around the knotted towel, trying to grab it and run back to their masking-tape line without getting tagged by the other "Six." The kids were better at this game than the adults, snatching the rag and darting back to their line to the hoots and cheers of the rest of us on the sidelines.

When one team was declared the winner with ten "steals," Precious put a CD on the Manna House boom box, turned up the volume, and within minutes, had nearly everyone in the middle of the floor doing the Macarena—even me. Right arm forward, then left. Right palm up, then left. Right hand to left shoulder, ditto left . . . right hand to neck, then the left . . . hands to hips, wiggle the pelvis, turn ninety degrees and start all over again . . .

I was laughing, getting lost, trying again, slapping the wrong hip at the wrong time, when I heard the door buzzer. Probably Peter Douglass and his friend Carl—they'd slipped outside a while ago—now wanting back in. I was closest to the foyer, so I ducked out of the multipurpose room and opened the big oak door. Peter and Carl came past me, but a third man stood on the steps, wearing slacks and a sport coat, with a dark open-necked shirt and a gold chain circling his neck. He nodded a polite greeting, revealing a familiar bald dome. Brown face, short gray beard running from one ear around his chin to the other . . .

My face burst into a grin. "Mr. Bentley!"

Flying was not one of my favorite activities. I avoided window seats—or closed the shade if I had no choice—squeezed my eyes shut during takeoff, and kept telling myself I was just inside a big, long, noisy building. But I couldn't help grinning to myself on the American Airlines flight to Richmond the next morning. Mr. Bentley had been a big hit at the Manna House Fun Night. Once I introduced him as "a friend of mine," he was dragged into the middle of the Macarena—and his popularity skyrocketed when he insisted on teaching us the Mashed Potato. "Who else knows this oldie but goodie?" he'd teased.

His gaze had zeroed in on Estelle, who protested, "Hey, I was only ten when that one came out!" But then the two of them cut the rug with such hilarity that everyone else jumped in, filling the multipurpose room with music and laughter.

Everyone said the Fun Night was a huge success. It made me wish I'd invited Philip to come. Maybe it would have changed his attitude about my job and given him a chance to meet the staff firsthand.

Or not. But I'd never know unless I asked him . . .

The flight landed on time at 1:55 Eastern time, but it was nearly three o'clock by the time I got my bag, picked up my rental SUV, and headed down Route 295 toward Petersburg. Four o'clock by the time I drove into the countrified hamlet of Briarwood just outside Petersburg and into the winding driveway of the Fairbanks home.

The red brick home was lovely, almost like a large bungalow, with a low front porch along the main part of the house and three dormer windows jutting from the roof on the second floor. An addition had been built at some point to accommodate a large family room with a loft, a stone fireplace, and an attached garage. The house nestled among two acres of trees and lawns . . . a wonderful play space for grandkids. No wonder my boys loved coming here.

The front door opened, and eleven-year-old Paul came running toward the car. "I knew it was you!" he yelled, jumping up and down as I got out of the car and enveloped him in a mama bear hug. Then Philip Jr. appeared, a bit more subdued, but I still got a hug. I held both boys at arm's length, drinking in the sight of them: Paul, still scrawny and short, his school buzz cut starting to grow out into the chestnut curls he'd inherited from me. And P.J., dark haired like his father, starting to add inches. He'd soon be looking me in the eye.

Marlene Fairbanks appeared, smiling benevolently. "Well, come in, Gabrielle. You can have dinner, can't you, before you have to go to your hotel? Mike will want to see you. He had to go into the office today."

Like father, like son. "Dinner would be lovely. Thank you, Marlene. And then . . ." I knuckled both boys on their noggins. "I wondered if the boys would like to come to the Holiday Inn with me for the night. My room has two queen beds. They have an indoor swimming pool and a game room—"

"Yes!" Paul pumped his arm. "Can we, Nana?"

His question grated on me. But Marlene, ever the Southern gentlewoman, said, "Well, of course, if that's what your mother wants, though I'd thought . . . well, never mind. Shall we go in?"

Our supper was pleasant enough, served by the live-in housekeeper, and delicious as always: country ham, smothered potatoes, cornbread, green beans, and peach cobbler. Mike Fairbanks welcomed me with a warm squeeze but kept saying, "So why didn't Philip come with you? Too busy to come see his family?"

I found myself defending my husband, saying our plan had been to come for several days the following week, when P.J. graduated from eighth grade, and this trip was "a little extra gift from Philip to me for Mother's Day." That seemed to pacify the senior Mr. Fairbanks, and I even wanted to believe it . . . until I saw Marlene's face, and knew she'd undoubtedly heard a different story from Philip.

Marlene called the Holiday Inn that evening and asked if we wanted them to pick us up for church. "Always something special on Mother's Day Sunday," she purred.

But the boys and I had already talked about picking up the boys' bikes—the reason I'd rented the SUV—and riding along the paths of the Petersburg National Battlefield Park. "And if I could borrow one of the other bikes Mike keeps around . . ."

"Oh dear." I could practically see my mother-in-law pout over the telephone. "Mike will be so disappointed. He just lives to see those boys on the weekend."

I pressed my lips together so hard, I practically bit them. *Who* hadn't seen them for the past *five* weekends? Good grief. Couldn't the Fairbanks give me just one day without whining about it?! I was sure the good Lord would understand if we didn't show up for church tomorrow.

But in the end we compromised. The boys and I would spend the day together at the Battlefield, and then we'd come back to the house in late afternoon for a barbecue if the weather held. And I had to admit later, I was glad we had a place to go by three that afternoon, because the boys were tired of riding their bikes, tired of seeing the monuments they'd seen half a dozen times before, and I was tired of their bickering and complaining. Besides, the fog that had started the day held a chill that began to seep beneath our windbreakers, and we were all glad to get back to the Fairbanks' home, where Grandad Mike had built a fire in the stone fireplace . . . though I soon found myself warming my toes alone as the boys scrambled to play their video games.

Only when I finally got back to my room at the Holiday Inn around nine o'clock did I realize Mother's Day was almost over, and I hadn't called my own mother. Terrible-daughter guilt threatened to undo my joy at spending the past twenty-four hours with my own sons. It was only eight o'clock in North Dakota . . . *Still time.* But the phone rang and rang. No answer. I tried at nine thirty, then ten. Still no answer.

Anxiety put my nerves on alert. Was something wrong? Wouldn't one of my sisters have called me? I tried the number I had for Celeste in Alaska, and all I got was a recording that said the number was not in service. I tried Honor in California—thank goodness, it was ringing!—but her answering machine kicked in. *"Not here. Leave a message. Peace."*

I finally crawled under the thick comforter of the Holiday Inn bed, worried sick. Had my mother heard from any of us? *How could I let this happen?* As I lay in the dark, kicking myself for my selfishness, I had an inkling of how some of the mothers at the shelter must feel, crawling into their bunks on Mother's Day and not hearing from a single child.

chapter 27

A phone rang . . . kept ringing . . .

I woke with a start and grabbed the bedside phone. The boys? Philip? But it was only the hotel's automated wake-up call. I fell back into the bed, feeling disoriented. I was here in Petersburg . . . had spent the weekend with the boys . . . the visit with Philip's parents had gone better than expected . . .

So why did I feel sad, like it had all gone wrong?

My mother. I still hadn't talked to my mother!

Opening the room-darkening drapes and gulping water to clear my voice, I found my cell phone and pushed the speed dial for Mom. One ring . . . two . . . three . . . and then to my relief, the phone picked up. A wobbly voice. "Hello?"

"Mom?! Oh, thank goodness! I tried to call you several times last night and got no answer. I was so worried!"

A pause. "Who is this?"

What—? "It's Gabby! I should have called you yesterday morning, but—"

"Oh. Gabby. You girls all sound alike, you know."

Sound alike? My mother had never said that before. "Mom, I'm so sorry I didn't call you first thing yesterday. I'm in Petersburg, visiting P.J. and Paul for Mother's Day. And we were running around all day—"

"Petersburg? Didn't you move to Chicago?"

"Yes, yes. But the boys are still in school here in Petersburg . . . Mom, are you okay? You don't sound so good."

"Oh, yes. I'm fine. Just tired is all. Didn't feel too well last night, so your dad told me to go to bed early . . . no, no, that's not right. I think I was at Aunt Mercy's house for dinner, and she brought me home because I didn't feel good . . ."

Now I was really worried. That was the first time my mother had slipped up, talking as if Dad was still alive. Aunt Mercy was my dad's sister, our only other relative in Minot. Maybe that's why Mom got confused. I tried to keep it light. "Oh, well, that explains why you didn't answer the phone. You must be a sound sleeper, Mom. But . . . are you sure you're okay?"

"I don't know, Celeste. This house is too big. I can't keep up. Do you have to live so far away in Alaska? Maybe you and Tom could come live in the house and I could go to the nursing home. After all, it's just me and Dandy now . . ."

My eyes blurred. I didn't bother to remind my mother again that I was Gabby, not Celeste. Dandy was my parents' dog, also aging, a sweet mutt somewhere between a sheltie and a cocker spaniel, with a lot of hair. But in spite of the dog, she sounded lonely. Shouldn't be a surprise after forty-eight years of marriage, now a widow living alone—but her confusion was what worried me.

The phone call with my mother unsettled me long after I

checked out of the Holiday Inn . . . after taking the boys to Aunt Sarah's Pancake House for breakfast . . . after reluctantly saying my good-byes and heading the rental car north to Richmond International. Should I have gone home to see my mother this weekend instead of insisting on seeing the boys? Maybe Philip was right; it was silly to make this trip when we'd be flying down there in another ten days for P.J.'s graduation!

I buckled myself into the aisle seat of the American Airlines plane, due to arrive in Chicago shortly after noon. Usually I loved to chat up my seatmate when flying alone, but my inner tussle took up all my attention.

That verse in Proverbs Edesa showed me . . . what does it mean to trust God with all my heart and He will direct my paths? Am I trusting God? Did I make the wrong choice this weekend? Surely there isn't any-thing wrong with wanting to see my boys after a whole month, is there? But . . . should I have given up what I wanted and done what was best for my mom? Who needed me more?

"Uh . . . coffee. Cream, no sugar. Thanks," I said the flight attendant, who'd had to ask me twice if I wanted something to drink. But the possibility that my decision to go see the boys had more to do with standing up to Philip than choosing "who needed me more" made me squirm. To be honest, I hadn't even thought about my mom, hadn't even called her until Sunday night . . .

As the plane squealed to a wet landing at O'Hare Inter-national—Good grief, was it still raining in Chicago?—I blew out a long breath. What was the point of second-guessing myself? I did go to Petersburg, and I was glad I got to see P.J. and Paul. The question now was what to do about my mom. I probably needed to see her too—and soon.

I called Philip's cell from the taxi and got his voice mail. "Hi, Philip! I'm back; my flight was on time in spite of the rain. Since it's still early, I'm going to Manna House to put in a few hours this afternoon. The boys send their love and can't wait to see you next week. See you tonight. I'll make dinner. Bye!"

I flipped the phone closed, once again wrapped in my thoughts as the taxi driver—foreign, dark, maybe Indian?—darted into traffic on I-90 heading into the city. *Has it really come to this?* Philip hadn't called me once while I was gone. I hadn't called him either. And just now I didn't say "I missed you" or "Love you"—those little endearments that marked our early years. I missed those little whispers in my ears. And yet . . . was I at fault? Was I the one pulling away?

"Oh, God, I need help here . . ."

Only when the driver glanced into his rearview mirror at me did I realize I'd spoken out loud. Then he grinned, teeth stark white against his dark skin in the mirror, and he made curlicue motions with his fingers around his head. *My hair.* It always went bonkers in the rain.

I rolled my eyes and laughed back. "Where are you from?"

"Pakistan, two years! English I like to practice." He seemed eager to talk, and I was glad for the distraction as the car crawled through heavy traffic.

When the taxi finally pulled up at Manna House, I rushed in and tapped on Mabel Turner's door and opened it. She looked up from her paperwork. "What are you doing here? I thought you were in Virginia!"

"I was. But my plane got in at twelve thirty, so thought I'd come in for a few hours. Thanks for giving me the time off."

She gave me a sly look. "Didn't give you time off. We have ways of filling up your time card."

"In that case, I already did it." I smirked back at her. "I was here until eleven cleaning up after the Fun Night!"

The director laughed and waved me off. But Carolyn accosted me as I pulled my suitcase across the multipurpose room. "Hey, Gabby. What about the books you promised? I found a bookcase in the alley, not too bad. We could put it right over there in that corner, or maybe in the TV room, make it a library instead. And we need a new chess set too. The one we got is missing two pawns, have to use checkers." Then she looked at my suitcase. "You movin' in or somethin'?"

"Not today." I laughed. "But you never know. Thanks for the reminder about the books. I'll work on it." That and a zillion other things. Donations. I needed donations of books. And a resource list sent out to supporters and volunteers . . .

The rest of the afternoon I worked on a *Manna House Needs Donations* sheet for board members, staff, and volunteers to hand out to their churches, friends, and coworkers. And mailing list. I needed access to the shelter's mailing list of supporters.

By the time I left Manna House at five o'clock, the "shelter kids"—about five of them school age—were ricocheting around the rec room, letting off steam. A crew of people I didn't recognize—volunteers?—were banging around the kitchen, making supper. On the main floor, a couple of toddlers and their mothers were making use of the playroom, while the TV room bleated some kind of sitcom laugh track. Aida Menéndez yelled at me from across the multipurpose room, "The Fun Night was awesome, Miss Gabby! Can we do it again this Friday?"

"Not this week, Aida! Maybe—" I caught myself just before I said, *"Maybe next month."* No way did I want to set up expectations I couldn't make good. "Maybe we can do it again sometime, though."

Since I had my suitcase and it was still drizzling, I broke down and called a taxi for the ride home. And somewhere between Manna House and Richmond Towers, I came to some direction about my mother. First of all, I needed to call her more than once a week. Maybe even every day for a while, to keep an ear on her situation. And I really needed to be in contact with my sisters about our mother, if nothing else. Last but not least, I needed to plan a visit—maybe even a trip to North Dakota with the boys this summer. They'd only been to Minot twice—when they were about five and seven, and later to my dad's funeral two years ago. The outdoor community swimming pool had been a favorite, plus all the comic books they'd found in my parents' attic from when we were kids. Even better . . . what if Honor and Celeste came too, and we had a family reunion?

As the taxi drove into the frontage road and pulled up in front of Richmond Towers, I made another resolution. I was going to start praying about my mom. And trust God to work something out.

With a lilt in my step, I pushed through the revolving door, then managed to get my suitcase stuck outside and had to back up . . . but finally I wrestled it through the door and crossed the lobby, in a hurry to get upstairs and see what ingredients might magically be on hand to make a nice supper for Philip. But I dreaded what I might find. Philip wasn't good at "baching it." An overindulgent mother and a live-in housekeeper had pretty much inoculated him from catching any domestic skills. But that was the way it was. So be it.

"Hello, Mr. Bentley!" I called out to the doorman. "Thanks for coming to our Fun Night at the shelter." I simpered at him. "You were definitely the life of the party."

Mr. Bentley gave me a little bow with a smile. "Thank you for inviting me, Mrs. Fairbanks. I looked for you this morning but didn't see you. Did you"—he tipped his head at my suitcase—"go somewhere this weekend?"

I smiled big. "Yes. I flew back to Virginia to see my boys for Mother's Day. They'll be coming next week. Afraid your job may never be the same. They're lively."

"Mm. Wonder who they get that from? . . . Oh, by the way." Mr. Bentley glanced into space, his voice super casual. "The woman named Estelle . . . I think she's a volunteer at the shelter. Seemed like a mighty fine woman. I was, uh, wondering if you happen to have her phone number. She said something about doing elder care, and I thought maybe sometime I could talk to her about my, um, mother, in case she, you know, needed some in-home care. Just in case."

I stared at him, listening to him stumble and blather, remembering how he and Estelle had cut the rug doing the Mashed Potato at the Fun Night—and ended up dancing or being partners for games the rest of the evening. And I burst out laughing. "Mr. Bentley! Elder care, my foot. I do believe you have a crush on Miss Estelle Williams!"

chapter 28

I chuckled all the way to the thirty-second floor. Mr. Bentley and Estelle . . . now, that would be a pair! I promised him I'd get her phone number—with her permission, of course—and somehow finagled his age out of him. ("I don't know, Mr. Bentley, she's just a young *chica*, and you—" "What do you mean? I'm still this side of sixty, got lots of miles left, and she's a mature woman, at least fifty.")

He'd wanted to know more about her, but I had to admit I didn't know much—just that she lived in the Rogers Park neighborhood up north, attended SouledOut Community Church, was licensed to do elder care, and volunteered at the shelter. I didn't tell him she herself had been a Manna House resident at one time. I didn't know that story, didn't know how she became homeless, and I didn't want to speculate. She could tell him if he got brave enough to ask her out.

I unlocked the door to the penthouse, wondering if I'd have time to pick up the house, clean the kitchen, *and* cook supper before Philip got home—but to my surprise, the house was as tidy as when I left Saturday morning. Kitchen counters clear . . . bed made . . . no dirty clothes on the floor. In fact, the only evidence that my husband had even been there all weekend was a used towel in the bathroom, hanging over the shower door.

"What do you know?" I said to my reflection in the bathroom mirror as I dried my damp hair with the blow dryer. "Guess old dogs *can* learn new tricks." I'd have to really thank him for the nice welcome-home surprise.

The answering machine light was blinking. *Eight messages?* That was a lot for a Monday . . . unless Philip hadn't bothered to answer them all weekend. I touched the Play button to listen as I opened the refrigerator to scout our meal possibilities. The first two were telemarketing recordings. I hit Delete twice and kept rummaging in the fridge.

The third was Henry Fenchel. *"Philip? You still there? Mona says she wants to stay Sunday night too, okay with you? We can get back to the office by midmorning Monday . . . Philip? Pick up if you're there, buddy. Okay, guess I'll try your cell. Bring plenty of Horseshoe money! And clean shorts. Ha-ha-ha."*

I stood stock-still with the refrigerator door wide open. Stay *where* Sunday night?! What did he mean, "Sunday *too*"? Had Philip been gone all weekend without telling me? Was he doing that to spite me? And where did they go? Henry said bring plenty of "Horseshoe money" . . . what did he mean by that? I'd seen billboards advertising a Horseshoe Casino but had never paid any attention where it was. Indiana maybe . . .

I pushed Play to listen to Henry's message again, a shaky mad building in my gut. Maybe Philip didn't agree with me going to Petersburg this past weekend, but at least I'd told him! After the third time through, I let the answering machine run through the other messages: a call from his mother . . . two more telemarketing reps . . . then my spinning mental wheels did a U-turn as I heard my name.

"Gabby dear? Please give me a call. This is Aunt Mercy. Your mother had a fall this morning at home. Didn't break anything, thank God. Good thing I was picking her up to go to church. I heard Dandy barking, so I let myself in. I took her to the ER just to be sure she's all right, then brought her to my house. Just wanted to let you girls know where she is if you call her today."

Now I was really upset. My mother had fallen yesterday? She hadn't said anything about that when I talked to her this morning!

The last message was from Aunt Mercy, too—6:10 last night. *"Gabby? I don't know if you got my other message, but I'm taking your mother home now. I wish she'd stay overnight, but she wants to go home to take care of the dog. I'll check in on her on Monday. Please call me. We need to be able to get in touch with you in an emergency. Do you have a cell phone? All right. Guess you're not there. Good-bye."*

I forgot all about making supper for Philip and used the caller ID to return my aunt's call. I apologized all over the place for the missed communication, told her I'd been out of town, gave her my cell number, told her to call me at any time day or night, told her I'd tried to call my mom on Sunday and finally got her this morning, but Mom hadn't said anything about a fall . . .

I held off crying until I hung up with Aunt Mercy, and then I had a good bawl on the living room couch, feeling like the proverbial no-good, rotten, terrible daughter. And that's how Philip found me when he came in the door at six thirty, surrounded by used tissues. And I yelled at him. "Where were *you* this weekend, Philip Fairbanks?! My mother had a fall, and, and Aunt Mercy called here, and if you'd been here, you could have let me know! Why didn't you *tell* me you were going to be away too?! What did Henry mean, bring Horseshoe money? Did you and those, those Fenchels go gambling at one of those casino hotels?" I pulled my knees up to my chin and sobbed some more.

Philip just stood there, tight-lipped. Then he said, "Is your mother all right?"

I nodded, hiccoughed, and blew my nose again.

"Good. Then let's talk about this when you get control of yourself." He stalked out, then returned. "Did you make anything for dinner?"

I shook my head. "I . . . I was going to, but—"

"Never mind." A moment later I heard him on the phone, ordering something to be delivered.

Philip had been unapologetic when we finally talked over Chinese takeout. "It came up at the last minute, Gabby. Henry tossed me the idea on Friday, and I said I'd think about it. But you didn't get home till late that night, remember? After I dropped you off at the airport the next morning, I realized it was going to be a long, lonely weekend until you got back on Monday, so, heck, why not? I called Henry; we drove to Indiana and had a great time. Snazzy hotel, great food, a good show . . . If you'd been here, they'd have invited you too."

"But . . . gambling, Philip? It's a big racket! People lose money. And it can be terribly addictive, as bad as a . . . a drug addiction or alcohol."

"Good grief, Gabby. What do you take me for? I didn't take any more than I could afford to lose—but the fact is . . . I won."

His boyish grin widened. "Seventeen hundred bucks. Not bad for a weekend's work."

I'd been floored. What could I say?

The whole fiasco troubled me for days, but I tried to drown my worries at work. Josh Baxter showed up on Tuesday to drop off a packet of ESL materials from his mother and Avis Douglass. I wanted to ask him how Gracie's adoption process was going, but he seemed to be in a big hurry, so I let it go. I passed the ESL materials on to Tina and told her to look them over. "They're geared more toward kids than adults, but it'd be a start," I told her. She nodded, came back to me the next day, and said she'd give it a shot. She seemed both nervous and excited. We set up an ESL class to start the next Tuesday at 5:00 p.m.

I talked Estelle into bringing as much leftover knitting yarn and extra needles as she could muster and encouraged her to teach knitting to women on Wednesday morning while they waited their turn to see the nurse. At least five women took a pair of needles and labored on and off for two hours learning how to "cast on" and do simple "knit and purl" stitches before and after their turn behind the nurse's room divider. Even Hannah the Bored picked up a pair of needles and tried a few rows—though it was a bit awkward with her long nails. Today they were decorated with flourishes and tiny rhinestones. Where did she get money to do *that*?

But I swear, when I told Estelle that Mr. Bentley had asked for her phone number, the woman deepened at least two shades to raspberry chocolate. But she gave it to me, muttering, "*Humph*. I need a business card."

Lucy hadn't been at the shelter when I got back on Monday, but she showed up again Wednesday morning to see the nurse about her cough and to get something for her "rheumatiz" . . . and signed up for a bed when a thunderstorm cracked overhead, unleashing a torrent of spring rain. The woman was still a mystery to me, but she usually rebuffed my attempts to get her to talk. But I took my lunch tray on Thursday and pulled out a chair at her table. "Mind if I sit?"

"Free country." She stabbed a forkful of kielbasa, potatoes, and cabbage.

I took a bite. "Mm. This is good." I was surprised how tasty the stew was. "Wonder what's in it?"

Lucy gave me her "dumb question" look. "Whatever ya got on hand is what's in it, missy. Ain't your ma never made stuff like this? Cabbage, taters . . . some kinda meat if you're lucky."

"Hm." I swallowed my mouthful. "I don't think so. We kids didn't like cabbage."

"*Humph.*" Lucy shoveled in another mouthful. "That didn't make no difference at our table. Head o' cabbage went a long ways. Sometimes that's all it was. Cabbage soup . . . cabbage stew . . . rice rolled up in cabbage leaves . . . Used to grow the things on our two-bit farm down in Arkansas 'fore the drought drove us out."

My ears pricked up. Lucy grew up on a farm in Arkansas!

"Drove you out?" I tried to keep my question light, not prying.

Lucy eyed me up and down sideways for half a minute. "Huh. You too young to know anything 'bout the big migration. Where'd you grow up anyway? Chicago? . . . Nah, you just moved here."

I could hardly contain my excitement. Lucy and I were having an actual conversation! "Yes, from Petersburg, Virginia. My husband's home. But I grew up my first twenty years in a small town in North Dakota." I laughed. "Most of the farms around us were wheat and cattle ranches. But not my family. My dad owned a carpet store."

Lucy just looked at me with her rheumy blue eyes as she chewed on cabbage and sausage. To my disappointment, she didn't say any more.

As I went back to my office, I tried to put together the bits of information she let drop. *A two-bit farm in Arkansas . . . "the drought" drove them out . . . the big migration . . .* Lucy was likely in her seventies, at least. Which probably meant her family was hit hard by the Dust Bowl and the Great Depression. But where did the Tuckers "migrate" to? And what brought her to Chicago?

I shrugged, dug out my cell phone, and hustled upstairs where I got better reception. Lunch seemed a good time to catch my mom, and it was already one o'clock.

Philip and I had been civil but distant most of the week. Thursday night I suggested we make plans for our trip to Petersburg for P.J.'s graduation and work out the details for bringing the boys to Chicago. Philip said he'd already made plane reservations for next Wednesday so we could be present for the academy's award night, as well as the graduation ceremonies the next day.

"Oh. Well, that's good." I looked at the computer printout. Return flight was scheduled for Saturday. *Drat.* I'd been hoping we could return on Friday, but . . . oh, well. At least we'd be with the boys.

"Their bicycles," I said. "How are we going to get them here? They'll want them, I'm sure. There are a lot of bike trails along the lakefront. In fact, that'll be fun if the four of us—"

"Leave them."

"Leave them?" I was startled.

"Of course. It doesn't make sense to ship them here when they'll want to have their bikes on weekends next school year."

"*Next* school year?" Dismay and panic fought with a familiar anger. I wanted to scream, *"Over my dead body!"* But instead I said, "Philip! We *moved* to Chicago, remember? It's one thing for the boys to finish out this school year, but we need to find a school for them here in the city. I'm sure there are plenty of good private schools—"

"I already checked it out. The enrollment for most decent schools closed months ago. Besides, Fairbanks males have always gone to George Washington Prep. It's family tradition."

I was speechless. When I finally found my voice, it was shaking with anger. "No! I will not be a thousand miles away from my sons for a whole school year! That wasn't part of the deal! They're just *boys*, Philip! They need their parents!" *And I need them*, my heart cried. I'd never realized how much the boys had filled up the cracks in Philip's and my marriage . . . until we came to Chicago.

"Oh? If they need their parents so badly, why did you get a job that's going to take you out of the house during the summer while they're here? Who's going to take care of them during the day while we're both at work? Did you think of that, Gabby?" He snorted. "Of course you didn't. You never do."

chapter 29

I woke Friday morning with a ferocious headache. The same headache that started during the fight with Philip the night before. Philip had nailed me. In the past few weeks, my mind had conveniently separated into two tracks, job and family. When I was at work, I got excited about all the possible activities for Manna House residents that summer. I'd also imagined doing all sorts of fun things with the boys once they got here—swimming at the beach, exploring the lakefront bike trails, getting family passes to the museums, taking in the ethnic festivals that went on all summer . . .

I'd stammered, "I—I'm sure I can work something out . . ." but before I could finish my sentence, Philip drove in another nail. "Never mind. I've already signed them up for sailing camp the second week of June. You'll just have to take time off from work until then." And that was that.

Dragging myself out of bed the next morning, I downed a couple of extra-strength Tylenol and brewed a strong pot of coffee. I stayed at the penthouse long enough to get Camila started on the housecleaning, then ducked past Mr. Bentley in the lobby on my way out the door. The man was too perceptive. One kind word from him, and I'd be blubbering my mascara down to chin level.

I decided to walk the two miles to work. I needed the exercise to help clear my head. The sky was cloudy, the air damp, but at least it wasn't raining. When was Chicago going to dry off, for heaven's sake?! No way did I want the boys to arrive and be stuck in the penthouse five days a week, or we'd have mutiny on our hands.

My insides clenched. Rain was the least of my worries. I dreaded the boys getting caught in all the tension Philip and I seemed to generate like static from walking over a wool rug.

At the shelter, I somehow managed to sign in and make it down to my cubbyhole without getting caught in any conversations. *Turn on the computer . . . call up e-mail . . . go over Mabel's staff notes and announcements . . .* But all the words on the screen seemed to run together and reformat in my brain: *"Fairbanks males have always gone to George Washington Prep. It's family tradition."*

I grabbed fistfuls of my hair. *No, no, NO!* I'd go crazy if the boys went back to school in Virginia next fall, leaving their father and me to navigate rough waters alone. It took too much energy trying to keep an even keel when Philip's "gusts" hit my sails. My life kept tilting off balance like Lester Stone's sailboat—"heeling up," he'd called it—and it was my side that kept skimming dangerously close to those choppy waves. One more gust, and I'd be in the drink.

Drowning.

Okay, I needed to get a grip. The Bible I'd set on the back corner of the desk caught my eye. Hadn't I promised God I'd start reading the thing again if He answered my prayers and helped me get this job? Well, God had kept His end of the bargain. I pulled the book toward me. But where to start? Too many times as a girl I'd made a New Year's resolution to read the Bible straight through and started with Genesis 1, only to get bogged down in Exodus and never get any further.

Suddenly my eye caught something on the computer screen. Mabel's staff announcements included Edesa Baxter's topic for her Bible study today: "Isaiah 54—The Barren Woman." That seemed like a curious topic. But maybe it was as good as any to read today. I could go to the Bible study prepared.

I found Isaiah 54 and began to read—and within moments the tears I'd been holding back all morning flooded over. *"Sing, O barren woman,"* the chapter started. *". . . burst into song, shout for joy . . . because more are the children of the desolate woman than of her who has a husband . . ."* I groaned. The verses seemed to be talking about *me*. I had a husband, I had children—but I was the one who felt desolate.

Grabbing a ready supply of tissues, I kept reading through blurry eyes and came to verse six. *"The Lord will call you back as if you were a wife deserted and distressed in spirit—a wife who married young, only to be rejected, says your God . . ."* The flood of tears spilled over again. Oh, yes, I'd married young—and been rejected. But that was then. I should be over it now. Why did I still feel so . . . so deserted?

I backed up and read the first several verses again, reading and rereading the fourth and fifth verses. *"Do not be afraid; you will not suffer shame. Do not fear disgrace; you will not be humiliated. You will forget the shame of your youth, and remember no more the reproach of your widowhood . . ."* Except it wasn't true. Even though I had married again and had thought I'd be living the fairy tale of my dreams, if somebody asked me right now, I still felt afraid. Humiliated. But mostly, I felt . . . alone. Like a widow.

So what in the world did verse five mean? *"For your Maker is your husband—the Lord Almighty is His name . . ."*

I never did make it to Edesa's Bible study, because all I could do was sit at my desk behind a closed door . . . and weep.

I ran into Edesa in the line for lunch, Gracie riding her hip. "Gabby!" She gave me a hug. "I thought you weren't here today."

"I know. I missed your Bible study." I gave her a wry smile. "It's all your fault."

Her eyebrows went up.

"Yeah. I decided to read your Scripture passage before I came to the Bible study, and . . . well, it touched a few raw nerves."

Now her eyebrows came together, putting wrinkles of concern into her smooth, brown skin. She lowered her voice. "Do you want to talk about it, *Gabriela*? Or pray?"

I shook my head. "Not right now, but thanks anyway."

She smiled. "At least you are reading the Bible, *mi amiga*. That is good."

Gracie reached toward me. "Gaaa."

What a cutie. I leaned close to give her a kiss, and the eight-month-old grabbed a fistful of my hair.

"Ow!" I gently untangled the little girl's hand from my curls. "Uh, what's happening with Gracie's adoption? Any news?"

Edesa instinctively drew the child closer to her body and

nuzzled her soft hair. "*Sí y no*. Next week we go to a hearing about our petition to get guardianship of Gracie. This must happen before we can proceed with the adoption. But now this ex-boyfriend of the mama's—at least that's what he claims—says he's the daddy and wants to take her."

"But, didn't you get guardianship when you became her foster parents?"

"*Sí! Sí!* But now they say it is only 'temporary' guardianship—an emergency, because her mama died of a drug overdose while she was here at the shelter, and she needed *una familia* right away. But I know Carmelita wanted me to take care of Gracie, to bring her up! She left us a note! That is how we got custody of her in the first place."

We had stepped out of the lunch line in order to talk off to the side. "And other people witnessed this note?"

Edesa nodded, eyes determined. "*Sí*. Many staff members and residents here, they all knew. Reverend Handley, Mabel, and others will have to come to this hearing and testify . . . and even then, the judge will also talk to this man. The social worker at DCFS told us blood family usually has priority." The young woman's full lips trembled. "But I *know* God put Gracie into my arms! It is why Josh and I got married—"

She must have seen my startled look, because she quickly added, "I mean, it is why we got married *now* instead of waiting longer. Though . . ." She looked away. "Well, it is not so easy."

I pulled her farther away from the lunch line. "Are you two okay? I mean, you and Josh seem very much in love."

"Oh, *sí*, of course I love Josh. It's not that. It's just . . ." She sighed. "The apartment *es minúsculo*! Only two rooms and a bath. And the walls . . . like paper! The *familia* we are renting from must hear every time we *a-choo*, not to mention . . ." She rolled her eyes. "They are good friends—one of my Yada Yada sisters—which makes it worse."

"Oh Edesa." I wanted to hug her. "Have you looked for a bigger apartment?"

She shook her head. "We have no money. I mean, Josh works part-time, but we are both going to school. Money, so tight. Sometimes we fight." She sighed. "I wish—"

Heavy feet coming down the stairs caught our attention, and a second later Josh Baxter materialized from the stairwell, backpack slung over one shoulder, looking this way and that around the dining room. "There you are! Am I in time for lunch? My afternoon class got canceled, so I thought . . . hey there, Gracie girl, come to Daddy?" The overgrown college guy held out his arms.

Edesa surrendered the baby and grimaced at me behind his back. I gave a single shake of my head. I didn't think he'd heard us talking.

"Hey, you three!" Estelle's voice sailed across the room from behind the kitchen counter. "You goin' to eat or what? I gotta sit down. My feet are killing me."

We hustled over to the counter, where Estelle handed us plates of sliced ham, cooked carrots, and what looked like corn pudding. As Josh jiggled Gracie on his lap and hand-fed her bits of corn pudding, he said, "Oh, hey, Mrs. Fair—um, Gabby . . . my mom wants to know if you'll be at the Sunday Evening Praise this weekend. It's SouledOut's turn to do worship here, and she and my dad are coming. She'd like to meet you and talk to you. Something about a typing class?"

"Sure. I'll make it a point to be here. And I've been meaning to ask you two—do you know where I could get a CD of that song the New Hope worship team did two Sundays ago? The chorus went something like, 'I go to the Rock . . .'"

Josh scratched the back of his head. "I kinda remember. I think it's an old Dottie Rambo song. I don't know if it's been recorded lately . . . but I'll check around."

Saturday, I had to admit, was a perfect spring day—low seventies, sunny. I stood a few steps back from our floor-to-ceiling wraparound windows, drinking in the sun sparkles on the lake. *I might even like Chicago if there were more days like this.* But as tempting as it was to go out and play, I spent the weekend putting the finishing touches on the boys' bedrooms, making chocolate-chip cookies and freezing them, and shopping for groceries so we'd have their favorite foods on hand—boxes of macaroni and cheese, frozen hamburger patties, hot dogs, both kinds of buns (plain and poppy seed), and cans of spaghetti and meatballs. And frozen Pizza Bites.

At least they still preferred my homemade cookies.

When Philip went running Sunday morning, I got on the computer and searched online for Memorial Day activities in Chicago. We were bringing the boys home on Saturday, which meant we still had Sunday and the Monday holiday. I found lots of things going on—the Memorial Day parade, an Irish Fest, fireworks at Navy Pier . . . *whoa.* The Cubs were playing Atlanta at Wrigley Field next Sunday! Could I get tickets this late? Maybe Henry Fenchel could help me. Philip would be dazzled.

My spirit lifted. I was *not* going to let the fight with Philip over my job ruin the boys' homecoming. I'd work out something. After all, my job was part-time and the schedule flexible. I'd cut my hours if need be—which should be possible once I got a number of activities up and running. And if I did have to take some time off . . .

A tickle of an idea brought a smile to my face. Why not? I picked up the phone. What time was it in Alaska, anyway?

chapter 30

✽ ✽ ✽

When I told Philip I'd managed to get four tickets to the Cubs game next Sunday—with Henry's help—he was elated. "No kidding! Good thinking, Mop Top."

Building on this goodwill, I asked for the car to go to the Sunday Evening Praise at Manna House, promising I wouldn't come home without it. Then, in a burst of good intention, I asked if he'd like to go with me. "You could see where I work," I said. "And we haven't been to church together since we came to Chicago."

Philip snorted. "You call that church? When you're ready to go to *church*, Gabby, we can talk about going to church."

My face burned. A quick retort rose to my lips. As if Sunday Evening Praise at Manna House was stopping us from going to church somewhere Sunday morning! But I decided to leave it alone. "Okay. Maybe when the boys come, we'll find a church."

He didn't answer.

Park it, Gabby, I told myself—and I didn't mean the Lexus, though I did find a parking space halfway down the block from the shelter, and I was able to leave two feet of room between me and the next car. It was still light at six o'clock, but might be dark when I came out. As I *beeped* the remote car locks, a couple came walking up the sidewalk, then stopped.

"Mrs. Fairbanks?"

They looked familiar—and I realized I'd met them once. "You're Josh's parents!"

The man laughed. "Gee, I thought when the kids moved out, we'd get our names back." He held out his hand. "Denny Baxter. And this is my wife—I mean, Josh's mother."

"Denny!" "Josh's mother" backhanded her husband with a smart left, then held out her right hand to me. "I'm Jodi—and don't mind him. You're Gabby, right? We talked on the phone."

I smiled and shook both their hands. "Yes, of course! Thanks so much for the ESL materials. We'll put them to good use." I wanted to laugh. Finally! "First name" people. I'd never seen a man with dimples as deep on both cheeks as this guy. They were both probably a few years older than I—early forties?—but both were pleasant looking. Denny had short-cropped hair, still brown but graying. Jodi wore her dark brunette hair shoulder-length, bangs swept to one side.

"I'm so glad we're getting a chance to meet you," Jodi said. "Josh and Edesa talk about you all the time—oh, there's Avis and Peter. Hey, you two!"

Another couple came from the opposite direction as we converged on the Manna House steps. I recognized Avis Douglass as the woman who spoke at Sunday Evening Praise the first time I'd come, and her husband, Peter, was on the Manna House board. The two couples seemed very cozy with one another, which was interesting, since the Baxters were white and the Douglasses black. But I remembered that about SouledOut the last time the church had come to Manna House—the praise team and others from the church were a rather diverse crew. Not a "black church" like New Hope Missionary Baptist, or a "Spanish church" like the time Rev. Álvarez spoke, or Rev. Handley's white suburban church that came on Mother's Day last week, the Sunday I'd missed.

As we all stood in the foyer and chatted, my thoughts drifted. If only Philip had come with me, I wouldn't feel like a fifth wheel . . . and it'd be good for him to meet men like Peter Douglass, who owned his own software business, and Denny Baxter, who said he was athletic director at a Chicago public high school. Respected people in the Chicago community who supported shelters like Manna House.

What was Philip's *problem?* The jerk.

"Gabby? Come sit with us." Jodi Baxter took my arm. "If you don't have to rush off afterward, maybe we can talk about that typing class you asked about—though I teach third grade, and they're not typing yet!" She laughed and hustled us into the multi-purpose room, where the SouledOut instrumentalists and singers were starting on their first song.

My eyes blurred a little bit as the saxophonist pulled the words along. *"We bring a sacrifice of praise . . . into the house of the Lord!"* But it wasn't the song. Not even the rather poignant image that this homeless shelter was "the house of the Lord."

It was a longing deep inside I'd buried for a long time. I needed a friend. A *girlfriend.* Someone who wasn't a coworker, as friendly as all the volunteers and staff at the shelter were. Someone who wasn't half my age, as much as I adored Edesa. Someone married, with a husband near Philip's age, someone with the potential to have good times as a couple. Someone who called me Gabby and would like me just for myself.

Someone like Jodi Baxter.

On Monday morning, I asked Mabel Turner if I could take a week off the first full week of June, no pay, to take my sons to North Dakota to see their grandmother. With our trip to Virginia in a few days, and Memorial Day weekend coming up, that only left six working days in the next two weeks, but I promised I'd try to have a slate of activities up and running by then, which hopefully could function for a week without my oversight.

"Jodi Baxter is willing to do a Saturday typing class starting next week. And once school is out, she'll consider doing another on a weekday. Peter Douglass said he'll look into getting us a couple more computers. Carolyn wants to start a book club, as soon as we can settle on which book . . . and I've got a couple other ideas I'm pursuing."

I couldn't read Mabel's face. What if she didn't want to let me off? I'd already left messages for both my sisters suggesting a family reunion in Minot that week. I'd just assumed I could work this out with the job! And the more I'd thought about it, the more I realized I had to do this—for my mother, for the boys, for my marriage . . .

"I'm sorry to ask for time off again so soon after our trip this week to pick up the boys, Mabel. But I really need to check in on my mom. And the boys don't begin their summer camp until the following week. This would take care of both, and I'd—"

Mabel held up a hand. "Gabby, stop. You don't have to convince me. If that's what you need to do, we'll swing by somehow here. What concerns me is . . . what's going on at home? You seem to be juggling some delicate plates in the air, acting as if you're afraid they'll fall and break into a thousand pieces."

I wasn't prepared for that. But I couldn't answer either. I didn't want to paint Philip as some ogre before Mabel and others here had even met him. And Philip and I *were* going to work this out, weren't we?

"Sorry," I said weakly. "We're still . . . adjusting to our move, new jobs, boys coming home—you know how it is. Thanks for understanding about taking the week off." I fled downstairs to my office.

When I switched on the light, I realized someone had already been there. On my desk was the shelter's CD player and a plastic CD case. I picked up the plastic square. The soundtrack from *The Preacher's Wife*. I glanced at the list of songs, and there it was: "I Go to the Rock." But when I opened the CD case, it was empty. Already in the CD player.

I grinned. *Bless Josh Baxter.* I wondered where he'd found it. Clicking through the songs, I got to the number I wanted and pushed Play. The music pulsed and filled my cubbyhole . . .

Where do I go . . . when there's no one else to turn to?
Who do I talk to . . . when nobody wants to listen?
Who do I lean on . . . when there's no foundation stable?
I go to the Rock, I know that He's able, I go to the Rock . . .

I practically wore out that CD in the next few days. I even found one of the boys' old portable players with earphones and listened to it as I traveled to and from work on the El. The CD contained some other neat songs too, most of which I'd also never heard. How could I be so ignorant of really great gospel music? To tell the truth, my repertoire of "Christian music" consisted mostly of hymns and Sunday school songs I'd learned growing up, with a few contemporary songs and choruses that were popular with my youth group when I was a teenager. Twenty-plus years ago.

I had a lot of catching up to do.

I was soon caught up in the whirlwind of washing clothes Tuesday evening, packing, canceling Camila on Friday, trying to reach my sisters again and finally sending e-mails about meeting up in Minot in June, calling my mom and aunt ahead of time to let them know we were heading for Virginia . . . and finally Philip and I were on the plane Wednesday afternoon heading for Richmond.

Philip buried his attention in a copy of *BusinessWeek*, with the complimentary glass of wine provided in business class, leaving me to close my eyes and begin to relax. We were going to see the boys in a few hours . . . and then bring them home. *"Home"* . . . that wasn't a word I applied easily to the penthouse in Richmond Towers. But maybe with the boys there, we would begin to feel like a family again.

Oh Lord, please, make us a family again.

My thought-prayer bounced to my sisters, who still hadn't responded to either my phone messages or e-mails. What had happened to our family? The last time I'd seen either of my sisters was at my dad's funeral two years ago, and we rarely communicated. *Lord, can you make us a family again too?*

On the other hand, for the next few days I was going to be

wrapped once again in the tight-knit web of Philip's family—where I felt not so much included as caught. *Huh.* Could I pray the same prayer for the Fairbanks family?

We drove our rented luxury SUV directly from the airport to George Washington Preparatory Academy for the annual end-of-the-year award night, with plans to meet Mike and Marlene Fairbanks, who were getting a ride with another set of grandparents so we four could return together. Philip was his charming self, joking with his parents and escorting me with a gentlemanly hand on my elbow. I warmed to his touch and started to relax, his self-assurance flowing to me. I suspected he felt good about returning home to Petersburg—and to his alma mater—on the upswing of a new business.

The stately auditorium with its dark wood wainscoting and pewlike seating was abuzz with proud parents, siblings, and grandparents as we found our seats, just before the academy's middle school students marched in, dressed in their maroon, navy, and royal blue school blazers, depending on the class.

"There's P.J.! Do you see Paul?"

The evening was long, but I felt like cheering when Philip Jr. received a second-place science award for his astronomy project on black holes, as well as a "team participation" trophy in soccer. But to my surprise and delight, Paul received a band award for original composition.

"Since when is Paul musical?" Philip stage-whispered.

"You knew he signed up to play trombone in the band."

"Yeah, well, every boy goes through a stage when he wants to play the trumpet or trombone or something big and brassy.

Usually doesn't last long."

A lump settled in my throat. I hated that I hadn't known he'd composed a piece for the band. What else didn't I know about my youngest son?

Afterward, amid congratulations and hugs and excited babble, we went out to eat—along with scores of other family groups. I wasn't really hungry, just kept sneaking peeks at my sons as they chattered. P.J.'s dark hair and Romeo lashes preempted the few pimples that had erupted on his chin. Paul's childish flush still bloomed beneath his chestnut curls trying to grow back. I could have soaked up their faces all night, but we had to have the boys back to the academy by eleven. The school expected all its students to be present for the graduation ceremonies, so report cards and room clearances were deliberately scheduled for the following day.

The SUV hummed its way back to the Fairbanks' "country suburban" home near Petersburg in the warm night air, still in the midseventies. Mike Fairbanks rode in the front seat with Philip, while Marlene and I chose our corners on the soft leather seat in back. Chatter about the award ceremonies and how proud we were of "our boys" turned to polite questions about Chicago. With a note of pride, Philip confidently described the accounts he and Henry had been able to land in the last six weeks.

"That's right," I chimed in. "I'm proud of Philip. Fairbanks and Fenchel has gotten a good footing in Chicago in a short time."

His father *harrumph*ed. "Well, that's good, Philip. I'm real happy for you. Just don't lose those accounts by getting cocky and trying designs that are more fluff than functional."

"Fluff!" A flash of anger hardened Philip's voice. "I don't do *fluff*, Dad. I do bold, I do cutting-edge . . . I just don't do old and tired."

"Watch your mouth, young man!" the senior Fairbanks snapped. "The Fairbanks name means something here in Virginia. Quality. Heritage and tradition."

Even in the dim interior, I saw Philip's mouth turn into a thin line and his eyes dart to the rearview mirror, where he caught his mother's eye. Marlene blew her son a silent kiss. "Don't you worry, Mike dear," she purred. "Philip is going to make a name for himself in Chicago."

"*Humph*. Make a name for himself . . . He already had a name here to live up to—if he could."

The tension in the car thickened until I thought I might suffocate. I pushed the button to roll down my window, inviting a snap from Philip. "Gabby. I've got the air on." I rolled it partway up.

We rode in silence through the winding roads. Then Mike Fairbanks growled, "I'm just thinking about the boys, Philip. It's one thing for you to have your fling, get some of these newfangled ideas out of your system—"

I saw Philip's hands tighten on the steering wheel at the word "fling."

"—but what are the boys going to do in a big city like Chicago? They've already got a good start at George Washington; they've got their friends *and* a family business to take over when the time is right."

Philip's mother took over. "Well, of course they'll continue their schooling at George Washington, darling. Philip knows the boys love it here, and he knows they're always welcome to stay with us."

Of all the—! How dare they talk as if I had no say in my sons' future! I opened my mouth, ready to blast them all. *"Forget it! The boys aren't coming back to Virginia in the fall. They're our sons, and they belong with us!"* But all I got out was, "I'm sorry. We haven't made that decision yet—" before Marlene interrupted, still purring, but more like a bobcat than a kitty.

"I'm not worried about Philip, darling. He'll do the Fairbanks family proud . . . if certain people don't tarnish the name with their own foolish ideas."

I stiffened in the darkness. *Wait a minute.* What did she mean by "certain people"? Did she mean Henry Fenchel? . . . or me?

chapter 31

Even after we unloaded our suitcases and squirreled away in the guest suite of his parents' beautiful home, Philip was still fuming. "The old fart! I thought he'd be over his little tantrum about me starting my own business by now. Well, he can just stuff his opinion up his you-know-where—"

It wasn't a conversation. I let him rant while I brushed the snarls out of my Orphan Annie hair, wishing I had the nerve to complain about his mother's little dig. I did suggest maybe we could change our tickets to leave Friday instead of Saturday, but he just rolled his eyes. "No way. I'm not going to let him run me off." He flopped on the bed, the steam dissipating. "Let's just make the best of it and enjoy the graduation tomorrow. I don't want to disappoint my mom. They do adore the boys, you know."

Argh! Now I was fuming. Why didn't he just stand up to his parents? His father goaded him, made him feel like a failure waiting to happen, while his mother dripped sweetness that stuck like flies on flypaper.

Only later in the darkness, listening to Philip's soft snoring, did I realize that the little interaction in the car between father and son was a mirror of how Philip treated me.

Summer temperatures settled over Virginia the next day like a wool blanket with no sheet. Hot. Sticky. Scratchy. We sweated in the ancient hall that still boasted no air-conditioning, fanned our way through the graduation ceremonies with our programs, and glared at the families who cheered when their son's name was called even after the headmaster requested that applause be held until *all* the graduates' names had been called . . . Then it was over, and the four of us stood outside under a shade tree, watching indulgently while P.J. and Paul tussled with their friends on the wide lawn, acting out because all the adults were watching.

Philip and I did the final room checks with the boys in their dorms. Good thing, since we found an overdue library book, a single dirty sock, and a wadded-up T-shirt under P.J.'s bunk, and Paul's suitcase wouldn't close because he'd just stuffed everything into it willy-nilly. But the resident assistant finally stamped their room inspection cards, which the boys and I had to have in hand at the registrar's office in order to pick up their report cards. When we got back to the car, waving cards that were mostly Bs sandwiched between an occasional A and C, Philip and his father had loaded the boys' suitcases, trunks, and sports equipment . . . and then we were off.

"Can I play lacrosse next year, Dad?" P.J. hollered from the third seat as we headed down the long drive that led off-campus. "Most of my friends are going to sign up for the Upper School's junior team."

neta jackson

"Don't see why not, son."

I turned in my seat. "What Dad means, P.J., is that we'd love to see you play lacrosse. But with the move to Chicago, we can't make any promises about anything just yet."

"But, Mom! Dad just said—"

"We'll talk about it, okay, P.J.? Just not now. Hey, I'm hungry. How about you boys? What would you like? This is a special day. P.J., you choose."

But P.J. had flopped back in his seat, arms folded, lips tightly pressed, glaring out the window.

"Pizza Hut!" Paul offered.

Philip groaned from the driver's seat. "At least let's do Sal's and Brothers pizza."

I tried to laugh off P.J.'s sulk. "Hey, did you boys know Chicago has the best pizza in the world?"

I let out a long sigh of relief once our American Airlines flight to Chicago was in the air on Saturday. Paul was in the window seat next to me in business class, playing with a handheld electronic game, a gift from his grandfather. Philip and Philip Jr. sat across the aisle. Finally it was the four of us. A family again.

I leaned my seat back and closed my eyes. The rest of our visit with the Fairbanks had gone reasonably well, I thought, with the exception of a conversation between Philip and his mother I'd overheard the previous night . . .

"Of course the boys will be returning to George Washington Academy in the fall, Philip! You said that was the plan before you moved to Chicago. They're already registered! I don't understand why Gabrielle—"

"I know, Mother. But she's their mother, and of course she misses them. Right now she doesn't want to think about them coming back. But things may look different after a couple of months. Give her time. And like you said, they're already registered. It won't hurt to look at the Chicago academies and consider our options."

I glanced across the aisle, where P.J. was plugged into his own iPod world—a graduation gift, also from his grandparents. Of course the boys were already registered at George Washington Academy, but so what? We'd done that last January, before moving to Chicago had even blipped onto the family radar. All we had to do was tell the school we'd moved out of state and get our deposit back . . .

A flicker of uncertainty licked at the edges of my thoughts. *What if it's too late to register for any of the Chicago-area private schools?*

No. I wasn't going to let doubt make me afraid. Didn't Philip say it wouldn't hurt to consider our options? Said it to his mother's face, in fact! But why hadn't Philip and I talked about this before? *Really* talked, and come to a decision. Decided who was going to check out the Chicago schools, make applications . . .

"When I am afraid, I will trust in God . . . I trust in God, why should I be afraid?"

I let slip a small smile. I wasn't used to thinking Scripture verses, but Edesa's Bible studies at the shelter seemed to stick on me. Okay, I was afraid. I wished I'd brought my Bible so I could look up those verses in the Psalms, but that was a habit I hadn't revived. *Yet.* I needed to get one of those travel-size Bibles I could tuck in my purse so I wouldn't look like some fanatic Bible-thumper . . . if that mattered. What was a "Bible-thumper" anyway? People like Edesa Baxter, who loved to study the Bible?

Mabel Turner, who always had the right scripture for me? Avis Douglass, the classy elementary school principal who preached at the shelter once a month, encouraging women on the down-and-out?

I felt a tad guilty. Okay, forget whether I'd look like a Bible-thumper or not. But a travel-size Bible would still be a good idea.

Paul seemed awestruck by the view from the penthouse's glass wall in the front room. "We *live* up here? Wow! Is that really a lake? It looks like the ocean!" Then my youngest turned eyes of concern on me. "Don't you get a little, you know, queasy up here, Mom?"

I nearly melted.

His brother was already staking out territory. "Awww-riight! My own room. Mom, I want a lock so I can keep Punkhead here out."

I delighted in all the noise and chatter, giving the boys time to explore while I started a "welcome home" dinner sure to please—Southern fried chicken, mashed potatoes, creamy gravy, buttered green beans. Philip called for a cart to get the boys' luggage up the elevator, then disappeared into the den to check phone and e-mail messages and go through the mail, which was fine by me.

"Hey, P.J.! Paul! Come set the table, okay? Supper's almost ready!"

Twin groans radiated from both bedrooms down the hall. "Aww, do we have to?"

Philip appeared, waving an envelope. "Oh, give 'em a break, Gabby. It's their first night in Chicago. But I think they'll like what Henry sent us . . ."

Philip handed the envelope to P.J. as we sat down to dinner.

Our oldest crowed. "Cubs tickets! Hey, look, Punkhead! Four tickets to a Cubs game at Wrigley Field!" P.J. squinted at the fine print. "Tomorrow? Against Atlanta? Aww-riiight. Thanks, Dad!"

"You're welcome, buddy. Now, how about passing some of that chicken over here?"

I flinched. The Cubs tickets were *my* surprise. Why did Philip take the credit? *Well, just say so, Gabby. It's not a big deal.* "Actually, boys, the tickets were my idea—but they're from both of us." *Or something.*

But the opportunity passed, and the more seconds that ticked away, the more awkward I felt bringing it up. *So let it go, Gabby.* I did, smiling as the boys poured too much gravy over everything. But a too-familiar crack tore wider in my spirit.

The boys were totally berserk with excitement as we joined the crowd of Cubs fans on the Red Line El Sunday afternoon. Ninety percent of the riders got off at the Addison El Station, where Wrigley Field towered just a block away. The weather cooperated, draping Chicago with a bright, sunny day and temps heading into the nineties. I smiled happily. Looked like Chicago's rainy season might be over.

I had brought a backpack full of water bottles and snacks, but a security guard wouldn't let us in unless I dumped it all. "No food or beverages allowed inside the park," he growled. "Club rules. You can buy it inside."

I started to argue, but Philip took the backpack away from me and dumped the offending contents into the nearest trash can. "Come on, Gabby. That's just the way it is."

It was all I could do to keep from diving back into the trash can to retrieve it. Dump perfectly good food and water just so we could pay twice as much for it inside? When there were people like Lucy digging through Dumpsters, hoping for something to eat? Felt downright sinful to me.

Let it go, Gabby.

The game was exciting, even though I didn't follow the baseball teams much. Wrigley Field roared with happy fans as the score nudged upward, first the Cubs ahead, then the Braves. Between innings, Philip and the boys put away three hot dogs each, plus nachos and peanuts, washed down with soft drinks and two large beers for Philip. Well, at least he wasn't driving.

At the close of the ninth inning, the Braves won by one measly run—13 to 12. But the loss didn't dampen the boys' gusto. Philip bought Cubs caps and pennants for them on our way out of the stadium, and Chicago suddenly had two new Cubby fans.

I felt pretty smug. A Cubs game was a perfect way to help our sons own the move to Chicago. Even the ride on the El was exciting to them, in spite of having to stand in the swaying car, jammed like human sardines. I tried to think . . . was this Philip's first time taking public transportation? Well, good. Now he had some idea of how I got to work each day.

As the train passed the Sheridan El stop, I nudged P.J., who was hanging on to the nearest pole. "This is where I get off to go to work."

He looked at me funny. "Where do you work?"

"At a homeless shelter. You know. I told you. I'm the program director."

He wrinkled his face. "That's weird."

"I'll take you sometime—so you can see where I work." I looked at my watch. Sunday Evening Praise would be starting in an hour or so. Pastor Álvarez's Spanish church would be there. I was halfway tempted . . .

No. One step at a time.

The four of us got off at Berwyn and walked toward Richmond Towers, which rose in the distance. My mind was tumbling over things Philip and I needed to talk about in the next few days. Sailing camp didn't start till mid-June, but then ran for four weeks. If I took the boys to see their grandmother in North Dakota next week, that just left the rest of this week—four measly days after the Memorial Day weekend—to juggle between us. But even before we planned the boys' summer, we had to talk about school—

"*Streetwise*! Get your new issue of *Streetwise* right here!"

Just ahead of us on the first corner, a black man in a knit hat and a few missing teeth was peddling the newspaper. "*Streetwise*! Only one dollar! *Streetwise*!"

I rummaged in the backpack for my wallet, pulled out a dollar, and got a copy of the newspaper and a "God bless you, lady!" in exchange. I hurried to catch up to Philip, who had already walked ahead several yards, then realized the boys had fallen behind. Turning, I saw P.J. mimicking the man, covering his teeth with his lips as if he were toothless and pretending to call out, "*Streetwise!*" while Paul snickered. Before I even thought about it, I grabbed my firstborn by the collar, practically jerking him off his feet.

"Ow!" P.J. yelped, trying to pull away.

I put my face nose to nose with his thirteen-year-old mug. "Don't let me *ever* catch you doing something like that again, young man!" I hissed.

chapter 32

Hustling the boys out of earshot of the *Streetwise* vendor, I turned both of them to face me. "That man has had troubles you can't even imagine, but he's working for a living and trying to make a better life. He deserves to be treated with respect. He has a *name*. It's on his *Streetwise* badge. Maybe he has kids your age he's trying to support. Did you ever think of that?"

"You don't have to yell." P.J. looked at me beneath sullen eyelids.

"You think this is yelling?" I had deliberately lowered my voice to avoid embarrassing the boys in public. "Yelling is what I'm going to do if you *ever* disrespect someone like that again." I turned on my heel and marched off to meet up with Philip, who had turned around, frowning.

Behind me I heard Paul mumble, "Gee, if that homeless guy has kids, I bet they don't want anyone to know *he's* their dad." I ignored it and marched on.

Philip didn't see what the big deal was. "Good grief, Gabby," he said when I told him what happened. "They were just goofing around. They're kids!"

"That's no excuse! Philip, I work with homeless people like that—not with men, but some of the women at Manna House sell *Streetwise* too. What if that had been one of the women I know by name, someone I've eaten lunch with, who's told me her story, someone who's excited about some of the program ideas I've started?"

Philip looked back to be sure the boys were still following, then started to push through the revolving door of Richmond Towers. "Ah. I get it. This is about you. You don't want the boys to embarrass you."

My mouth hung open as the door swallowed him and spit him out on the other side. I pushed myself through to make sure he didn't get away. "No! I just made it personal, because it's easy to mimic someone or laugh at them when you don't know them, don't know anything about them. It doesn't have anything to do with me being embarrassed."

We passed the weekend doorman—"door dude" was more like it—who ignored us as Philip swiped his security card for the inner door. As he held the door open, waiting for the boys to catch up with us, Philip leaned toward me and lowered his voice. "Maybe not, Gabby. But did it ever occur to you that your choice of company might embarrass your *sons?*"

The boys, being boys, forgot about our little spat by the time we got to the top floor. Philip rode above it as though it had nothing to do with him. But I was upset. Upset that the boys had behaved so rudely—P.J. in particular, with no apology—and upset at Philip's insinuation. It just made me determined: I was going to take the boys to the shelter this week, introduce them to the staff and residents, let them hang out, and find something they could do to contribute.

Memorial Day turned out to be a bust, holiday-wise. Big clouds rolled up over the lake, throwing lightning darts and growling thunder just as we were getting ready to go downtown to see the Memorial Day parade. The boys stomped off to flop in front of the TV, but Philip didn't seem too disappointed. "I've got a lot of catch-up work to do anyway. You and the boys do . . . whatever." He headed for the den.

"Philip, wait a minute." I followed him into the den and shut the door behind me. "We need to talk about school for the boys next fall. I don't want to send them back to Virginia, not with us so far away. So we have to do something *now*."

He was already booting up his computer. "So what's stopping you? You're the one who's hot to find an alternative. When you find something that compares to George Washington Prep, then let's talk."

That took me aback. I thought for sure Philip would want to be in the driver's seat when it came to choosing a school for any child of his carrying the Fairbanks name. I'd held back, not wanting to step into territory he'd already claimed. But I wasn't about to question this turnabout.

"All right. I will. Thanks, Philip."

He was already calling up his spreadsheets and opening files. "Mm-hm. Shut the door behind you, Gabby."

Oh my goodness. If I'd known it would be this easy, I would have started weeks ago, as soon as he'd set his sights on Chicago.

Today was a holiday, so schools would be closed. But at least I could get the phone directory and start making a list—

"Mom. I'm bored. There's nothin' to do." Paul drifted into the kitchen, right behind his whine.

"How about . . ." I racked my brain, then picked up the phone and dialed 0-1. "Mr. Bentley? Oh, good, you're here today. Be right down." I turned to Paul. "Where's P.J.? I have somebody I'd like you to meet."

I managed to pry P.J. away from the widescreen TV in the living room, which was televising the rather wet Memorial Day parade, and we rode down to the lobby in the elevator. Mr. Bentley was standing in front of the half-circular desk, spiffy as usual in his blue uniform. I gave him a wide smile. "Boys, I'd like you to meet my friend, Mr. Bentley. You'll see a lot of him. He *rules* this roost."

"Mrs. Fairbanks," he said, doffing his cap. "You're back from Virginia, I see. And this must be the young man who just graduated from middle school." Mr. Bentley held out his hand to P.J. "Congratulations, young man. And welcome to Chicago."

P.J. shook Mr. Bentley's hand with all the enthusiasm of a limp noodle. Mr. Bentley didn't seem to notice—or chose to ignore it. He turned to Paul. "What about you, young man? Do you have a name, or should I give you a street name? Like your mom." He looked side to side, as if casing the lobby for spies. "Her street name is Firecracker."

"Wha—what?" I giggled, feeling my cheeks flush.

Mr. Bentley leaned closer to Paul's eye level and patted his own bald head. "You know. The, um, hair."

Paul laughed out loud. "Nah. My dad calls her Mop Top. But

only when he's in a really good mood." He held out his hand. "I'm Paul. He's P.J."

Mr. Bentley's eyebrows went up. "Ah. Now, what would that stand for? Pearl Jam? Para Jumper? . . . I know. Peter Jackson! *Lord of the Rings*—"

Uh-oh. I saw P.J.'s eyes flash. "No. It stands for Philip Fairbanks, *Junior.*" P.J. turned to me. "Come *on*, Mom. I thought we were going to do something."

Mr. Bentley straightened. I wanted to apologize for my humorless son, but Mr. Bentley pulled a couple of coupons out of his pocket. "Well, then. Maybe these will come in handy. Good for free doughnuts or ice cream at the Dunkin' Donuts a couple of blocks north of here." He gave one to each of the boys. Paul's eyes lit up. P.J. gave a grudging nod of thanks. "And it seems to have stopped raining. Just in time."

The doorman smiled, put his cap back on, and turned to greet another Richmond Towers resident coming in. I headed for the revolving door, eager to get out of there to cool off my flaming cheeks. I had so looked forward to introducing Mr. Bentley to my sons. Why was P.J. acting like such a jerk?

Give them time, Gabby. Give them time. Right. They'd been in Chicago all of two days. They'd grown up in Deep South Suburbia. Had to be some culture shock.

We found the Dunkin' Donuts on Bryn Mawr and used the coupons to get ice cream for the boys while I splurged on an iced latte. As we came out of the shop, the sun was drying up the puddles, and the thunderheads were drifting westward. "Hey, guys. I know what let's do. Come on!" I headed for Richmond Towers once more—only this time, we skirted the high-rise for the park on the other side. Feeling a tickle of excitement, I started to run, leading the boys through the pedestrian tunnel beneath Lake Shore Drive . . . and introduced them to kicking off our shoes and splashing in the gurgling edges of Lake Michigan.

After all, I giggled as I chased first Paul and then P.J. along the wet sand, the boys and I were still dressed in the shorts and T-shirts we'd planned to wear to the parade. Even if we ran into Lucy Tucker—Miss Beach Police herself—she couldn't fuss at me.

Philip wasn't happy about my plan to take the boys to North Dakota for a week. "Good grief, Gabby, they just got here."

"Yes, but you said yourself sailing camp doesn't start for another two weeks, and you wanted me to take time from work to spend with them. So I'm taking that week off."

"I meant give up the stupid job, Gabby."

I tensed. The boys were finally in bed and we were heading that way, but I didn't want to fight with Philip. I chose my words carefully. "Don't be unfair, Philip. You've already got them signed up for sailing camp, and after that there'll probably be something else. It doesn't need to be either-or. Besides, I need to go see my mom, and this would be the best time to take the boys too. It all works out."

Philip pulled off his gym shoes and tossed them. "What about this week? You taking this week off too?" Socks came off, then his T-shirt, all ending in a pile with the shoes.

I bought time picking up his clothes and putting them into the laundry hamper. "No-o. But it's only four days. I thought I'd take them to work with me one day and show them around, then maybe do one of the museums for a half day. If you took them to work with *you* one day, why, that's three days already—"

"Take the boys to work with me?" Philip looked at me as if I'd suggested hanging the boys by their thumbs.

"Well . . . sure. I thought you'd want the boys to see your new office, meet your partner, and, you know, get a feel for what their dad does."

"Sure. But that would take, what, one hour? Why don't *you* bring them to the office one day, on your way to the museum or something. And let me know exactly when you're coming. I've got a busy week."

I kept back the tears until I was in the bathroom by myself, door locked, water running in the sink as I washed my face. *Oh God, why is this so hard?* I looked at my face in the mirror—snarly curls askew, cheeks sunburned from our afternoon at Wrigley Field, mascara smudged from tears. Was I being stubborn? Should I have taken the job at Manna House? It had seemed like such a God thing. Mabel even said as much. But maybe I *should* quit—

No. That made no sense. We only had four days to cover for the boys! A week to visit my mom . . . then they'd be gone all day to sailing camp for a whole month. It was a good plan. Philip was the one being unreasonable. If he'd just meet me halfway, we could work this out.

Burying my face in a towel, I wished I had someone to talk to. Or pray with. It seemed so much easier when Mabel or Edesa talked to God. But right now it was just me. *Jesus,* I started—but instead of a prayer, the gospel song on the CD Josh gave me filled my head. *"Where do I go . . . when there's no one else to turn to? Who do I talk to . . . when nobody wants to listen? . . ."*

I groaned into the towel. Good question.

chapter 33

Taking the boys to Manna House the next day went better than I expected. Of course, before we left the house, I threatened to take P.J.'s iPod away for the rest of his natural life if he showed the slightest disrespect to any living soul that day.

"O-*kay*, Mom, I get it. But what are we supposed to do all day while you're working? It's going to be so *boring*."

"So? Nobody ever died from being bored. But tell you what. If you're so bored you can't stand it at two o'clock, I'll knock off and take you home—but you'll have to cook supper tonight so I can get some work done at home. However, if you hang with me until four, I'll cook supper *and* even do your dishes tonight. Deal?"

The boys brightened considerably. I knew they liked to mess around in the kitchen—mile-high hamburgers and doctoring frozen pizzas were their specialties—so the whole deal probably felt like win-win to them. They even seemed to get a kick out of riding the Red Line again, choosing to hang on to the poles rather than sit as the train jerked and swayed around corners.

I'd called Mabel to ask if it was okay to bring the boys along, but I was surprised when she met us in the foyer when we arrived at nine thirty and presented the boys with orange and black "Manna House Volunteer" T-shirts, which said in small lettering beneath, "I'm part of God's miracle."

"Is that black lady the boss?" Paul whispered to me.

"Top dog." I grinned. This was going to be a good education for my sons. George Washington Prep had its small share of minority students, but except for the maintenance and grounds crew, the entire administration and teaching staff were white.

I was hoping we'd run into Lucy, but Mabel said she hadn't been in for about a week and a half—which meant my conversation with Lucy about growing up in Arkansas had been the last time anyone had seen her. But I did see several new faces in the multipurpose room, including a busty young woman still in her teens who was falling all out of her half-buttoned blouse. I hustled the boys to the lower level on the pretext of showing them my office. P.J. was unimpressed. "Gosh, Mom. Our bathroom at home is bigger than this."

I laughed. "Of course it is. This used to be a broom closet."

Just then Estelle Williams hollered at us from the kitchen. She'd whipped up a batch of chocolate-chip cookies in the boys' honor and gave P.J. and Paul the task of passing out the hot-from-the-oven cookies to everyone on the lower and main floors, which made them immediately popular with the current crop of residents. "Top floor is off-limits though," Estelle warned.

"What's up there?" Paul's eyes widened, as if he suspected hidden corpses.

Estelle chuckled deep in her chest. "Sleeping rooms. This is a *women's* shelter, son. No men allowed."

Between delivering cookies and playing Ping-Pong in the rec room, the boys managed to entertain themselves while I caught up on responses to my recent e-blast requesting donated supplies. Two boxes of books had come in from Rev. Handley to start the Manna House library, and Carolyn had already appointed herself Head Book Honcho and invented an honor-based "checkout" system. An e-mail from Josh Baxter's mom, Jodi, confirmed that she was all set to teach typing in the schoolroom this coming Saturday at eleven, and three people had signed up, including Kim, even though we only had two computers. And Tina left me a note saying she would try teaching the first ESL lesson tonight— Tuesday—from five to six, just before supper.

So far, so good.

When the bell rang for lunch, I went through the line with the boys and got them settled at a table, then caught Estelle by herself when I went back to the counter for napkins. "Did Mr. Bentley call you?" I whispered.

"Mm." Estelle didn't miss a beat refilling the bowl of butter pats.

"Well?"

"Well, what?"

"Estelle!"

"Well nothin'. We talked about care options for his mother."

"And . . . ?"

"And none of your business, Gabby Fairbanks." She flounced over to the heavy-duty refrigerator to replace the plastic container of butter pats.

Chuckling, I returned to our table, only to find Miss Bulging Blouse sitting across from the boys, talking loudly with someone at another table. But there was no mistaking the way the older teenager cut her eyes at P.J. or her sultry smile. P.J., on the other hand, wasn't looking at her smile . . .

With a start, I realized P.J. was going into *high school* in a few months, looking for all the world like a junior version of the dreamboat I fell in love with in France on that fateful day sixteen years ago in the Place de la Comédie.

I gulped. I wasn't ready for this!

Making a quick getaway after lunch, I let the boys watch a Spiderman movie in the TV room on the main floor, while I made up an activity calendar of weekly events so far: ESL on Tuesday late afternoon . . . Typing on Saturday morning . . . Knitting on Wednesday while the nurse was here . . . plus the Friday Bible study . . .

I still had a few more "life skills" ideas I wanted to get off the ground—basic cooking classes (Estelle?), basic sewing (Estelle again?), maybe a dance exercise class (Precious?). And Josh had suggested a sports clinic for the shelter kids on the weekend. Was he volunteering? His dad was athletic director for a high school in Rogers Park . . . *Hmm, that might be a good resource.*

Somehow I also managed to squeeze in a few calls to Chicago-area private schools, but the answers were all the same. "I'm sorry, registration is closed" or "We can put you on a waiting list." My heart was starting to sink. *Oh God, please help me find a good school for the boys . . .*

I sighed. Seemed like most of my prayers were still the *"Oh God, help!"* variety. How did Edesa and Mabel and that Avis woman learn how to pray? Seemed like the prayers of all those women were full of praise and thanksgiving, no matter what disaster was pending. *I need someone to teach me how to pray.* Funny thought, given that I'd grown up going to church until I gave it up in college. Correction: until Damien left me. But how could I go to church all that time and still not get it when it came to prayer?

I glanced at the clock. Almost four. We'd been here almost all day! The boys' movie should have been over an hour ago . . . what were they up to? Gathering my bags, I hustled up the stairs to the multipurpose room. Carolyn's ponytailed head was bent over a game board in the far corner, matching wits with P.J. and Paul in a game of Stratego.

"Time to go, guys," I called out. "Thanks, Carolyn."

"Aw, Mom, do we have to?" P.J. fussed. "We're right in the middle of a game!"

A smile started somewhere inside and popped out on my face. P.J. didn't want to go home yet? *God, You really do have a sense of humor.*

Somehow we made it through Wednesday and Thursday too. On both days I put in three or four hours of work, then took the boys to see the beluga whales at the Shedd Aquarium on Wednesday, and on Thursday we took the El downtown to the Aon Building so the boys could see the offices of Fairbanks and Fenchel—yes, there it was, a large nameplate beside the door— and have a late lunch with their father. My eyes nearly bugged out when I saw the professional décor: sandstone and fawn on the walls, tan leather couches with deep brown and ochre-red throw pillows, a rug that picked up the rich brown and sandstone colors, desert prints on the walls, and large, leafy plants.

My kind of room, exactly.

Uh-oh. Did Mona Fenchel think I pushed for my idea instead of hers? I was amazed she was still speaking to me. Or was she? Come to think of it, we'd been on Lester Stone's sailboat together all one Sunday afternoon, and I couldn't remember more than three sentences she'd said to me that day.

But on Friday the boys balked. "Can't we just stay here and play video games?"

"I wanna go to the beach," Paul whined. "Can't we go to the beach?"

Frankly, I'd run out of ideas. *Just one more day. One more day to juggle—*

The intercom chimed. That would be Camila. I buzzed the security door so she could come up and briefed the boys. The three of us were waiting in the gallery when she got to the door. "Camila, these are my sons, P.J. and Paul. Boys, this is *Señora* . . ." My glance pleaded with the woman to please provide a last name.

Blushing, she seemed to understand. "Sanchez. Camila Sanchez. I am very happy to meet your fine sons, *Señora* Fairbanks."

To their credit, both boys gravely shook hands before disappearing into their rooms. I ran a hand through my hair, which seemed to be getting frizzier as the June humidity hiked up. "I—I hope we won't be in your way, Camila. I had planned to go to work, but the boys want to stay home today, so I'm not sure what I'm going to—"

"Oh, you go. You go." Camila Sanchez flicked a hand at me, as though shooing a fly. "Your fine boys can stay with me. I am here until two o'clock. I will watch them. Just give me a phone number where I can call you. It is no problem. Go, go."

I gaped at her. "Oh, Camila—and please, call me Gabby—are you sure? I'd be happy to pay you extra." I couldn't believe how this answer had dropped from above right into the gallery, almost like that Bible story where a bunch of friends lowered their sick buddy right through the roof to get to Jesus. I grinned at the analogy. Camila Sanchez's generous offer felt like a little miracle.

The boys seemed okay with the arrangement, and agreed to stay out of Mrs. Sanchez's way in whatever room she was cleaning. I made them promise not to leave the premises until I got back, and if they behaved, we'd go to the beach as soon as I got home that afternoon.

I had to admit I felt relieved going to work without having to worry about entertaining the boys. Couldn't blame them, either, for not wanting to tag along with me every day. Had Philip given *any* thought to his kids when he bought the penthouse at Richmond Towers? Even if I wasn't working, what were they supposed to do every day? It'd be different if we lived in a neighborhood where they could ride their bikes or run outside to play with their friends any time they wanted . . .

One thing at a time, Gabby. Right. At least the boys would have a great time romping with their cousins for a week in my old hometown—which reminded me. Celeste and Honor still hadn't confirmed that they were coming home next week! The three-hour time difference in Alaska made finding a convenient time to call my oldest sister difficult. And Honor tended to view time on a sliding scale. "I'll call you tomorrow" might be tomorrow—or a week later.

Well, I'd try when I got to work. Celeste ought to be up by then.

But my first phone call after I dumped my bags on my desk was to the penthouse. "Camila? How are the boys? . . . Good. Good. Yes, I know it's only been an hour . . . But you'll call if there's any problem, all right?"

Well, that was silly. Of course they're all right. Those two could play video games for hours. I'd wait until noon to make the next call, and maybe just before I left at two.

Next I tried Celeste. She should be up by now, even with the time difference. But I immediately got a recorded voice saying, "That number is being checked for trouble." *Rats.* That usually meant a dump of snow had hit Denali National Park, disrupting their landline. And the geography made cell phone access spotty at best. I dialed her cell anyway and left a message.

At ten thirty I went upstairs to catch Edesa before the Friday Bible study, hoping to find out what had happened at the adoption hearing while we were in Virginia last week, but they'd already started. I tried to slip in quietly, but Edesa stopped mid-sentence and said, *"Hola!* Gabby's back!" She flashed her familiar megawatt smile as I sat down. "We missed you last week, Gabby. I was just telling the ladies that today we're going to ask the same question the disciples asked Jesus: 'Lord, teach us to pray.' Has everyone found the book of Matthew, chapter six?"

Well, this was ironic, given that I was wishing someone would teach me how to pray earlier this week. But . . . the Lord's Prayer? I'd memorized that as a kid, and it was a regular part of the liturgy at Briarwood Lutheran. But repeating a rote prayer wasn't exactly what I had in mind.

I considered slipping out, but that seemed rude after just sitting down. So I stayed put—and then forgot about leaving as Edesa Baxter broke down the prayer into tiny parts. "First, Jesus encouraged His disciples to give God praise! 'Hallowed be Thy name!' *Hallowed* means holy, sacred, blessed. When we come into the presence of the King of kings, this is the first thing we do. We worship Him!"

I listened in amazement as the young black woman from Honduras—who seemed too young to be so wise—went phrase by phrase through the Lord's Prayer, encouraging these women off the street to get familiar with the Bible, so they could pray *in* the will of God. "Because prayer is powerful, *mis amigas*. Prayer changes things. But that doesn't mean God's going to answer your prayer for security by sending you a smooth-talking pimp who's promised to take care of you if you'll just take care of his johns." Nervous snickers and a few guffaws consumed the room.

The discussion got a bit dicey when she got to the part about confessing our sins and asking God to forgive us. "Jesus said we also need to forgive people who sin against us."

"Man! I ain't forgivin' my daddy for what he done to me. He can burn in hell for all I care."

"What if the scumbags don't confess *their* sins? Do we still have to forgive 'em?"

"Jesus did," Edesa said simply. "While He was hanging on the cross, after being whipped and nailed through His hands and feet, He said, 'Father, forgive them, because they don't know what they're doing.' But that doesn't mean it's easy. I know." Her lip trembled. "I admit I'm very angry at the man who got Gracie's mother pregnant, probably got her hooked on drugs, too, and then abandoned her to die. And now he's trying to take Gracie away from us."

Suddenly everyone wanted to talk about the crackheads and slicksters in their lives who didn't deserve to be forgiven. I slipped out of the room. This didn't seem to apply to me. Nothing in my life matched what these women had suffered—not even Edesa's fight for Gracie.

But I decided to take another look at the Lord's Prayer.

Starting with praise . . . I was definitely weak on that one. *Asking God to meet my needs* . . . Yeah. When I got desperate. But it talked about "daily bread." Basic needs. Why not *before* I got desperate? *Confessing my sins* . . . Didn't do that too often. *Huh.* It was bad enough constantly having to apologize to Philip for all the ways I didn't measure up to his expectations. *Forgiving others*—

I stopped with my hand on the doorknob to my office.

Could I forgive Philip for making me feel like I was nothing more than sand in his shoes?

chapter 34

I phoned the boys at noon and talked to Paul. The natives were getting restless. "It's eighty degrees out there, Mom! I wanna go swimming."

"I know, hon. Hang in there. Let me talk to Mrs. Sanchez."

Camila said everything was fine, but she had to leave at two o'clock.

"That's fine, Camila. The boys can stay by themselves for a little while. I should be home by two thirty or so. I'll check in with them by phone."

I made a point to catch Edesa at lunch and ask about the hearing, but she just shook her head. "It got postponed, Gabby. Nobody said why." The anxiety in her large, dark eyes contradicted her wry smile. "Makes it hard to practice what I preach—you know, what I said this morning, about forgiveness. And patience!"

Frankly, it was good to know she was human. I gave her a sympathetic hug, told her to keep me posted, and went looking for Mabel. I hadn't seen the director at lunch, so I tapped on her office door, my list of current and proposed activities in hand.

"It's open!"

I peeked in. She and Stephanie Cooper, the case manager, had their heads together—beauty-shop-relaxed black coif and wash-and-wear light brown bangs—poring over a stack of manila file folders. "Oops, excuse me. I can come back later."

Mabel looked up. "That's okay. Just doing progress reports. What's up?"

I waved my list. "I can just leave this with you. There are some life skills I'd like to add to the program—and Estelle Williams could do it all. Sewing. Cooking. But she's already making lunch five days a week, and she's teaching some of the women to knit when the nurse is here. I hate to ask her to do more as a volunteer." I took a deep breath. "Have you thought about adding her to the program staff? Even part-time?"

The director cast an amused glance at Stephanie. "How did you know we were talking about adding to our staff? Stephanie needs another case manager too."

Mabel invited me to write a memo to submit to the board meeting in two weeks, listing the need and Estelle's qualifications. "Personally, I like the idea. What else is on that list?"

By the time I got back to my office and typed up the memo, it was already after two. I grabbed the phone and dialed the penthouse. The phone rang seven times and went to voice mail. "P.J.? Paul? Pick up! This is Mom." Nothing.

Oh, great. They probably have the TV on and can't hear the phone. But I knew Camila had to be gone by now, and I didn't like not knowing if the boys were all right. Grabbing my purse and backpack, I signed out and headed for the El. I tried again while I waited for the Red Line. Still only got voice mail.

An uneasy thought niggled at me as I paced on the platform.

What if the boys got tired of waiting in the house and decided to go swimming on their own? Did the beaches have lifeguards yet? Chicago schools weren't out, but it was after Memorial Day . . .

By the time the train finally opened its doors at my stop, I was that jumbled bag of nerves familiar to parenthood—furious that the boys hadn't answered the phone, plotting dire punishments if they had disobeyed me, and scared spitless that something had happened to my kids. I practically ran the three blocks to Richmond Towers, pushed through the revolving doors, heart pounding . . . and stopped dead in my tracks.

A chunky white man I recognized as another resident in the building had the shirt collars of both my sons locked in his grip, one in each hand, and—neck veins bulging—was spouting off to Mr. Bentley. "Call the police right now!" he was yelling. "If you don't, I will!"

P.J. was writhing like a wild feline. "Let me go, you jerk! I'll tell my dad."

The doorman patted the air with both hands as though trying to calm everyone down. "Now, no need to call the police. I know the parents. Just let me—"

Paul spotted me and burst into tears. "Mom! Make him let us go!"

Heart pounding, I finally found my voice. "Mr. Bentley! What's going on?"

Before Mr. Bentley had a chance to say anything, the red-faced man had let go of my sons and was shaking a finger in my face. "These your kids? You live here? What kind of parent are you, letting them run loose around the building, raising Cain?!"

"What—what did they do? . . . Mr. Bentley?"

But the man wasn't finished. "Snuck into the parking garage

281

and ran around rocking cars, setting off a dozen car alarms." He stabbed his finger at me again. "You better believe management is going to hear about this!" He stormed off, but he had one parting shot for Mr. Bentley. "If you can't keep hooligans like these brats from running amuck in our building, mister, I'll have your job!"

The man's words burned in my ears. *"Hooligans like these brats . . . I'll have your job."*

But I tried to focus on the real issue with P.J. and Paul when we got up to the penthouse. "He shouldn't have said that, but he was angry. With good reason. You boys know better than to create a ruckus like that! What were you thinking?!"

P.J. flopped on the couch, arms folded, face molded in an angry pout. "But, Mom, we got so bored! There's nothin' to do here."

"No excuses. I told you not to leave the house until I got home."

"Yeah, but you didn't come, and the whole day was almost gone."

That got me. It was so tempting to relent, pack a snack, grab our swimming suits, and let the sparkling waters of Lake Michigan wash this whole ugly incident into oblivion. But I braced myself to follow through. "I'm sorry I wasn't here when Mrs. Sanchez left. And I'm sorry you had to wait so long. But that's still no excuse for setting off car alarms, for heaven's sake! You have embarrassed your dad and me and . . . and you even put Mr. Bentley's job in jeopardy."

P.J. shrugged sullenly. That did it. I realized neither boy had so much as said, "I'm sorry."

"Both of you. To your rooms. You're grounded the rest of the day—and maybe longer. Depends on what Dad says when he gets home."

Twin wails went up. "Aww, Mom!"

"Go!"

I pressed my fingertips to my scalp as bedroom doors slammed. *Oh God. Please don't let this get Mr. Bentley in trouble too.* Heating water for tea to calm my nerves, I realized I was less concerned about us getting kicked out. In fact, I almost hoped it would happen. Maybe we could look for a house—on the *ground*—or even buy one of those charming row townhouses in one of the "gentrified" urban neighborhoods.

Get a grip, Gabby. Philip would blow a gasket—

Philip. I groaned as I steeped my chamomile tea. I'd give anything if I didn't have to tell Philip. But I had no doubt we would hear from management about this, and it would be even worse if he found out that way.

By the time my husband got home, I had a pot roast in the oven—I figured a heavenly "welcome home" smell never hurt—and had steeled myself to tell him right away what had happened. Personally, my own mad at the boys was over, and I was going to lobby that not getting to go swimming today was punishment enough for a first offense . . . but I should have known better.

Philip was furious with *me*.

Somewhere in the back of my mind, I had hoped the boys and I could pack Friday evening and take off for North Dakota on Saturday. But Philip insisted on taking the boys to Navy Pier for the day—"Since you kept them holed up here like moles yesterday," he'd hissed at me—to ride the enormous Ferris wheel, eat lunch at Bubba Gump's, and take a sail on one of the masted "tall ships" that gives rides by the hour to tourists.

My eyes burned with unshed tears as I washed and folded clothes, ordered a rental car for the trip—a minivan, no frills—and packed duffel bags for the boys. Nothing I'd done yesterday had been right according to Philip, from leaving the boys with Camila Sanchez in the first place, to not being there when she left, to not fulfilling my promise to take them swimming. Of *course* they got into trouble. What did I expect?

I'd said nothing. From his point of view, he made a good case. None of this would have happened if I'd been home with them instead of at work.

I argued my own case to the laundry basket. "Good grief! P.J. is thirteen, old enough to stay home a few hours by himself—*and* look after his younger brother! . . . Many families have working parents . . . I was home for years when the boys were small . . . Philip is the one who sent the boys off to boarding school nine months out of the year! . . . A job for me at this time in our life makes sense. My job is a worthy one, and I'm good at it . . . Since I do have a job, there will be times we have to pull together as a family and adjust. I can't just work a few months and quit, then start up again . . . Good grief! One day of boredom isn't going to kill the boys. And I *am* taking a week off to take them on a vacation trip . . ."

But it was no use. Philip's words continued to beat me over the head in the silent penthouse. *"Selfish"* . . . *"Pigheaded"* . . . *"My mother is right about you"* . . . *"Might as well send the boys back to Virginia right now"* . . .

I buried my head in a still-warm-from-the-dryer T-shirt. Was I just selfish and pigheaded? Was I the crazy one here?

Frankly, I was glad to be leaving for a week. We both needed time to cool off. By the time I got back, the heat would be off, the boys would be in sailing camp for a month, and we could settle into a workable routine.

But the silence in the empty penthouse was starting to give me jitters. I called Manna House at noon to ask how the first Saturday typing class went. I waited for several minutes while someone went to see if Jodi Baxter was still there, then she picked up.

"Checking up on me, are you, Gabby?" Her voice was teasing. "Actually, I was surprised you weren't here to make sure I showed up." Jodi laughed. "I'll have to tell you sometime about the first time I volunteered at Manna House. The place burned down." She chuckled again. "But seriously, the class was good, I think. That Kim is a real go-getter. She's still in the schoolroom practicing. A couple other people dropped by and asked if they could learn to type, too, which would be fine with me, but you'll need several more computers." She paused a mere nanosecond, as if shifting gears. "How are you doing, Gabby? Everything okay?"

The question took me by surprise . . . and for some reason I found myself telling this woman I barely knew about the juggling act all week, trying to entertain my boys *and* keep up with my job.

"Oh, boy, tell me about it. I've been teaching third graders ever since our youngest started school. At least Denny and I both work for the public schools, so when school is out, so are we. Well, technically. Except Teacher Institute Days. And athletic meets on weekends, ad infinitum. But if one of our kids got sick? There went all *my* sick days."

For some reason, I found Jodi's homily strangely comforting. Lots of families had to juggle schedules. I was not crazy. "The worst part is," I found myself saying, "I let them stay home yesterday since the woman who cleans for us was there until two o'clock, which was fine, but I didn't get home until three—which turned out to be just long enough for them to get into trouble."

"Oh dear. What did they do?"

Why was I telling her this? "It's so embarrassing. I guess they were exploring the building we live in, got into the parking garage, and started rocking cars to make the car alarms go off. Like ten or twelve all at once."

I heard a gasp at the other end, and mentally kicked myself for saying *anything*—now she thought I was a terrible mother!—but to my shock, Jodi Baxter started laughing. I mean, howling.

"Oh. Oh. Oh." More belly laughter. "That is so *funny*! I mean, I know it isn't right now, but it's the sort of thing you and your husband will tell on your kids and laugh about later. I mean, I'm sure they meant it as a prank, and there was no real harm done. But, oh dear. I can just imagine. *Yikes*. The noise! Just be sure you guys stuff a sock in your mouths so the kids can't hear you laughing behind closed doors. *They* can't know you think it's funny until they're at *least* eighteen."

Her laughter was contagious. I couldn't help it. Pretty soon I was giggling too. And that night, after the boys had come home, talking a mile a minute about their exciting day at Navy Pier with their dad and getting excited about our road trip to North Dakota, the world no longer felt like it was falling apart. Of course not!

What the boys did was naughty, yes. They had to be disciplined, yes. But it wasn't the end of the world.

As I lay in bed after Philip had fallen asleep, I wondered what it would be like to giggle in the dark with my husband about what had happened yesterday, and laugh so hard we had to stuff socks in our mouths.

chapter 35

A cloudless sky arched over the city Sunday morning, and the TV weatherman promised mild temperatures in the low seventies. Perfect travel weather. I sent up a heavenly thank-you. The weekend "door-dude" called the penthouse at eight to tell us Enterprise had delivered the rental minivan. While Philip rode down the elevator with the boys and the luggage, I did a last-minute sweep of the house. Good thing. I found the earphones to Paul's portable CD player, my cell phone still charging in the bedroom, and our damp swimsuits still in the washing machine where I'd washed them last night. I guiltily whisked them into a recloseable plastic bag. My name would be mud if I forgot those.

At the last minute, I also stuck my Bible into my bulging backpack. I'd been telling God I was going to start reading the Word more regularly. Maybe this week while I was on vacation I'd have time to actually make good on that promise.

Outside by the car, Philip gave me a peck on the cheek, smelling faintly like his Armani aftershave. Sea breezes and tropical forests. He'd already picked up a tan from the outing on Lester Stone's sailboat, our afternoon at Wrigley Field, and another layer yesterday. Gosh, he looked good. I had a sudden urge to slide my arms around his neck, feel his body pressed against mine, satisfy this hunger for skin touching skin . . . but the moment passed as he opened the car door and waited for me to get in.

"You're sure you know how to get out of the city?"

"I think so." I showed him the maps I'd printed out from the computer.

"Looks okay. Just be sure you get on I-90 to Wisconsin, Gabby, and not I-94, or you'll waste a lot of time." He leaned in a side window. "'Bye, guys. Don't give your mom any grief. Call me when you get there, okay?" Philip stepped back and waved us off. When I looked in my rearview mirror just before leaving the frontage road, he was gone.

It seemed to take forever to get out of Chicago's sprawl, even without major traffic delays. Finally we were zipping northwest on the toll road, past newly plowed fields, pretty farms, and the occasional oasis for gas, restrooms, and fast food. The day was so beautiful, I drove with my window down, the sunroof open, and no AC. The wind felt so good, I didn't even mind that my curls would probably end up a snarly mess. And the farther we drove away from Chicago, the lighter I felt.

My cell phone rang the "William Tell" midmorning just as we were entering Wisconsin. I snatched it up and recognized the area code for Alaska. "Celeste? Thank goodness you called! . . . What? . . . Yeah, the boys and I are on the road now, heading for Minot. Are you coming? . . . Can't hear me? I *said*, are you coming home?!"

I pressed the cell phone to my ear, my sister's voice fading in and out. But I got the gist of it. She wasn't coming. Late snow. Some stranded hikers. Tom needed her there. Maybe later in the year when their daughter Kristi was home from college . . .

I finally flipped the phone closed, fighting the lump in my throat. I knew it'd been a long shot, trying to get my sisters and their kids home all at the same time. But I'd been hoping . . . no, *needing* to try to tie up the loose ends in my life. We'd been distant too long.

I shook off my disappointment, stuck an *Eighties Faves* CD in the car player, and turned up the volume. It would've been great to have a family reunion, but the boys and I were going to have a good time anyway.

"What's love got to do, got to do with it . . ." I bellowed with Tina Turner.

"Mo-om! I can't hear my CD player!"

"Too bad. It's my turn."

"I'm hungry!"

I tossed the bag of snacks into the backseat and kept singing. "Who needs a heart, when a heart can be broken . . . !"

Nothing was going to stop me from enjoying every second of this trip.

We stopped just west of Minneapolis at a chain hotel for the night. *Eight hours on the road, not bad . . .* though it took a twenty-ounce Pepsi to keep me awake in the late afternoon, and I had to move P.J. to the front seat to end the jabbing and poking.

But once in a booth at a local Outback Steakhouse, I actually managed to get the boys talking. Well, Paul anyway. "Tell me about this piece of music you composed for the band, Paul. I wish we could have heard it."

"Aw, I was just horsing around with my trombone and came

up with a tune, and my band director showed me this really neat composition program on the computer, and, well . . ." As he prattled on, I mentally made a note to ask Philip about getting the software for our home computer.

The boys spent an hour in the hotel pool after supper, while I soaked in the Jacuzzi, watching them horse around, letting the forceful water jets coax the last of the tension from the past several weeks out of my body. I didn't think about Philip. I didn't think about Manna House. I didn't think about anything at all except how warm and relaxed and . . . and *safe* I felt, five hundred miles away from my life.

The next morning, we were on the road again by eight o'clock after a carbohydrate-heavy continental breakfast in the hotel lobby. P.J. elected to sit up front, and as the long miles clicked by on the odometer, I had a momentary hope he'd open up and tell me more about what was happening at school, but he pretty much kept plugged into his iPod.

However, both boys did reasonably well on the second leg of the trip, as long as I stopped every two hours and reloaded the snacks and drinks. Between Minneapolis and Fargo, we played the License Plate Game and called out thirteen different state plates plus two Canadian provinces, then ran Twenty Questions into the ground. Paul decided he'd annoy us by starting in on, "Ninety-Nine Bottles of Beer on the Wall," and was delighted when I joined in the old camp song. But at around sixty-five bottles left on the wall, P.J. hollered, "Enough already!" I couldn't have agreed more.

My heart was singing. I wanted to keep driving forever.

As we crossed into North Dakota around noon, the topography had definitely changed from compact family farms to sprawling prairie. Cattle dotted the slightly rolling grasslands, which were still reasonably green in early June, though miles went by without seeing a single tree—just shrubs, sagebrush, and occasional sandstone formations. Mega-acre fields sprouted the first mantle of spring wheat, looking like a military crew cut.

Both boys pronounced it "boring," but to me it was beautiful. The pungent smell of sagebrush made me feel slightly drunk, and my pulse quickened as we turned off I-94 at Jamestown and headed north on a two-lane highway. MINOT—170 MILES the sign said.

Home . . .

For the first time in months, that word formed in my conscious thought and rolled around on my tongue.

"There's Grandma!" I pulled into the driveway of the boxy beige house that had been my childhood home and beeped the horn. My mother, grayer than I remembered her, got up stiffly from the flower bed where she'd been weeding, turned, and shaded her eyes from the five o'clock sun. A four-legged bundle of wispy yellow hair erupted from the grass and charged the car, barking.

"Hey there, Dandy," I said, trying to keep the dog from jumping up on me as I crossed the yard and threw my arms around my mom. Had she always been this short? But she still smelled like lavender, the same soft smell I remembered from nighttime kisses when she'd tucked us girls in bed.

Paul was already tussling with the dog. I waved P.J. out of the car. "Hey, guys. Come give your grandma a hug."

"Hi, Grandma!" Paul ran over, gave his grandmother a noisy smack, and ran off again with the yellow mutt, who led him on a merry chase around the yard.

P.J. climbed out of the car and sauntered over to where we stood by the flower bed. He gave his grandmother a polite hug. "Whatcha doing—planting flowers?"

My mother looked at my oldest quizzically. "Is this Ryan?"

"No, no, Mom. This is P.J.—Philip Junior. You remember."

"Oh, yes, of course. Philip's boy. He's just grown so much. Looks so much like Ryan now."

P.J. rolled his eyes at me. His cousin Ryan was Honor's oldest, at least two years older than P.J. *An easy mistake*, I decided, since my mother hadn't seen any of the grandchildren since my dad's funeral two years ago. Except that even then, Ryan had been a beanpole, blond and freckled.

I made a quick call to Philip and left a message on his cell that we'd arrived safe and sound. Then we unloaded the car, and I had the boys put their stuff in the second-floor bedroom with the two dormer windows that Honor and I had shared for years until Celeste left home, at which time Honor inherited her bedroom.

P.J. made a face. "Aw, Mom. It's all full of, you know, girl stuff."

"I won't tell anyone." I laughed. "I'm going to help Grandma with supper. But I'll tell you a secret. Behind that little door into the crawl space, I bet you'll find a whole box of superhero comic books. Go for it."

I left the boys diving into the crawl space. To my surprise, the oven was cold, no supper makings in sight. In fact, the refrigerator was surprisingly bare. A half gallon of milk, half-empty. A carton of orange juice. A wilted head of iceberg lettuce. A bag of raw carrots. A package of shredded cheddar cheese. A carton of eggs—full. An array of condiments in the door. Several containers of leftovers. A partial loaf of wheat bread. And in the freezer, two TV dinners and a package of Mrs. Stouffer's Homemade Lasagna.

"Uh, Mom? Did you have any plans for supper? How about if I make some cheese omelets? We can eat at the kitchen table, make it easy."

"No, honey, we can't eat in the kitchen. I've got the dining room all set with the good china. Tonight is special, having you and the boys here."

I peeked into the dining room. Sure enough, the dining room table was covered with my mom's antique lace tablecloth. Her rose-patterned wedding china sat at each chair—six place settings in all. A silk flower arrangement graced the center of the table.

China on the table, but no supper? Six place settings? What was going on here?

I woke up in Celeste's old room the next morning, sunlight streaming in through its single dormer, and stretched. What a good sleep! And we'd had fun the evening before, eating our cheese omelets on china and lace, pretending to ignore the two empty place settings, and then all four of us had played a rousing game of Pit, yelling and trading and hoarding. My mother had laughed triumphantly when she *won*.

It felt so good to just lie in bed this morning, cuddled in the faded lavender-flowered comforter. *Funny* . . . Celeste had been the girly-girl of the family. Now she was married to a park ranger in Alaska with, I guessed, very few frills. Honor had always been the "wild child," doing things differently just to be different. She'd been born in '62 and came of age in the early seventies, and flower-power stuck to her like a permanent tattoo. As the youngest, I was the tomboy my parents never had, climbing trees, always running, never walking, living up to all the stereotypes of redheads with tempers, fighting for my place in the family.

Trouble was, I didn't fight for my place in the world. Got married right out of high school—even before Honor. Got divorced two years later—even before Honor. At least I got married again—unlike Honor. *But, oh God, look at me.* I hardly recognized the person I used to be.

Sudden tears blurred the sunshine, and I brushed them away. *Get a grip, Gabby. This week is your gift. Don't waste it on spilled milk.*

I grabbed a tissue, blew my nose, and reached for my Bible. Okay. Might as well put first things first. Trouble is, I didn't know where to start. Maybe one of the Gospels, the story of Jesus. After all, He was the main point. Right?

I'd read the first two chapters of Matthew about the birth of Jesus and was trying to imagine the headlines if that had happened today—PREGNANT TEEN DENIES HAVING SEX WITH A MAN or WORLD LEADER KILLS ALL INFANTS IN TOWN TRYING TO GET RID OF A POSSIBLE SUCCESSOR—when I heard the *click click click* of doggy nails on the stairs, and Dandy poked his nose into my room and cocked his scruffy ears quizzically. I smiled. The dog had a sweet face. "Hey, boy," I murmured. "Anybody else up? You need to go out?"

And then I remembered. I had planned to get up early and make a quick trip to the nearest Miracle Mart so we could have breakfast. My mom had obviously forgotten how much food two adolescent boys could pack away in a day, much less a week!

When I let the dog out into the backyard, I realized something else my mom had forgotten. Dog poops. The yard was full of them.

By late morning of our first day at Grandma Shepherd's, I was feeling that things were a little more under control. Old leftovers and expired food had been tossed out. The refrigerator and cupboards had been restocked with fresh food. I'd called Aunt Mercy and invited her to come over around four and stay for supper. And I'd corralled the boys into helping me do pooper-scooper duty. I sweetened the deal by saying we'd not only go swimming at the public pool after lunch, but I'd let them go to the movies on their own afterward if we got the yard clean.

The public pool I remembered as a kid—shallow end, deep end—had been replaced by a larger pool with a water slide. I bought the boys waterslide bracelets for unlimited trips through the curlicue and let them run off. As Mom and I looked around for a place to set up camp, I thought, *Odd. Everyone here is white.* Which wasn't that odd, given that Minot was in the heart of Scandinavian country. What was odd was that I even noticed. My reality had changed.

Both Paul and P.J. were good swimmers, so I let them horse around in the pool on their own, while I sat with my mom under a shade umbrella and talked. She seemed perfectly fine . . . except for the occasional long pause in the middle of a sentence, and then she'd say, "My, my, what were we talking about?" But mostly she smiled a lot and patted my hand, happy for company.

On the way home, I dropped the boys off at the neighborhood theater, which had a four o'clock showing of the latest blockbuster animated movie. "Pick you up at six!" I yelled after them. I watched them go. *Could I do this in Chicago?* Probably not. I'd have to go with them, which wasn't such a bad thing. But today I had a reason for getting them out of the house.

I needed to talk to Aunt Mercy about my mom.

Aunt Mercy was my dad's younger sister, ten years his junior and still working as a reference librarian at the Minot Public Library, even though she was nearing retirement age. "They won't let me retire." She laughed as we peeled potatoes and diced ham for scalloped potatoes. She tapped her head. "I know too much. That's what they get for letting me work as a reference librarian for thirty years."

I'd talked my mom into lying down for a nap, telling her not to worry about supper, Aunt Mercy and I would take care of it. Dandy curled up on the rug beside my mom's bed and gave me a look. *Dog on duty. Beat it.*

Aunt Mercy shrugged. "Even if they did, I need to work another two years to get my full pension. And I only have a one-bedroom apartment. Otherwise I'd invite Martha to come live with me until her name comes up on the list for assisted living. They said it would be another three to six months at least. Maybe longer." She shook her head. "I don't think your mom can wait that long, Gabby."

I stopped slicing and stared at my aunt. She was an attractive woman in her sixties, her short shag turning silver (or tinted, I couldn't be sure). And she was dead serious. "What do you mean?"

Aunt Mercy pointed a paring knife at me. "Gabby, we've got a problem. Your mom's still driving that old Ford Galaxy, but she had three fender-benders last fall. Drove into the birch tree in the front yard in December. But it's not just the driving—it's her memory. I come to pick her up for church and she thinks it's Tuesday. Gabby, she calls me Mary all the time—*her* sister." My dad's sister sighed. "The doctor says she's had a series of small strokes. Nothing major—yet. I try to check on her at least one other time during the week, but I live on the other side of town, Gabby. I can't do it every day."

I was silent as I stirred the white sauce for the potatoes. What was she saying? I'd been hoping we could get Mom moved into an assisted-living situation—but Aunt Mercy had already answered that. Waiting list.

Aunt Mercy broke the silence. "What about you girls? Have any of you considered moving your mom closer to one of you?"

Move Mom closer to—? I was sure Mom wouldn't want to leave Minot. Even getting her to sell this house would be tricky. But even if she did, I couldn't imagine moving Mom to Denali National Park in Alaska to live with Celeste! And moving her to Southern California with Honor was just as laughable. Honor lived in a trailer with two kids, for goodness' sake! It was some artsy trailer park for aging hippies, and she made jewelry for a living, more or less. Plus, I didn't know whose forgetfulness would be worse—Mom's or Honor's. I snorted to myself. Honor would probably call me back about my proposed "family reunion" next week. *"Oh, when did you say it was, Gabby?"* Yeah, right.

I stopped stirring and stared out the window at my mom's poop-free backyard.

That left me.

chapter 36

Oh, great. In my haste to grab my cell phone at the last minute, I'd forgotten to unplug the charger and take it too. *Well, no big deal.* I'd just turn it off and save it for the trip home. The boys could use the house phone to call their dad while we were here. And my mom's number was in our address book at home, if Philip bothered to look.

Besides, I had bigger problems. Aunt Mercy's question niggled at me all the next day, most of which we spent at the pool again since the weather forecast threatened rain at the end of the week. My thoughts bounced around like a pinball trying to find the right hole. What was I going to do? I couldn't just take my mom home with me! We didn't have an extra bedroom, not since we decided to give the boys their own rooms. And Philip . . . I didn't even want to go there. Maybe we could set up something like Meals on Wheels, so she'd at least get a decent meal once a day . . . find a housekeeper to come in once a week . . . hire a kid to walk the dog . . .

I tossed aside the magazine I'd been flipping through and scanned the bobbing heads in the pool until I found Paul's curly head and P.J.'s dark one. *How am I going to do all that in just two days? We have to leave on Saturday!* I suddenly felt like throwing something. *Grr! Celeste and Honor should have come home like I'd asked them to! Then we could talk about what to do together.*

I looked over at my mom in the other deck chair. She was asleep. Her hair looked as if it needed a cut and a perm. Definitely didn't get my curly hair from Mom. I sighed. One more thing to do . . .

I got up and dove into the deep end of the pool, letting the cool water slide over my body and black tank. In the underwater silence, a line from the gospel song on the CD Josh Baxter got for me floated through my head. *"Who do I talk to . . . when nobody wants to listen . . . ?"* I came up gulping for air, hearing the chorus in my ears: *"I go to the Rock of my salvation, go to the Stone that the builders rejected . . . !"*

I felt like yelling, "Okay, God, I'm listening!" But what I really wanted was a husband I could call who'd listen to the pain in my heart and help me decide what to do.

I called my aunt that evening to ask what she thought about Meals on Wheels. She sighed in my ear. "I tried that a few months ago, Gabby. Your mom would eat a little, then stick the leftovers in the refrigerator to 'save for another day.' I came over one weekend and found six or seven half-eaten containers and threw them all out. I was afraid she'd get food poisoning."

"Mom? Mom!" Paul was tugging on my shirt.

I frowned at him and held up a finger to wait.

"But Mom—"

I covered the phone receiver. "Just a minute. I'm talking to Aunt Mercy."

"But Mom! There's an empty pan on the stove, and the gas burner's turned up on high!"

Okay, that was it. The pan-on-the-stove episode scared me. What if she set the house on fire someday? I had to do *something* about my mom, and do it quick.

Since I woke up Thursday morning before working people were even out of bed, I dutifully turned on the bedside light and read chapters five, six, and seven of Matthew's gospel—three whole chapters devoted to Jesus' famous Sermon on the Mount. I skimmed most of it. Didn't want to deal with radical stuff like "turn the other cheek" and "love your enemies" right now.

But I skidded to a stop in the middle of chapter seven, where Jesus said, *"Ask and it will be given to you; seek and you will find; knock and the door will be opened to you. For everyone who asks receives; he who seeks finds; and to him who knocks, the door will be opened."* The verses were familiar. I'd probably even memorized them in Pioneer Girls club as a kid. But today, something about those promises felt like wide-open arms, and I wanted to fling myself into them.

Instead, I flung the comforter off. *Get a grip, Gabby.* I wasn't likely to get any answers about my mom until I got on the phone, knocked on some doors, and asked about services I could line up for her. I still had two days. Maybe I could put together something that would fill in the gaps until the assisted-living unit opened up. After all, Aunt Mercy said it *might* be only another three months—I hoped.

The temperature had dropped into the fifties under a gray cloud cover that matched my glum spirit as I served up old-fashioned oatmeal for breakfast. P.J. frowned at his bowl of oatmeal. "Doesn't Grandma have any instant stuff?"

"I want cold cereal." Paul plopped into a chair. "What are we gonna do today?"

I kept a watchful eye on my mother as she sorted her medications and vitamins into a plastic seven-day pillbox, while I heaped brown sugar and raisins on the boys' oatmeal. I'd have to double-check that pillbox later. "First, you're going to eat this hot cereal. Then Paul is going to walk Dandy, and P.J. is going to mow Grandma's lawn before it rains, while I make some important phone calls this morning—"

"Aw, Mom! I thought this was supposed to be vacation!"

"—And if we get that stuff done, then maybe we can go to the Dakota Air Museum this afternoon. I hear they've got a replica of the Wright Brothers' flyer."

That mollified them briefly. As soon as I heard the lawn mower start up, I got out the yellow pages and looked up Senior Services. A lot of listings . . . in other towns. Fargo. Bismarck. Burlington. The list for Minot was pretty short. I called one church group that had an "in-home companion" program and was told that their current volunteers were all assigned. But they'd be happy to put my mother on a list for when they got new volunteers. "We are usually able to assign a companion within a month or so who can give five to ten hours a week. How many hours a day does your mother need a companion?"

I thought about the pan on the stove. Twenty-four hours a

day would be about right. But I agreed to put my mom on their list. It was better than nothing.

I next tried the local Agency on Aging. The person on the phone explained their list of services, which included day care at the local senior center, transportation to medical appointments, home-delivered meals, and hot meals available at various sites around the city. "We'd be happy to set up a home visit to assess your mother's needs. How about next Wednesday at eleven?"

The piano in the living room tinkled a jazzy tune. Didn't sound like my mom. I stuck a finger in my ear so I could hear the phone. "Uh, I'm only in town this week. Could we do this today?"

"I'm sorry. The best we can do is a ten o'clock tomorrow here in the office."

Tomorrow?! I gritted my teeth. "Fine." What was I going to do between now and then?

I poked my head into the living room. Paul was sitting at the piano, playing with both hands, while my mother sat nearby, beaming. I listened. Not bad. "Where did you learn that, kiddo?"

Paul shrugged. "Made it up myself. Can we go to the air museum now? Are you coming, Grandma?"

I hesitated. I really should make more calls! But my mother was already getting her hat. "Just so we're back in time for prayer meeting tonight," she said.

Was she assuming we were all going to church? I opened my mouth to protest . . . and was surprised to realize I actually wanted to go. Maybe *needed* to go was more like it. I could sure use some help praying.

At the last minute, I tore out a page from the yellow pages and stuck my cell phone in my pocket. No way could I waste several hours wandering around a museum while there were still stones to be turned.

In spite of the change in weather, the boys had a great time at the air museum. The huge DC-3 World War II Troop Transport standing out in an open field, named *Gooney Bird* by its now-silent heroes, was the boys' favorite, while inside the museum a replica of the Wright Brothers' famous flyer and a two-winged, red-and-white aerobatic plane came a close second and third.

Mom tired fairly quickly, so I parked her on a bench while the boys ran their batteries down. Stepping away a few paces, I turned on my cell phone and dialed all the social service agencies I could find. But the answers all ended at the same place: zero. "We would need a doctor's referral" . . . "Why don't you call the Agency on Aging?" . . . "I'm sorry" . . . "Would you like to put her name on our waiting list?"

And then the battery died. *Drat!* Tomorrow's appointment was my last chance.

Trying not to be panicky, I picked up a pizza and a video for the boys on the way home, and let them stay home with Dandy and the TV remote while I drove Mom to church.

Only a smattering of people were at the prayer meeting at the little stone church, maybe fifteen max. I didn't know anyone there, for which I was glad. My parents had changed churches shortly after Damien dumped me nineteen years ago. The scandal of a divorce in a "no divorce—ever" church had been too much for them. A few people shook my hand and murmured, "That's nice," when my mom introduced me as "my daughter from Virginia." I didn't bother to correct her. Someone started a

song a cappella, and I was surprised how quickly the words came
back to me . . .

> *What a friend we have in Jesus,*
> *All our sins and griefs to bear*
> *What a privilege to carry*
> *Everything to God in prayer . . .*

A stack of prayer request cards were passed out. I got two—
someone's sister who had breast cancer, and another for a
husband who drank too much. I was surprised when everyone
got down on their knees along the wooden pews, and I heard
murmurings all around me as people prayed aloud. But I got
down on my knees, too, wishing I'd worn slacks instead of a
skirt, and dutifully prayed silently for the cards in my hand.

But Jesus' words kept rolling around in my mind. *Ask and you
will receive. Seek and you will find. Knock and the door will open.* I
squeezed my eyes shut even tighter. *Okay, Jesus, I'm asking. What
should I do about my mom?!*

I stayed on my knees, head buried in my hands, listening to
the rise and fall of the murmured prayers all around me. I kept
thinking about my mom living alone, thinking about having to
get the boys back by Sunday night so they could start sailing
camp, realizing there wasn't enough time to do everything I
needed to do to get my mom set up here and keep her safe . . .

"Come to Me."

The words were so clear, they seemed to echo in my head.
Where did that come from? Was that supposed to be God's
answer? What kind of answer was that? That's what I was doing,
wasn't it—coming here to prayer meeting to pray?

But I couldn't get the words out of my head. *"Come to Me."* Not even the next morning—the last day of our visit before heading back to Chicago—while I read another three chapters from Matthew. *"Come to Me."* I shook them off. What I needed to do was get up, get dressed, and get Mom and me over to the agency to see what my options were.

That was before my mom backed into Dandy, who was standing underfoot in the kitchen as we made breakfast, and tumbled backward over the dog and thumped her head on the floor.

"Mom! Mom! Are you okay?" I tried to get to her, but the dog still stood in the way, looking confused. "Dandy, get out of here, you stupid mutt." I grabbed the dog by the collar, pulled him across the kitchen floor, and shoved him outside. *Oh God, no . . . what if Mom broke her hip . . . I should call 9-1-1 . . .*

My mom sat up, rubbing her head. "Oh, it's nothing. Just a bump." She looked at me reproachfully. "Go say you're sorry to Dandy, Gabby. It's not his fault."

I blew out a relieved breath. "Okay, I will. Later." I helped my mother up from the floor. "Are you sure you're okay? Come on, I want you to lie down on the couch with an ice pack." After I checked her pupils to make sure she didn't have a concussion, she let me lead her into the living room, prop her feet up with some pillows, and make an ice pack for the back of her head. I told the boys to get their own breakfast, then went back into the living room to sit with my mom. Concussion or not, I decided I had my answer.

Mom was going back to Chicago with me.

I made my peace with Dandy, who wagged his forgiveness and promptly curled up on the couch with my mom. But the dog

was a problem. I called Aunt Mercy at the library, told her I was taking my mom back to Chicago, and could she please keep Dandy?

"Oh, Gabby. I'm sorry. My apartment complex doesn't allow
pets. But I've got a key to the house. I'll be glad to check on things
and water her plants. You better have her mail held—on second
thought, she has a slot in the door, so I'll just collect it and forward anything that's important. How's that?"

It would have to do.

I took the boys upstairs and told them Grandma was coming
back with us. P.J.'s eyes narrowed suspiciously. "Where's she
going to sleep?"

I'd steeled myself for that question. "In your room for now.
Paul's still got a bunk bed. You can sleep there—"

"That's not fair!" P.J. yelled. "I'm the oldest. Let Grandma
sleep in Paul's room."

"Keep your voice down," I hissed. "And don't give me that
look, young man. You and Paul share a room at your Nana
Marlene's house. It's not going to kill you for a few weeks." Who
was I kidding? A few months was more like it. "Grandma just
can't stay by herself right now."

P.J. flopped on one of the twin beds, his back to me. "Still not
fair. You and Dad didn't ask *us* if we wanted to move to Chicago.
Didn't want to come on this dumb trip, either." He buried his face
in the pillow.

I almost snapped, *"Dad didn't ask me if I wanted to move
either!"*—but P.J. suddenly rolled back over and faced me, his eyes
challenging.

"How come Dad didn't come with us to Grandma's?"

"Well, uh . . . he had to work. You know, just starting the new
business and all."

P.J. glared at me a long moment, then rolled back over. "Just go away. Leave me alone."

My eyes blurred. I pushed Paul out of the bedroom and started down the stairs. This trip wasn't turning out like I had hoped. I'd wanted to spend some special time with my sons, getting to know them again, just having fun together. But P.J. seemed so distant, hard to reach. The move had been tough on me . . . what else should I have expected from him? But now I felt so consumed trying to figure out how to care for my mom that—

Paul was tugging on my arm. "Can Dandy come too?"

"What?" I stopped on the staircase.

"You know, back to Chicago."

I hesitated.

"Mom, please! Grandma would cry without Dandy. I'll help take care of him. I can run him in the park. I'll even pick up his poops."

I pulled my youngest into a bear hug and rumpled his curly head. If only it were that simple. But what other choice did I have? My mom would never agree to leave her dog locked up in a kennel for a couple of weeks, much less three months. She'd fuss about the cost, anyway.

I canceled the appointment with the Agency on Aging and spent the rest of the day washing clothes, packing a suitcase for my mom, cleaning the house, and even packing a duffel bag for the dog: leash, brush, food and water bowls, sleeping rug, bag of dog food, plastic bags. "Guess that makes you official," I muttered to Dandy, who seemed quite anxious about the suitcase on my mom's bed.

The weather was still coolish, with occasional drizzles, so the boys didn't even beg to go to the pool. They discovered an ancient

Monopoly game with most of its parts, which helped kill the afternoon and kept my mom company in the living room while I made a quick trip to the Miracle Mart for trip food.

But I knew I was stalling.

I had to call Philip.

Tonight.

chapter 37

❋ ❋ ❋

The car was a little crowded with four of us plus a dog in the minivan, but Dandy turned out to be a good traveler, curling up on the floor under Paul's feet, only getting up from time to time to check on Mom in the front passenger seat. Paul was true to his word, snapping on the leash and taking the dog for runs at rest stops, a plastic bag in his back pocket in case the dog did his business.

My mom still had a lump on her head, but otherwise she seemed fine, sitting quietly in the front passenger seat, taking in the scenery, a little smile on her face. Casting an occasional glance her way, I realized she probably hadn't been anywhere since my father had died two years ago.

"Did you tell Dad that Dandy is coming too?" Paul asked. "What he'd say?"

I glanced at my youngest in the rearview mirror. Did he have a sixth sense that his father was not going to be happy with this whole plan? "Ah . . . I had to leave a message." Which was true.

The house phone rang seven times last night, and then voice mail picked up. At first I thought God must be smiling on me, because I was able to leave a matter-of-fact message, saying my mom and Dandy were coming for a visit, even adding that my mom really couldn't stay alone any longer. But then I realized it just put off the inevitable: Philip's reaction.

Still, when he hadn't called back by the time I locked the house Saturday morning and got everybody into the car, I began to relax. My cell phone was dead. I had a whole day before I had to try calling again from the hotel tonight. I started to hum. Might as well enjoy the trip.

Funny thing, though. When I tried to call the penthouse that evening from our hotel room, I only got voice mail again. I sucked up my courage and tried Philip's cell. Same thing.

Odd.

We were a wilted bunch when we piled out of the minivan in front of Richmond Towers Sunday evening. I sent Paul over to the park with Dandy on a leash and asked P.J. to get a luggage cart from the weekend doorman while I helped my mother out of the car. P.J. was back in five minutes, holding the nonrevolving door open for Mr. Bentley, pushing a luggage cart.

"Mr. Bentley!" I was so happy to see him, I threw decorum to the wind and gave him a big hug. "What are you doing working on Sunday? I thought the door-dude—"

Mr. Bentley burst out laughing. "The 'door-dude,' as you so aptly call him, got himself fired. I have to fill in until they hire his replacement. And who is this lovely lady?" He tipped his head in a little bow toward my mother, who stood beside the car trying to juggle her sweater, pocketbook, a plastic bag of car trash, and a magazine.

"Oh . . . This is my mother, Martha Shepherd, from North Dakota. Mom, this is Mr. Bentley. He's the doorman here at Richmond Towers, and also a good friend."

Mr. Bentley doffed his cap. "I'm very pleased to meet you, ma'am—"

A happy bark, followed by a breathless Paul, announced the rest of our crew. "And, uh, this is Dandy, my mom's doggy companion," I finished. The little yellow mutt danced and turned circles in front of my mother until he got his rump scratched and a pat on the head, then Dandy bounced over to Mr. Bentley and sniffed his shoes.

"I see. You've multiplied." Mr. Bentley replaced his cap and glanced at me with a twinkle. "Are you expected?"

I flushed. I knew what it must look like, Gabby Fairbanks bringing home more strays. *Mr. Bentley knows me all too well.* "Uh, I hope so. It was kind of a last-minute thing. I left a message . . ."

"Mm. A message." Mr. Bentley helped P.J. lift bags out of the rear of the minivan and pile them on the cart. Then he straightened. "Would you like me to call upstairs and tell Mr. Fairbanks you've arrived?"

My brain *cha-chinged* in light speed. Appear en masse at the penthouse front door . . . or have Philip meet us down here in public? "Uh, that would be great. Thanks, Mr. Bentley. We can load the rest of the bags."

The boys wanted to go right up, but I made them pick up all the trash in the car, brush out all the crumbs as best they could, and then wait with their grandmother while I parked the rental in a "Visitor" space until Enterprise could pick it up. When we finally pushed the luggage cart into the lobby, Mr. Bentley shrugged. "No answer upstairs."

A funny feeling prickled the back of my neck. Should I be worried?

We were sitting around the dining room table an hour later, passing around the makings for tacos, when I heard the front door open and close, then a bag being dropped in the gallery, and Philip appeared in the doorway. Tan. A stray wisp of dark hair falling over his forehead. Sunglasses. Open-necked silver-and-black silk shirt. Gray slacks. As if he'd just stepped out of *GQ* magazine.

"Dad!" Paul screeched, jumping up from the table and throwing himself on his father. Dandy immediately came to life, barking at this stranger.

"Dandy! You hush," my mom said. "Come here, boy. Lie down." Dandy obeyed, still rumbling throaty little growls.

I saw Philip's face twitch, but he hugged Paul and then walked over to P.J. and rumpled his dark hair. "Hey, guys. Good to have you home. Save any of those tacos for me?" He pulled out a chair by the empty plate and sat down, removed his sunglasses, and stuck them in his shirt pocket.

My husband did not look at me. But he nodded at my mother. "Mom Shepherd. You're looking well."

"And you." My mom gave him a smile. Then she stage-whispered to me, "You have a very handsome husband, Gabrielle."

I flushed, my eyes hot, afraid I was going to cry. But I smiled. "You bet." I forced myself to look right at Philip. "Hi, honey. Looks like we beat you home. I've been trying to call—"

"I got your message." His voice was even. Emotionless. "Tried to call your cell."

I grimaced. "Sorry about that. The battery died, and I forgot the charger." I forced brightness into my voice. "The boys are excited about sailing camp tomorrow. Couldn't wait to get home."

"Yeah, Dad!" Now even P.J. jumped in. "What kind of boats do we get to sail?"

Philip disappeared into the den after supper. I put clean sheets on P.J.'s bed and got my mom bedded down after promising to take Dandy out one last time. P.J. was still bent out of shape that he had to give up *his* bedroom, and I heard the boys squabbling over who was going to sleep in which bunk. Well, it'd take a few days to work out the kinks . . . maybe I could rearrange Paul's room so P.J. could have space for some of his own stuff . . . plus Mom would need a couple of drawers for her clothes and personal things . . .

On the way out of the house with Dandy, I saw Philip's leather overnight bag still sitting in the gallery. *Huh.* He had some explaining to do too.

It felt weird to take Dandy down the elevator and across the frontage road for his last "outing" in the dark. I saw a couple other Richmond Tower residents out with their dogs. A pit bull. A Pekinese with a bow in its hair. Come to think of it, most of the dogs I'd seen at Richmond Towers were actual breeds. Not another mutt in sight. But as far as I was concerned, Dandy was cuter than any of them. I wasn't sure how he related to other dogs, so I kept him on a tight leash and didn't venture far into the park, even though the night was mild. How did people do this in the dead of winter? Or in the rain?

Back in the penthouse, I put Dandy into P.J.'s room. The dog sniffed at my mom, then curled up on his rug beside the bed. "Good dog," I whispered and closed the door.

The light was still on in the den. Might as well face the music. I tapped on the door and peeked inside. Philip was at the computer, his back to me. I went inside, closed the door, and leaned against it. "Hi."

Thirty seconds went by. Then Philip slowly turned around in his swivel chair and leaned back. The desk lamp outlined his striking features with light and shadow. More seconds went by as he looked at me. Finally he said, "Just tell me, Gabby . . . Do you get a kick out of turning our household upside down? No warning, just showing up here with your mother. And the *dog* too! Good grief! What were you thinking?"

I held on to the doorknob behind me. "I didn't plan it this way, Philip. But when we got to Minot, it was obvious my mom shouldn't be living alone any longer. She—"

"That's what retirement homes are for."

"She's on a waiting list, Philip."

"What about your Aunt Grace, or Mercy . . . whatever. She lives right in town."

I shook my head. "I asked. She works full-time—"

"Like you don't?" His voice was hard.

"She doesn't have a spare bedroom, either. She lives in a—"

"And you think we do?"

I counted to five. "Look. Will you let me finish? I spent most of the week trying to line up in-home care for Mom—*something* to fill in the blanks until her name comes up for assisted living. But it wasn't like I had two or three weeks! I only took a week off, and I had to get the boys back here in time to start sailing camp. And then Friday morning she tripped and hit her head—"

"How long?"

"How long what?"

"Until her name comes up on the list for assisted living."

"Ah . . . maybe only three mon—"

"Months?! *Three months!*" Philip vaulted out of his desk chair. I flinched. But he just threw up his arms. "Uh-uh. No! There is *no way* this penthouse is designed to be a mother-in-law apartment!" He stopped and jabbed a finger at me. "You know what the trouble with you is, Gabby? You just up and do whatever you want to do without considering anyone else. You go off half-cocked to see a homeless bag lady and end up with a job. You pine for the boys to come here, then leave them alone to get in trouble. You say you're going to Minot for a visit, then you bring your mother *and* her mutt here, without even discussing it with me."

I pressed my lips together. He flopped into the chair again, one elbow on the armrest, rubbing his chin. After a few moments, I spoke. "I left you three messages—two here at home, one on your cell. Where were you this weekend?"

His face darkened. "What does that have to do with anything? Did you expect me to sit around babysitting the phone all weekend?"

"But I couldn't get hold of you."

"I wasn't *here*, Gabby. The Fenchels invited me to spend the weekend with them."

"At the casino again, no doubt." It was a stab in the dark. But I could tell by the way his eyes twitched that I'd hit the bull's-eye.

"And the problem with that is . . . ?"

"It's *gambling*, Philip. Is that what we're working for, to throw our money away like that?"

He started to laugh, a mirthless sound that was more like a sneer. "Good job, Gabby. Turn this around, make me the bad guy, just because I got to relax this weekend after putting in sixty hours at the office. But let's get down to the bottom line. Tomorrow morning. I go to work. The boys go to camp. You'll probably waltz off to work. So . . . just what are your plans for your mother—who, according to you, can't stay alone? Drag her to the shelter with you? They'll love that for sure."

"Exactly. For a start."

Philip rolled his eyes. "Of *course*. That's your plan. Well, get this, Gabrielle Fairbanks." He stood up abruptly and stabbed his finger at me again, making shadows on the wall that pierced the dim light. "You have one week to find another place for your mother and her mutt. *One week*. Or she goes back to North Dakota."

chapter 38

We spent the night with our backs turned to one another. I woke up at two and couldn't get back to sleep. Sliding out of bed and pulling on my robe and slippers, I felt around in my backpack for my Bible and tiptoed toward the living room, hoping I wouldn't wake up the dog. I hadn't kept up with my Bible reading the past two days, and I doubted the morning would be conducive, getting everyone up and out the door. On the way, I heated a mug of milk in the microwave, doctored it with honey, then curled up on the couch with just one lamp on.

So quiet. Peaceful.

Unlike the knot in my spirit.

I had to do something to get my mind off that disastrous conversation with Philip the night before. Even though I was only half-awake, I found my bookmark at chapter eleven of Matthew's gospel, and plodded through the verses—until suddenly three words leaped off the page. *"Come to Me . . ."*

There it was! That *was* God talking to me, after all. I feasted on the verses at the end of the chapter. *"Come to Me, all you who are weary and burdened, and I will give you rest. Take My yoke upon you and learn from Me, for I am gentle and humble in heart, and you will find rest for your souls. For My yoke is easy and My burden is light."*

A yoke. I knew enough about farm animals to know that a yoke was a wooden frame that harnessed two oxen together so they could pull a load. I read the verses again and again, wanting so much to know what they meant. But all I knew for sure was that I fit the description of someone who was "weary and burdened." *Oh, God. I am so tired. Tired of the tension between Philip and me. Tired of trying to keep the peace. Tired of trying to live up to Philip's expectations.* And now, a big load on my shoulders. My mom needed care—but what? It felt like it was all up to me. And Philip had given me *one week* to figure it out?

I turned out the light and pulled an afghan over me right there on the couch. *God, I sure could use some of that rest . . .* And I fell asleep, dreaming that a voice kept whispering in my ear, *"Come to Me."*

Philip took the boys to Burnham Harbor for the Youth Sailing Camp on his way to work the next morning, but he asked me to pick them up at four. "Call Enterprise and tell them we need the minivan for another week. Maybe we'll lease a second car for the rest of the summer so you can cart the boys around."

Philip's announcement both surprised and pleased me. I didn't mind taking the El to work, but we really did need a second car now that the boys were here. And if he was willing to take the boys to camp in the morning, I could work with that. Now all I needed to do was figure out what to do with my mother.

"Mom, would you like to see where I work? I plan activities at a shelter for homeless women. I know the staff would love to meet you—no, no, Mom. You already took your meds today. Those are for tomorrow, see? It has a *T* for Tuesday."

"Oh." She stared at the pillbox. "Would we be gone all day?"

"Well, yeah, pretty much." Especially by the time I picked up the boys.

She shook her head. "I can't. I need to stay with Dandy. I wouldn't want to leave him in a strange place all by himself."

She had a point. Could Dandy hold it all day? Would he get frustrated and chew up the furniture? But there was no way I was going to leave my mother alone all day either. Which is why the three of us ended up in the rental, heading down Sheridan Road toward Manna House, while I tried to devise some kind of brilliant excuse for showing up at work with a dog. *He's a therapy dog . . . I'm thinking of having a class in pet care . . . a watchdog would be a good idea for a women's shelter . . .*

In the end, I did what I always did—threw myself on Mabel Turner's mercy. We showed up in the foyer of Manna House and I introduced my mother to Angela in the reception cubby, while making soothing noises to Dandy.

"Oh, what a sweet dog!" Angela came out of the cubby and bent down, letting Dandy lick her face. Instant friends. The Asian-American girl stood up. "And how nice to meet you, Mrs. Shepherd. Gabby keeps things interesting around here." She laughed.

I could have kissed her. A perfect welcome.

Mabel heard the commotion and came out of her office. She looked professional as always—black slacks, tangerine short-sleeved sweater that brought out highlights in her warm, brown skin. Her eyebrows went up at the sight of the dog, but I hastily introduced her to my mother and then said, "We, uh, have a situation. I'll explain later. But for right now, can I keep Dandy down in my office?"

Mabel gave a slight roll of her eyes but waved us off with a tolerant smile. The woman had the patience of Job—though I figured she'd used half of it up just on me in the past two months. So far, so good. I'd park Mom in the multipurpose room, take Dandy down to my office, and—

What I hadn't figured on was the terrified screech that met us when we walked into the multipurpose room. "Eeek! Get that dog out of here! I'm scared of dogs!" A heavy-chested black woman I'd never met before jumped up, grabbed the nearest person, who happened to be Carolyn, and hid behind her, still yelling, "Go 'way! Go 'way!"

I don't know who was more upset—the new resident, my mother, or Dandy. I expected Mabel to come bursting in any second and order us out.

"Oh, gimme a break, Sheila." Carolyn untangled herself from the woman's grip and came over to us, bending down and stroking Dandy's head. "Atta boy. Good dog." She called over her shoulder, "See? This dog's a sweetie pie. What's his name?"

Carolyn, bless every hair in her ponytail, chatted with my mom and glared at Sheila every time the woman started to freak out again. We finally made it downstairs, where I shut Dandy into my office, got two cups of coffee—black for my mom, cream for me—and tried to wrap my mind around catching up on the activity program after a week away while I had a dog underfoot, a list of senior facilities to call, and two boys I was supposed to pick up at four o'clock at Burnham Harbor, wherever that was.

As it turned out, Burnham Harbor was a straight shot down Lake Shore Drive, just beyond Soldier Field, the Chicago Bear's "remodeled" football stadium. I snickered when my mom murmured, "Oh my. Looks like a flying saucer landed on top of a Roman coliseum," because that's exactly what it looked like. But at least there was no way I could miss my turnoff, and I managed to get to the harbor at ten after four.

The boys bragged all the way home about their new "expertise" handling a two-man 420 sailing dinghy. "And then we get to try a one-man Pico all by ourselves!" Paul was excited that Dandy had come along to pick them up, and immediately took the dog to the park for a good run when we got back to Richmond Towers.

I'd had a good long talk with Mabel before I left work, trying to bring her up-to-date on my latest crisis. She gave me her blessing to bring my mom to work that week and make calls to various senior facilities. I needn't have worried about entertaining my mom. She seemed content to read or watch television or just sit, playing audience to the comings and goings at the shelter— much like many of the residents did between their case management meetings and trips to public aid. That is, until Carolyn the game-meister discovered that "Gramma Shep," as the younger residents soon dubbed her, liked to play Scrabble and old card games, like Rook. My mom started to look forward to "going to work" each day.

As for the dog . . . I really needed to find another solution. So far we'd had no major problems at home except for an excess of dog hair and Dandy's tendency to growl when Philip first got home. But the dog was developing a real attachment to Paul. I even discovered Dandy on Paul's bed one night when Mom's door wasn't tightly closed.

On Wednesday, the dining area outside my office clucked like a henhouse since the nurse was there. I put my mom's name on the list and kept my office door cracked to hear when her name was called. Dandy kept wanting to nose the door open to check out all the excitement, but I finally got him to lie down and stay under my desk.

Estelle had a regular knitting club going with several of the women as they waited for their turn with the nurse. My mom's eyes glittered, and she ended up helping two or three of the residents untangle the messes they made and pick up their stitches. But she was surprised when Delores Enriquez called out, "Martha Shepherd? You are next."

I shut the door on Dandy and went behind the makeshift privacy booth with my mom, watching as Mrs. Enriquez gently did a brief workup—heart, breathing, reflexes, weight and height, eyes, organs. "You seem in good health, Señora Shepherd." The sweet-faced nurse smiled encouragingly. "But your daughter says you had a fall last week?"

"Oh, that." Mom seemed embarrassed. "It was nothing. Dandy didn't mean to."

Mrs. Enriquez eyed me curiously.

I nodded. "The dog was in the way, and Mom fell backward, hitting her head."

"Mm. Probably should have had her checked out, but—"

"Hey!" a familiar voice croaked on the other side of the privacy divider. "What does a lady gotta do to see the nurse around here?"

I didn't have to peek to know who it was, but I did just the same, and grinned.

Lucy Tucker, purple knit hat and all. And wet. It must be raining.

"That lady with the purple hat is interesting."

"What?" I'd been thinking about the calls I'd made that day as we drove down Lake Shore Drive, windshield wipers on, to pick up the boys. All the retirement homes had waiting lists. Huh, big surprise. I did have a couple of good leads for in-home care, as well as elder day care—*if* Philip would back off his one-week ultimatum. Big *if*.

"That lady with the purple hat is interesting," she repeated.

"You mean Lucy?"

"Yes. Her real name is Lucinda. Isn't that a pretty name? She ran off with a boy when she was only sixteen because she got tired of moving from place to place every few months. I think they were migrant farm workers back in the thirties and forties. But she said Romeo—isn't that funny? That's what she called him, 'Romeo'—dumped her when they got to Chicago. Never did find her family again, poor soul."

I stared in astonishment at my mom as we pulled up to the clubhouse at Burnham Harbor. How did my mom know this? She'd only met Lucy this morning, yet she knew more about my favorite bag lady than I'd managed to discover in two months!

I wanted to ask if Lucy said anything about how she ended up on the street, but just then P.J. and Paul jumped into the minivan, grousing about not being able to go out on the boats because of the rain. They'd spent the day tying sailors' knots, learning how to pack sails, and touring some of the big yachts moored at the harbor. Don't know what they were complaining about. A day at the docks sounded like fun to me.

Fortunately for the boys, the sun was out again the next day . . . but I was surprised to see Lucy still at the shelter. "Why shouldn't I stick around, Fuzz Top? *Somebody* 'round here needs ta spend time with your mother, her bein' a guest an' all. Respect your elders, ya know? Come on, Martha, we can watch us some TV."

I kept a straight face. Respect your elders? If I figured right, Lucy was at least five years older than my mom, maybe more. I peeked into the TV room an hour later, and the two of them were trying to outguess each other how the TV judge was going to rule in one of those civil courtroom shows. Correction: *uncivil*, by the tone of the plaintiff.

That day was the warmest we'd had so far, mid-eighties. Too nice to be inside all day. I let the boys take Dandy *and* their grandmother for a walk in the park before supper, as long as they took my cell phone and promised to call if Grandma got too tired.

I was just about to call them to say supper was almost ready when the front door opened. "P.J.? Paul? That you?"

Philip appeared in the kitchen door, loosening his tie. "No, it's me. Where are the boys?"

"Out in the park with my mom and the dog. I was just going to call—"

"Don't." My husband parked his briefcase on the counter. "We need to talk. It's not that easy, you know, with a houseful of other ears."

"O-kay." I turned off the stove under the pan of pasta water and leaned against a counter. I had a feeling what was coming.

Philip sat on one of the counter stools. "So . . . have you found a retirement home for your mom?"

I felt like rolling my eyes. "You have to know they all have waiting lists. But I did find some good possibilities for in-home care—or, if we want, elder day care. I could drop her off every morning and pick her up after work. Really, Philip, she's coming up on the list back in Minot. All we have to do is fill in a few months until her name—"

"No!" He got up and paced. "You said it might be three months. *Might.* I know how that goes. Three if we're lucky, but probably six or eight or, who knows." He stopped pacing and threw an arm wide. "Have you *looked* at this penthouse lately, Gabrielle? Dandy underfoot. Dog hair on the couch. More bickering because the boys have to bunk up when all could be solved if they had their own rooms again. And coming home to peace and quiet? Forget it. Everywhere I turn, there's a warm body! Dog on the couch. Your mom watching some lame rerun on the plasma when I want to relax and watch TV." He sat down again on the stool. "No. She's got to go back."

"Go back to what? She still shouldn't be alone. She's had two falls, Philip!"

"I don't know. Get her a live-in companion. Whatever."

"And how am I supposed to do that from Chicago? I'm already taking time from work to make calls. My boss has been very patient."

"So *quit* the job already, Gabrielle. How many times do I have to tell you?"

I could feel my spine stiffening. "Why? According to *you*, my mom has to be out of here *this week*. The boys are perfectly happy at sailing camp for the next month. What am I supposed to—"

He snorted. "That's just it. They're not."

I blinked. "They're not what? Not happy?"

"Not going to sailing camp next week." Philip's jaw muscles tightened. "Some goofball got our application mixed up and put the boys down for only a one-week camp. Now they tell me the four-week camp is filled. There's not another one until late July."

I stared at him, speechless. Finally I licked my lips. "And you were going to tell me this when?"

"I'm telling you now. Good grief, Gabby. I just found out this morning."

I felt like I was gasping for breath. "But . . . I can't quit work just like that. I'd need to at least give two weeks' notice, find people to cover my responsibilities, give them time to find someone else."

"Oh. Well, then"—his tone was sarcastic—"maybe I'll just have to send the boys back to Virginia where there *is* someone who wants to take care of them."

chapter 39

As I lay awake in bed that night, I kept telling myself Philip didn't really mean it. Sometimes he threatened stuff just to bully his point. But the news about sailing camp was a huge blow. *Humph.* Was it really some administrative "goofball" who messed up? Maybe Philip had filled out the wrong application and didn't want to admit it.

Does it matter, Gabby? Whatever happened, come Monday, the boys had no activities scheduled. Not to mention I was under the gun to find a place for my mom, or send her back to North Dakota . . . no, I couldn't just send her. I'd have to take her. *Oh God,* I groaned. *What am I going to do?* I felt as if walls were closing in on me, pressing in, no windows, no light, and I only had a fraction of airspace left . . .

In the bright light of day, as Mom and I drove to Manna House the next morning with Dandy sitting in the backseat, pressing his nose to the two-inch window opening, I realized I only had one choice. I would have to quit my job—or at least take several weeks off, maybe even the whole summer, until I got my family stuff squared away. Would Mabel hold my job for me? They'd been looking for a program director when I fell into the job. If I took off too much time, they might have to get someone else.

For some reason, the thought of not returning to Manna House was almost a physical pain, like a stab wound to my gut. *Get a grip, Gabby. It's just a job.* I blinked away the tears before I ended up blubbering in front of my mom. *Just do it, Gabby. Sit down with Mabel and tell her what you have to do. See what she says.*

Except . . . Mabel wasn't in. Again. "What?" I said to Angela at the front desk. "But I have to talk to her! Today!"

Angela shrugged, her black silken mane falling over one shoulder. "Sorry, Gabby. She's at the hospital. Something about her nephew."

"Her nephew?" I'd almost forgotten about the boy she was raising. She called him C.J., or something like that. "Was he in an accident?"

Angela shrugged again. "She didn't say. Just said she wouldn't be in today and couldn't use her cell at the hospital."

Oh, great. Now what was I going to do? Philip was in no frame of mind for me to tell him I couldn't quit because my boss wasn't in. But I couldn't just not show up next week without talking to Mabel first! How unprofessional was that?

"*Hola*, Gramma Shep! You too, Dandy dog." Aida Menéndez hopped off a chair as we came into the multipurpose room and gave my mother a hug. "Would you like some coffee? Black, right?"

My mother beamed.

"There she is!" hollered Lucy. "Carolyn's been buggin' the daylights outta me to play her some Scrabble, but them word games ain't my thing. C'mon over here, Miz Martha, and take her down a peg or two."

In spite of feeling like my life was spinning out of control, I had to laugh. You'd think my mother was a regular fixture at Manna House, the way the residents had taken her under their wing. And Lucy, of all people! Here it was, hiking into the nineties today, and Miss Disappearing Act was still hanging around the shelter. *Thank You, God. That's all I can say . . . thank You.*

Estelle was banging around the kitchen, already working on lunch, when I came downstairs. I tried to sneak into my office with Dandy without her seeing me, but no sooner had I shut the door and got Dandy settled than it opened again, and Estelle stuck her head in. "I know when I'm being avoided. What's goin' on, girl?"

I shook my head, but all that did was slosh out the tears that I'd been holding back for the past twelve hours, and the next thing I knew, I was bawling into Estelle's broad bosom, her warm, brown arms around my shaking shoulders. When I finally got hold of myself, I told her about the catch-22 I was in. ". . . And even if I—*hic*—quit my job here," I added, "I still don't know how I'm going to take care of the—*hic*—boys *and* take my mom back to North Dakota. I mean, it might take me a week or more back there to line up the care she needs until her—*hic*—name comes up on the list for assisted living."

"*Mm-mm-mm.*" Estelle brushed my hair back off my damp face, tucking a misbehaving curl behind my ear. "Now listen, Gabby Fairbanks. I don't believe God brought you this far to leave you now. He's gonna make a way, just you wait an' see. *Mm-hm.* But I sure would like to give that man o' yours a piece o' my mind. Or . . ." She started to chuckle. "Maybe I oughta sic Harry on him. Now, *there's* a man."

I sniffled and blew my nose. "Harry? Who's Harry?"

I could swear Estelle blushed, though it was hard to tell under her creamy brown skin. "You know. Harry Bentley. The doorman at your place who—"

My mouth dropped open—and then I started to laugh. "His name is Harry? *Bald* Mr. Bentley's first name is *Harry?*" My shoulders started shaking again, but this time it was laughter draining all the tension from my body. And before I knew it, Estelle was laughing too, laughing so hard *she* had to wipe away the tears.

I was glad I'd spilled my guts to Estelle and got that out of the way. By the time Edesa Baxter came flying in the door to teach her Friday morning Bible study, her hair enveloped in a multicolored head wrap and Gracie riding in a sling made from a long length of cloth on her hip, I was able to give her a warm hug without falling apart. But I felt a pang as I held out my arms to the baby. Would this be the last time I'd see Edesa and Gracie for a while?

"Where has your mama been keeping you all week, *chica?*" I said, smooching Gracie's cheek and neck until she squealed with laughter. I turned to Edesa. "I haven't seen you, 'Desa, since I got back from North Dakota. Did you finally have the hearing while I was gone? What happened?"

Edesa nodded, her expression tentative. "*Sí.* Mabel Turner and Reverend Handley both came to the hearing to testify about the note Carmelita left me before she died." Strain crept into her voice. "The honcho's DNA test came back positive, though. As far as they know, he *is* Gracie's father. The caseworker at DCFS tried to encourage us. He's on parole and has no income right now, though the judge gave him a month to get his life together, and then she'll make a ruling." She swallowed. "But we are still praying. We . . . have to trust God."

"Oh, Edesa. I will keep praying too." I wrapped my arms around her and gave her a long hug. Then . . . "Hey, come on. There's someone I want you to meet. The residents have dubbed her Gramma Shep, can you believe it?"

I left my mom in Edesa's Bible study but didn't stay, and I didn't offer to look after Gracie either. I had too much to do. I tried Mabel's cell several times that day, but only got her voice mail. I didn't leave a detailed message, just asked her to call me at her earliest convenience, even on the weekend. I still had a few leads to call about my mom—one was like a "group home" for senior adults, only five other residents, and yes, they had an opening for one more. My heart beat faster. Was this our answer?

I made an appointment for tomorrow—Saturday—at eleven o'clock.

At the end of the day, I didn't say good-bye to anyone. I couldn't tell others I was resigning before I had even told Mabel. I would just have to come in on Monday. Philip would have to grant me that much, especially when he saw I had decided to resign. And to be honest, I still needed a couple of days to leave the program—such as it was so far—in good shape for someone else to pick up.

I was surprised, however, when I picked up the boys and they talked as if they were going back to sailing camp next week. Didn't Philip say anything to them? Well, I wasn't the one who was going to break the news to them . . . and I told Philip as much when he got home that evening.

"Don't break into a sweat, Gabby." Philip actually seemed in a good mood. "I've got a surprise for the boys that ought to make up for sailing camp. I was telling Lester Stone about the boys learning how to sail, and he invited me and the boys on a two-day sail this weekend—perfect for Father's Day, eh? He said they'd learn more in two days of sailing his yacht than in four weeks on a dinghy."

I flinched. P.J. and Paul on a sailboat all weekend? "But what about the weather? Isn't it supposed to rain this weekend?"

"Don't worry about it! You know Chicago weather—a thunderstorm rolls through, and then the sun comes out. Besides, Lester says if the lake gets too choppy, we'll just pull into the nearest harbor."

I wasn't convinced, but told him I had news too—a group home that might work out for my mom. "And I've decided you're right. I need to resign from my job, or at least take an extended leave. But I couldn't put in my resignation today. My boss had an emergency and was out of the office. I'll have to go back at least one or two days next week to finish up."

Philip narrowed his eyes. "And what's supposed to happen those days? You always do this, Gabby! Take a simple request and bend it like a pretzel to go your way."

"I'm trying, Philip! It's *not* a simple request, and I'm doing my best!"

"Yeah?" He snorted. "Well, as usual, your best just isn't good enough, Gabrielle."

I was so glad Philip and the boys left early the next morning for their sailing date with Lester Stone. Philip's words had stung, and I really needed some time to get my head together. Or my heart.

Mom was still asleep, so I took Dandy out and then got another cup of coffee and curled up on the couch with my Bible. Hadn't cracked it even once in the past week . . . where was I? Dandy jumped up and rested his head in my lap. I found my place at chapter twelve and started reading. Good grief, Jesus really lit into the religious leaders who kept finding fault with Him, calling them a "brood of snakes." I laughed out loud. I'd have to remember that next time Philip criticized me. I mean, if Jesus could do it . . .

As I read further, Jesus said He couldn't expect anything else from them. Their hearts were evil. And, He said, the stuff that comes out of our mouths reflects what's in our hearts. I thought about that. I didn't think Philip was evil. Maybe that's why I felt devastated when he said hurtful things—I kept expecting him to be good. That's all I wanted, just to love my husband and be loved back, to be a family.

Which is why I teared up at the end of the chapter when Jesus' family interrupted what He was doing and wanted Him to come with them. Jesus basically said, "Who is my family? The people who love God and serve Him—that's my family."

I closed the Bible and hugged it to my chest. Dandy snuggled closer now that there was more room on my lap. I remembered that scripture from my Sunday school days. I always thought Jesus' reply was kind of rude. But it made more sense to me now.

"Oh, God," I moaned. "I don't want to have to choose between my husband and kids and the new family You've been giving to me!" But I knew which "family" had been feeding my spirit and bringing me closer to God.

chapter 40

Mom took forever to sort out her various meds and vitamins into the seven-day pillbox, but at least I still had the rental car, so we made it to our appointment on time. This time I left Dandy behind. We weren't going to be gone that long.

The "group home" was a Victorian three-story in Rogers Park, with a wraparound porch, wedged between two six-flats. The whole neighborhood was oddly incongruent—older, once-noble homes in various stages of upkeep left standing here and there as apartment buildings crowded in.

The houseparents seemed nice, a white couple in their mid-fifties, and the home was pleasant enough. Three meals a day and housekeeping. A social worker came once a week to assess needs and arrange transportation to medical appointments. But I was perturbed to learn that the other five residents were all men. "We'd be happy to accommodate your mother if she'd feel comfortable here," the husband said.

"What about Dandy?" Mom said. "My dog."

"I'm sorry." The woman smiled. "No pets."

I should have seen that coming. "Mom, any retirement home we find will have the same rule. Maybe"—I went out on a limb—"we can take care of Dandy for a while."

But my mom was still shaking her head. "No. I would be the only woman. That wouldn't feel right."

"Mom," I said, lowering my voice. "It's only for a few months. Then we can take you back to Minot when your name comes up on the list for the home there!"

"A few months?" The male supervisor shook his head. "I'm sorry. We require at least a twelve-month contract—which, of course, is void if the guest, um, passes before that time. We try to keep our guest list as stable as possible. Turnover is always an adjustment in a home this small."

My mind scrambled. Should I sign up anyway? This was the only choice I had! But if Mom's name came up back in Minot in three, or even six months, she might lose her place there if we didn't take it right away. And if we took her back there when her name came up, we'd be stuck having to pay the unused months here!

"Uh, thank you so much." I stood up. "We need to think about this a bit more."

But I hit the steering wheel in frustration when we got back in the car.

"I'm sorry, Gabby." My mom's lip trembled. "Why can't I just stay with you?"

"Oh, Mom . . ." How could I explain? "I wish you could." But the wistfulness in my mother's voice wrenched my heart. We were both in danger of losing it. "Hey. I've got an idea." I'd seen a Supercuts near the El stop where I got on the train. "Let's stop by the beauty shop and get your hair done. What do you say?"

As we headed down Sheridan Road, it suddenly occurred to me that my mom hadn't called me by the wrong name for a whole week. Maybe consistent presence and regular interaction helped her memory.

The answering machine was blinking when we finally got back to the penthouse around two o'clock. "Let me check this, and then I'll make some lunch!" I called out to my mom, who was laughing at Dandy's excited welcome-home dance in the gallery.

"Do you like my new hairdo, Dandy?" I heard her say. "You think it's too short?"

I punched the Play button. *"You have one new message"* . . . *"Gabby? Are you there? It's me, Henry. I just got off the phone with Bill Robinson, and we've got a problem. I know Philip's out on the boat with Lester Stone, but I really need to get him on a three-way with Robinson before Monday. Do you know how to reach him? I tried his cell, but it didn't even give me his voice mail. If he calls, or if Stone has a radio or something, just tell Philip it involves the Robinson deal and to give me a call ASAP—today if possible. Thanks, Gabby."*

Oh, great! Why did Henry have to leave this in my lap? Philip had said their cell phones might be out of range, and I could contact the Coast Guard in an emergency. The boat had a ship-to-shore radio. But I didn't think the Coast Guard would think a business call was an "emergency." All I could do was—

Wait a minute. I listened. The house was too quiet. "Mom? Dandy?" A quick look through the house confirmed my suspicion. Mom must have taken the dog down the elevator to do his business! I ran into the hallway and jiggled the Down button. *Oh, Mom, please don't get lost . . .*

But there she was, across the frontage road along the edge of the park, walking Dandy on his leash while the dog sniffed at bushes and lifted his leg. I laughed in relief and joined them until a light drizzle chased us inside. "My goodness!" Mom said as we rode back up the elevator to the thirty-second floor. "And I thought it was hot in North Dakota! But this humidity . . . I was already wet before the rain started."

By the time we ate our lunch, it was three o'clock, and Mom was ready for a nap. I took a peek out the windows in the front room—gray and rainy across the lake. *Oh, dear. Not the greatest day for a sail.* And then it occurred to me that I had a perfect excuse to find out how my kids were doing: Henry wanted me to contact Philip.

I grinned as I dialed Philip's cell. No one could accuse me of being an anxious mother. I had to deliver a message to my husband, right? But all I got was a funny beep. It didn't even ring. Just in case, I tried leaving a quick message for Philip to call Henry ASAP and hung up. Okay, plan B. Philip had left Lester Stone's cell number on the fridge along with the Coast Guard number. I dialed. It rang . . .

"Yeah? Stone here."

"Oh! Lester? This is Gabby Fairbanks! Sorry to bother you. I need to speak to Philip. It's business."

"Ha-ha. Knew we should've left our phones home. Your husband's a little preoccupied right now. He and the boys are trying to bring down the jib. We've got some waves here . . . Can I give him a message?"

My heart lurched a little at what "we've got some waves here" meant. But I said, "Sure! Tell him his partner, Henry, needs him to call ASAP. Something about the Bill Robinson deal."

"Hang on . . ." There was a lot of wind static in my ear, then Lester Stone came back on. "Did you say Bill Robinson?"

"Yes! But Philip should call Henry about it, not Robinson, okay?"

A slight pause. "Okay, got it. Gotta go."

I'd wanted to ask if they were going to pull into a harbor and get out of the weather, but the phone went dead. Oh, well. I delivered the message. That ought to earn me some brownie points with Philip.

I turned on the TV and kept it on the weather channel the rest of the afternoon. And tried to remember the psalm that said, *"When I am afraid, I will trust in God . . . I trust in God, why do I need to be afraid?"*

I swam up out of my dreams into consciousness the next morning, fighting off panic. Not about the boys. God had given me peace that they were going to be all right—wet, maybe, but not in danger. But I realized it was Sunday, Philip was coming home, and the only possibility I'd found for my mom had fallen through.

It was all so unfair!

I made coffee, rehearsing a speech in which I would ask Philip for more time. Begging for mercy was more like it. And I hated feeling that way.

My mom came into the kitchen dressed in a navy blue suit and a white blouse with the tag sticking out. "What time are we leaving for church, Gabby?" I started to tuck it in when I realized she had the blouse on inside out.

I put on a smile. "Uh, nine thirty. Church starts at ten." I knew my mom would expect to go to church. At work on Friday, I'd looked at the schedule and realized that SouledOut Community Church was on for Sunday Evening Praise this weekend. Of all the groups who led the weekly evening service, so far SouledOut had been my favorite. But it was likely that Philip and the boys would just be getting home from their sailing trip Sunday evening. Why not go to SouledOut in the morning? It was just Mom and me. At least we'd see some familiar faces—Josh and Edesa, Josh's parents, Avis and Peter Douglass, even Estelle!

The directions I'd gotten from Estelle took me straight up Sheridan Road to Howard, and then west about a half mile to a shopping center by the Howard Street El Station. I pulled the minivan into the parking lot at five minutes to ten.

My mother craned her neck. "I don't see any church."

I pointed to a sign on one of the large storefronts: "SouledOut Community Church." The air was still misty with leftover rain as we dodged puddles on our way across the parking lot. *Drat.* My hair would be totally frizzed by the time we got inside.

When we walked through the double glass doors into the large friendly room, however, I forgot to worry about my hair. "Mrs. Fairbanks!" Peter Douglass gripped my hand, his smile warm, his dark eyes delighted. "What a pleasure to see you here. And who is this charming lady?" The well-groomed businessman took one of my mother's pale hands in both of his brown ones. She seemed startled.

Smiling big, I introduced my mother and added, "Mr. Douglass is one of the board members at Manna House."

"Oh, that's lovely." Mom gave me a quizzical look. "What's Manna House?"

I barely had time to remind her that that was where I worked, when Josh and Edesa Baxter swooped down on us, and right on their heels, Josh's parents. Denny Baxter was carrying Gracie, his smile betraying the two large dimples in his cheeks. Edesa gave me a big hug. "Oh, *Gabriela*! I have good news! . . . Well, it's bad news in one way, but good—"

Just then the worship band launched into a song. and over the music a woman called out, "Good morning, church! Let's find our seats and begin our worship this morning with 'Shout to the Lord'!" I thought the voice sounded familiar and looked over Edesa's head. At the front of the room I saw Peter Douglass's wife, Avis, face glowing as the song began to roll: *"Shout to the Lord, all the earth, let us sing . . ."*

"Tell you later!" Edesa kissed my cheek and scampered off with Josh.

"This must be your mother!" Jodi Baxter whispered, giving my mom a warm hug. "Come sit with us." She found four seats, but everyone was standing, many arms lifting in praise as the music continued to swell . . .

". . . Nothing compares to the promise I have in You . . ."

Still trying to take it all in, my eyes swept the room. Dark faces, creamy brown, fair-skinned . . . African braids, brunettes, blondes . . . wow, what a diverse congregation. And there was Estelle, decked out in one of her roomy caftans that hid her extra pounds! I tried to catch her eye and then did a double-take as the bald African-American man next to her tilted his head and winked at me.

My mouth dropped open, and I tried not to laugh. Mr. Bentley!

By the time the service ended, I was so full, I felt like I'd just eaten a ten-course meal. The songs were a mixture of upbeat and worshipful—I really did love that saxophone wailing beneath the melody on some of them—and the sermon by one of the copastors, a tall, gangly white man with thinning hair, was punctuated by "Amens" and even an occasional, "Thank ya, Jesus!" from the congregation.

My head was in a whirl afterward as Jodi and Edesa and Estelle tried to introduce me to several women—"our Yada Yada Prayer Group sisters," they called them. Estelle's housemate was a stylish, slender blonde in a red beret she introduced as Stu. I could hardly imagine two people who looked more different. I was surprised to learn they lived upstairs in a two-flat over Josh's parents.

Edesa introduced me to the African-American family she and Josh rented their "studio" from. I'd seen Carl Hickman before—he'd come with Peter Douglass to our party at the shelter. His wife was a wiry woman named Florida. "How ya doin', Gabby?" She shook my hand in an iron grip. "We been prayin' for you at Yada Yada—'scuse me. Girl!" Florida's hand shot out and grabbed a youngster darting past. "You know better than ta be runnin' in the house of God!"

I was grateful when Jodi Baxter showed up with two cups of coffee and pulled me aside. Mr. Bentley, even without his uniform, had graciously taken my mom under his wing, keeping her company and her coffee cup refilled, so I sat down with Jodi, blowing out a big sigh. "This was quite a church service."

"Yes, praise God! I love the worship here." Jodi brushed her soft bangs back. She wore her brunette hair with its slight wave just skimming her shoulders. *Wouldn't mind hair like that for a change.* "We used to be two different churches, but we merged because God told us we needed each other . . . long story." She chuckled. "We're still in training, but we love it." Jodi cast an affectionate glance toward her son, who was holding little Gracie in one arm, the other draped around Edesa, talking to an excited knot of people. "And it's good for our kids, who don't have to give up their own culture to feel at home as a family."

I noticed Josh and Edesa seemed especially happy. "What's this bad news–good news Edesa was going to tell me?"

"She didn't tell you yet? Gracie's birth father violated his parole and landed back in prison. So his petition to take the baby got thrown out! I can still hardly believe it, after all the worry of the past few months—but God really answered our prayers."

"Oh, I'm so glad." That's what I said. But I felt a pang. *God really answered their prayers . . . why not mine?*

"Are you okay, Gabby? You look a bit strained. What's going on?"

And just like that I found myself telling Jodi Baxter my whole saga—moving, feeling adrift, finding the job at Manna House, tension with my husband, now triple complicated with needing to find a place for my mom and summer plans for the boys falling through. I shook my head. "I don't know what to do, Jodi. I was going to resign Friday, but Mabel wasn't there—"

"I know." Jodi's face clouded. "Her nephew, C.J., tried to commit suicide."

I gasped. "What?! That little boy? Oh, Jodi. I had no idea. Is he going to be OK?"

"I think so. We've been praying around the clock since we found out yesterday."

I looked at her. "Does God really answer prayer, Jodi? I've been praying and praying about my mom and about my job and about what's going wrong with me and Philip, and it seems like the only answer I got was, 'Come to Me.'"

Her hazel eyes got round. "'Come to Me?' God said to you, 'Come to Me'?"

I felt embarrassed. "Well, those are the words that popped into my brain while I was at the prayer meeting at my mom's church. It didn't seem to make a lot of sense—not exactly an answer to my prayer about Mom. But a couple of days later I was reading my Bible—I've been trying to read Matthew—and I came to those verses, you know, the ones that go, 'Come to Me, all you who are weary—'"

Smiling, Jodi chimed in. "'—and bearing a heavy burden, and I will give you rest. Take My yoke upon you and learn from Me, for I am gentle and humble in heart, and you will find rest for your souls. For My yoke is easy and My burden is light.'"

I gave her a wistful grin. "Yeah. That's the one."

Jodi Baxter took my coffee cup, set it aside, and took both my hands in hers. "Gabby, that *is* God answering your prayer! Don't you see? All these other things—your husband, your kids, even your mom—yes, they're important. And God really cares about them. But the thing God cares about most is *you*. I think . . . it sounds to me like God is calling you, Gabby. To come home."

chapter 41

"There were a lot of black people at that church, weren't there?" My mom was still watching people spill out of the doors of SouledOut as I snapped her seat belt in place.

Her comment took me by surprise, but I tried not to show it. "Mm-hm. All kinds of people. It was nice, wasn't it? Maybe that's what heaven's going to be like."

My mom nodded thoughtfully. "I didn't know there'd be so many nice people in Chicago. Mr. Bentley is very nice. And the lady named Estelle."

I pulled out of the parking lot. "We didn't have much of a chance to know many black people back home, did we?" In Petersburg, either, for that matter. Our own fault. Everybody tended to stay in their own little neighborhoods and their own churches.

"But they're not really black, are they? Brown. And all different shades too."

I felt a little impatient with Mom getting so chatty. It was nice that she was being observant, but what I really wanted was some time by myself to think about what Jodi Baxter had said—and get myself psyched up for the inevitable talk with Philip tonight. Maybe Mom would take a nap after lunch, and I'd have a few quiet hours to just think and pray before the sailors got home.

But to my surprise, the TV was on and the boys were sprawled on the wraparound couch, watching a *Pirates of the Caribbean* DVD when we got back to Richmond Towers. "Look who's here!" I gave them each a hug. "I didn't expect you back so early! The weather get too rough for sailing?"

P.J. shrugged, his eyes locked on the movie. "The weather was OK. Ask Dad. He's the one who called it."

The door to the den was closed. I hung up my coat, found the makings for tuna fish sandwiches and put my mom to work, filled the teakettle and turned on the burner . . . before tapping on the den door and sticking my head in. Philip was slumped in the leather armchair by the reading lamp.

"Hey. You guys are home early."

My husband looked up, eyes hard. "That's right. Thanks to you."

I tensed. "What do you mean?"

"Close the door."

I did but stood with my back against it, hand on the handle. *Déjà vu.*

Philip threw his hands wide. "You just cost Fairbanks and Fenchel our business with Lester Stone, that's what."

"Wha—what are you talking about?"

"The phone call to Lester? Dropping Bill Robinson's name into the conversation?"

"But Henry asked me to get a message to you! He said it was important!"

"Fine. Talk to *me*. But you don't tell my business to *anyone*, Gabrielle!" His voice was hard, clipped. "Do you understand?!"

I was totally confused. "I tried to call your cell. Henry tried too, but he couldn't get through. That's why he called me."

"Doesn't matter. You had no business talking to Lester Stone about Bill Robinson."

"But . . . I thought that was the message, so you'd know why Henry wanted you to call."

Philip pushed himself out of the chair. I flinched, but all he did was jab a finger at me. "Did Henry tell you to go through Lester? Huh? Did he?"

"Well, no, but—"

"I'm telling you! That phone call cost us our contract with Stone! And it's your fault!"

I gripped the doorknob harder. "But I didn't tell Lester anything! I just said what Henry told me, for you to call about the Bill Robinson project."

"'But I didn't tell Lester anything,'" he mocked in a high-pitched voice. "You told enough just dropping Robinson's name. Turns out Lester Stone is involved in a lawsuit with Bill Robinson, and he didn't like it one bit that Fairbanks and Fenchel are working with him. Said it was a conflict of interest for him to employ the same developer." Philip threw up his hands. "Zap. We're done. Just like that."

My heart was pounding now. "But I didn't know that! How could I—"

"You don't have to know it!" He was yelling now. "All you have to know is not to talk about my business with *anyone*! Do you understand me, Gabrielle?"

The teakettle whistled. Jerking the door open, I fled to the kitchen to silence it, catching frightened glances from the boys as I ran through the living room. I needed time to pull myself together—but I forgot my mother was still puttering in the kitchen, taking her sweet time making the tuna sandwiches. I flipped the burner off under the teakettle and kept going to my bedroom, where I flung myself on the bed.

Philip followed me, slamming the bedroom door behind him. "I'm not through with you, Gabrielle. You just don't get it, do you? Ever since we moved here, you've done everything you can think of to undermine my new business."

I sat up, hugging a pillow in front of me. "That's not true, Philip!"

"Shut up. That's the problem with you. You don't have any business savvy. You don't know what a corporate wife should be doing to help make her husband a success. You turn up your nose at Mona Fenchel's connections that would help us break into a business class social strata. You puke all over Lester Stone's sail-boat. You bring your mother and her . . . her dumb mutt here just after the boys come home for the summer, turning this pent-house into a three-generation madhouse . . ." He stopped and glared at me. "Speaking of your mother, what's the deal with the group home? When is she moving in?"

I was too scared to speak. I shook my head slightly.

"I knew it!" he yelled. "This is the last straw, Gabby! The last straw!"

Philip stomped out without saying where, and the whole house-hold felt like a graveyard the rest of that day. The boys holed up in their room. My mom shut herself and Dandy in her borrowed bedroom. Moving like a zombie, I finished the sandwiches my mom had started, set out fruit and chips on the kitchen counter, tapped on doors, told my sons and my mother they could get something to eat when they got hungry, and spent the rest of the day in my bedroom, blinds pulled, crying until I'd sucked out every drop.

Philip still wasn't back when I turned out the light at nine o'clock.

But I woke with a start when I heard Philip yell, "What the—!" followed by a string of curses. Then, "Where's that dog! Who didn't take the dog out?"

I grabbed my robe and went flying down the hall to the gallery. Philip was hopping on one canvas boat shoe, ripping off the other. A pile of dog poop had been deposited right beside the front door, now mashed and stinking where Philip had stepped in it.

"Oh no! Paul must've forgotten to take him out before bed . . . I'll—I'll get the dog and take him out now. Just give me a sec to get my clothes on."

"Just clean up this mess, Gabby," Philip said between clenched teeth. "I'm dressed. I'll take the stupid dog out. Just . . . just get my other gym shoes and take this one and clean it off."

I carried the stinking canvas boat shoe into the laundry room, got Philip's other shoes from the bedroom, then went for paper towels, a bucket, rag, and pine cleaner. When I got back to the gallery, Philip was trying to clip the leash onto Dandy's collar, who was pulling backward and growling.

"Let me do it."

"Forget it!" Dropping the leash, Philip grabbed the dog up under his arm and disappeared into the elevator. The doors closed.

I cleaned up the mess in the gallery, washed the entire marble-tiled floor with pine cleaner, and then tackled Philip's shoe. I got the poop off as best I could, then threw it into the washing machine. A half hour passed. Philip still wasn't back, so I went to bed.

I woke at three-something and realized the other side of our king bed was empty. Putting on my robe, I wandered through the dark penthouse. The gallery light, which I'd left on, was out. Philip was sacked out on the couch, snoring gently.

Well, fine. I didn't want to sleep with the big jerk anyway.

I woke the next morning, a dull headache throbbing above my eyes. I could hear the shower running in the bathroom. Philip was getting ready to go to work.

I put on my robe and dragged myself to the kitchen, feeling like Charlie Brown with a cloud of gloom over my head. I had no idea how to dig myself out of the pit I was in. I should go in to work today to drop the bomb on Mabel that I needed to take an extended leave of absence and offer to resign. Mom would prob-ably be happy to go with me. But that left the boys hanging . . .

To my surprise, the pungent smell of fresh coffee greeted me. I stared dumbly at the coffeemaker, which was dripping mer-rily. Philip had made the coffee?

A tiny ray of hope broke through the gloom cloud. Maybe Philip was over his mad. Maybe I should call Mabel, tell her I have a family emergency, take the day off, try to work out plans for the boys and my mom with Philip, and go in tomorrow to have the face-to-face talk about—

"Celeste?" My mom's voice was plaintive. "Have you seen Dandy? He wasn't beside my bed when I woke up."

I frowned. That was the first time Mom had called me by the wrong name in over a week. Had she heard the dog-poop-in-the-gallery fiasco last night? "Oh, he's probably sleeping in Paul's bed. I'll get him." I needed to take the dog out soon, anyway.

I headed for the boys' bedroom and peeked in. Both boys were still asleep. But no Dandy. Picking up my pace, I did a quick search through the main rooms and was just heading for the master bedroom when Philip appeared in the hallway, clean-shaven, tan slacks, black silk short-sleeve shirt, smelling like his Armani aftershave.

I stood in his way, arms crossed, knowing I looked like a frowzy housewife in my robe and uncombed hair. "Where's the dog?"

He looked down at me, unperturbed. "I put him out. What did you think I was going to do after he crapped all over our floor?"

"He's been out since *last night*?"

Behind me, I heard a plaintive wail and felt my mother clutch my robe. "Oh no! No, no . . . he'll get lost! Oh, Celeste, we have to find Dandy! It's too cold in Alaska!"

"You rat!" I hissed through my teeth at my husband as he calmly squeezed past us and headed for the kitchen. I pried my mother's fingers off my robe and patted her hand. "Don't worry, Mom. He's probably hanging around outside, wanting breakfast. I'll get dressed and go right down, okay?"

I pulled on jeans and a T-shirt and was heading for the elevator when Paul came running after me in shorts, pajama top, and sockless gym shoes. "Mom! What happened? Where's Dandy? Why is Grandma crying in her room?"

I tried to be matter-of-fact as the elevator door dinged open and Paul followed me in. "Your dad, uh, took Dandy out last night, and I guess the dog got away. I'm sure he won't have gone too far."

351

It seemed to take forever as the elevator stopped again and again to pick up residents leaving early for work. In the lobby, Mr. Bentley was already on duty, passing out newspapers, whistling for taxis. But I shouldered in. "Mr. Bentley? Did you see Dandy outside this morning?" I pointed toward the frontage road exit. "We . . . lost him last night."

The doorman shook his head. "Sure haven't, Mrs. Fairbanks. I'll keep an eye out and let you know soon as I do."

But Paul and I were already flying out the revolving door toward the park, and we spent the next half hour running up and down the jogging path, calling the dog's name. We even went through the underpass and out toward the beach, barely noticing the calm blue of the lake under a perfectly clear sky. We stopped joggers, described Dandy, and asked them to keep an eye out, pointing back toward the high-rise where we lived.

But no dog.

chapter 42

Paul was in tears. We walked back to Richmond Towers with my arm across his shoulders. "I know, kiddo. But we'll keep praying, okay? Maybe somebody found Dandy and took him to the animal shelter. I'll call, okay? He has a tag on."

"But it has Grandma's North Dakota phone number!"

"Well . . . but if the shelter has him, we can use it to identify him."

Back upstairs, I tried to soften the bad news. "Mom . . . Mom. Don't cry. I'm sure we'll find him. Look, I'll stay home today with you and the boys, and we'll look for Dandy and—"

"Don't you have to go to work today, Gabrielle?" Philip broke in, coffee cup in hand. "To finish things up, talk to your boss?"

I glared at him. "Yes. But I can't leave now, can I? There's the boys and—"

"Yeah. Just like I figured. Look, you just go. I've got the boys."

I gaped at him, my thoughts ricocheting. Was Philip actually going to pitch in and take care of the boys? "What do you mean? Are you going to—"

"I *said*, I've got it covered." My husband turned on his heel and disappeared into the den. Not out the door. Into the den.

Well. This was an interesting turn of events. Maybe Philip felt guilty for throwing the dog out last night. Maybe he and the boys would go look for the dog while I was gone. If Philip was willing to stay home from work and cover for the boys while I took Mom to Manna House and finished business there, maybe there was hope we could work things out bit by bit.

Mom was reluctant to leave with Dandy still missing, but on the other hand she didn't want to stay there ". . . with that mean man," she whispered to me. I hustled to get ready before Philip changed his mind. On the way out, I fished in the wooden bowl in the gallery where we kept car keys but couldn't find the keys for the rental car. I poked my head into the den. "Have you seen the keys for the minivan?"

Philip looked up, all nonchalance. "Oh. Enterprise picked it up yesterday afternoon, or maybe early this morning. I left the keys at the front desk downstairs."

I counted to three. "You could have said something."

"I did. Last week we said we'd keep the rental another week. Week's over. And you can use the El today, Gabby, since you don't have to pick up the boys at camp." He turned back to the computer.

We'd also talked about leasing a second car. But . . . so be it. I wasn't going to get bent out of shape about this. The El was fine with me, though it meant more walking and stairs for my mom.

It took longer to get to the shelter, but we finally walked in at ten o'clock. I signed in, got my mom settled in the multipurpose room with a cup of coffee, and came back to the reception cubby to ask if Mabel was in. Angela shook her head. "Not yet. But she called. She'll be in around lunch." She stood up and peered over the counter. "Where's Dandy today?"

"Don't ask."

It was hard pretending that this was a normal day. I gave a wave to Estelle as I scurried for my office, but she leaned over the kitchen counter, hairnet covering her usual topknot, apron covering her roomy dress. "I hear you the one told the board I should get paid for all the cookin' I do."

"What? Oh! Estelle!" I'd totally forgotten that the Manna House Board was supposed to meet last Saturday and consider new staff. "They offered you a job?"

"Yep." A wide grin pushed her dark eyes into half moons. "Twenty hours a week. Which means I got a few extra hours left over for them cookin' and sewin' classes you talked to me about."

"That's wonderful! I'm so glad, Estelle." I leaned across the counter and gave her a hug. *And really, really awkward,* I thought, as I escaped into my broom closet office. *Now what am I going to do?*

I booted up the computer. Well, I would type up a proposal for the cooking and sewing classes, ask Estelle to list materials needed, suggest a time slot, and turn it in to Mabel with my resignation. Estelle could probably launch those classes by herself and wouldn't need me to look over her shoulder.

But first, I needed to type up my resignation. After addressing the letter to Mabel Turner and the Manna House Board, however, my resolve faltered. *If I quit this job, I'll wither up and die.* My head sank into my hands. It wasn't just the job. It was the living faith of the staff and volunteers. I'd lost my way, but I was beginning to find it again . . . here, in this unlikely place! Here I'd felt accepted, needed, appreciated. I'd made all kinds of mistakes, and they still loved me.

What was I going to do once I walked out of those doors tonight?

I got another cup of coffee from the kitchen to steady my nerves, punched the Play button on the CD player sitting on my desk to distract my thoughts, and started typing again as gospel music filled up my little office. But I flipped it off when the Dottie Rambo song came on. *"Where do I go when there's no one else to turn to . . . ?"*

It hurt too much.

My phone rang just before lunch. It was Angela at the front desk. "Mabel's here."

I took a deep breath, folded my resignation letter and the proposal for Estelle's classes, and went upstairs. A small circle of shelter residents were clustered around my mother, and I heard Lucy mutter loudly, "What kinda lowlife would kick out yer dog?"

I slipped through the room and through the double doors. Angela looked up from the desk. "She said go right in." I took a deep breath and opened the door.

Mabel Turner's eyes had bags under them, and I suddenly remembered what she'd been through the last few days. "I . . . heard about C.J. Is he okay?"

The director nodded wearily. "He's going to be all right. Physically. But . . . I don't know. You've met him, Gabby. He gets teased a lot at school, called 'pretty boy' and 'faggot'—all the cruel things kids say. He's had a real tough time—but I didn't expect this." She sighed. "He really needs your prayers. Me too." She was quiet a long moment, then seemed to remember I was there. "Anyway, Angela said you needed to see me. What's up?"

I sat down, though I was tempted to flee. Mabel didn't need more bad news. But I had no choice. I spilled it all . . . and used up thirty minutes and a whole wad of tissues in the process.

"I'm so sorry, Mabel. I wanted to tell you Friday, to give you more warning, but I don't know what else to do." I blew my nose, sure by now that I looked a sight. "In fact, even if I resign today, I'm still in a fix. Unless I find a situation here, I'll probably have to take my mom back to North Dakota, but—"

A loud commotion suddenly erupted in the foyer, and then Mabel's door burst open. Lucy Tucker stood there, purple knit hat crammed on her grizzled head, dragging my mother in by the hand. Several other residents crowded in behind them.

"So why can't Gramma Shep stay *here*, is what I wanna know. That scumbag Gabby's married to—don't mean no offense to you, Gabby—already kicked Martha's dog out, now he's sayin' Martha can't stay. She don't wanna go back there anyway, an' she don't have nowhere else to go right now. Don't that make her homeless? Ain't this a shelter for homeless ladies? Ain't I right, girls?"

"Yeah, that's right." . . . "They's a couple beds open up-stairs." . . . "Uh-huh."

I looked in astonishment from Lucy, to my mom, then to Mabel. I practically stopped breathing. Had the answer to the dilemma about my mom been under my nose all the time?

"Oh, Mabel, if . . . if she could. Just for a few days, or maybe a few weeks, or—" What was I saying? This was my mother! I turned and looked at her. My mother had a triumphant look on her face. "Mom?"

"I like it here. They're my friends." She held up her hand, locked in Lucy's.

I went out the double oak doors into the late afternoon sun, my heart and my feet lighter than they'd felt in weeks, even though my backpack was heavy with stuff I'd cleaned out of my desk. I'd hunted high and low for the CD Josh had given me, but someone had borrowed the CD player from my office—must have had the CD still in it.

Didn't matter. I'd be back soon. Manna House was willing to give my mom shelter up to the usual limit—ninety days—as long as I was working on alternative solutions. Surely I'd find something before then, or maybe her name would come up on the assisted living list back in Minot.

I told my mom I'd be back later that night with her clothes, but just in case, Estelle rustled up the basic "kit" that was given to women just coming off the street: personal-size toiletries, new underwear, and pajamas. Estelle had even offered to stay a night or two to help get my mom settled, walk her through the routines, and make sure she took her meds, which Mom always carried in her purse, at the right times. She'd brushed off my profuse thanks. "Hey, might as well piggyback my jobs. I'm still licensed to do in-home elder care, ya know."

I had turned in my resignation letter, though Mabel said she was willing to consider it an "extended leave," depending on what happened at the Fairbanks household in the next few weeks. Just before I got ready to leave, Mom tugged on my arm. "Please look for Dandy, won't you, Gabby?" Her lip trembled a little.

I wrapped her in a hug. "Absolutely, Mom. I'm sure we'll find him." At least she'd used my right name. A good sign. "Where's Lucy? I want to say good-bye."

My mother shook her head. "I don't know. She went out. Said she had to do something. She'll come back, won't she, Gabby?"

Drat. After making that big show about my mom staying here, the least Lucy could've done was hang around! "I'm sure she will, Mom." Well, she always did—sooner or later. I would've felt better leaving my mom if her new buddy, Lucy, had been there.

Still, I felt eager to get home, impatient with how slowly the El rattled along during rush hour, loading and unloading scores of passengers at every stop. I'd tried calling home with the news, but only got voice mail. Philip and the boys were probably out doing a museum or something. Just as well. I wanted to see Philip's face when I calmly announced I'd found a place for my mom, he didn't have to worry about her staying with us anymore . . . *Where, you ask? Oh, a homeless shelter.*

The scumbag. Let him live with *that* on his conscience.

But that, and the news that I'd turned in my resignation, ought to calm things down on the home front. Give me time to focus on the boys. And find Dandy.

"Hello, Mr. Bentley!" I threw the doorman a smile. "Guess what? *Estelle*"—I winked at him—"is looking after my mother at Manna House for a while. Ought to ease things upstairs—oh, did Dandy show up?" I looked toward the glass doors that faced the frontage road and the park, hoping to see a mournful mutt tied to the bike rack outside.

"Haven't seen him, Mrs. Fairbanks. Your boys went out looking after you and the missus left this morning, but they came back empty-handed . . . and then they took off on their trip, so I kept a lookout for the dog whenever I could. Never did see him, though. Sorry."

I shrugged. "Well, thanks anyway. I'll go change my clothes and do another run through the park. Oh—the other big news. I quit my job at Manna House. Didn't want to, but I need to spend more time with the boys . . . long story."

A puzzled look crossed Mr. Bentley's face, but I really didn't want to go into detail right then. "Tell you more later, okay? Right now I've got to run." I gave him a wave, ran my card through the security door, and headed for the elevators. If Philip and the boys were still out, that would give me time to thaw something for supper and go outside to look for Dandy. Maybe make a few calls to nearby animal shelters. After all, a cute mutt like Dandy was sure to get someone's attention, and they'd see he had a collar and a tag, maybe even call the number. I should call my aunt, have her go to Mom's house and check any messages—

Ding! The elevator slowed its upward journey, and the door slid open on the thirty-second floor. I pulled my house key out, still lost in thought as I crossed the foyer, so that at first I didn't notice the pile of stuff beside the front door. I stopped in midstride. What was all this?

My mother's two suitcases were standing next to the door, bulging and presumably filled with her things. Had Philip packed her clothes already? But I hadn't called. How did he know—?

Wait. What was all this other stuff? An even larger pile of suitcases, boxes, and bags stretched on either side of the door. I opened a box and stared at the contents. Dandy's rug, bowls, dog food, and leash.

And then I saw my suitcases. The tan-and-green set my parents had given me when I finally graduated from college several years ago.

Starting to feel frantic, I opened each bag and box. My coats. My shoes. A box with all my personal stuff from our bathroom—toothbrush, deodorant, makeup . . .

I stared at the door. What was on the other side? Trembling, hardly daring to think, I stuck my key in the lock and turned.

Nothing happened. The lock didn't budge.

And then I knew.

When Philip said, "That's the last straw," he'd meant it.

My husband had thrown me out.

chapter 43

I just stood there, mouth agape, staring at my belongings stacked in the foyer. A growing fury gradually swallowed my disbelief. I pounded on the door. "Philip?" I screamed. "If you're in there, open this door right this minute!" I pounded until my fist was red, but no answer. Was he in there, pretending not to hear? "*Paul! P.J.!* Are you in there? Let me in! It's Mom, and this isn't funny!"

Silence.

I grabbed one of my clogs and threw it as hard as I could against the door. "You've gone too far this time, Philip Fairbanks!" I screamed.

My words ricocheted like echoes in the Box Canyon.

Dumping my backpack, I pressed my back against the wall next to the elevator and slid down until I was sitting on the floor, trying to catch my breath. *Think, Gabby, think! . . . Okay. Okay.* So he and the boys were still out. He wanted me to get home first, *wanted* to shock me. *Well!* If he thought I was going to sit here bawling like a baby and lick his shoes when he got home, that . . . that *snake* had another think coming. I'd sit right here and wait for the dirty rat to show up. And then he was going to get an earful, and I didn't care if the whole building heard me! He had to show up sometime. He couldn't keep the boys out all night—

Wait. My thoughts did a sudden tailspin. Mr. Bentley had said the boys had gone looking for the dog that morning, and then "took off on their trip." *What trip?* I thought he just meant some day trip around Chicago—

My mouth suddenly went dry.

Scrambling to my feet, I punched the call button for the elevator, which took forever to arrive and even longer to reach the ground floor. *No, no, no, no . . .* I burst through the security door into the lobby. Mr. Bentley was chatting amiably with one of the other building residents, but I ran up and grabbed his arm. "Mr. Bentley!" And with a wild look at the other man, "I'm sorry! It's urgent!"

The other man shrugged good-naturedly and caught the security door before it closed.

I was practically hyperventilating. "What did you mean, the boys took off on their 'trip'? *What* trip?"

Mr. Bentley gave me a strange look. "What did *I* mean? Don't you know? It just looked like they were going on a trip is all. Your man and the boys came out that security door each pulling a suitcase, you know, the kind with wheels—"

"*When?* When did they leave? Did they take a cab?"

He shook his head. "Didn't ask me to call a cab. But they came through the lobby, *mm*, maybe 'round two o'clock, and went out that door." The doorman jerked a thumb toward the frontage road exit. "Car must've been parked outside."

My heart was pounding so hard I could hardly get a good breath. *No, no, he wouldn't—!* But Philip's words a few nights ago stabbed me with vicious reality: *"Maybe I'll just have to send the boys back to Virginia . . ."*

I grabbed my purse off my shoulder, dumped the contents on the half-moon counter, and snatched up my cell phone. I had to catch them before they got on that plane! I punched Philip's speed dial . . .

"Mrs. Fairbanks. What's the matter? Are you—"

I held up my hand for silence. But even when Mr. Bentley stopped talking I couldn't hear any rings. I ran outside to the frontage road for a better signal and tried again. Still nothing. Dead.

I stared at my phone. Had he—? He had! Philip had cut off my cell phone too!

That's when I lost it. I threw the phone as hard as I could as a wail ripped from the bottom of my gut. *"No, no, no, nooo . . . !* Oh God, Oh God, he took my boys away!" I collapsed against the building, bent over, hands on my knees, sobs coming so hard I thought my lungs would turn inside out.

A few moments later I felt big hands lifting me up and pulling me into his arms. I struggled, beating my fists on Mr. Bentley's chest, but he held on, the fingers of one hand threaded through my mop of curls, holding my face to his chest, the other around my waist, holding me up until I went limp in his arms and just cried and cried and cried.

Finally spent, I pushed Mr. Bentley away and stumbled across the frontage road to the nearest park bench. *Oh God, oh God, what am I going to do?* A few minutes later, Mr. Bentley followed, handed me a bottle of water, my purse, and my cell phone, which had landed in the grass. I took a few gulps of water and then muttered dully, "He's gone. The boys too. I'm locked out. Can't get in." I lifted raw eyes to the kind, brown face. "You don't happen to have a master key or something?"

Mr. Bentley nodded slowly. "But don't get your hopes raised. A service guy came in this morning, said he had an appointment with Mr. Fairbanks. I didn't think anything of it, just called the penthouse and your husband buzzed him in. Honey, if your key doesn't work, I don't think mine will either. But come on . . . come on now. Let's check it out."

Reluctantly, I let Mr. Bentley lead me by the hand back into Richmond Towers and up to the thirty-second floor. Neither one of us spoke. I was embarrassed for him to see all the suitcases, bags, and boxes—the shreds of my life—piled up against the wall of the foyer. One lone clog lay on the sparkling ceramic tile floor where I'd bounced it off the door.

The doorman pulled out his master ring and tried several keys. None of them worked. He surveyed the piles, absently scratching the grizzled gray beard along his jaw line. "What are you going to do?"

"I—I don't know. I need to think."

"Well, come on now. Come down to the lobby and sit. You can have my chair at the desk."

"No, no . . . you go on." I grabbed both sides of my head. "I need to think!"

"You sure?"

I nodded. "Please. Just . . . leave me alone."

When the elevator door closed behind him, the suitcases and piles of bags and boxes began to taunt me. I paced back and forth, unable to stay still. *Did the boys see Philip bagging my stuff and tossing it out here? . . . What did they think? . . . Did they try to stop him? . . . What lies did he tell them? . . . Why didn't they call me to say good-bye? . . . Are they on a plane heading for Virginia? . . . Do they think I have abandoned them?*

I had to get out of there! Frantically, I pushed the elevator button. On the way down, the elevator stopped at three other floors and people got on. But I turned away, my back rigid, willing no one to speak to me—or I might lose it again right there in the elevator. On the ground floor, I managed to slip through the lobby and out the revolving door without Mr. Bentley seeing me, then walked in a daze across the frontage road to the park and along the jogging path until I found an empty bench out of sight of Richmond Towers. I sank into it . . .

Joggers ran past, plugged into their iPods.

The evening air was sweet, still warm after washing Chicago with sunshine most of the day.

A gentle breeze off the lake ran its fingers through my hair.

The only sounds were the drone of traffic on Lake Shore Drive and the trill of birds darting here and there in the trees.

I felt as though I could sit there forever . . .

I might have to.

That thought jolted my numb brain and a hundred questions crowded into my head. What was I going to do? My phone was dead . . . Did I have any money? I fished in my purse, all a-jumble after Mr. Bentley had stuffed everything back in. Thirty dollars in my wallet. A couple of credit cards. A debit card to my household account . . .

How much was in my household account? Philip and I didn't have joint accounts. I was supposed to use a credit card for everything from groceries to clothes, and Philip paid the bills. Other than that, he put a hundred dollars into a household account every week that was mine to use for anything that required cash. My paychecks from Manna House had gone into that account too—though I'd used a good deal of that for the trip to North Dakota.

I groaned. The checkbook for that account was up in the penthouse. *Okay, Gabby, don't panic. You have your debit card.* But if I remembered correctly, there was only a couple hundred left. And I'd just quit my job.

I fingered the credit cards. Had he frozen my credit cards too? I already knew the answer.

"Oh, God!" My head sank into my hands. "What am I going to do?!"

"Come to Me, Gabby . . ."

I looked up, startled. The words were so clear I thought someone had spoken them out loud. But the path in front of me was empty. That Voice in my spirit . . . Jodi Baxter had said it was God calling me. Just like that verse in the Bible, the one where Jesus said anyone who was weary and carrying a heavy burden could come to Him, and He would give them rest.

Pulling my feet up onto the bench and hugging my knees to my chest, I held on for dear life. "Help me, Jesus! I don't know what to do! . . . I can't lose my boys! . . . I'm so tired of fighting, trying to keep my life from unraveling . . . But I can't do it by myself! . . . I need You, God! *I need You!*"

A cold nose poked itself between my ankles and then nudged my arm. Startled, I looked up. A muddy yellow dog very much in need of a bath was pushing its muzzle into my lap, the rest of its body wiggling all over. I blinked in disbelief. The dog was now trying to crawl into my lap. I gasped. "Dandy!"

That's when I noticed a bandana knotted to the dog's collar—and another knotted to it, and another, making a rope. I followed the bandana rope with my eyes and found myself staring at a wrinkled face wearing a purple knit hat.

"You an' God havin' yourselves a private tête-à-tête, or can a body sit down on that there bench too? My feet are tired." Lucy Tucker plopped all six layers of her clothing down on the bench beside me.

"You found Dandy!" I croaked. By this time the dog *was* in my lap, and we were both a muddy mess. I pushed Dandy off and wiped my eyes and nose with the back of my hand. I felt like laughing hysterically. I'd just told God I needed Him—and He sent *Lucy*?

Lucy eyed me skeptically. "So what's wrong with you? You look worse'n the day I first found you in this park, wet as a drowned rat and bleedin' like a stuck pig."

Now I did laugh hysterically. *Who found who?* My shoulders shook from the sheer insanity of it all, the tears started again, and my story came out in little gasps. No penthouse. No husband. No kids. Locked out. Nowhere to go. Just a bunch of suitcases, bags, and boxes sitting in the foyer on the thirty-second floor of Richmond Towers.

"Hey, hey, hey," Lucy said, patting me awkwardly. "It's gonna be all right." She sat beside me for a while until the shaking and crying died down once more. Then she rose stiffly from the bench. "C'mon, let's go. You got enough for cab fare? My feet are killin' me."

"Go?" I blubbered. "Go where?"

"Manna House, of course. Nobody's ever locked outta Manna House."

Dandy's ears perked. He tugged on his bandana leash and barked.

I stared at her. But I didn't move. "What about my boys? I can't just let Philip take my boys!"

"That's right. But one day at a time, Missy. Them boys are all right. Now, you got cab fare or not?"

I nodded, stood up on wobbly legs, and let Lucy the bag lady walk me back along the jogging path toward Richmond Towers. Handing me Dandy's bandana leash, the old woman in her unmatched layers of clothes pushed through the revolving doors. I could see her gesturing to Mr. Bentley, who got on the phone. Within minutes, a cab pulled up on the frontage road. Mr. Bentley came out and opened the rear door.

"Hey!" the cabbie said. "I don't take dogs." I saw Mr. Bentley slip him a folded bill. "Well," the man grumbled, "maybe this once."

Mr. Bentley leaned into the backseat before shutting the door. "Don't worry about those suitcases and stuff upstairs, Mrs. Fairbanks. I've got a car. I'll bring it all later tonight when I get off work."

I nodded, not trusting myself to speak. The cab pulled away, and we rode in silence down Sheridan Road. Lucy rolled her window down, and Dandy stuck his head out, his mouth open in a doggy-smile. Within ten minutes, we pulled up in front of the shelter that had been my workplace for the past two months.

Now it would be my home?

I fumbled in my purse, paid the cab, and the three of us walked up the steps to the double oak doors. "I—I think I still have my key. Forgot to turn it in."

"Good," Lucy muttered. "What time is it, anyway? Did we miss supper?"

I turned the key and opened the door. Late evening light still shrouded the peaceful foyer with muted colors from the stained glass windows. The receptionist's cubicle was empty. Beyond the swinging doors, sounds of chatter and laughter came from the multipurpose room. And music. Turned up loud.

I stopped and listened. Someone was playing my CD! I closed my eyes as fresh tears slid down my face, but strangely, this time they felt like a spring rain washing out the crud as the familiar words sank deep into my spirit . . .

> . . . *The earth all around me is sinking sand*
> *On Christ the Solid Rock I stand*
> *When I need a shelter, when I need a friend*
> *I go to the Rock . . .*

reading group guide

1. The Yada Yada House of Hope series introduces a new primary character. Who *is* Gabby Fairbanks? Describe her as a person— her personality and character . . . her emotional strengths and weaknesses . . . her spiritual assets and debits. How do you *feel* about Gabby? What do you want to say to her?

2. What do you think has happened internally to Gabby between the time she first met Philip in the Prologue, and when we meet her sixteen years later in Chapter One? Are there ways *you* feel you've lost part of "who you are" or had to give up hopes and dreams while simply coping with life's circumstances? If you could get back that lost part of yourself, what would it be?

3. How would you characterize the tension in Gabby and Philip's marriage? In what way does Gabby feed into this tension? Do you see yourself or your marriage in their relationship in some way? What feelings does it bring up for you?

4. Mr. Bentley and "Mrs. Fairbanks . . . penthouse" are probably as different as two people can be. And yet, why do you think Gabby thinks of the doorman as her "first—and maybe only—friend" in Chicago? Who in your life has proven to be an "unlikely" but genuine friend?

5. In Chapter 10, Lucy the "bag lady" asked Gabby, "Why ain't you prayin' for me 'bout this bronchitis?" Gabby assured her that she, um, had been (intending to make it "retroactive"). What do you think Lucy meant by, "Huh. Ain't what I meant"? What is *your* usual response when someone asks you to pray for them?

6. Even though Josh and Edesa Baxter—whom you met in the original Yada Yada series—are quite a bit younger than Gabby, in what ways do they help open Gabby's spiritual eyes and heart? Even though they have a temporary reprieve in their efforts to adopt Baby Gracie, what challenges do you anticipate they may face in the future as a multicultural family?

7. Gabby is caught in the "sandwich generation"—parenting not only her two growing sons, but "parenting" her mother as well. In reacting to the crisis in her mother's life, how is she missing what her kids need? In what ways have you experienced (or are experiencing) a similar family squeeze? If you are discussing this question as a group, how can you encourage and support one another in times of family stress?

8. The setting of this story alternates between a *luxury penthouse* and a *homeless shelter*. In what ways do these settings symbolize what's happening in the story itself—with Gabby in particular, but also some of the other characters (Philip . . . Lucy . . . Estelle . . . etc.)?

9. In spite of what happens in the last chapter, what do you see as glimmers of hope for Gabby? Do you think there can be any redemption for Philip? Why or why not?

10. In what ways do Gabby's encounter with Lucy in the first chapter and their encounter in the final chapter act as "bookends" to this story? What are the similarities? What is the significance of the differences?

To my readers . . .

Thanks for joining me on this new journey. Don't know about you, but this one knocked the wind out of me! Hang on for the next episode in the Yada Yada House of Hope series, Who Do I Talk To? *coming out in September 2009.*

Until then . . . be blessed!

The Yada Yada Brothers: A New Series

BY DAVE JACKSON

As her life unravels, Gabby Fairbanks, whose story is told in *Where Do I Go?*, finds a friend in Harry Bentley, the affable doorman of her luxury Chicago high-rise. What she doesn't realize is that Harry lives with his own drama—a forced retirement from the Chicago Police Department for blowing the whistle on corruption in the elite Special Ops and a budding romance with the fascinating Estelle Williams.

Through Estelle, Harry meets the Yada Yada brothers—Denny Baxter and his son Josh, Peter Douglas, Carl Hickman, Ben Garfield—who provide a new circle of friends to replace his old CPD cohorts. But when Harry discovers he has a grandson he didn't know about, will he find the faith to take on the boy as a "second chance" to be the father he'd failed to be to his own son—even when the boy creates new dangers in Harry's fight against corruption, and may derail his "second chance" at love?

Enjoy the following short story, an introduction to *Harry Bentley's Second Chance*, the first Yada Yada Brothers Novel.

Dave Jackson lives in Evanston, IL with his wife, Neta, the author of the popular Yada Yada Prayer Group series and the new Yada Yada House of Hope series.

> ➤ To order the novel *Harry Bentley's Second Chance*, ask your favorite bookstore to order it for you (ISBN # 978-0-9820544-0-6) or go directly to www.daveneta.com.

Harry Bentley's Second Chance

Cindy Kaplan pulled the unmarked cruiser into the lot behind Chicago Police Headquarters and found a parking space. She left the engine running, the whine of the air conditioner cycling on and off to beat the summer's heat. But sweat still glistened on the bald head of the older black man sitting beside her. In the four years they'd been the salt-and-pepper duo in the elite anti-gang unit, she'd seen the frown lines between his eyebrows deepen into permanent grooves. They'd watched each other's back, covered for one another on little things, and saved each other's life more than once, but now she was afraid she was losing him.

"Harry," she sighed, brushing back the shock of straight, ash brown hair that fell perpetually over her right eye, "you know you don't have to do this. What's to be gained? Really . . . think about it. Even if you make your case against Fagan, your career's over the moment anyone finds out you blew the whistle."

She saw him glance at her out of the corners of his eyes, then he sighed. "Cindy . . . in all the time we've ridden together, when was the last time I backed down over somethin' like this?"

She shrugged. "Well, when was the last time we ever faced something like this? I know you're a straight-up guy, but this is different. Different than anything we ever faced before. Fagan's popped guys for less."

"Oh, come on." He tugged at the vest under his shirt that always seemed too tight in hot weather. "Don't start trippin' on me now, partner. We don't *know* that for sure 'bout Fagan."

"Maybe not, but we've heard it more than once. Why take the chance? I mean, given what we've actually seen Fagan do, why wouldn't he smoke you if you tanked his little racket?"

She watched the big man lean forward again, cradling his head in his large hands, his elbows on his knees, face inches from the air-conditioning duct in the cruiser's dash. She could imagine him sitting like that in his little apartment for hours struggling over what to do and she knew if she talked him out of it now, she might save his life but crush the self-respect he had rebuilt.

When he leaned back again, he stared straight ahead. "Look, Cindy. I'm goin' on up in there to make my report like I said. I'm a lot of things, but I ain't no quitter. What Fagan and his crew been doin' ain't right, and someone's gotta shut him down. You young. You got your whole career 'heada you, and I wouldn't be s'pectin' you to put that on the line. But me? It don't matter what happens to me no more. This is just somethin' I gotta do. Know what I'm sayin'?"

He turned and looked at her, dark eyes glistening. She could tell his emotions were churning when his speech got "homey," as he called it. She broke eye contact, not wanting to embarrass him.

"Don't worry 'bout it," he added, his voice a little husky. "No way am I gonna drag you into this. I'll make sure of that."

"Harry, that's not what I'm saying. It's you I'm concerned about."

"I know, and I 'preciate it. But I gotta do it. No way 'round it."

She heard the door click open. He turned once more and gave her a little mock salute, grinning like a school boy. "See you. I shouldn't be too long." Then he stepped out of the cruiser and headed for the Office of Professional Standards.

"Detective Bentley, please sit down."

It was a warmly decorated conference room, not a police interrogation cell like so many in which Harry had spent hours questioning suspects. But as he took his seat on the other side of the polished mahogany table from the three "suits," he felt like he was as much on the grill as any perp.

"I understand from this report that you feel there's been a few problems in your Special Operations Section."

"That's what it says. But . . ." Harry looked back and forth at the three of them. "Perhaps you gentlemen would be so kind as to let me know just who I'm speaking with before we dig in too deep."

"Of course. I'm Captain Roger Gilson, chief investigator for the IPRA. And"—motioning to the man to his right—"this is my assistant, Carl Handley." He turned to his left. "Bill Frazer sits in on these hearings as counsel for the city. And that little tape recorder between us is here in place of hiring another court recorder . . . Tight budget, you know."

Harry Bentley slid his chair in a little closer. "You did say this was the IPRA, the *Independent*"—he emphasized the word as he raised one eyebrow—"Police Review Authority, right? Even though two of you are from the department and Frazier, here, represents the city?"

"*Entirely* independent." Gilson waved both hands over the table like an umpire signaling *safe*. "We have no contact with any of the line officers, completely insulated. And we take orders from no one, not even the mayor's office."

Harry rolled his eyes . . . not in Chicago, but he took a deep breath and plunged on. "As you can see from my report, I've been in the SOS for six years. At first we were doing a lot of good putting away dope pushers and gangbangers. And there are still good men and women in the unit, don't get me wrong. But it's been taken over by rogues, particularly . . ." Harry took a deep breath. "Particularly Matty Fagan."

"What do you mean, 'taken over'? This Fagan, he's your boss, isn't he?"

"Yeah, Lieutenant Matthew Fagan. Irish, you know. Likes to be called Matty. But . . . well, if you read my report, it details three raids where we had no warrants but broke into citizens' homes anyway. On two of those occasions we found large quantities of drugs, cash, and weapons. We confiscated them all but did not make any arrests—probably couldn't have made them stick without warrants. But a short time later, all that contraband disappeared, back onto the streets. Then—"

"Mr. Bentley," interrupted Frazier, the lawyer, "you lost me there for a minute. How do you *know* this money and dope and guns ended up back on the street?"

Harry rubbed his hand across his smooth head. "I don't have any proof about the drugs, but they did disappear. And I'm sure the money went into the pockets of a few members of the unit, because they talked about it—"

"Wait, they *talked about it*? And you think they'll admit to that?" Frazier snorted.

"'Course not. But the guns . . . now there I have evidence. I recorded the serial numbers from those guns, and three weeks later I pulled one off a perp. The number matched! It's even in my arrest report."

The three investigators looked at one another. "Harry," said Captain Gilson, his voice confidential, "would you consider any of the men in your unit your enemies? Any racial problems going on?"

Harry's gut clinched. He wasn't about to dignify that one with a direct answer. "Captain, look at my report again. We had no warrant for the third incident, either. Didn't find any drugs *or* weapons. But we did find $6,420 in a Ziploc bag in the back of an old woman's freezing compartment. Fagan walked out of the house with the woman's money in his pocket. No criminals apprehended. No arrest. Just a raid!"

"Why didn't you say something at the time?"

"Oh, I did. But Fagan shrugged it off. 'It's drug money, Bentley. Those gangbangers do it all the time—stash their cash with grandma, auntie, or their girlfriend, wherever they think we won't look. Well, we looked and finders, keepers!' That's what Fagan said."

Gilson leaned toward his assistant and mumbled out of the side of his mouth, "Fagan's probably right."

But Henry heard him. "You think so?" Intensity furrowed his brow even deeper as he hunched forward over the table. "You think I don't know that happens all the time? I'm no rookie. But that's not what happened *this* time. I'm tellin' you, this old woman wasn't holdin'. Even if she was—whether that was drug money or not—Lieutenant Fagan had no right taking it for himself. This kind of thing happens all the time with him. The guys talk, but on these three occasions—the ones in my report—I was there. I saw it go down. And I'm willing to testify."

Captain Gilson busied himself flipping through Harry's report. "Okay, okay, Bentley. Let's say everything in your report's accurate—"

"It is!"

"All right." Gilson held up his hand. "I just want to ask, why are you entering a complaint *now*?" He turned both palms up in a helpless gesture. "A lot of people might consider your unit a service to the community even if it does cut some corners, know what I mean? They're happy for an all-out war on the scumbags. But here you are, turning on your own. Why?"

Harry leaned back in the chair. Good question. He had a lot to lose. But he shook his head. "I . . . I got a kid—or at least I had a kid—who I lost to the streets. I joined the SOS to make a difference . . . but what do I find? The SOS is at the rotten core of the whole problem. That's why!"

Cindy watched Harry Bentley push open the glass door of the office building and stride across the parking lot, his tread heavy, head forward. Uh, oh. Didn't look like it went too well. What would Harry do, now that he had made his play?

"Hey, Partner. How'd it go?"

"Eh. Okay, I guess. Let's roll."

"Nah, nah, nah. You don't get by me with that." She put the cruiser in gear and turned to back out of the parking spot. "Come on. Spill it. What'd they say? They gonna open an investigation?"

"Yeah, but . . ."

"Yeah, but what? Didn't they believe you? What happened?"

"They probably believed me, but I'm not so sure how eager they are to bust it open. They're more worried about the bad press it'll give the whole department."

"But they're gonna do it? Right?"

"They gotta do it since I made a formal report. But . . ."

"But what? Come on, man, don't make me pull thread by thread. What happened?"

Cindy watched Harry out of the corner of her eye as she turned into traffic along 35th Street. He leaned back against the headrest. "They want me off the force."

"*What?*"

"Ah, it kinda makes sense. They say if the time comes I have to testify, I'll be seen as a more independent witness . . . nothing to gain or lose."

"So, how's that gonna happen?"

"Take early retirement. I got twenty years in, so they can put out the word that I was 'encouraged' to retire because of . . . of . . ." He turned and stared out the side window.

"Because of what?"

"Because of the problems I was havin'."

"You mean the drinking? But you're on top of that now! You've been in AA for over a year. Everybody knows that."

"Yeah, I know. They're just saying it'd be a good cover. No one would suspect me of being the whistle-blower until the hearing. But believe me, Cindy . . ." He shook his head. "I don't wanna go out with a cloud hanging over my head either way—for still having a problem or for being a whistle-blower."

"But Harry, it's not a bad plan. It might keep you alive, you know. And besides, you'd have your pension. You're not *that* old. You could start over, new career, whole new life. It'd be like a second chance. Man, I'd go for it! And you know I'd come around and check on you from time to time." She grinned.

"Yeah, maybe."

Cindy looked over at him. It *was* a good plan, but she knew the downside. Even if Fagan and his gang got sent up river, Harry had broken the blue code of silence. Once it got out that he was the whistle-blower, there wouldn't be a precinct in the whole city where he could go in and get a cup of coffee.

Eight months, and Harry still had to think twice before automatically strapping on his Glock when he got out of bed each morning. But he was beginning to adjust to his new job as doorman for Richmond Towers. Occasionally he could read on the job and now that he had landed the day shift, he could relax and get other stuff done in the evenings. "Copacetic" is what his old grandmama would have called it—with just enough "characters" around to stave off boredom.

Like now. He watched through the rain-streaked floor-to-ceiling windows as a hunched figure dragged something toward the door. A second figure emerged out of the mist, limping along behind. Harry stepped quickly around his chest-high desk to confront them both just as they came inside the revolving door.

"Hey! Get that rickety cart outta here," he barked at the homeless derelict hauling all her worldly possessions. "You can't come in here. Residents only!"

But the person behind the frizzle-haired woman looked slightly familiar—late-thirties, attractive, in spite of the dripping ringlets hanging down around her face. She grimaced and waggled her fingers toward him in a tentative wave. "Uh, she's with me, Mr. Bentley . . . I'm Mrs. Fairbanks."

Fairbanks? Henry looked more closely. "Fairbanks? Penthouse?" He nodded toward the old woman, frowning as deeply as ever. "Whatchu doin' with this old bag lady?" Then he noticed a bloody rag around the younger woman's bare foot. "Are you all right, ma'am? What happened to your foot?"

"It's all right, Mr. Bentley. I, uh, we just need to get up to the, uh, apartment and get into some dry clothes." She smiled and flipped up her ID card with a *ta da* flourish, then swiped it through the scanner that opened the glass security door leading to the elevators.

Harry walked back around his crescent-shaped desk and settled onto his high-backed stool. Some of these rich people were a piece of work. He could keep the riffraff out of any place, but making nice to the residents at the same time could get complicated. Like the kid on twenty-two who kept bringing in his punk friends, smelling of dope and banging their skateboards against the walls. Harry raked his knuckles over the wiry gray horseshoe beard that ran along his jaw line and wished the management would create clearer guidelines.

The house phone rang and he picked up the black receiver. "Richmond Towers. Can I help you?"

"Is this Harold Josiah Bentley?"

He hesitated. "Who's askin'?"

"My name's Leslie Stuart and I'm calling from the Department of Children and Family Services. I need you to verify whether I'm speaking to Harold Josiah Bentley."

"I'm Bentley. But did you say *DCFS*? I don't have any kids." He pulled the receiver away from his ear and frowned at it, the grooves in his forehead growing deeper. "How'd you get this number, anyway?"

The woman was quiet for a moment. "Do you have a son named Rodney?"

Rodney! Harry stiffened. It had been years. What had Rodney done now? Hearing someone coming through the revolving door, Harry swung around on his stool and lowered his voice. "Look, can't talk now. Got people here. Besides, this phone's supposed to be for internal use only. No personal calls." He slammed down the receiver and stood up with a placid smile on his face.

"Oh, Mr. Bentley, I'm so glad you're here," said a white-haired woman. She was probably the same age as Harry, but he thought of her as much older. "I forgot my cash. Could you run out and pay the cabby for me? I'll take care of you later."

Knowing he hadn't been "cared for" since the last time, Harry still smiled broadly and said, "Happy to, Mrs. Worthington. How much does he need?"

"Oh, I think it was fifteen-something. But be sure to give him a dollar tip. You know, Mr. Bentley, I want to thank you so much. That kid who works here on the weekends when you're gone would never be so nice."

Harry went out and tossed a twenty through the window of the cab and came back in before his shiny dome could catch too many raindrops. The phone was already ringing again. He reached over his counter and picked it up more slowly this time. *"Richmond Towers . . ."* He emphasized the name. "Can I help you?"

"Mr. Bentley, I do need to speak to you today. If this phone's not good, do you have another number where I could reach you?"

"Yes, but I'm on duty right now. Can't this wait? Couldn't you call me some other time . . . like on Saturday? I'm off Saturday."

"I'd rather not work on Saturday if I don't have to, Mr. Bentley. Look, we need to talk ASAP, so can't we just do it now?"

Harry blew through pursed lips and gave her his cell number. Within a minute his *Law and Order* ring tone sounded.

"Now, Mr. Bentley, if you would just confirm your birth date for me, we can—"

"Wait a minute. Before I confirm *anything*, what's this about?"

There was a deep sigh on the other end of the line. "It's about your son, Rodney. With him not making bail, he's likely to be in Cook County for—"

"What'd he do?"

"Well . . . for now he's pled innocent, so his case will take at least six months. In fact, it could be a couple years before he's sentenced. And who knows what after that. So we've gotta place your grandson in foster—"

"*Grandson*? What grandson?"

"Rodney's nine-year-old, DaShawn . . . You do know about DaShawn, don't you?"

Harry's shoulders slumped. Rodney had a kid? "Uh, I kinda lost touch with Rodney some time ago."

"Listen, Mr. Bentley, I do need you to confirm your date of birth before we continue. Confidentiality, you understand. Wouldn't want to be discussing these matters with the wrong person. So when were you born?"

Harry Bentley swiveled around on his stool so that his back was to the revolving door. He sighed again. Dealing with Rodney always meant drama. "February 23, 1948. When did he have a baby?"

"February 23, 1948? Okaaay"—she dragged out the word as though she were writing down the date—"and you *are* Harold Josiah Bentley, right?"

"Yes, yes, and I was born on the south side and served as one of Chicago's finest for twenty years. You wanna do a background check on me?" He cringed as soon as he'd said it. He didn't need anyone plowing through his past, turning up the supposed reason he'd been encouraged to retire from the force.

"A background check won't be necessary at this time, Mr.

Bentley, but if you could come on down to DCFS tomorrow, we'd like to talk about the possibility of you taking the boy."

"Wait a minute. Wait a minute. What about the mama? Why don't she take the kid—hold on. I got a call on the other line." He laid down the cell and spun around to pick up the house phone even though his cell continued to emit the tinny scratch of Ms. Stuart's voice as it lay there on the desk.

"Hello."

"Mr. Bentley?"

"Yes." At least *this* call was an internal one.

"Uh, it's, uh, Mrs. Fairbanks. Top floor. Do you know the whereabouts of a homeless shelter for women in the area?"

Harry chuckled to himself. The "pet" she'd brought home wasn't working out so well. "Yeah, I think there's one just a couple blocks from the Sheridan El stop."

"Is that nearby?"

Harry began to give directions when Mrs. Fairbanks cut in again. "I'm lost. Could you just call a cab for my, uh, friend? We'll be down in a few."

Harry hung up and glanced at his cell. He was tempted to close and forget it, but he picked it up. "You still there?"

"Sure am—"

"Hang on. There's somethin' else I gotta do."

He laid it back down and called the cab.

Finally, he picked the cell up. "Okay, Ms. Stuart, now . . . Oh, yeah. Why isn't that boy with his mother?"

"She's in rehab. Crack. So, can you come down?"

Harry rested his elbows on the counter, head in hands. "Ms. Stuart, I'm not off until Saturday—"

"Then Saturday'll have to do. *I'll* come in on *my* day off. You be here—100 West Randolph—at 10 A.M. and give the security my name, Leslie Stuart."

She hung up before Harry could object. He slapped the desk. He'd left himself wide open for that one, mentioning he'd be off Saturday. Maybe he shouldn't show up . . . but he knew he would.

In a few moments, Mrs. Fairbanks came down with the bag lady in tow and handed him a ten to put the old woman in the waiting cab.

What? Harry Bentley has a grandson? What will that do for Harry's chances with Estelle Williams? What if Fagan discovers Harry was the whistle-blower on the rogue cops? And what about those "Yada Yada brothers" Harry meets when he goes to church with Estelle at SouledOut Community? Will they become as tight as the sisters?

» To order the novel *Harry Bentley's Second Chance*, ask your favorite bookstore to order it for you (ISBN # 978-0-9820544-0-6) or go directly to www.daveneta.com.